Emyr Humphrey  resort of
Prestatyn, the son ucated at
the University of velop his
lifelong interest in s. He has
worked as a teach producer
for the BBC, and sity.

Winner of the Hawthornden Prize and the Somerset Maugham
Award, his highly acclaimed novels include: *Flesh and Blood*, *Salt of
the Earth**, *A Toy Epic* and *Jones*. He has also published books of
poetry and non-fiction in Welsh and English, and in 1983 he won
the Welsh Arts Council Prize for *The Taliesin Tradition*, a book
about the Welsh character. He lives with his wife in Anglesey.

* soon to be published by Sphere Books

Also by Emyr Humphreys
in Sphere Books

FLESH AND BLOOD

THE BEST
OF FRIENDS

Emyr Humphreys

Sphere Books Limited

First published in Great Britain by
Hodder & Stoughton Ltd 1978

Copyright © 1978 by Emyr Humphreys
Published by Sphere Books Ltd 1987
27 Wrights Lane, London W8 5SW

TRADE
MARK

Set in 10/10½ Plantin

Printed and bound in Great Britain by
Cox & Wyman Ltd, Reading

I
Siôn A Nan

Part One

1

The train puffed with tantalising slowness into the great station. Compartment doors were flung open long before it came to a halt. Passengers in a hurry to make their connections plunged into the shadowed tide of those advancing urgently towards the opening doors. Enid pulled down her little straw hat, grabbed her hand-luggage and jumped out with athletic ease. Amy followed her with no less confidence even though she was making the journey for the first time. Both girls wore their new college blazers and knee-length pleated skirts. They dragged their luggage back into the sunlit side of the platform and stood for a moment to gaze at the jostling crowd and consult the station clock.

'My goodness, did you see him? And all the room he took!'

Amy could no longer stifle her indignation and excitement.

'He trod on her foot. With that great hobnailed boot of his. And not a word of apology. And the pain on the poor woman's face. I was dying to tick him off.'

'So was I.'

Enid peered into the endlessly shifting crowd.

'Have they gone?'

It was still possible they could run after them and give the hulking male a piece of their mind.

'And did you see him scoff all those sandwiches she gave him? The greedy monster.'

Amy was staring indignantly at her friend. The expression on Enid's face was already softening.

'To tell you the truth, that made me a little sorry for him.'

A porter in baggy trousers passed by and extended an arm towards their luggage without much hope of being engaged. Amy shook her head and the porter went on, dragging his noisy trolley behind him.

'Sorry? What do you mean "sorry"?'

'She wanted him to eat to keep up his strength. They were going to somewhere near Birmingham to look for work. He didn't want to go. Not one little bit. That was why he was in a bad temper.'

'I don't know.'

Amy sounded mildly irritated.

'You always find reasons for being sorry for people.'

They gathered their luggage together and walked towards a large indicator board. They put their things down again and looked up to study it. A scraggy youth was enjoying cranking up a flapping canvas of boldly printed information: times, destinations, numbers of platforms.

'I suppose our trunks are alright?'

Amy voiced a fleeting inclination to worry. She was the less experienced traveller. In itself the five-hour journey was a new adventure.

'I used to stand here.'

Enid pointed to the indicator board.

'Mother was always here first of course. But she had this silly trick of hiding on the other side of the board. Then out she would pop with a new frock from Brown's for me to wear in chapel. There was a white one with frills I remember particularly. The frills excited me so much. Now why was that, do you suppose?'

A dreamy look passed over her face. Here was a mystery she could contemplate indefinitely and a memory of the past as real to her as this present moment.

'Aren't children funny?'

Amy was silent just long enough to signal respect for her companion's well-known habit of asking herself unanswerable questions, before nudging her cheerfully in the ribs and once more picking up their bags.

'Living is moving,' she said. 'Come on. The Shrewsbury train. If we don't get a move on, we're going to miss it.'

At the foot of the iron passenger bridge they forgot their attempts to appear sophisticated and experienced travellers.

Spurred by the clack of their heels on the fretted stairway, they both broke into a trot. The crossing became a race. Amy wanted to take the lead. Her legs were longer but Enid was determined not to be overtaken. The smart little scarf around her neck billowed out gaily behind her. The pedestrian bridge was long and sagged in the middle. Suddenly Enid was running downhill and unable to reduce her speed. She was heading straight for a portly clergyman in a silk hat. He interrupted his comfortable progress to jump out of her way: but one of her cases caught his black thigh. He let out a sonorous roar of pained protest. She might have stopped to apologise, but Amy shot by, calling out with great presence of mind that their train was in and about to leave. Pointing over the side of the bridge she urged Enid to take notice of a squat old-fashioned engine raising steam, the four carriages behind it with nearly every door closed and the platform almost deserted except for the vital figure of the guard, the green flag tucked underneath his arm, studying his watch on the end of its silver chain. A harassed looking man, dashing out of the refreshment bar, looked like a prototypical misser of trains. He was followed through the swing door by a strong smell of beer and brown soup. A shaft of sunlight, like an apotheosis, suddenly pierced the grimy glaze of the station roof and glinted brightly on the shiny peak of the guard's cap as he craned his long neck from one side to the other to indicate to any latecomers the folly of being late when the man in charge was dedicated to departure strictly on time. Amy weaved her way towards him, avoiding stationary obstacles, and one moving truck, like the practised wing she was on the hockey field. She cried out loudly to gain the guard's attention and deprive him of the least excuse about not having seen them. Then she turned to watch Enid stumbling down the last few steps and lifting her cases in outlined gestures of comic desperation. At the first open carriage door, the two girls clambered in. Overcome with relief and laughter, they were both too weak to hoist their bags up to the sagging nets of the luggage racks.

'Did you hear him?'

Enid tried to control her voice but it came out in a squeal. '"Savage!" That's what he said. "Female savage".'

She pointed helplessly at herself.

'That's me ... I've never been called that before. Do you think it counts as an official curse? Was he a bishop or some such?'

Amy abruptly became an authority on the Anglican hierarchy.

'No. Not a bishop. He wasn't wearing gaiters. Bishops have to wear gaiters.'

Enid found this, too, very droll. She clasped her sides and gasped for breath. This encouraged Amy to further speculation.

'He could have been a dean of course. A gloomy dean.'

The wizened features of a diminutive porter suddenly appeared just above the level of their feet. With a lifelong hostility to all late arrivals and noisy young persons in particular, he looked up with sour disapproval before slamming the door with spiteful vigour. It was sufficient to make both girls blink and preserve a well-behaved silence until they felt sure the train was moving. They looked around with exaggerated wonder to notify each other of the blissful fact that they had the compartment to themselves. Amy snatched Enid's hat from the seat, tossed it in the air, caught it as it fell and then threw it accurately up on the rack. The irresistible forward movement of the train broke the last chains of constraint. There was nothing now to prevent them behaving just as they liked. As the train gathered speed they began to laugh and shout, tottering from one end of the compartment to the other, making half-hearted attempts to tug up the leather straps of the door windows, slapping each other on the back, intoxicated with a new level of freedom that neither had ever experienced before.

'We're away!'

Amy shrieked with such uncharacteristic abandon that Enid lay still, sprawled on the seat, her mouth open, watching her with unconcealed wonder. Then to show her full support, she raised both her clenched fists in the air and shook them in as unladylike a fashion as she could manage.

'It's an escape!'

Amy stood swaying in the middle of the compartment, her feet wide apart to keep her balance.

'An escape from a trap. People can go on about a new age

4

dawning for women and all that kind of rot. But for me it's more than that.'

Her eyes sparkled with emotional excitement.

'And I owe it to you.'

She stretched out her hand and Enid took it.

'I'll never forget that, E.P. Never.'

She tumbled back to sit in the middle of the seat opposite and put up her feet. She felt like singing and burst out into song. Enid listened intently to her voice above the accelerating clatter of the wheels of the train. It had a bell-like clarity that she always admired. She wanted to listen. Like the late September sunlight that poured into the compartment it made the world seem delightful. Amy made her join in. They sang a folk song which merged into a revival hymn and ended up as 'Bye Bye Blackbird'.

'I've got to eat.'

Pretending to be desperate, Amy dragged down a case and extracted a bag of four red apples.

'Travelling always makes you hungry. Have you noticed that?'

The world seemed as delectable and edible as the apples the two girls held in their hands. Amy trilled a few more bars before sinking her teeth in the apple.

'I'll tell you something.'

She spoke with her mouth full.

'I've never been so happy. Never in my whole life. Never. Never.'

She waved the apple about merrily before taking another bite. The girls leaned towards each other, their heads as close as hazel nuts in the centre of the compartment.

'I've spent weeks imagining just what it will be like.'

She was not satisfied with Enid's sympathetic smile.

'I have. Day after day. Especially when you were off enjoying yourself in that University Women's Camp. It kept me going. Washing visitors' dirty dishes is a marvellous way of making you dream. I'd stare at these piles of dirty dinner dishes and they became college towers. Are there college towers?'

Enid seemed unable to remember exactly. She was anxious to be truthful.

5

'Well, I suppose there are in a way. There's one anyway. Didn't you see the postcard?'

'I suppose I did. I didn't take it in. There are some things I just can't take in. The force of what's inside won't let them in. Do you know what I mean?'

Enid made a profound effort to understand.

'Yes. I think I do. The imagination is so powerful it holds out reality.'

'Those are just words.'

Amy was impatient of abstraction.

'I'm talking about an over-all thing. A new world. A new life. Oh, gosh. I'm never any good at saying what I mean.'

'Yes, you are.'

Enid's natural generosity spurred her to a further effort.

'Buildings like palaces. Full of wonderful people. Great occasions. Wise men. And . . .'

She stopped suddenly. Enid was able to help her.

'And Val Gwyn.'

Amy frowned. She looked unwilling to have the man's name mentioned. But Enid had done it so pleasantly. A characteristic exercise of friendly, sympathetic tact. Amy did not need even to blush. Their comfortable isolation in the moving train removed restraints and resentments. Between friends, frankness was everything.

'Yes, well, him if you like.'

Amy tried her best to be matter of fact.

'I have thought a lot about him. What else can you do when you're washing dishes?'

'You poor old thing.'

'No wonder housemaids are romantic. That proves how near I was to being one. I admit it. I did daydream about him. He was my "beau-ideal". It was just like those cheap films, you know. The heroine tied to a sink full of dishes and the perfect hero floating about in a cloud just above her silly head. "My Val", "My Valentine", "My Valentino". My goodness! Even the silly name fits. It's the kind of thing that helps to keep the working class going.'

'There's a bit more to Val than Valentino,' Enid said laughing.

Amy narrowed her eyes dramatically and pointed at her friend.

6

'It's all your doing, E.P. "Her image is stamped on my heart." I bet you made it up.'

'Cross my heart, I didn't. Would I want you to have him? It was reported speech. "The girl who brought the flag," he said, "she is the future. Her image is stamped on my heart".'

'Well,' Amy said cheerfully, 'any day now it is likely to be stamped on his foot. We've got to improve our dancing. You do realise that, don't you? Ready for all those Victory Balls.'

'You mustn't expect too much, Amy. I mean it will be pretty dull most of the time, surely?'

'Not if I can help it.'

'After all, it's only a small university, stuck on top of a pretty mediocre seaside town.'

'That's sacrilege!'

Amy's mock annoyance was only half-feigned.

'Blasphemy! Or whatever the word is. We've got to be loyal. Remember the Col. spirit and all that.'

'All I mean is that if you don't expect too much, you won't be disappointed. From what I could gather, it leaves a lot to be desired.'

'E.P., you've had all sorts of relatives going through the place no doubt. And your aunt of course who has made it possible for me to go. Don't think I'm ungrateful.'

'She only pointed out the means,' Enid said. 'The ways and means of getting there.'

'With all due respect to your family, and I don't know of a family I respect more, I have one huge advantage over you.'

They smiled at each other trustingly. Because their friendship was so deep, they had no more need of secrets from one another.

'I'm an orphan.'

Amy leaned back with some degree of self-satisfaction and listened contentedly to the rhythm of the train.

'Is that an advantage?'

'Yes, it is.'

Amy was profoundly pleased with the conclusion she had come to.

'I am not hemmed in by family. Tied down by family ties. By preconceived ideas. For example if I don't like the place as it is, I'll change it!'

She waved her apple core like a magic wand.

'Shatter it to bits! Remould it nearer to the heart's desire!'

She studied the apple core, pondering where she could throw it. Enid went to the window and used both her hands to pull up the leather strap with the remains of her apple in her mouth. The window dropped with an unexpected bang. Enid jumped back and the apple fell out of her mouth to land in the dust on the floor of the compartment. Amy threw her core through the open window and leaned back to fold her arms and think. She decided to open another of her cases. She plunged her hand under the clothes and felt about until she found what she was looking for. She extracted a small leather-bound Bible and held it up for Enid to see.

'See this?'

She smiled and breathed deeply to show that she was acting with considered calm.

'I am about to chuck it out of the window. Which side is that? England or Wales?'

Enid was disturbed but she made an effort to appear light-hearted.

'This is Border Country,' she said. 'It's all ours really. Ours and not ours. Gwalia Irridenta and all that.'

Amy was barely listening. She got up to her feet and held the book above her head.

'Well, here we go,' she said. 'Let's see how far I can throw it.'

She held the book out through the open window so that the leaves fluttered helplessly in the slip-stream. Below the track two women were gathering blackberries in a wild hedgerow. Amy waved the book at them as if to invite them to catch it. One of them waved back but the other went on blackberry picking without lifting her head.

'Well, here we go...'

Amy repeated the phrase with marginally less enthusiasm. Enid was too upset to notice. She could bear it no longer. She rushed to her friend's side and tugged at her arm in a last desperate rescue operation, her eyes screwed up with the effort.

'Amy,' she said. 'If you don't want it, just give it to me. I'd like to have it. It's an awful thing to throw it away.'

Amy teased her briefly with a pretended resistance.

'Going,' she said. 'Going, going, gone.'

She twisted about and threw the book to the other side of the compartment. It bounced from the seat to the floor. Enid waddled across unsteadily to pick it up.

'From today,' Amy said, 'I am going to be an Atheist. Full-time. Dedicated.'

She turned and put her face outside to shout to the green countryside at large while the train roared noisily by.

'I am an Atheist. And anything else I want to be. Now and for ever and ever, Amen.'

'That's just rubbish. And you know it.'

Enid was muttering to herself as she dusted the small Bible with some care. She opened it to read aloud a dedication written in bold black copperplate on the brown flyleaf. '*To Amy on her departure for the University with the prayers and good wishes of her uncle, Lucas Parry.*' Faint pencil marks were visible that Amy's Uncle Lucas used to assist his penmanship.

'Amy...'

Enid sighed and shook her head. She was evidently troubled.

'Amy,' she said. 'How could you?'

'You can keep it. Old History swot. Relic of the Past. I shan't be needing it again. I'm for Science and the Future.'

'"Prayers and good wishes"... nobody can afford to do without those!'

Amy shook her head.

'I don't agree,' she said. 'It's only his way of trying to extend his hold. His authority. Don't you see? It's the long arm of the Law and the Prophets. The gospel according to Lucas Parry. He would never want me to be free. He's what you can call a jealous god. He would have kept me in a cage all my life if only he could have afforded to feed me. I say, shall we have a sandwich? I'm ravenous. I really am. Travelling makes me so hungry.'

'We've a long way to go yet.'

Enid was studying solemnly the little Bible in her hands. Amy unwrapped a packet of sandwiches.

'Just one each,' she said. 'To keep the wolf from the door.'

Enid bent her head to look closely at the early nineteenth-century print. She read a verse aloud as if she was happy to have stumbled on it.

9

' "These are the words of the Covenant which the Lord commanded Moses to make with the children of Israel in the land of Moab, beside the covenant which he made with them in Horeb".'

Amy had taken a sandwich and filled her mouth with food. She held out the packet and urged Enid to take one. Her closed mouth stretched in a smile until dimples appeared in both cheeks.

'What's the joke?' Enid said.

'Horeb and Moab. Sounds as if God and Moses were two special preachers making a tour of the chapels around Melyd.'

'But it isn't an accident, Amy. The names of the chapels were chosen for that very reason. You know that surely?'

'Horeb-moreb,' Amy said. 'What do I care.'

Enid looked at the imprint of the book.

'This Bible was printed in Carmarthen,' she said. 'That's interesting.'

Amy pointed her bitten sandwich at the book.

'You have a superstitious reverence for a block of old paper. Do you realise that? Like the Romans with the entrails of cockerels.'

'It's much more than that . . .'

'Are you going to take a sandwich or aren't you?'

Obediently Enid took a sandwich. She put the little Bible down on the seat beside her. She pulled a face.

'What's the matter?'

'It's something I'm trying to remember. Uncle Peter used to say it, but he was quoting someone else. "There is always light enough for those who wish to seek and always dark enough for those who want to hide" . . . Something like that.'

'And what on earth is that supposed to mean?'

Enid blushed as Amy stared hard at her.

'I don't know quite. I'm sure it does mean something. Maybe I haven't remembered it properly.'

'I don't want to hide,' Amy said. 'If that's what you mean. I want to seek as much as anybody and more than most.'

'Of course you do. I don't quite know what I'm trying to say.'

She picked up the Bible again.

'I'm no religious fanatic as you well know,' Enid said. 'But

10

we are the People of the Book after all. I mean in that sense, historically speaking, you could argue we are a Chosen People. Chosen for what of course is another question.'

Enid gave an academic little laugh and began to nibble her sandwich.

'Well, there you are.'

Amy brushed her hands against each other as she swallowed the last mouthful of sandwich.

'That's exactly what's wrong with us. We're buried under a load of old Bibles like insects under a heap of stones.'

She raised her eyebrows naughtily.

'Do you think we could sneak another sandwich? Half each. Just a half.'

2

The railway junction was in the middle of the country. From a modest cluster of buildings three hard planes of platform stretched imposingly into a soft world of hedgerows and green fields. A strong smell of bitumen rose from the brown railway sleepers. The polished surface of the rails gleamed in the sun. The girls left all their luggage in one pile on a wooden seat in order to stroll together towards the very end of their platform. They had noticed a deserted garden and a mass of blue Michaelmas daisies leaning on the points of the wooden fence.

'Cambrian ... G.W.R. ...'

Amy spoke in a dreamy voice as they walked.

'They sound much more romantic than L.M.S. Don't you think?'

At the end of the platform Enid pointed towards the flowers.

'Look at those butterflies,' she said. 'Did you ever see so many? Aren't those Painted Ladies? Isn't it a gorgeous day?'

There was barely a cloud in the blue sky. Beyond the overgrown garden they could see an empty cottage with a broken thatch and small windows roughly boarded. Above the cottage a great ash tree flourished. The leaves were beginning to turn yellow and some were already falling, twirling slowly in the still air before landing softly on the discoloured thatch. Both girls raised their heads to listen to the great peace of autumn that surrounded them. What sounds they heard were like mysterious hieroglyphics left on the edge of an empty canvas, until a colony of rooks became active in a soft explosion of muted croaking and black marks above the brilliant colours of a little wood.

'There's no sign of anybody.'

Amy sounded a little disappointed.

'Who were you expecting? We've got a long way to go yet.'

'Do you think we are lost?'

Amy whispered excitedly and then executed a little waltz to amuse herself.

'Wouldn't that be gorgeous? The train has steamed up the wrong line. Dropped us in the middle of nowhere. In ten minutes we shall be turned into a pair of turtle doves. We'll spend the rest of our lives cooing in the sun.'

'Crows.'

Enid pointed at the rooks throbbing more urgently in the blue sky.

'A pair of ancient crows. Waiting for a train that never comes.'

'Crawc ... crr ...'

Amy was about to make noises like a crow when she stopped abruptly.

'Look out.'

'A train?'

'No, a crow.'

Amy muttered under her breath.

'There's one coming straight towards us.'

She was referring to the figure of a woman in black hurrying down the platform in their direction. She was dressed in a skirt of almost pre-War length, but her black hat had the high crown which had just come into fashion, with a narrow turned-down brim. It shone in the sun like the helmet of some newly-raised army. There was a skimpy black fur over her bony shoulders. She wore spectacles and she was frowning anxiously as she approached the girls, until she came close enough and then she drew back her thin lips in a tremulous smile.

'Aber?'

She jerked her clasped hands to indicate their college blazers and the black handbag dangling from her arm shook excitedly. The girls nodded politely. Amy tried hard not to stare at the tuft of long hair growing from a mole on the woman's chin. The woman smiled more confidently.

'I was at Aber,' she said. 'Many years ago of course. You must be waiting for the train.'

She turned suddenly to look back at the modest buildings of the isolated junction. For the first time the girls noticed an exceptionally tall girl standing in solitude with her baggage around her feet.

'That's my daughter,' the woman said. 'My only daughter. Going up for the first time.'

She swallowed and blinked hard, suppressing her emotions.

'So are we.'

She turned to Enid and seemed ready to embrace her in gratitude for information so freely given.

'Are you? Are you really? You are freshers then. Just like my Mabli.'

She stared hard at them both, her lips pressed together and stretched in an expectant smile like a nervous shopper about to make a sudden but wholly worthwhile purchase.

'You won't tell her I told you, will you? But my poor Mabli has just lost her father. The Rector of Cymmer with Talywern. The Reverend Gwilym Herbert. We married late in life you might say. He passed away three months ago. Mabli is our only child. Our only chick. We may have protected her too much. And now she is going out into the world alone.'

She paused to look closely at the two girls and assess the degree of sympathy they were showing for her account of her daughter's situation.

'She would be so cross with me if she knew I was telling you so much. But what else can I do? I am a mother and a widow. What else can I do?'

'It's alright, Mrs. Herbert.'

Enid sounded so sturdily comforting that the woman's lined features became wreathed in smiles.

'We'll look after her. Won't we, Amy?'

Amy nodded hurriedly.

'I know I shouldn't ask you. But time is so short now. I have to set aside formalities and ask you to listen to the outpourings of an over-anxious mother. Where are you from, my dears?'

'Llanelw.'

Enid was brisk and prompt with her answer.

Mrs. Herbert quietly repeated the name of the seaside town.

'Llanelw?'

She looked so anxious she could have been saying 'Sodom'. But she recovered quickly. Even in towns and cities of the most dubious reputation, there could always be remnants of the untarnished chosen. Clearly it was from such islands of grace that these girls came. She had every right to breathe a deep sigh of relief and contentment and to clutch her handbag closer to her person as she gazed at the pleasing sight of two fair maidens clad in their new college blazers.

'This is Amy Parry. My best friend. And I'm Enid Prydderch.'

Enid's smile was so open and friendly, Mrs. Herbert's arms rose and fell in gratitude.

'Which Chapel do you attend? You are Chapel of course. Although I don't know why I should say that, being Church myself.'

Enid nodded cheerfully, while Amy looked up at the crows as though mildly displeased to note a fresh disturbance among them.

'Sincerity is the thing. Not dogma. That's what my Gwilym always used to say. "By their fruits ye shall know them." And yet curiously, he was inclined to High Church in the matter of worship. A strong aesthetic sense, you see. But his instincts were evangelical. He and Mr. Williams the Calvinistic were the best of friends. As Christians they knew how to co-operate. The archbishop never approved. That's why Gwilym never gained preferment.'

Mrs. Herbert turned away from them suddenly to attain a measure of privacy for an unavoidable spasm of bereave-

14

ment. Her hands fumbled for a white handkerchief in her handbag. Noisily she blew her nose.

'Mabli is like her father. Tall and original. There's nothing original about me.'

She packed away the handkerchief in her handbag.

'I was quite a good scholar in my younger days. But there's nothing *original* about me. Do you know what my husband used to do, many a Saturday in summer?'

She was eager to take the girls into her confidence and they were obliged out of politeness to listen.

'He would ride down here on his great big bicycle to spend the afternoon on this platform. He would bring his work with him. His translation of the *Divine Comedy*. Dante, you know? He would sit on the seat over there and when a train arrived he would leave his books on the seat and walk down alongside the carriages to see who he might know and have a chat with. He said he enjoyed it more than fishing. Such surprises he would have. Sometimes it would be like a miniature eisteddfod. Five or six trains on a summer afternoon and he'd never fail to catch a friend or good acquaintance. Often men who lived in distant parts of the Empire. Old college friends he hadn't seen for years, changing trains here. It gave him so much innocent pleasure. And inspiration too, he said. It's a great tragedy that he never finished the translation. Do you know what I hope?'

She leaned forward to take the two girls into her deepest confidence.

'It's my hope that Mabli will finish it one day. She has the talent, I know that. But she's terribly shy. I want to travel down with her to Aber, to tell you the truth. But she prefers that I shouldn't. And I wouldn't want to embarrass her.'

'I think the train is coming.'

Amy raised a stiff arm to point down the track. A puff of smoke was visible above the green hill and they could already hear the extra effort the steam engine was making. Mrs. Herbert was suddenly struck by panic. She pressed her gloved hand against her mouth.

'Oh dear,' she said. 'I've been here chattering away like an old woman with loose wits and I haven't introduced you ...'

'There's plenty of time ...'

Enid tried to exert a calming influence but Mrs. Herbert

15

was already moving up the platform waving her arms. Her daughter Mabli remained as still as a statue watching her mother's disorganised approach from the corner of her narrowed eyes. Her head was small in relation to the length of her body.

'Mam...'

She whispered when her mother was close enough to hear.

'Mam. Try and control yourself.'

Mrs. Herbert was too intent on expressing joy and relief to take in what her daughter was saying.

'Such charming girls ... I couldn't have wished ... I mean if one had the pick! They are perfect for you, my little Mabli. And companionship is such a marvellous thing. You know I still correspond with some of my old college friends. Just think of Jess Watson coming all the way from Suffolk for Dada's funeral.'

The girl could only listen to her mother as if she were standing alongside a mountain stream swollen with rain and trying in vain to empty itself. Patient silence had a more calming effect than trying to argue or reason with an emotional mother. Mrs. Herbert's eyes moved constantly as she scrutinised her daughter's face in a desperate effort to improvise some new mode of communication more immediate, more comprehensive, more instantly telling than words.

'I shall be alright,' she said.

As the sound of the train grew louder she was making a last supreme effort to put herself in her daughter's place.

'You mustn't worry at all about me. I've lived alone before, you see – when I was a teacher. Before I married your father. Before you were born. I'm quite used to it. I know how to keep myself busy.'

Mabli's gaze had strayed from her mother to watch the two girls in their bright blazers collecting their luggage on the station seat. Mrs. Herbert noticed instantly where her daughter's attention had wandered.

'Don't worry, my pet. They're coming and they'll be very nice to you.'

She smiled and sighed a sigh of pleasant melancholy.

'Alas and alack. How I wish I were coming with you. What wonderful times you are going to have ...'

16

Her voice was drowned by the great bluster of the train entering the station, but she continued to speak through the cloud of steam, pressing her hands together and closing her eyes in a muted ecstasy of hope and expectation. When she opened them and the steam had cleared away she saw that Enid and Amy had been joined by a new arrival who was already addressing her daughter with cheerful effusiveness.

'Mabli, old thing! How long have you been here? By gosh, I nearly missed it, didn't I? That idiot Jim couldn't start the van so we had to ring up Davies the Castle for what he laughingly calls a taxi. Hello, Mrs. Herbert.'

Mrs. Herbert nodded primly.

'Hello, Gwenda.'

She tried to extend to her daughter a cautionary glance but Mabli was too absorbed in greeting Gwenda to see it. Gwenda's copper-coloured hair was cut in an Eton crop. Mrs. Herbert looked with ill-concealed disapproval at the white skin exposed at the nape of her neck. Gwenda's college blazer showed a year's use and seemed ill-matched with the striking green frock she was wearing and the flesh-tinted silk stockings. She wore conspicuous make-up and there were nicotine stains on her thin fingers.

'Well, there's one thing you won't have to worry about, girls. You won't have to waste time learning the ropes. You'll have old Gwenda G. to look after you and steer you safely through the labyrinth!'

'Do you know each other?'

Mrs. Herbert looked from Gwenda to Enid and then from Gwenda to Amy unable to hide her perturbation.

'Sort of.'

Gwenda's cheerful manner of speech and friendly swagger seemed to affect Mrs. Herbert's nerves. Gloom had descended like a cloud on her lined and malleable features.

'Enid and I met in the University Women's Summer Camp at the end of July. Very jolly it was, except for the weather. Small world, isn't it?'

Mrs. Herbert nodded dismally. Mabli leaned towards her, ready to console her before they parted.

'It's a Christian thing, Mam. The camp, I mean. With study circles every morning. And then recreation and long excursions. All the orderly work shared by the campers

17

except for the cooking. I wanted to go, remember? I would
have gone but for ... Dada ...'

Overwhelmed by a fit of weeping, Mrs. Herbert groped
about in her handbag and pressed her large white
handkerchief to her eyes. Mabli signalled the other girls to
board the train. They took charge of her luggage while she
put her arm around her mother's shoulders and walked her
gently up and down the platform whispering last words of
comfort in her ear.

3

The sun, declining in the west, filled the well of the large
chapel with an intense haze of golden light. There were
classes situated there, groups of elderly men and elderly
women. They sat apart, each faced with its own teacher.
Hidden as they were in the aura of suffused and dazzling
light, they were more easily located by the hum of studious
sounds they made: the men a steady continuous almost
subterranean rumble; the women more intermittent, a
twittering liable to variations in tempo and more prolonged
silences.

The young college women were provided with a class of
their own. They occupied the three curving pews in the back
of the chapel: about thirty young women in their Sunday
best, all wearing hats, with pale green commentaries open on
their knees. The young men were in the gallery immediately
above them. These were traditional locations, so that neither
group should be distracted in any way by the presence of the
other. Everywhere there were murmurs of subdued study
like the sound of work in the hive on a warm summer day.

The children's classes were conducted in the vestry and
the smaller children had their own large room behind the
organ loft. From time to time one or other of the polished
pine doors on either side of the mass of organ pipes would
open and some wayward toddler would issue forth calling for
his mother: and emerge a second time perhaps, determined

to explore the more silent reaches of a great commonwealth of wood and stone to which he was gradually getting more acclimatised before taking out full naturalisation papers. His teacher would catch up with him as he began to enjoy wandering between the gallery pews and causing a pleasurable diversion to the classes that noticed him. She would grasp him gently by the shoulder with a gloved hand and steer him back to the harbour from which he had detached himself, answering his loud questionings in a firm but comforting whisper.

In the deacon's pew beneath the large pulpit, three deacons were deep in hushed discussion with the young minister. The silver vase of flowers on the table under the pulpit had been set aside to make room for an open ledger. Mabli was making discreet efforts to stretch her neck and follow what was going on in the deacon's pew without being observed by the class teacher, a large and ornate figure liable to shift and block her view.

'It's the War bonds. I'm sure of it.'

Mabli's whisper was intense and excited but barely audible. Amy, who sat wedged between her and Enid Prydderch, just clenched her teeth. She too kept a wary eye on the class teacher, a woman whose thick expressive features glowed with benevolence and goodwill towards her young ladies. A rope of heavy beads passed twice around her solidly sculptured neck, and she fingered them delicately with the broad fingers of one hand as she studied her india-paper Bible in its soft black cover balanced with the other hand on the crest of the pew in front of her.

'He'll have his way.'

Mabli continued to whisper.

'He'll put it to the school any minute now. You mark my words.'

'Well, now . . .'

The class teacher projected her soothing alto towards her young ladies.

'We come to a passage that I still find quite alarming to read. Miss Griffiths . . . would you, please . . . I think it's your turn . . .'

A young woman at the end of the first row cleared her throat and began to read in a low measured monotone. The minister in the deacon's pew turned to look at the industrious classes scattered around the vast chapel and shaded his eyes against the dazzle of the light.

'Tom Arthog'll get his own way.'

Mabli's enthusiasm vibrated through her cautious whisper.

'He really is a wonderful man.'

Amy looked unwilling to share her opinion. She moved her head so that she could whisper fiercely into Enid's ear through her clenched teeth.

'What am I doing here?'

Enid grinned and waited for her chance to whisper back.

'Better than sitting on your own in that draughty Common Room.'

Amy gave her a quick indignant scowl.

'And you'll be able to see Tom Arthog himself in action.'

'How exciting.'

Being obliged to whisper took all the bite out of Amy's sarcasm.

'Just imagine . . .'

The class teacher raised her voice a fraction to command the full attention of all her charges.

'When I was a young girl there were certain officials in our church at home who declared quite categorically that Jeremiah was too indelicate a book for young ladies to read.'

Her smile was enough to indicate the kind of reaction she expected. The rows of young women she faced set up a ripple of subdued amusement.

'Mind you, I would never want to try and scoff at them in any way. They were good old men. But the world has changed so much since those days. I wonder if your generation can really grasp the extent of the change? I just wonder. And for that matter would they have recognised a world at war. That's part of the great difference, isn't it? The Great War is also the Great Divide. We know, we can grasp what war means in a way that wasn't possible for them. But just listen to this. Do you mind if I read it again, Miss Griffiths? I still find this quite terrible . . . "*I looked to the earth to see a formless waste: I looked to the heavens and their light had gone . . . the mountains trembled and all the birds of the heavens were fled*".'

She paused to let the words attain their full effect and then resumed her customary honied conversational tone.

'You must all of you have seen those frightful photographs of the Western Front. Well, to me, you see, in its own way of course, this passage is just as terrible.'

Mabli began to whisper excitedly.

'Oh, my goodness. He's coming to us first. He's coming here.'

The minister, the Reverend Thomas Arthog Williams, was approaching with exaggerated care, indicating an unwillingness to interrupt. He sidled his long body along in the vacant pew behind the class teacher. He was a man in his middle thirties who still cultivated a boyish manner. His bright eyes darted about as he registered as many reactions as he could to the details of his behaviour. His cheeks were of a high colour and his black hair stood up in front like a courting signal on the crest of a nervous bird. His false teeth were new and shone with too much perfection when he smiled. He waited behind her until the class teacher turned to greet him with a large forgiving smile.

'Mr. Arthog Williams,' she said. 'The commentator draws our attention to a difficulty the scholars find in this passage. Jeremiah 4, verses ten to thirty-one. Is the prophet describing an invasion, or a catastrophe, that has already taken place, or is he giving voice to a prophecy of terrors still to come?'

'Ah, yes.'

The minister smiled understandingly. He suspended his long jaw momentarily before speaking.

'It's the old problem, isn't it? Partly a question of tense and partly a question of when the document was put together.'

He looked at her to pick up any signals of reward for his rapid and well-informed response. Then he looked at the young women to make a census of any variants in appreciation. He placed a bony knee on the pew in front of him and stretched himself forward until he was almost level with the teacher the other side of the pew back.

'Mrs. Hughes-Davies,' he said. 'Could I disengage you and your class from the Prophet of Sorrows for just a few moments? It's not an entirely unrelated matter either, in its implications, shall we say. There are related principles involved. Shall I put it to the class, Mrs. Hughes-Davies? Do you mind?'

'Of course not, Mr. Arthog Williams. Please carry on.'

'I want to stimulate thought in a certain direction,' he said. 'We have a practical problem to solve and I have persuaded the officers of our Sunday School to allow me to put the matter before the adult assembly. That is everyone over the age of eighteen. For my part I would have put the age limit at fourteen, but that is almost another question. Our youngsters contribute well and therefore in my view they should have a voice in this matter. However I shall not press that point. This is the issue. This Sunday School does not flourish as it used to do in the palmy days before the War. But we are facing up well to a difficult situation. Our attendances compare very well with any of the larger churches in our Connexion and we are taking vigorous steps to round up the strays, as the saying goes. As you know we have a sub-committee in session to deal with the problem of backsliding and they have many very novel ideas to cope with this very ominous post-War phenomenon. Now this Sunday School has funds and it intends to use them. Quite substantial funds, I'm happy to say, because it has always been well organised and the finances have already been in the care of experienced businessmen devoted to our Cause. And please don't imagine for one moment that I'm not deeply grateful to them for all their long patient voluntary efforts. A lifetime of devotion in almost every case.'

He turned for a second to draw their attention to the three white-haired men in the deacon's pew still deep in conference over the open ledger.

'But a large amount of our funds are invested in War bonds. Now I tell you quite frankly that I am opposed to this. It does not seem to me right that the cause of the Prince of Peace, the cause of our Lord and Saviour Jesus Christ, should be investing money in what is perhaps the greatest social evil of our time and the scourge of Western Civilisation – war and preparation for war.'

It was clear that the whole class was on his side. Mabli's cheeks were flushed with enthusiasm. When she nudged

Amy in the ribs, Amy was obliged to show her measure of agreement. The smile carved on Mrs. Hughes-Davies' face was beatific.

'Mr. Arthog Williams,' she said, 'as far as voting is concerned the University Women's Class is unanimously in favour of your proposal.'

'Good. Good.'

The minister looked down at the Bible to conceal his obvious pleasure. His position as a leader of opinion in his church and in the life of the town would seem to be reinforced with every step he took.

'Jeremiah,' he said, ready to be briefly lighthearted before leaving on his rapid tour of the classes and more difficult constituencies.

'He's a hard old nut. And there's no getting round him. But I'll be quite frank with you. I find this the most desperately depressing book in the whole of the Old Testament. I'd like to know what you think. Are things really as bad as old Jeremiah paints them?'

He was waiting for some further appreciation of his frankness and modernity. Mabli's lips were moving but she was too shy to speak. On the whole there was a demure lack of response.

'Is he speaking to us do you think? Is he relevant?'

He was ready to leave. He had too many visits to make. A deacon had raised his arm for some attention. The minister waved back to indicate that he still had other ports of call to make. He did not hear Amy's voice muttering with a disconcerting degree of indifference.

'Not really.'

But Mabli and Enid heard and so did other members of the class including Mrs. Hughes-Davies. She stretched out her left hand without letting go of her string of beads. She turned her head out of respect for the minister's hurried departure to another class and then raised her eyebrows gracefully before speaking.

'Would you care to enlarge, Miss . . .'

'Parry.'

Enid was ready with the name.

'Amy Parry.'

'Yes, of course. Our very welcome guest. And that's Miss Herbert. We are delighted to have you both. And grateful to Miss Prydderch for bringing you.'

Mabli was blushing and nervous about whatever Amy would be liable to say next.

'There is nothing more stimulating than a positive reaction,' Mrs. Hughes-Davies said.

She waited patiently for Amy to speak.

'It's so primitive,' Amy said.

It was a reasonable statement. A defensible point of view. Having put herself in an exposed position where it could have been easy to look foolish, she had contrived to utter words that no one could condemn as ill-considered or silly. Relief showed all over her face. She breathed deeply and found it easy to continue.

'It's not really civilised. He sounds like a savage, talking about some bloody, vengeful, war god. And the thing is, as Mr. Arthog Williams was just saying really, the world has had enough of war.'

Mabli smiled at her forgivingly. The reference to the minister showed that Amy was not, as she had at first suspected, lacking in respect and admiration for the man she had been so anxious for her new friend to see and hear.

'"*I looked to see the wooded country and the meadows a wilderness...*"' Miss Griffiths was reading again in her steady monotone.

'"*And all her cities were in ruins in the presence of the Lord, laid waste by the heat of his anger*".'

'That's it.'

Amy had acquired enough confidence to lead the discussion. Mrs. Hughes-Davies was smiling at her, pleased perhaps that a flash of sullen rebellion was developing into a civilised debate. The class had become more interested and animated. The young women shifted about and spoke or muttered, pleasantly stirred by a breath of controversy.

'A savage God,' Amy was saying. 'For a savage people.'

'Who says we're not savage?'

Mabli looked pleased with herself for finding the courage to intervene brightly.

'We may not look it, of course...'

She couldn't find the words quickly enough to complete

what she had to say and she lowered her head to taper off her intervention into a self-effacing giggle.

'Isn't that the whole point?'

Having taken the lead, Amy was loath to lose it.

'People, societies, always create the God that suits them. That's what I'm trying to say. Take the War for instance. The Germans praying for victory to their God and the British to theirs. That sort of thing.'

The class became so immersed in the discussion they were quite taken aback when the bell was rung for the last assembly and all the scholars trooped in to recite the Ten Commandments; to listen to the day's statistics concerning attendance and absence, collections and verses; to sing the last hymn, recite the Lord's Prayer and bend their heads for the minister's final blessing.

4

The two girls hesitated on the street corner. Everywhere was so quiet they could hear the tide sucking the pebbles on the beach beyond the promenade. Amy turned on her heel to study uneasily her own reflection in a shop window. She made no pretence of taking in the goods on display. Not a single shop was open. On a Sunday afternoon the town seemed deserted.

'This is too ridiculous,' Amy said. 'We don't even know where it is.'

'It must be this street.'

Enid sounded apologetic.

'There's the back of the cinema. And there's the Baptist chapel. It is Baptist, isn't it?'

'How should I know?'

Amy wrinkled up her nose.

'They all look equally repulsive to me. I never thought I'd live to see a town with so many chapels in it, to be quite honest. It is the most awful dump on a Sunday. It really is.'

Amy looked so morose Enid was ready to comfort her with a bright suggestion.

'If we hurried back to Hall we'd be in time for tea with Tom Arthog.'

Amy pulled a face.

'You've got to be fair, Amy. He's not that bad. At least his outlook is modern. You've got to admit that.'

'Just go,' Amy said. 'I'm sure they'll make you very welcome. Mabli will lend you one of her joss sticks.'

Amy took her friend's arm suddenly and weighed on it in an attempt to make her lose her balance.

'We may as well find it,' she said. 'Finish what we set out to do. Let's just march down and then back again. Just once. And if we don't find it, we'll go back. Isn't that fair?'

Arm in arm they walked down the short street. They were both nervous, both conscious of being too easily observed. In the street there were two chapels, one Baptist and one English Presbyterian, the rear exit of a cinema protected by a locked steel fence, the back of a public building and a terrace of substantial red brick boarding houses set back from the street and protected by railings, laurel bushes and front gardens.

'There it is.'

Enid whispered excitedly under her breath.

'That's the one. "Tadmor". Did you see it?'

They had arrived at the end of the street where it joined a larger thoroughfare which ran parallel with the promenade. The discovery had not solved their basic problem.

'What do we do?'

Amy appeared to be seized with an uncharacteristic burst of panic.

'Did you see the name? Carved on the piece of slate alongside the front door. "*Tadmor*". The one and only "Tadmor".'

Enid was excited.

'There's a joke about it.'

'Is there?'

Amy was ready to listen as she considered their next step.

'There's a librarian who lodges there. Mr. Francis or some such. Very know-all. He was holding forth on the meaning of the name. All very scholarly, you know, interpreting the name. "Tad", says he, that's "father" and "mor" is a common contraction of "mawr" meaning "great", "large", "big". So that's what we have here, gentlemen. "Big Father".'

Amy was showing mild disapproval of Enid's attempt at mimicry.

'Anyway, John Cilydd was there, listening quietly. You know. In that sardonic way of his. He just said, "First Kings, nine, eighteen", and walked out of the room.'

'What's so brilliant about that?'

'Well, apparently "Tadmor" is the Hebrew for a palm tree. What are we going to do?'

Confidently Amy took her arm. They wheeled around with a comic precision that amused them both and marched back this time on the same side as the terrace of boarding houses.

'That bike!'

Enid pointed at a large motor bike alongside the pavement outside "Tadmor".

'That is the immortal "Zenith". John Cilydd's "Zenith"!'

They approached it with awe. Tentatively Enid touched the pillion seat with a gloved finger.

'It can do more than sixty miles an hour. It looks powerful, doesn't it? He must be in there. Visiting Val, I expect.'

They stood like a pair of startled deer ready to run but their feet rooted to the ground. They both looked up the path and studied the lace curtained windows. Someone in one of the windows could have been watching them. Amy was breathing rapidly, fighting to restore her self-confidence.

'I think I fancy driving a tank,' Amy said. 'Up and down and over hedges. With "Women For Ever" on the front, and "Wales For Ever" on the back.'

'What are we going to do?'

Enid was trembling with nervous hesitation.

'What do we say if we go up to the door?'

Amy tightened her lips, refusing to be nervous.

'"Good afternoon",' she said. '"Does Mr. So and So live here by any chance?"'

'But we've got to have a reason. An excuse for calling.'

Amy thought for a moment.

'We are fed up with waiting for Mr. Val Gwyn to call on us. So we are calling on him.'

'Yes, I know that's true. But an excuse, Amy. A polite excuse.'

Amy was looking at the garden. It was in an untidy state. Under a stunted cherry tree with half its dead leaves blown off, an old brown bath tub had been left upside down.

'I know!'

Enid cheered up wonderfully.

'We want to start a branch of the Movement in Hall.'

'Do we?'

'Of course we do. You know we do. So we need his advice. That sounds fine, doesn't it? And on our way back from chapel, as it were, we just thought we would call.'

'Off we go then.'

Amy was ready for action. She led the way up the path and rang the bell. The upper half of the wide door in front of them was filled with coloured glass. In the portico there were stands for umbrellas and walking sticks, and, in the corner, a golf bag filled with wooden clubs.

'Does Val play golf?'

Amy was plainly nervous now. Curiosity brought her no relief.

'It's awful really. I know so little about him.'

She looked at Enid. Her confidence had collapsed suddenly. She was weak and imploring for help.

'We are silly coming here, aren't we?'

The portico was floored with a neat pattern of black and white tiles. In the centre of the main door, made of mahogany, there was a highly-polished ornamental brass knob. Amy caught a glimpse of their distorted images in the curved polished surface. They were no longer two smart young women from the college but absurd caricatures in soft cloche hats.

'Let's go.'

Amy was changing her mind rapidly.

'Before anyone answers. After all, it's up to him to call on us. After all, he's the man. And he knows we've come up. It's not our place to run after him.'

Enid was reluctant to turn back.

'We're here now,' she said. 'It was your idea. Anyway it's you that he likes. That is a fact. So he's bound to be glad to see us. Ring the bell again. Pull harder.'

Amy began to blush; far more than she had realised, she needed information, she needed reassurance, at that moment.

'How do you know? It's only what your brother told you somebody told him. He could be quite wrong. I mean if he were really interested he would have been around days ago. At least he would have written. Oh dear, I should have thought it all out much more carefully. I don't want to look a fool, E.P. Ever. That's one thing I can't bear.'

Enid was calm and soothing.

'It's alright. We have every reason to call. We really are going to start a Cell in the Hall. Mabli and Gwenda have promised to join already. And those two girls from Tregaron. Anyway, educated women are the equals of educated men. There are more important things than outworn social conventions.'

'I don't know why I always listen to you. I really don't.'

Amy was striving to frown darkly at her friend. She did not see the inner door had been opened by a small frightened-looking maid in uniform. She was so small and thin she did not look strong enough to drag the outer door open. It sagged on its hinges. As she pulled, it scraped unpleasantly along the tiled floor, but the maid's pale face seemed incapable of registering any reaction: her senses had been dulled by unremitting labour. The sound made no impression on her. Her shoulders drooped under the weight of an invisible yoke. Behind her in the passageway there was a large overloaded coal scuttle. The lumps of coal on top were in danger of falling off. The little scullery maid would need both hands to transport it in the direction of the drawing-room fire.

'Good afternoon,' Enid said, cheerful and polite as ever. 'Is Mr. Val Gwyn in, please?'

The maid lifted her gaze momentarily to take in the face of the speaker and then quickly lowered it again.

'No, he's not, I'm afraid.'

Her answer was barely audible. One small red hand lay on the door knob as though it were glad of the rest.

'He's out then? When will he be back?'

The little maid's head moved slowly from side to side, displaying just enough resilience to bear her up above a sea of hopelessness.

'I don't know.'

She spoke so quietly the girls had to strain to hear the answer.

'That's it then,' Amy said.

She was ready to leave. The maid stood by the door ready to watch them go. They turned around, prepared to walk down the path. Enid remembered the motor bike.

'Wait a minute. How silly of me. We should have asked for Cilydd.'

She addressed the maid in a bright pleasant manner, intended to put her more at her ease.

'Mr. More. Mr. John Cilydd More. Will you tell him we are here, please. Miss Parry and Miss Prydderch.'

Before the maid could move a young man appeared in the doorway. He was smartly dressed in a grey suit with a double-breasted waistcoat and his blue tie was allowed to protrude conspicuously on his chest. His nose was flattened in his handsome face and there were gold fillings in his teeth. His red hair was cut very short, the top set in immaculate waves that gleamed with brilliantine. He spoke English.

A clipped nasal style and a slight lisp that softened his 'r's', helped to disguise his native accent.

'This is very nice,' he said.

He stepped down on to the black and white tiles with the neat step of an athlete. He fingered one shirt cuff and then the other, drawing them out a little so that his gold cuff-links came into view. He grinned happily at the girls.

'I must be able to help you. Old Gwynnie-Binnie can't really speak English.'

'Neither can we.'

Enid's sharp reply came so quickly, he blinked. Then to show his equanimity was undisturbed he jerked his head back like a skilled boxer avoiding a blow to the head.

'My goodness,' he said. 'I suppose I asked for that one. Leading with my chin.'

He smiled broadly to demonstrate that the feathers of his self-confidence were not easily ruffled.

'Winnie.'

He addressed the maid with his own kind of kindly contempt. Inside her black uniform, the maid had begun to shiver with the cold.

'You go and put the coal on the fire, there's a good girl. I'll look after these young ladies.'

He swivelled his neck to watch her lift the heavy coal scuttle with both hands. When she had struggled through the drawing-room door which he had left open he turned to speak pleasantly with Enid and Amy.

'Our little Maid of the Mountains,' he said. 'Now, who was it you wanted to see?'

The girls looked at each other, uncertain what to say.

'We have a small selection of bachelors in this establishment. Not *all* eligible, I regret to say.'

He rubbed his hands in comic imitation of an obsequious shopwalker.

'Professional men of slender means for the most part. But full of promise. Full of promise. Anyway, won't you come in?'

The girls declined the invitation.

'We would like to speak to Mr. Cilydd More.'

Amy spoke the name with particular clarity.

'Ah. The Bard himself! I'll get him this instant. He's busy writing in the back parlour. Or said he was. For all I know he was taking his post-prandial snooze. Excuse me.'

They could see him marching lightheartedly down the passage. He even managed to practise a side-shuffle before tapping briskly on a door beyond the divide of gathered curtains.

'Cilydd! This is your lucky day.'

He opened the door, but they could still hear his penetrating tenor voice.

'There are two beautiful young ladies asking for you at the front door. If you need any assistance, old fellow, please don't hesitate to call on me.'

Amy spoke to Enid in an urgent whisper.

'I don't think we should go in. Do you?'

'No. It's probably against the rules anyway, come to think of it.'

'I don't care about that. It's that awful fellow. And there are probably more like him inside. He thinks he's God's gift to the female sex.'

They retreated from the doorway so that they could enjoy a giggle together without being heard.

'He's so ridiculous.'

Enid placed her gloved hand over her mouth.

'Not to look now, but he's standing in the window. He's lighting his pipe with a flourish. Do you know what I think. I think he thinks he's on the pictures.'

'Girls.'

Cilydd was standing on the path behind them. They had not heard him come down from the house. His dark suit and narrow trousers looked old-fashioned in comparison with the grey suit of the red-haired young man. His fingers were thrust into his waistcoat pocket and his chin lifted high above his stiff collar as he tried to smile. He was shy but anxious to be friendly.

'I'm very glad to see you. Why don't you come in? I could offer you some tea.'

Amy was shaking her head.

'We ought to shake hands anyway.'

Solemnly he shook hands with them both. His hand was cold and there were ink stains on his fingers. His spectacles intensified his searching stare and made them both a little uneasy.

'You were looking for Val, I expect,' he said.

Their silence suggested their disappointment.

'He's not here, I'm afraid. And I am. That's the pity of it.'

Enid protested first and Amy quickly joined in.

'Oh no, John Cilydd. We are delighted to see you. We recognised the bike. Well, I did anyway. We knew you'd be here.'

'Why don't you come in?'

He stretched his right arm stiffly to indicate the door, as though it were an object they had not noticed before.

'We are first-years.'

Amy outlined the situation in her most helpful manner.

'We're not sure, but we think there is a rule about first-years entering boarding houses in the town. It's silly of course. But there could be eyes watching.'

32

The idea of being watched seemed to make him suddenly self-conscious. His back stiffened and he became too shy to speak.

'Where is Val then?'

Enid asked the question gently. She seemed acutely responsive to Cilydd's condition, as though she never forgot that he was a poet with one skin less than ordinary men.

'That is the whole trouble.'

Cilydd looked morose.

'He is in Paris now. As far as I know. But the danger is, in a matter of weeks he will be in America. For good.'

'Oh, no.'

Enid gave voice immediately to her alarm and distress. Amy went pale and moved away a little to hide her feelings.

'That was exactly my reaction. We can't afford to lose him. Wales can't afford to lose him. That sounds a little pompous and inflated. But I believe it to be true.'

'Oh, so do I. So do we. Don't we, Amy?'

'And in my own case, of course, I have thrown in my lot with him.'

He breathed hard and pressed the palms of both hands against his ribs like a man trying to ward off an asthma attack.

'I mean this quite literally. My firm has opened a branch office in the town. I more or less volunteered to come here. In order to be with Val. So that we could start putting some of our plans into operation.'

'John Cilydd!'

Enid's voice was so full of admiration he allowed himself a frosty smile.

'How wonderful of you.'

'I don't know about that. I may have been just foolhardy. Or stupid. The poet getting the better of the 'torney.'

He was making a dry joke at his own expense and he shook his shoulders to indicate this in case of any misunderstanding. It appeared characteristic of him to take pains to be precise about meaning. Both girls were watching him closely and this made the obligation to be accurate even more pressing.

'I've rented a house,' he said. 'In the old courtyard behind our office. It would be more exact to describe it as a warehouse. A small warehouse.'

He paused as if to review what he had just said, and test it at every point.

'What for?'

Curiosity made Enid less patient than usual.

'A printing press. A publishing house. Something like that. Any movement with political and social aims must have one. It's quite vital that he should come back.'

'Well, he will, won't he? Of course he will.'

Enid was wishfully optimistic. She snatched a quick glance at Amy. Her friend's face was still pale. She was staring fixedly at the motor bike beyond the garden gate.

'I thought so. That's why I am here. But there's no word about his return. Not one word.'

'We must have faith.'

Enid was smiling cheerfully. He studied her closely through his gold-rimmed spectacles: although he derived obvious comfort from the presence of both girls, he found it easier to communicate with Enid.

'It's not only him,' he said.

Amy turned to look at him, alarmed by his grim cryptic manner of speaking. It seemed to suggest complications in Val Gwyn's life about which they knew nothing. The hero had another life, like another universe outside the reach of their imagining. She looked resentful of the pontifical manner in which John Cilydd was eking out his store of information.

'It's the Gwyn family,' he said. 'Arminians with Arian inclinations for several generations.'

He was amused by the puzzled look on the girls' faces.

'Would you know an Arian if you saw one?'

He did not notice how little appeal his humour had for them.

'Well putting it very crudely, people who do not believe in the divinity of Christ. People who do not believe in the doctrine of the Trinity. It's interesting, isn't it, our nation has been obsessed with theology for two hundred years and now quite suddenly it doesn't mean a thing.'

Caught up with his own idea, he mockingly half pointed to each of the girls in turn.

'Brilliant as you both are, it doesn't mean a thing to you, does it?'

34

It was not a line of speculation that Amy was inclined to follow. She showed that she was not amused.

'What has it all got to do with Val?' she asked.

'Quite a lot.'

He hastened to prove that nothing he said was ever irrelevant.

'For four generations someone in the Gwyn family has emigrated to America. At first for religious freedom. Then for political freedom. Then for economic freedom. Now Val has to face the choice. The Old Wales or the New Wales in the New World. I imagine that's exactly what he's doing now in Paris. Sitting in a café somewhere making his choice.'

'He has no choice.'

He was startled by Amy's sudden indignation.

'What right has he got to make a choice? Ordinary people don't have any choice.'

'That's the point.'

Cilydd spoke with his customary precision.

'He's not ordinary.'

'He's started something.'

Amy was blushing furiously but determined to have her say.

'It's his business to finish it. If he wants to make a new Wales he can do it right here. The old one is dead and dying.'

Cilydd was studying her like a man observing a landscape suddenly revealed in a burst of light from behind the clouds.

'I'm sure he'll come back,' Enid said.

She had given the problem deep thought.

'America is no choice at all. Not by now, surely? It's just like a rabbit running out of one trap into another. Amy is quite right. He has no choice at all.'

The red-haired young man was tapping the drawing-room window with the stem of his pipe to attract their attention. He made signs to indicate that there was a nip in the air and that they should come inside and enjoy the welcoming warmth of the stoked-up fire as well as the splendid entertainment his company would afford. Fleetingly the faces of other men appeared, drawn by curiosity and then quickly withdrawn as if to demonstrate that they had no desire to compete with the red-haired young man in importunate display or showy boldness.

'That's Rees.'

Cilydd smiled grimly as he uttered the name.

'Articled clerk and amateur Englishman. He worships two Gods. The golden calf and the English calf. In that order. He has a certain wayward charm. Surprisingly enough he and Val get on quite well together. How does one ever fathom the depth of the human personality?'

Amy had cheered up. She confronted Cilydd boldly.

'Enid would like a ride on your bike,' she said.

'Amy!'

Enid laughed reproachfully. Cilydd's head jerked as he looked from one to the other. He was pleased with the good fortune of having their attention and very willing to be made use of; to give them whatever they asked for.

'Just let me get my coat,' he said. 'I shan't be a moment.'

Before Enid could speak, Amy took her arm and led her to the gate. She put her head close to Enid's.

'If you ask me, I think he's quite keen on you. And so he should be too.'

'Now you are just making excuses. It's you that wanted a ride on the bike. And it's probably you he's keen on if the truth were told. He gets tongue-tied in front of you.'

'Rubbish.'

Amy was unshakably confident in her own analysis.

'To put it quite plainly, he is in love with you, E.P. And you think his poetry is marvellous. So Q.E.D. Let us not to the marriage of true minds etcetera etcetera!'

'Amy... You mustn't... You shouldn't...'

Enid was alarmed by the possibility that her friend would take charge of the situation and embarrass her further with more outright statements.

'Shush.'

Amy squeezed her arm.

'Here he comes. Like a knight in armour.'

Cilydd's tweed overcoat was made more bulky by the sleeveless leather jerkin he wore underneath it. He carried a motoring cap to match the brown coat, leather gauntlets and a large pair of dust goggles.

'You can laugh if you like,' he said. 'I bought these in Caernarfon and they've been a great boon. I've got leather breeches too, but I shan't bother with those for now. Well? How are we going to manage?'

As he lowered his dust goggles carefully over his spectacles he saw that Amy was laughing and that Enid too was having to struggle to keep a straight face.

'One lesson I've learnt in life,' he said, grinning. 'You'll never do anything worth doing if you are afraid of looking ridiculous. Now then, who's first?'

Amy slapped the pillion seat gaily with the palm of her gloved hand.

'Isn't there room for us both? I could sit on Enid's shoulders like they do at the circus.'

Cilydd was in the saddle. He kicked the starter and the engine soon began to roar. In the boarding house the men rushed to the drawing-room window. Enid and Amy began to shout, and then waited for the engine to quieten down.

'To the Hall of Residence!'

Enid shouted close to Cilydd's ear.

'Take Amy first. And I'll walk up the main street to meet you on your way back.'

Cilydd smiled and saluted in mock military fashion. Amy sat on the pillion sideways and hung on to the belt of Cilydd's thick coat. The motor cycle shot forward down the empty street. Amy crouched behind him and cried out with delight as the bike picked up speed. He drove first through the deserted side streets that led towards the college buildings and then out to the promenade so that Amy could enjoy the speed of the bike from one end of the bay to the other. Outside the granite mass of the women's Hall of Residence she jumped off, clapping her hands and laughing. Young women appeared in the windows, curious at hearing the rumble of a motor bike at the dead end of the prom on a Sunday afternoon.

'How fast did we go? Did we touch sixty? You know, I would just love to have a motor bike. It must be the perfect form of travel.'

Cilydd stopped the engine and took off his cap and goggles. The afternoon sun was low on the horizon and the great heaving expanse of western sea was alive with glutinous light. On top of the dark headland that towered immediately above the end of the promenade the sun had turned the unshuttered windows of a summer restaurant to steady signals of blazing light.

'Miss Parry. Amy.'

He cleared his throat nervously.

'Would you mind if I asked you something? I wouldn't ask ... I wouldn't dream of asking if it wasn't important. Important to me, that is. Does it matter very much to you whether or not Val comes back? I suppose he will, mind you. I'm pretty sure of it.'

'Of course it does.'

Amy was blushing but she met his close gaze without flinching.

'What's the matter? Don't you believe me?'

He was taken aback by her challenge.

'Of course I do. Of course.'

'I suppose you think I'm too young to understand his great significance and all that sort of thing.'

'Oh no. No. I didn't mean that.'

'I understand how much a new movement will need men of that calibre. Certainly I do. Leadership and so on. But I think it will need women too.'

'Of course. Of course.'

He looked uncertain whether to nod or shake his head. He seemed impressed by Amy's maturity and self-confidence.

'Not that anyone is indispensable. I don't think I believe that. Do you?'

Cilydd tried to compose himself by folding his arms. They were bulky inside the thick sleeves and gauntlet gloves.

'I was talking on another level,' he said. 'More personally. Not that I have any right to ask you. But it is important to me ... on that level.'

Amy showed her unwillingness to face his implied question.

'You are forgetting about Enid,' she said.

She turned to study the front of the Hall of Residence. She could see Mabli in the window of the Common Room waving and beckoning. Gwenda was with her and a male figure hovered in the dimmer light behind them holding his cup of tea. By the crest of hair and the clerical collar she could identify the Reverend Tom Arthog Williams.

'Enid is the most brilliant girl in Hall. Everybody says so. I think she's a genius.'

Amy looked at him as if defying him to qualify her unrestrained enthusiasm.

'She's the most wonderful person I know,' she said. 'I can tell you that much. Totally unselfish. But for her I can tell you, I wouldn't be here. I'd be working in a cake shop or something. I don't know whether you know that?'

He licked his dry lips and shook his head respectfully. In spite of her youthful good looks, the girl seemed to be speaking with the considered wisdom of the ages.

'You must go and pick up Enid. She'll be tired of waiting.'

He lowered his head obediently to replace his cap and goggles.

5

The study bedroom was arranged precisely as she wanted it. Through the tall window the afternoon light showed up the glistening marble top of the washstand and the carefully laundered linen splashback. A block of clear soap lying on a white soapdish was reflected in a bulging highlight on the ewer, and again, on a smaller scale, on the curve of the basin. The walls were distempered white. Two coloured reproductions of Watteau were hung in simple wooden frames. The linoleum on the floor was swept and polished. There was a mat by the bed and a rug by the fireplace. A neat coal fire was already laid in the black-leaded cast-iron grate.

Amy herself was in bed. Outside it was windy. The noise of the rough sea made the room more cosy. She hummed to herself as she studied the substantial text book she was supporting with her raised knees. On the locker there were more books and a tin of blackcurrant-flavoured throat pastilles. Amy had washed her hair and her fair curls were mostly hidden by a decorative blue nightcap that she chose to wear like a comic crown with the white lace frill turned up to provide the coronet. She dabbed the end of her nose with a handkerchief and then put it down in order to help herself to another blackcurrant lozenge. A gust of wind rattled the window. She wriggled her toes under the bedclothes and pressed her feet against the stone hot water bottle wrapped in a blanket. As she closed her eyes to mutter a formula, there was a tap on the door and Enid hurried in.

'That Vi Atkinson! I just can't stand her.'

She was carrying an overcoat over her arm and a hat in her hand.

'What's up?'

Amy remained deliberately calm.

'Overbearing. Supercilious. Patronising. Bossy.'

'Oh, I see. Just being her usual cheerful self.'

'Do you know what she said?'

Enid paced up and down the narrow room.

'Shut the door, my dear. And tell me.'

The words burst out before the door was properly shut.

'She was so cool and smiling as she said it. As if she was talking about the weather.'

'Just what did she say?'

'I was standing by the notice-board. You know, putting up an invitation for people to put down their names to join our Cell. Which I am quite sure I am perfectly entitled to do. She said I had no right to do it without asking the Warden's permission. She told me to take it down. As Head of Hall she said she had a right. I refused to. So she tore it down herself.'

'The old woodpigeon.'

'And do you know what she said? "We have an Empire, Prydderch, which touches every corner of the Globe".'

Enid was making a laboured effort to imitate an East Midlands English accent. Amy sucked her lozenge and her cheeks dimpled with enjoyment.

'"The whole earth belongs to the English-speaking peoples and you have to go on about this piffling little country and its piffling little language all the time. It's boring, Prydderch. Don't you realise that? Very boring".'

Enid breathed hard.

'And she was so cool and smiling as she said it.'

'She's a bitch.'

Amy derived great satisfaction from her brief statement.

40

As though suddenly deflated, Enid sat down on the foot of the bed.

'The maddening thing was I couldn't think of a really effective answer. I wasn't prepared somehow. And she was standing there like a great bulldog with her feet apart just waiting to knock me down.'

'We'll get her.'

Amy was chewing confidently. Enid looked at her eager for reassurance.

'Will we?'

'Of course we will. It will take time. We've got to consolidate our positions. Dig in. Prepare new ammunition. It's like a war really. It's got to be.'

Enid became distressed.

'I mean ninety per cent of all those women standing around laughing at her stupid jokes were Welsh. The very people who voted her Head of Hall. They put her there to rule over them in a position of pseudo-authority.'

'Well, that's exactly what Val Gwyn says, isn't it?'

Amy determined to remain cool and scientific.

'"It is in the nature of conquered peoples to become servile, imitative, unoriginal and incapable of facing the truth".'

'That's exactly what the students of this college are,' Enid said. 'A race of servile toadies.'

'Now steady on, E.P.'

'Why? You've more or less just said it yourself.'

Amy tapped her crown with her fingers to make sure it was on straight.

'If you take against the place too much, you'll never be able to do anything about it.'

Amy sucked wisely on her lozenge.

'I don't like it. It's so false. It nauseates me.'

'That's exactly what I mean.'

'It's an imitation of an imitation of an imitation.'

Enid was vehement. Her cheeks were still red with embarrassment and humiliation.

'If only I could have had something ready on the tip of my tongue to say. That's another good reason for this magazine. Val's got to come back. He's got this gift of crystallizing issues. Summing up in a way that everybody can understand.

41

That's the only sound basis for propaganda. And it's what we need. He's got to come back.'

Amy was staring hard at her text book. She shut her eyes to practise memorising a sentence.

'*Chromosomes vary in size and shape, but two chromosomes of each kind are present in every normal nucleus.*'

Her eyes opened. She was pleased with herself for memorising.

'Isn't this just like the book of Genesis! "Two of every sort thou shalt bring into the Ark..." Did you used to think it was naughty? And exciting. "Male and Female"! The great thing about science, E.P. It gives you a balanced view.'

Enid squeezed Amy's foot under the bedclothes.

'Come on,' she said. 'We're going out, don't you remember? Let's get out of this place.'

'Don't you want to hear me holding forth on the subject of sex? My cool scientific view. Very stimulating. No. That's the wrong word. Very absorbing. That's what I meant.'

'There's not one single rule that says women students are forbidden to enter solicitors' offices. Isn't that nice. Come on, Amy. Tea and toast with an intelligent grown-up man, instead of a set of cackling idiotic imitative poultry. Come on, Amy. We'll be late. John Cilydd is a stickler for punctuality. Have you seen the way he glances at his watch?'

'The thing is...'

Amy spoke with elaborate tact, dabbing her nose with her handkerchief.

'I've got a chill. And without thinking, I've washed my hair. Force of habit. Anyway, I'm sure I shouldn't go out.'

'Oh, Amy...'

Enid was sharply disappointed.

'We've promised him. We should keep our promise. You know how sensitive he is. He's so easily hurt.'

'It's no problem at all.'

Amy held out the fist that clutched her handkerchief.

'You go. Tell him I'm unwell. A chill. I'm losing my voice. And my throat is sore.'

'Oh, Amy...'

'It's the truth. Also I'm miles behind with my work. To tell you the truth, I've taken on too much. I've got a problem. I like Geog. and I like Biol., but the two departments don't like each other. Can you imagine it? Robinson and Bowen just hate each other's guts. It's too ridiculous for words. But I could get caught in the crossfire.'

'You are deep.'

Amy had been smiling winningly at her friend. What she received in return was a long hard stare.

'Am I?'

'You keep everything so close. You hide it all deep down inside you. And you look so open and forthright. You can smile like a summer's day and in fact you are just about the most secretive person I've ever known.'

Amy was not pleased with the criticism.

'That's not very nice,' she said. 'Especially coming from you, E.P. I've always told you everything.'

'It's as if you are always on your guard. Always.'

'So would you be, my girl, if you came from where I come from.'

'We come from the same place, surely.'

'That's just where you're wrong, Enid Prydderch. I come from the very bottom. And I'm obliged to crawl up on my hands and knees. And don't you forget it.'

'That's not fair . . .'

Enid was upset.

'After all, Mr. Parry and your aunt. They are very respectable people. Very intelligent people.'

Amy relented a little.

'I have to work,' she said. 'I have no other choice. If I want to make something of my life, I have to put my work first.'

Enid was near to tears. Her defence sounded childlike.

'You were the one who said the world needed changing.'

'Of course it does.'

'Well, we've got to start. Or this place will suffocate us. It's changing you already. That's what I mean. Instead of us changing the place, the place will change us. It can so easily happen.'

Enid was excitedly in pursuit of a new idea.

'You could easily be "included".'

'Me?'

'Easily. Good at games. Lovely singer. Popular. Plenty of social graces. They'll make an idol of you and you won't be able to resist it.'

Amy laughed out loud. The text book slipped over and she scrambled to rescue it.

'I'll say this for you, E.P. You are never short on imagination. You were born to be a poet or a playwright or something. It just bubbles up and down inside you, all day long.'

Enid sat still on the edge of the bed. Her face was long and despondent.

'I used to believe I was creative,' she said. 'I know now I'm not. Then I thought perhaps I had a good critical mind. And I suppose I have in a way. But what's the use if I can't win arguments? Get a point of view across.'

Amy leaned forward to pat her gently on the back of her hand.

'You go and see old John Cilydd,' she said. 'You've got everything in common.'

Enid lowered her head. Her voice was barely a whisper.

'You're throwing us together,' she said. 'It's you really he wants to see.'

Amy struck the bed with her fist.

'Now that is rubbish, E.P., and you know it. Complete and utter rubbish. Anybody would think you had one of those inferiority complexes. You're bright and you're beautiful.'

Enid was shaking her head.

'It's true and I'm telling you! And there's nothing in the wide world he likes more than talking to you. He likes it even more than talking about Val, and that's saying something.'

'Val.'

Enid spoke the name and gazed questioningly into Amy's eyes. Amy was not to be put off.

'Do you know what I think? You must never tell him this, E.P.'

Enid lowered her head slowly, unwilling and yet eager to listen.

'It's not something I know anything at all about, of course. But I can use my eyes. And my common sense. I'm very good on common sense. I think you inspire him. No! Just listen. That's what he is, after all. A poet. And a poet can't exist without inspiration. He may not know it and you may not know it. But I'm your friend and I can see the game better than the players, by chasing up and down the touchline. You should be where you should be at the right moment. He is a good poet, isn't he? You believe that. I don't know anything about that sort of thing.'

'It's not very nice to discover your limitations,' Enid said. 'I'm so feeble.'

She sighed deeply before she spoke again.

'You are strong. All the way through. The world will never be too much for you.'

'Nor for you, Enid Prydderch, while I'm around.'

Amy straightened her back to exude protective power.

'I let that Vi Atkinson walk all over me,' Enid said.

'Don't you worry. We'll settle her sooner or later. Your trouble, my lovely, is perfectly obvious. You're too good and too sensitive for politics. Well, I'm not good and I'm not sensitive. If politics is a game, you can learn to play it. That's what I think. You wait till I get Lady Vi on the hockey field. I'll make her shins smart.'

Amy's blue nightcap was slipping down over her left eye. Enid was looking more cheerful.

'Now you go and see our master-poet. And if there's any news of Val, you know where to bring it.'

Amy smiled wistfully, confident now that she could appeal for a little sympathy.

'We all have our little dreams,' she said.

'I wish you'd come. You can't be all that ill.'

There were urgent knocks outside the door. They heard Gwenda's voice.

'Amy! You there? Can we come in?'

Gwenda appeared first. She was breathless with indignation but still intent on preserving her sleek and soigné appearance. Behind her Mabli's head kept turning to look over her left shoulder to make sure the support in the corridor was in no danger of melting away.

'Look here, we've got to do something about this,' Gwenda was saying. 'Vi Atkinson had no right to pull that notice down. Who is she to say the Hall has too many societies already?'

Amy tugged at Enid's sleeve.

'There you are,' she said. 'What did I tell you?'

Gwenda swept on.

'This is what I suggest. I suggest we've got enough bodies

here and now to form a good solid society right away, this very minute. Isn't that so, girls?'

There were loud noises of agreement from the corridor. An abortive cheer was followed by a spasm of good-natured laughter. Mabli was grinning happily, enjoying the occasion. Gwenda waved for silence.

'Moreover, my friends, we shall compose a masterly letter and send it to the Principal and to the Senate, informing them that our Cell exists and demands the rights and privileges accorded to any other college society.'

'That's very good, Gwenda.'

Amy was nodding her agreement so vigorously her blue crown fell and her hair slipped down about her ears.

'Therefore I propose we have a meeting here and now. Have I said that before?'

Gwenda's fingers were straying urgently through the pockets of her cardigan.

'Anyone got a cigarette? I think better when I'm smoking.'

In no time the narrow room was crowded with excited young women, all talking at once. Amy replaced her blue nightcap. A plump girl stood near her locker and stared expectantly at the open tin of blackcurrant pastilles. Gwenda raised her empty cigarette-holder and rapped it on the iron frame at the foot of the bed. The tinkle of sound was too ineffective. Amy smiled happily and clapped her hands to win some silence.

'Girls. Please be quiet. Gwenda wants to say something. Shush.'

Gwenda stabbed the air with her cigarette-holder.

'This is the way to do it! Officers of the Society. Secretary, Enid Prydderch. Treasurer, me, Gwenda Gethyn. Lots of experience with other people's money. Chairman, Amy Parry. Any other nominations?'

The girls all laughed and cheered and raised their hands to show complete and untroubled agreement. Amy reached out to tug at the coat on Enid's arm, and draw her close so that she could mutter fiercely in her ear.

'Off you go. Now you've got something extra to tell him.'

Enid was overwhelmed with the warm response of her friends.

'You see. It's not such a bad place, E.P.'

Amy grinned and pushed her on her way. When they saw her make for the door some of the girls began to protest.

'Steady on. Where's she off to?'

'That's our new secretary. Where does she think she's going?'

Amy raised her hand like a policeman holding up traffic.

'There's something you all ought to know.'

She raised her eyes to indicate she was going to be funny.

'I didn't want to let on, but the fact is I'm suffering from the bubonic plague. My good friend and your good friend, Miss E. Prydderch, is just off to the chemist to collect a ton of antidotes and a small bottle of the elixir of life. The Cell exists. Long live the Cell!'

Enid waved before she hurried off.

'What about the minutes?'

Amy lifted the tin and offered the fat girl a lozenge as an answer to her question.

'Don't you worry. Like all good chairmen, I'll invent them,' she said.

6

The discreet hotel sign was almost hidden by overgrown laurel. Cilydd stretched out his leg to keep the motor cycle upright and raised his dust goggles to read the sign in greater detail. Enid sat on the pillion, gripping the belt of his thick coat.

'"Doferchen Hall Hotel"... and in brackets: "patronised by H.R.H. The Duke of Connaught, K.T. Hot and Cold Luncheons. Afternoon Teas. Under personal management of the resident proprietors, Mr. and Mrs. Sidney Hale"... in brackets and very small print: "late of Eastbourne". Do you think it is good enough for us, Miss Prydderch?'

Enid could not hear all he said above the noise of the engine, but she could tell he was joking and she laughed obligingly into the woollen scarf wrapped around her face. They set off up the gravelled drive at a suitably majestic pace.

Cilydd left his goggles on the peak of his cap and looked about with alert interest. A flash of movement in a hazel copse below them made him brake suddenly. Enid was jerked forward and the right side of her head collided with his back. He called out an unintelligible apology at the same time indicating he would like her to get off. She stood well back as he cut off the engine, kicked down the parking stand and tugged excitedly at the heavy bike.

'Did you see it?'

'See what?'

He was in too much of a hurry to explain. He jumped over a moss-covered fallen wall and raced towards the copse. Enid hesitated and then tried to follow him. The ground became marshy and churned with the cloven feet of grazing cattle. Cilydd was leaping from clump to clump of green rushes to reach the hazel copse. Where the park opened out the grass was cropped low except for the rushes. The sun scattered the grey clouds above the quiet valley. Cilydd's activities had disturbed a flock of curlews and Enid shaded her eyes to watch their flight. As they rose up they melted into the sunlight and only their melancholy cries marked the line of their retreat. A noble cluster of great fir trees stood out against the bright sky. The bark of the lower tree trunks was a strange pink colour which merged upwards into black as though the outstretched branches had been singed in an attempt to snare the golden fire of the sun. Left alone Enid also ventured to raise her arms. The place was a new discovery in the calm October afternoon. She was willing to stay still and patiently enjoy it.

Eventually Cilydd came back to her. He was out of breath and his boots were caked with mud.

'Did you see it?'

'Did I see what?'

'The pig. It was a young sow in fact. And there were more pigs. All young sows rooting around in the wood.'

He waited for her to marvel a little and then they made their way back carefully to the motor cycle. He wiped his boots in the tufts of coarse grass between the fallen stones.

'I suppose you know that pigs can see the wind?'

She knew that he was teasing her. Since it appeared to give him pleasure she did her best to respond.

'And they can disappear too, can't they?'

He jerked the bike forward off its stand.

'My great uncle was very fond of pigs. He used to say that the pig is a very clean animal. It's human beings, he said, that are dirty.'

He straddled the bike, holding it firm while Enid mounted the pillion.

'Would that be the uncle who taught you the strict metres?'

Her tact was too apparent. It made him reply in a brief irritable manner.

'No. Who says he taught me?'

Enid hesitated to answer. He was not an easy person to know. And she was under no obligation to push their friendship beyond an intermediate stage. He had an intimidating habit of pausing and giving a sudden upward tilt of his head before committing himself to a statement. It was as if some alarmingly impartial mechanism sifted everything she said ready to reject the spurious or the counterfeit. She settled herself comfortably on the pillion and spoke up cheerfully.

'He's mad about billiards.'

He turned to glance at her sharply over his shoulder. The pupil in the corner of his eye looked so intensely suspicious that she laughed at him openly.

'Who told you?'

'You did of course.'

She punched him in the back. He appeared to register the action and find it unexpectedly pleasing. He breathed deeply, leaned forward with his hands on the wide handlebars and his feet planted firmly on the ground. He heard the crying of the curlews and his head moved from side to side.

'They say it will all be here tomorrow. But it won't, you know.'

He bent forward and pushed the heavy motor cycle forward with his feet. He listened to the crunch of the tyres on the gravel.

'That's why we have to do it. Weave out of worn words ghostly worlds that can't rot or wear out. There's a paradox for you.'

His boots dug harder into the gravel. Her silence behind him lured him to go on speaking, against his natural inclination to cautious silence.

'And there's nothing clever about it. In fact you have to be a bit stupid to do it. Especially in our language. Not stupid, ignorant.'

He stopped the motion of the motor cycle and straightened his back, recklessly pleased to be speaking his mind.

'The ignorance of a child learning to speak. A two year old. Distinguishing for the first time between snow and sugar.'

Without seeing her, he knew Enid had raised her head. To their left a plantation of fully-grown beech trees was firmly rooted in a wide hollow. They towered eighty feet into the air. A breath of wind had sent down a golden shower of leaves.

'There you are. You see what I mean. The trees are moulting!'

'So that's what a poet is.'

Enid was tapping his back in the friendliest manner with both her fists.

'A grown-up child.'

'Precisely. Can you imagine anything more useless?'

'Oh, I don't know. I think every village ought to have one.'

Her answer pleased him. He kicked the starter with hopeful energy. They cruised forward happily until the hotel came into sight beyond a wide lily pond bounded by a bank of rhododendron trees. Most of the surface of the pond was covered with a smooth carpet of green algae and dead lilies. There were lights already switched on in a drawing-room with glass doors that could open on to the terrace. The room gave the best view of the lawns and the ornamental gardens. Cilydd drew up several yards from the entrance.

'Will you dismount, my lady,' he said, 'while I take the iron steed around to the stables and arrange for him to have some oats?'

Enid looked a little nervous. She unwound her scarf and then waved it a little with her right hand.

'Shall I talk in a loud voice like an Englishwoman, my de-ah?'

He smiled encouragingly and drove off. Enid waited for him on the terrace. Beyond a high hedge a fire had been lit and the column of smoke writhed upwards between the roof of a summerhouse and the branches of an oak tree still covered with brown leaves.

In the east the faint moon had risen in the afternoon sky. The blue was deepening even as she watched it. A single starling arrived first on a corner of the lawn and was followed at once by a small flock urgently pecking at the soft dew-laden surface. Cilydd's boots on the gravel disturbed them. They fluttered upwards in a brief cloud and then landed again a few feet further away. He found Enid lost in reverie.

'Now then,' he said. 'A penny for them.'

'It's so beautiful,' she said. 'And I was thinking of what you said, John Cilydd.'

'What did I say?'

He slapped the gauntlets he was carrying together, determinedly cheerful.

'About it not being here tomorrow.'

Enid looked deeply thoughtful.

'Did you mean the world, or the moment or us?'

'My goodness. That is a very profound philosophical question. Much too difficult for me. Unless I have a cup of tea, of course. That could solve everything.'

In the entrance hall they hesitated, uncertain which way to take. Cilydd took a few steps in the direction of the reception desk. A plump woman appeared, smiling easily. Her hair had been dyed black and set in regular corrugated waves.

'We would like some afternoon tea.'

'Oh dear...'

The woman slammed the palm of her hand down on the large registration book. She confidently expected her guests to share the joke.

'I knew it would happen sooner or later. After all, this is Welsh Wales when all is said and done. *Dim Cymraeg*, I'm afraid. I've learnt that from Doris because she's got precious little *Saesneg*. Oh and I know *bara*. That's *bread* isn't it? And *llaeth* for *milk*. And that's my lot, I'm afraid. The trouble is, Sidney and I are getting on perfectly well without it.'

Cilydd waited for her flow of friendly reminiscence to stop.

'I asked for afternoon tea.'

His English was over-precise.

51

'Can you provide us with afternoon tea?'

'Of course we can, my dear. Just go down that way and make yourselves comfortable in the blue drawing-room.'

On their way in Enid was indignant.

'It's incredible when you think of it,' she said. 'In our own country. Just exactly where else in the whole wide world ...'

'Oh, I don't know.'

Cilydd was disposed to be more patient and understanding.

'Africa, I suppose. India. Anywhere where the British-stroke-English Raj holds sway. The language of the lords of the earth and all that. There is nothing that reflects social and political attitudes more accurately than speech, Miss Prydderch. Hotels, by and large, are for the convenience of the governing class when they feel like a little change. Where would you like to sit?'

A family group already occupied the positions closest to the fire: two prosperous middle-aged brothers in brown tweeds, and their wives. The women were knitting, contentedly aware that they were to be served tea at any moment. They glanced up from time to time as if to remind each other of this happy fact. The older man was describing a fishing experience in great detail. His loud Yorkshire voice did not succeed in holding his brother's interest. When Enid and Cilydd came in, their presence offered a faint hope of diversion and relief. His protruding eyes followed them like a dog's, hoping for some kind of greeting or anything that would relieve a wearisome stint of aching boredom.

Over by the window facing south, two spinsters sat side by side on a Chesterfield, engaged in deep and anxious conversation. They had been served with tea already and their cups tinkled in their porcelain saucers punctuating their intensely private discourse. Cilydd and Enid had little choice but to occupy chairs in the corner furthest from the other two groups.

'The world is a planet furnished for the convenience of Englishness.'

Cilydd was enjoying himself. He sat back in the tub armchair so that he could judiciously put the tips of his fingers together. There was a satiric grin on his face.

'This is what makes Englishness so accommodating, so reasonable and so tolerant and also so irritated by any

52

element that cannot be easily and effortlessly incorporated into the soothing anodyne universality of simple straight-forward pre-digested and reconstituted Englishness.'

Enid showed her appreciation with an imperfectly controlled burst of laughter. It sounded defiant and reckless. She could not help herself blushing. Her laughter made all the other occupants of the drawing-room turn their heads and look at each other questioningly. Cilydd was stimulated by her open admiration to further flights of analysis.

'If you find yourself stranded on a planet furnished in a particular way, your basic instinct for personal survival quickly educates you to fit in with the furniture. And that is the reason why we have so many educated idiots among our fellow countrymen. Last week I heard a certain medical man, who is a member of your college Council by the way, arguing that by now all the great riches of the world's culture were easily available through English and therefore English should be proclaimed the universal language forthwith. And your little *universitas* could best put its widow's mite in the collection by seeing to it that Welsh should never be used as a medium of instruction. And be put to death as quickly as possible. Gwalia, behold your gods.'

Enid raised her eyebrows to indicate that a waiter was standing behind Cilydd's chair. As if taken by surprise Cilydd lifted his head to look at him. He was a small man with a wrinkled face and his black clothes were too big for him. His attempts to smarten himself up had been concentrated on his hair which was flattened down at the front with oil but sticking out jaggedly at the back. He had been listening to Cilydd's animated discourse with an odd mixture of bold familiarity and ingratiating respect. The language being used was very like his own even though the meaning of the words escaped him.

'From what part do you come, then?'

He muttered as though he were conveying a secret message. He had discovered that the people he was paid to serve were closely related to him by language. This gave him the right to ask questions. Cilydd looked at him solemnly.

'China,' he said. 'We will take afternoon tea.'

He stared at the waiter until he shuffled off.

'Oh dear . . .'

Enid looked sorry for the man.

'You really have confused the poor fellow. You weren't very kind.'

'Kindness is for animals.'

Cilydd crossed his legs. He was unrepentant.

'This is what comes of our so-called national leaders talking about preserving the language on the hearth and in the chapel. It becomes like jam, sticky on the fingers. Instead of being invisible and healthy like the air we breathe. A healthy language is like a healthy climate. It should go unnoticed.'

He slapped his knee and groaned melodramatically.

'It's like a running sore,' he said. 'It's like a leprosy. He thought because he had the same disease that it gave him an automatic right to rub up against me. I wish Val would come back. That's one great thing to be said for political exercise. At least it eases the pain.'

'Why should we wait?'

Enid was eager to comfort him.

'You've rented that place. And you know this man with a printing press.'

For some reason her enthusiasm depressed him. He was quick to dismiss her suggestion.

'I've got no flair for it. I haven't got a political mind. I don't understand political logic. And I'm quite sure I haven't got his courage.'

'I wouldn't say that.'

Enid sounded quite indignant.

'You risked your job. That always needs courage.'

'Oh, I don't know. I was going to give it up anyway. No, I mean real courage. Being ready to die for a cause.'

When the waiter arrived with their afternoon tea, Enid tried to say one or two nice things to him but he behaved distantly as though he had decided it was wiser after all not to know strangers using his language. He glanced nervously at Cilydd and then murmured triumphantly in English.

'Everything is home-made.'

When he had retreated, Cilydd took the piece of bread and butter Enid offered him and stuffed it in his mouth to stifle a chuckle.

'There's no end to it,' he said. 'It's like an hereditary curse.

It's like original sin. And of course you can't write a thing about it. It's too endless. Too all-embracing. So you see, that's all I'm going to do all my life as a would-be poet. Collect fragments. Carve tokens. Volume One. Bits and Pieces. Volume Two Pieces and Bits. Ah, well. At least I won't peddle illusions about the human condition.'

Enid leaned forward to refill his cup with hot tea. She was enjoying the occasion. It was adult and intimate. It was an opportunity to discuss his work.

'Can I say what I think, John Cilydd? I think drama is the answer for a gift like yours.'

He set aside his normal distaste for discussing his own work, moved by her openness and sincerity. Her eyes were wide and sparkling with the opportunity of expressing herself on a subject obviously close to her heart.

'Why do you say that?'

'You have a mastery of the strict metres. Of prosodical form. You have a mastery over words in the central tradition. But I think the tradition needs expanding in order to contend with the complexities of new ways of living. Poetry can digest life best at the crisis point. And the crisis point has to occur in any dramatic form.'

He took a bite of home-made sponge cake and looked at the piece left between his finger and thumb.

'Are these your own ideas?' he said. 'Or is it something you've read? Forgive me for asking.'

Enid was blushing.

'They are conclusions I've come to. After reading your work. I read carefully. I'm not creative I'm afraid, but I have got a critical sort of mind.'

'I see. Press towards the mark. You are lifting the target. I shall have to think about it.'

They continued their meal in comfortable silence. They were both hungry and they were both confidently happy with each other. Cilydd made a mild joke about leaving one piece of bread and butter, one scone and one cake to demonstrate good breeding. It was something his grandmother had charged him to do when he first went into lodgings at the age of sixteen. The warmth of the room made them pleasantly drowsy. The waiter brought the bill. Cilydd gave him a shilling tip. The waiter bowed and murmured his thanks in English. When he was out of earshot, Enid whispered.

'He hasn't forgiven you.'

Cilydd was amused. As he stood up he tried to demonstrate a little regret in order to please her. Then he stretched his arms and legs to show preparation for further exertions. Before they left the room the older brother by the fire raised his arm and lifted himself out of his chair.

'Excuse me.'

His voice and his Yorkshire accent were as solid and as deliberate as the carved back of a wooden chair.

'I must ask you.'

His brother, his wife and his sister-in-law were all smiling in anticipation of a satisfying answer.

'That was Welsh you were talking, wasn't it?'

Cilydd stared at him solemnly. He seemed to be considering a barbed answer. With the instinct of a natural peacemaker Enid quickly made the reply for him.

'Yes, it was,' she said.

Cilydd turned away relieved of the responsibility and of any obligation to prolong the encounter. He went over to the coat-rack to collect their coats and scarves.

'I said it was.'

The older brother beamed benevolently at Enid and she was obliged to smile back.

'My brother here was of the opinion you were Swedes or Norwegians. But I told him I knew the sound of Welsh when I heard it. I've got two hobbies you see that have been bringing me to Wales for many years, fishing and antiques. I love Wales. We love Wales, don't we, mother?'

His wife hastened to agree with him.

'The scenery is so beautiful.'

She turned to her sister-in-law as if to reassure her of the authenticity of her information.

'There's just one thing, though.'

The elder brother held out his briar pipe in Enid's direction.

'And it's a question I've always wanted to ask an educated person like yourself. What use is it?'

He smiled cheerfully. He had asked a question he defied anyone to answer. He stood with his back to the fire and thrust his head forward in the most jovial and avuncular manner, his eye on Enid, fully appreciative of her youth and her fresh good looks. His sparse hair was parted in the middle. He looked as solid as Stanley Baldwin, but more ingenuous.

'What use is it? What use?'

Cilydd held out Enid's coat for her to put on. She was thinking hard and he left her to answer.

'I'll tell you.'

She inserted an arm in the sleeve of her overcoat.

'Ask yourself,' she said. 'Ask yourself, what use is civilisation. And when you find the answer to that, you will have the answer to the question you have just put to me.'

His jaw sank as he tried to fathom what she had said.

'Well, now... Hold on. Let's be fair now. That's no answer at all, is it? That's begging the question.'

He looked around his relatives for support, mutely asking them to show that they agreed with him. Cilydd had put on his own coat and was ready to leave.

'What do you say, sir?'

The elder brother was pointing his pipe jovially at Cilydd. Cilydd tightened the belt of his motor-cycling coat. He spoke with deliberation. His English was stilted. The English of a man who read the language more often than he spoke it.

'I'd say you got an excellent answer,' he said. 'Something for you to ponder. But now we must leave you, and bid you good afternoon.'

7

The road they took was an undulating ribbon leading down to the coast. Through half-closed eyes, with her head sheltered by the back of his broad coat, Enid watched the red rim of the sun dropping behind the watery green horizon. The pink clouds drew closer together as if it was their ceremonial function to close the curtains at the end of the last movement of a gigantic but totally inaudible symphony. The only sound Enid could hear as they drove through the soft quiet of the autumn countryside was the bold irresistible babble of the powerful engine that carried them forward like noisy ghosts on their way to an assignation. Cilydd switched on the headlight and it stretched ahead into a world that was only there because they had to pass through it. A white owl flew lazily through the precise segment of light and Enid tapped his back with alarm and excitement. He nodded and shouted something over his shoulder. There was no point in stopping. The owl had moved on just lifting itself enough to rise over the hedges. The hedges and the fields were merging into each other in the twilight that knitted together a secret world not available to travellers on powerful machines.

Cilydd shouted again over his shoulder and she stretched up to bring her ear closer to his mouth.

'Are you alright?'

'Yes. I'm fine thank you.'

'Not too cold?'

'No. I'm fine. Honestly.'

The wind created by the machine bound them together and they were willing captives. As it grew darker the bond grew tighter. The machine and its movement became the most sympathetic expression possible of their exalted isolation. It created a tunnel through which they could pass into a state of bliss governed by their joint imagining. Even the first drops of rain, stinging in their faces, became a substance to enhance their condition of glory. It had the cold purity of a dew arriving straight from a romantic heaven.

'Keep your head well down!'

She could barely hear what he was saying. Whatever it was, the sharp wind decorated and expanded it into an expression of triumph.

'I'm alright. Really I am.'

In the distance they saw the light of another vehicle. At first it seemed stationary. The light disappeared for a few moments where the road dipped abruptly to cross a small stream. When the lights appeared again it became apparent that it was a bulky cattle lorry moving at a bouncy speed that showed it was empty. The roar of a vehicle with a broken exhaust pipe challenged all comers. It made territorial demands and issued its own style of snorts and snarls.

Prudently Cilydd slowed down. The road had become little more than a lane with a ditch on the left side and a high bank on the right. Enid pressed her head against his back. Her eyes were closed in an expression of total trust in the man in the saddle. The driver of the lorry seemed too confident to slow down. As he passed the motor cycle the front wheel struck a pothole, the steering wheel swung momentarily in his hands and the tail of the lorry pushed against the protruding foot-rest of the motor cycle, sending it skidding into the ditch. Enid was thrown on to the road. Her raised arm and her right thigh took the brunt of the fall. Furiously Cilydd pulled at the bike, at first unable to move it. The rear wheel was still spinning helplessly in the air like the legs of a wounded horse. He abandoned the bike to run after the lorry, shouting and shaking his fists. But the lorry had gone. Its roar was fading mockingly into the night as it took a sharp corner and drove off in a new direction. Belatedly Cilydd became acutely aware of his lady passenger's condition. Overwhelmed with remorse he ran to her and kneeled at her side supporting her with his arms.

'Oh my God,' he said. 'What have I done? Are you hurt?'

Enid was trying to smile but her eyes were filled with tears.

'I think I've grazed my leg a bit. But it's nothing really. You mustn't worry about me.'

On its side in the ditch the motor cycle engine was still running. Cilydd drew her closer so that his lips were touching her cheek. He mumbled so intensely he could have been praying and begging at the same time.

'Oh my little angel,' he said. 'You're so brave. You're not even crying. I never saw a girl hurt who didn't cry before. And it's all my fault. I haven't taken proper care of you. You were my responsibility. You were mine to cherish and take care of and I've left you hurt in the road. Oh my darling, please forgive me. Each man hurts the thing he loves most and I've hurt you now, the thing I love most. Enid, I love you, will you ever forgive me, ever?'

She raised her left hand to touch his face with her gloved hand.

'Are you alright?' she said. 'Are you alright?'

He was becoming less coherent the more he spoke.

'I love you,' he said. 'Of course I love you. It's been

59

written inside me since I first saw you but I was confused and I couldn't read something I must have written myself. What am I saying? That I felt I was so much older than you. Seven or eight years is it? I know it doesn't matter but it seemed a great wall and, of course, you could be loving someone else. How was I to know? Why should anybody love me anyway? I'm not worth it. And you can see clearly enough now that I'm not worth it...'

'John Cilydd...'

She wanted him to help her to her feet. Her leg was hurting. She put her hands on his shoulders. Gently he lifted her. They embraced in the middle of the road. He kissed her face awkwardly, searching for her lips and repeating her name. She was patient and pleased until he squeezed her sore elbow and she gave a little cry. Once again he was instantly contrite, begging her forgiveness.

'The bike,' she said. 'Is it still working?'

He switched off the engine and tugged inexpertly at the inert weight of the machine. He stopped to breathe hard and to think. He approached the problem more rationally the second time. He managed to get the machine upright and pushed it back on the road. The front mudguard was slightly bent and impeded the free rotation of the wheel. He found a stone and battered the bottom of the mudguard until the wheel was completely free.

Enid stood in the headlight to try and assess her injuries. Her stocking was torn and hung around her ankle. She lifted her skirt. Her white thigh was heavily grazed. Cilydd stared at the red scratches with stupefied dismay. With a handkerchief Enid was dabbing bravely at the drops of blood.

'Oh my God,' he said. 'What are we going to do?'

He managed to put the bike on its stand and then started to take off his coat.

'Let me wrap you in this,' he said. 'It will keep you warm anyway. We'll get to the nearest house and ask for help. I'll leave you there and go and get a doctor.'

'No, John Cilydd. No. I'm alright. Really.'

She struggled to stop him taking off his coat. She made him get back in the saddle.

'Leave it on. I can shelter behind you. I'm quite happy

really. It's nothing. I'll hold on to you. You drive slowly. I'll hold on to you and we'll get back to Hall quite easily before seven. Anyway, I'm so happy I can't feel any pain.'

'Why?'

He was staring at her, apparently unable to understand and still borne down with worried concern and a sense of his own inadequacy.

'Because I love you, of course.'

She had moved out of the light as she spoke. Before she remounted the pillion she stood alongside him to give him a friendly kiss.

'A poet on a motor bike,' she said. 'That's what you are, John Cilydd.'

8

'You look marvellous,' Enid said. 'If only he were here to see you!'

She was on her knees plumping out the green velvet bows on the right side of the skirt of the dance frock Amy was wearing. The skirt hung low on the hips and was made of four rows of black fringe that shimmered when Amy moved. The black satin set off the whiteness of Amy's skin and the brightness of her golden hair. On the bed there was a large fan to be carried by the dancer. It was in jade green to match the velvet bows.

'I suppose I shouldn't be going really...'

With an effort Amy censored the smile that was breaking out on her face. She bit a fingernail, at the mercy of conflicting emotions. When Enid got to her feet she watched her closely for the slightest inclination towards agreement with the stern view to which she had given voice. But Enid was saying nothing. Just standing back full of generous admiration. She was a mirror in which Amy could have seen herself and been satisfied. But she was still plagued with nagging doubts. She eased herself by quickly transferring a share of the guilt or the blame on to her friend.

'It wouldn't look nearly so bad if you were coming as well.'

Enid smiled understandingly. Amy was ready to argue.

'I don't *have* to borrow your frock. I could perfectly well put that geranium red thing on. Ex Cranforth Royal. If it was good enough for Lady Alice it should be good enough for me. I could splash on some of Gwenda's Soir de Paris to take away the stink of mothballs!'

'Turn around,' Enid said. 'Let me see if your petticoat is showing.'

'There's nothing wrong with your leg any more,' Amy said. 'You can't really use that as an excuse. Does John Cilydd disapprove of dancing?'

'Of course he doesn't.'

'I'd just like to know what he expects,' Amy said.

'What do you mean?'

Enid struggled to her feet. Her right leg was still a little stiff from the motor-bike accident.

'Am I supposed to sit locked up in my room until the great white hope returns?'

'Oh, don't be so silly.'

'I wouldn't put it past him.'

'Amy!'

Enid grasped her arm and shook it.

'Stop criticising him. Please.'

Having made her appeal, she began to tidy the room. Amy looked cross and sulky as she watched her.

'I suppose you think you've been transferred to a higher level of existence. Above us ordinary dancing mortals. We are all too juvenile for words.'

In a fit of despondency Amy sat on the edge of the bed and frowned disapprovingly at the green fan.

'Amy.'

Enid stopped working. Her voice was gentle and appealing.

'Amy. What's the matter?'

'Can't you see?' Amy said. 'You have handed over your new dress to an old and trusted friend who is ungrateful and jealous.'

Enid came to sit alongside her.

'I don't like the way I'm feeling,' Amy said. 'It's horrid.'

She stared at her friend.

'Can't you see I'm eaten up with envy?'

Enid took her hands and shook them in gentle reproval. Amy's voice dropped to a whisper.

'What's it like?' she said. 'Is it something wonderful?'

Enid smiled and nodded.

'Just seeing him gets you all excited?'

Amy was driven on by her curiosity.

'And you always want to be alone with him? And there are no words to describe it?'

When Enid burst out laughing with happiness, Amy jumped impatiently to her feet.

'Well, that's it then. New Life. New Birth. New World and all that sort of thing. Good for you, Enid Prydderch.'

She examined herself critically in the wardrobe mirror.

'I do get the feeling sometimes he's putting me through a series of secret tests. Just to see if I'll be good enough for the great Val to consider, no doubt. There's something medieval about it. Does he send off daily reports to Paris by carrier pigeon?'

'Oh, Amy.'

'Do you have to report as well?'

'Amy!'

When Enid uttered her name again sharply, Amy saw that she had gone too far.

'You know I don't mean that, E.P. It's just that I'm so cross with you for not coming to the dance with me.'

'I've told you,' Enid said. 'I don't want to get trodden on by rugger forwards. I'm still a bit fragile and they're the only ones that ever rush up to ask me for a dance. Except the ones that want to get at you through me, Cinderella Parry.'

'If you were coming I wouldn't be feeling guilty for wanting to enjoy myself. So it's all your fault, Prydderch. And that's why I'm trying to get at you.'

She was appealing for forgiveness and Enid quickly gave it.

'You mustn't misjudge John Cilydd,' she said. 'He never says a single word against you. Ever.'

'I know. I'm sorry. But I get so fed up.'

Amy looked down reproachfully at the handsome dress she was wearing as though it should, in some way, be giving her more pleasure than in fact it did.

'I know he has this look on his face,' Enid said. 'As if he suspected the entire world of some primeval misdemeanour. As a matter of fact, I've told him about it. He was quite upset. He had no idea.'

'Well, it would help if he smiled a bit more.'

Enid was happy to enlarge on John Cilydd's facial idiosyncrasies. It was a subject to which she had given some study.

'The expression on his face is like that of a man peering into a microscope.'

'Oh?'

Amy was giving close critical attention to her own image in the mirror on the inside of the door of the single wardrobe in Enid's room.

'He is analysing experience as it occurs. Every little incident is being scrutinised under a microscope as it happens. Now this thing I'm calling a microscope for want of a better term is an integral part of his sub-conscious.'

'Is it?'

Amy resisted a temptation to be frivolous by moving closer to the mirror.

'It's a fundamental part of his poetic equipment.'

'Well, why couldn't he smile while he was doing it? He may as well enjoy it.'

She tried out an applied smile on herself but did not find it pleasing.

'On the other hand, a perpetual grin could be awfully annoying.'

Enid picked up the fan and ran the feathers through the tips of her fingers.

'Smiling is what I call a cultural twitch,' Enid said. 'Some peoples do and some peoples don't.'

'Is that a song?'

Amy took up the sentence and sang it to a popular tune from America. She bent her left elbow and rested her hand on an imaginary shoulder practising a few steps by herself in front of the mirror.

'And the fan,' Enid said. 'Don't forget the fan.'

'What would your aunt say if she knew I was waltzing around in a dress she had bought specially for her favourite niece?'

'She wouldn't mind one little bit. Come on. Hold the fan.'

'Oh no. I can't. Can I? Doesn't it look too silly for words?'

Amy slipped the ribbon over her wrist. The fan dangled languidly at her side, the feathers turning upwards like the necks of mythical animals stretching to catch any enchanted sound that might fall from their mistress' happy lips.

'You could at least come and watch,' Amy said. 'Come and keep an eye on me. I feel much safer when you are around. What are you going to do all evening? Write manifestos?'

The door opened before Enid could answer. Gwenda and Mabli hurried in. Amy lifted her fan theatrically to peep over it at her new audience. They were instantly enthusiastic.

'That's it! Exactly. Gorgeous. Belle of the Ball. Queen of the Evening.'

Mabli was giggling self-consciously in a white satin dress that exposed her knees. She clutched a heavy coat and stooped even more than usual like a brightly-plumaged bird in two minds between display and concealment. Gwenda was altogether more confident. Her dress was russet brown trimmed with dull gold. She wore her coat over her shoulders like a cloak and gave an extra length to her stride as she moved about the room flourishing her long ivory cigarette holder.

'We have transport!' Gwenda said.

Like a mannequin on a rostrum she strode about dramatically in the confined space.

'It appears that certain native youths are restless. Tom-Tom got wind of it in the back bar of the Black Lion. An ambush is laid for us. Isn't it exciting?'

'Ambush? What ambush?'

Amy was both anxious and incredulous.

'Something to do with a gang hiding behind the bandstand with dogs on leashes. As we pass they release them and they chase us along the prom. That was the idea.'

'I'd like to see any miserable dog trying to chase me.'

Amy waved her fan defiantly.

'Well that's it. You won't know. The President of the Students' Council has laid on a charabanc shuttle service. Tame really. No golden coaches. But safer I suppose? Enid P.! Why aren't you dressed?'

'She's not coming,' Amy said. 'I'm furious with her. And this is *her* dress.'

'You look heavenly in it,' Enid said. 'It fits you better than it fits me. Much better. I'm too broad for it.'

She turned to face Gwenda.

'Anyway, my leg is still hurting and I can't dance.'

'Isn't she impossible?' Amy said. 'I hate to think of leaving her here. Writing manifestos all evening.'

Mabli was eager to speak.

'Tom Arthog will be dropping in at the dance,' she said. 'For an hour or so.'

Amy raised her fan to tickle the end of Mabli's nose.

'The dancing minister,' she said. 'That's something to look forward to.'

This was a problem that Mabli had already faced up to and solved.

'Dancing is healthy,' she said. 'And it can be a natural expression of religious feeling. Take the Jews and the Negroes for example.'

Gwenda was laughing.

'Isn't she marvellous?' she said.

'It's a serious point,' Mabli said indignantly. 'Puritan non-conformity has deprived us of a major outlet of religious expression. My father always used to say that. He knew what he was talking about.'

Gwenda raised crossed fingers.

'Pax!'

'Anyway he wants to dance with each one of us,' Mabli said. 'So I said of course he could. He'll be very disappointed not to dance with you, Enid.'

'Never mind,' Enid said. 'You've got our chief attraction.'

'Yes.'

Gwenda wanted to add to the spirit of excitement.

'Just look at her.'

She pointed at Amy with mocking admiration.

'There she is. The mantrap.'

Angrily Amy stamped her foot and shook her fan.

'Stop it,' she said. 'What do you take me for? Who wants to be a mantrap for heaven's sake? What do you take me for? Some feather-headed fool? Any more of that rubbish and I'm not going. I warn you now...'

'Oh ... oh ... oh ...'

With playful energy Gwenda and Mabli were pushing Amy through the door.

'Now come on. We're depending on you. Aren't we, Mabs?'

'Oh yes, indeed. Men have got to be faced, after all, haven't they? Sooner or later.'

9

In spite of themselves Mabli and Gwenda were excited by the music and the two coloured spotlights that played above the heads of the dancers. They sat on either side of a small table just clear of the dancing floor, looking out for Amy in the long arms of a tall confident young man who clearly considered himself to be an accomplished dancer. Amy's green fan lay on the table between them and her prim programme card with its tiny pencil attached. Gwenda was able to hum the catchy tune and still look sophisticated and nonchalant. Mabli was more obviously keyed up. She kept glancing apprehensively towards a group of unattached males congregated in the space between the main entrance and the furthest corner where spare chairs had been stacked. Some of them had been drinking. A small group had turned in to face each other in order to create their own noise. One of their number stumbled back against the stack of chairs and then looked upwards prepared for them to fall on his head. A snatch of chorus was transformed into fuddled laughter. Enveloped by the glow of harmony generated by the band they could paddle contentedly in their own pool of sound.

'It's not nearly as bad as I'd feared,' Mabli said.

A cheerful young man with a comic face joined the group by the door. Much to their amusement he produced an evening paper. He began to slide towards the dance floor using the open paper as his partner. They gave him encouragement and a little cheer.

'Oh my goodness,' Mabli said, alarmed and amused.

It was clearly his intention to read aloud the rugby football results in a conversational tone as he gyrated around the edge of the floor. His effort was much applauded and encouraged by his friends.

A line-out specialist was in charge of the volunteer stewards. His large figure surged forward to lead the newspaper dancer gently off the floor. He was given a benevolent cheer for his efforts.

'Isn't Tom-Tom marvellous?' Mabli said.

She was full of admiration for the calm strength of the rugby forward and the influence he wielded over the unruly faction by the door. She clasped her hands together tightly in her lap and a contented smile spread over her face. The music was a massive receptacle of friendliness and cordiality. There was no need for anyone to feel left out. The elements of colour, movement and sound fused to give harmonious expression to the genius of the undergraduate community for creating an atmosphere of easy camaraderie. This was the true spirit of the place: a little world of young people bent on creating good will and happiness and on sharing it out among its inhabitants as evenly and as widely as possible. On the balcony young women were resting their chins on the rail and waved the tips of their fingers in benediction and greeting at their friends dancing below.

'Look at him,' Mabli said excitedly. 'He's watching her like a hawk. Have you noticed?'

At the corner of the gallery a small thin man pressed against the ornamented rail and stared down intently at the dancers. He still wore his overcoat. It was open and it reached down to his feet. His hands were thrust deep in the pockets. A cigarette hung in the corner of his sardonic mouth. His nose was sharp and slightly bent and viewed from below seemed designed to assist his deep-set predatory eyes in taking everything in. His hair was dark and thick and remarkable in being combed forward over his protruding forehead. He was one of the few men not wearing evening dress, and the only man wearing a narrow red tie with a stiff white collar. While they were watching him, Amy and her partner swept by. She called out gaily but they could not make out what she was saying. Her partner had pince-nez suspended from a black ribbon dangling on his dress shirt.

They contrasted oddly with the childlike pink of his cheeks. He flashed Gwenda and Mabli a generous smile which vanished quickly as he concentrated on executing a graceful chassé without colliding into another couple.

'Haydn is a lovely dancer,' Mabli said.

She was anxious to appreciate everything. She leaned over the table to speak more confidentially with Gwenda.

'Do you think he's keen on her?' she said.

'Who isn't?'

Gwenda's irony was unmalicious and free from envy.

'He's very nice isn't he?'

Mabli was on the verge of blushing.

'I know you think he's a bit pompous. A bit too old for his years. But underneath he's very kindhearted. Tom Arthog thinks a lot of him.'

Gwenda grinned at her in her most amiable manner.

'Well, there you are then,' she said.

'What do you mean "there you are"?'

Mabli simulated a little indignation as if it were a move in a game they could enjoy playing. Gwenda lifted the green fan and shook it at her mockingly.

'The hallmark,' she said. 'The stamp of approval . . . oh my God . . . He's coming down.'

'Who is?'

Mabli was ready to be excited.

'Ike Everett. The Bolshie.'

The man in the overcoat was in conversation with Tom-Tom the chief steward, just inside the doorway. He seemed to be making out a case.

'He's awful,' Gwenda said. 'Tom-Tom is asking him nicely to take his overcoat off. He just won't do it.'

Mabli watched over her left shoulder as if the mere act of observation had an element of danger in it.

'It's funny,' she said. 'Look at the difference in their size. Like a corgi sniffing at a St. Bernard.'

'Mabli! "Sniffing"?'

Gwenda pretended to be mildly shocked.

'I like Tom-Tom,' Mabli said. 'Don't you? There's something so appealing about strength and gentleness together.'

'Gentleness?'

Gwenda found the concept oddly incongruous.

'Have you see him on the rugby field? A juggernaut. He flattens everybody. A human steamroller. Oh my God, don't look . . . He's coming here.'

'Who is?'

'Ike Everett the Bolshevik. He does so like embarrassing people.'

Gwenda sat up to a more absorbed study of the dancing. Mabli followed her example. The young man in the overcoat stood between them looking down with intense but controlled interest at Amy's fan and her dance programme. He was in no hurry to speak. By the entrance two of the unattached males were accosting Tom-Tom and pointing indignantly in Ike Everett's direction. They were protesting against the fact that he had been allowed on the floor with his overcoat on. Like a referee who had been through the rule book and found no case for an infringement, Tom-Tom was shrugging his shoulders and turning up the palms of his large-fingered hands.

'Wallflowers, is it?'

He may have intended a pleasantry but his metallic voice rattled unpleasantly in his throat. Beyond the row of potted palms the brass section of the dance band snorted fortissimo and the bald-headed conductor, wagging his short arms, turned to the floor to seek endorsement and to give out a warning smile that the trick would be repeated. The girls took the noise as a reason to pretend that they were barely aware of a stranger's presence behind their table. The cigarette sagged in the corner of Ike Everett's mouth when he spoke. They could not possibly hear him. What he had to say would be conveniently obliterated by the music. He found an ashtray on an adjacent table and dropped it on theirs so that he could stub out his cigarette.

'Heard from Theo lately?'

He was sitting down. Gwenda could no longer ignore him.

'I suppose you keep in touch?'

Her look was intended to convey that the progress of her relationship with a person called Theo was no business of his. He crossed his legs calmly and leaned back in his chair, ignoring the signals.

'He had a good brain,' Ike said. 'But a bit fuddled with the

70

dregs of nineteenth-century notions. In Italy still, I suppose?
The Fascist paradise. Give him my regards when you write.
Tell him the class struggle is getting on nicely. Just as Ike
Everett predicted. You can give him some advice from me
too, if you like.'

At last Gwenda saw her chance to intervene swiftly.

'Why don't you give it him yourself?'

Ike was in no way put out.

'I haven't got his address. Tell him not to get lost in his
aesthetic preoccupations. And to take all that sex and
psychology stuff with a pinch of salt. Notice the metaphor?'

Ike was pleased with himself. He leaned forward and
looked at Mabli, inviting her also to listen to what he had to
say.

'Eating comes first, tell him. Economics. First, last, and all
the time ... the means of production, distribution and
exchange. The true facts of life.'

Gwenda sighed with sarcastic emphasis.

'Oh dear,' she said. 'Propaganda. Propaganda. Don't you
ever think of anything else?'

He picked up Amy's dance programme with the tips of
his fingers. He opened it to read the names already written in
it.

'Couple of vacancies here,' he said. 'Alright if I put my
name down? Pencilled in as they say in the trade.'

Mabli was roused to protest.

'You can't do that,' she said. 'You have to ask her
permission.'

Regretfully Ike let the card drop on the table. He stared at
Mabli.

'Who are you?'

'Mabli Herbert.'

She looked down at her fingers, overcome with shyness
and resentment. He made no further enquiry. This added to
her embarrassment.

'What's this about starting a Cell in the Hall of
Residence?'

He addressed his question to Gwenda.

'Oh, so you've heard, have you?'

'The question is, do you know what you're doing? I've got
to talk to her.'

He was watching the dancers, looking out for a glimpse of Amy.

'I don't know whether you understand,' he said. 'You're not unintelligent. In one sense this place is totally irrelevant. A puking little methodist academy jammed between the ice-cream carts and the hills. A piddling little Welsh petit-bourgeois information factory for turning out wage slaves for the Imperialist Capitalist System.'

'I've heard you say it all before,' Gwenda said.

It was a one-sided conversation. She would have preferred to be left alone to enjoy her fair share of the gaiety of the occasion. The tune that dominated the atmosphere would be coming to an end. He was depriving her of the right to hum it unobtrusively while it still lasted.

'That doesn't make it any less true.'

He grinned confidently. His teeth were brilliantly conspicuous in his sallow shadowed face. He licked his dry lips and pointed a crooked finger warningly at Gwenda.

'Revolution is like rain,' he said. 'The parched earth catches it. A pool here a pool there. Rivulets in the mountains. Every single one can contribute to the great river of change. Wash away the crumbling remnants of capitalistic oppression. Revolution is like a flood. And when the flood subsides, comes the dawn of a sparkling brand-new world.'

The band had finished playing. The dancers were clapping their hands before finding their way back to their seats.

'Ike Everett,' Gwenda said. 'You never give up, do you?'

He grinned at her to disguise his growing nervousness. Amy, escorted by Haydn Hughes-Jefferies, was making her way towards them.

'I don't need to,' he said. 'History is on my side. As day follows night.'

Amy reached for her fan. Haydn, her dancing partner, looked excessively pleased with himself.

'We managed it.'

His deep voice was so modulated and melodious that everything he said seemed to acquire extra significance. In spite of his youthful complexion his voice was already well on the way to middle age. Amy smiled at Ike. He shuffled to his feet, pale with the effort of controlling his emotions.

'I was talking to them about your Cell,' he said. '"Cell" is a

72

good word. Where did you get it from?'

'Biology, of course. Where else?'

Amy answered brightly. She picked up her dance programme to find out who she was dancing with next, and then slipped the ribbon over her wrist. Haydn inserted a hand elegantly in his trouser pocket and craned his neck, rather unnecessarily in view of his height, to stare at the entrance.

'It's a bit untidy around the door,' he said. 'Some of the fellows have been drinking, I suppose. Moderation in all things. That's my motto.'

He directed a stern glance at Everett but Ike had not heard him. He was watching carefully every move that Amy made.

'Can I have a dance, then?'

He muttered his request as if he hoped the others would not hear. Amy's smile had a disturbing effect on him so he avoided looking into her eyes.

'With your overcoat on?'

'That can come off.'

He lifted his hand in his pocket and the coat slipped back on his shoulders. Amy tapped her chin teasingly with the dance card.

'There he is!'

Haydn's deep voice drew attention to his announcement. In the door the Reverend Tom Arthog Williams was already deep in conversation with Tom-Tom, the chief steward. His head leaned first one way and then the other and his eyes were making a lightning census of any possible reactions to his arrival.

'I'd better go and welcome him,' Haydn said.

He spoke with particular dignity as though he were about to act in a private and a public capacity. He excused himself and hastened his advance to the door. There were men there who were making futile efforts to interfere in the conversation between the minister and the large benevolent rugby forward. Haydn frowned disapprovingly. Mabli rose to her feet ready with support if it should be needed but very nervous of anything the unruly men might do. The minister was in full evening dress with his overcoat over his arm and a white silk scarf, like a stole hanging about his neck. He shifted his stance to exclude the interventionists with his

73

back. But they were persistent and they shifted too, until Tom-Tom took a firm grip on their arms and pulled them to one side, without taking his polite attention away from the minister whose mouth continued to work at his argument as though there were no problems left through which he could not ultimately gnaw his way.

'Haydn does look smart,' Gwenda said. 'His height helps.'

'He could win a prize.'

Ike knew he was not included in the conversation. He put in his joke with a malevolent grin.

'Best dressed lamp-post of the year.'

Amy was laughing. He looked well rewarded.

'Ike Everett,' Gwenda said. 'You're just jealous.'

'Clothes.'

He spoke contemptuously.

'Clothes don't count.'

He stared urgently at Amy. His dark eyes were glowing.

'Do they? Do they?'

'No, of course not,' she said.

The answer satisfied him. He became quieter but did not move away. Tom Arthog arrived escorted by Haydn. His coat and scarf had been taken care of by one of the stewards but he still carried a pair of white gloves. When he offered one hand for shaking, he shook the white gloves in the other as if at any moment he might perform a conjuring trick with them. He suspended his long jaw and smiled roguishly at everyone before shaking the gloves again.

'My grandfather's,' he said, 'believe it or not. He had them when he first came to teach at this university in 1873. No dances then, of course. Just concerts and gala occasions. But I cling to them. My grandfather's gloves. Sentimental, I dare say. But I'm so very nervous. The saints in Ebenezer are not going to like it. Their minister taking time off to trip the light fantastic. They think I'm far too modern as it is!'

He directed his observations at each of the girls in turn, first raising his eyebrows in mock alarm and then smiling reassuringly. Haydn prepared to speak in his most modulated manner.

'Surely the point is, how can the minister understand young people and their problems in the modern age, unless he shares their experiences? In work and in play. And in any

74

case this ball is in aid of the Distressed Students' Fund. Practical Christianity, I would call it.'

Mabli was nodding her enthusiastic agreement. Her admiration for Haydn Hughes-Jefferies grew visibly as she watched the minister give him a smile of grateful approval. The argument put forward was conclusive. He could enjoy himself with a clear conscience. He put down his grandfather's gloves on the table and fumbled in his inside pocket for his fountain pen.

'Now I must put my name down,' he said. *'Comme il faut.* Oh dear ... This is too exciting for an old bachelor like me. You've kept little spaces for me, I trust? Now then who shall be first, dear young ladies?'

Because he was gazing at her so pointedly, Amy felt obliged to offer her card. It was still attached to her wrist. Like a man who suddenly sees himself losing his place in a queue, Haydn became uncharacteristically flustered.

'The statue dance,' he said. 'You promised me that.'

His hand thrust out wildly just as the minister's fountain pen was about to inscribe his name on the dance programme. The pen had been filled but the screw had not been replaced properly. A jet of bright blue ink shot over the front of Amy's dance frock.

'Oh no ...'

Her first helpless wail came as she looked down in horror at the ink still wet on the satin.

'It's Enid's ...'

'I'm so sorry ... I'm so awfully ...'

Haydn's voice was wobbling with childlike apprehension as he watched the anger mounting in Amy's face.

'Oh dear! Oh dear ...'

The minister was pushing forward to take a closer look at the damage. The offending fountain pen was still in his hand dripping with ink. Drops fell on the green bows and on the fan, and on his grandfather's white gloves. His head was close enough for Amy to hit.

'You clumsy idiot!'

The minister shot back dropping the pen on the floor. Mabli kneeled down to pick it up. The minister looked at Haydn as if he hoped that he would quickly volunteer to be the idiot referred to rather than himself. Amy pressed her fingers on the wet bodice and turned to Gwenda for comfort and advice. She was on the verge of tears.

'What am I to do?' she said. 'It's brand new. Enid will never forgive me.'

Together they hurried towards the door. Amy kept her head down like an injured player being taken off the field. Gwenda did all she could to protect her. Haydn followed after them, waving his arms apologetically. The minister accepted the pieces of the fountain pen from Mabli and gazed hopelessly at the ink on his fingers. He was so stunned he omitted to make his habitual quick survey of reactions to his behaviour. Mabli took charge of him. Gently she suggested he should sit down. When he had done so, he turned to smile at her vacantly like a man who has suffered a temporary loss of speech.

In the short interval a steady traffic had built up to the cloakrooms on the first floor. This gave the group of men near the door an opportunity to make their presence felt. The music had ceased. There was no longer harmony in the air to give cohesion to the evening. The disaffected wandered in and out, punctuating their random movement with out-bursts of badinage, fragments of choruses and concealed catcalls. Amy and Gwenda had difficulty in squeezing their way out. Over-anxious to make amends Haydn struggled to use his height to push a way through for the two girls.

'Now then, fellows. There *are* ladies present. Let's just pull ourselves together, shall we?'

All his deep voice succeeded in doing was to draw unfavourable attention from the jovial group pretending to control the traffic at the door. A plump young man was giving a poor imitation of a stage policeman. He held up Haydn with one hand on his chest, the other playing with his pince-nez.

'Who's this then?' he said. 'Mr. Gladstone or Mr. Asquith?'

He had instant support from his friends.

'It is none other than Hughes-Jefferies. Hugh Haydn, the Hanging Grudge.'

'The rising hope of the sinking fund.'

The pink colour retreated from Haydn's flat hairless

cheeks. His height left him curiously exposed. But he stood his ground.

'It's the curse of this college,' he said. 'Hooliganism disguised as fun.'

'Hark at him! Mother's best boy.'

'You want to degenerate the Col. spirit into mob rule,' Haydn said.

He had won a little support from some of the women and he was ready to wax more indignant. The plump young man snatched up the phrase.

'Mob rule! Now that's a good idea ... I tell you what, lads ... Let's debag him.'

'That's a good idea.'

'No. Listen now. Listen.'

The plump young man had something funny to say.

'They need a lamp-post in the dark alley behind the Black Lion. We could plant him there upside down and stick a light on his feet!'

Tom-Tom moved in with his burly trio of stewards. His manner as always was large, calm, reassuring.

'Now come on, lads. Don't upset the evening. Make a nice corner in the back there. Put your feet up, if you like. Relax a bit. I won't mind. How about this then? Llanelli 25, Newport 15.'

The men forgot about Haydn. There were some cheers and some boos. Tom-Tom lifted his arm and led the way to the corner where the chairs were stacked. Some followed straight away, begging for more details of the match. They looked like hungry calves following a farmer with a bucketful of mash. The band began to play 'The red-red robin goes bob-bob-bobbin' along'. Llanelli supporters gave a cheer. They took the song as a tribute to their team. An argument was developing in the corner that seemed more attractive than blocking the door. One by one they moved away. Haydn's face was flushed with triumph. He still wanted to speak.

'It's exactly the same in debates,' he said. 'Mob rule masquerading as democracy. There is no other way to describe it.'

Ike Everett in his long coat came up quietly behind him.

He poked him sharply in the back.

'Just move,' he said. 'And keep your big mouth shut.'

Haydn turned and looked down at him, his mouth gaping with astonishment. Amy and Gwenda hurried past him and made their way quickly upstairs. A few girls were still in the corridor outside the ladies' cloakroom, making a final inspection of their appearance in a long mirror on the wall behind a tattered red settee. The light was inadequate. The girls managed to kneel in turn on the settee to peer at their images and murmur their concern and discontent with what they saw.

Inside the cloakroom there was also a mirror above the twin washbasins. Access to the washbasins was completely blocked by a large blonde girl who was leaning forward to apply with care discreet make-up to her flushed face. Gwenda spoke to her urgently.

'Vi,' she said. 'Would you mind moving, please? Amy's got ink all over her dress. We want to get at the basin.'

Vi Atkinson continued to concentrate on her delicate operation.

'Fresher, isn't she?'

She spoke from the corner of her mouth. She was welcoming a heaven-sent opportunity of exercising her seniority. It was the perfect occasion to impress a factious element of the new intake with her authority as Head of Hall.

'We have to pull our weight...'

Unhurriedly she stretched her mouth to give her lipstick detailed inspection.

'... and wait our turn. That's what Col. life is all about.'

Her eyes opened wide with alarm as she saw in the mirror Amy's ink-stained hands threatening her head and shoulders.

'Just get out of my way,' Amy said. 'Or you'll have ink all over you as well. And be quick about it.'

Vi was speechless with indignation, but she was obliged to move. Amy turned on the taps. Gwenda unbuttoned her dress. She slipped out of it and stood in her petticoat and silk stockings, submerging her hands in the water.

'Don't think you're going to get away with this...'

Vi was by the door, muttering vengefully and calling on her companions to witness the outrage that had taken place in front of their very eyes. Amy looked at her in the mirror. The encounter seemed to have cheered her up. She lifted her wet hands and indicated a threat to splash water in Vi's direction unless she got out of the narrow room. But when Vi had gone, her distress returned. Together they soaked the satin top in the water. The fringes of the skirt and the pretty green bows hung helplessly over the edge of the basin.

'We're making it worse,' Amy said.

She could not prevent the low wail in her voice.

'It will shrink. I'm sure of it!'

'It will be fine when it's ironed,' Gwenda said.

She did her best to reassure Amy, who had begun to shiver.

'Here. Hold it. You'll catch cold. I'll get you my coat to put on.'

Amy stared at the ink clouding into the water.

'I'll have my own coat,' she said. 'I can't be for ever wearing other people's clothes.'

A spotlight followed the college singer as he moved among the dancers. They stood still, listening to him with admiration and respect. He was a good-looking young man with an exciting tenor voice. They seemed to take a particular pride in him, especially the women. The band accompanied him with muted care so that the quality of his voice could be displayed to the best effect. The expression on his face caught in the spotlight was white and wooden and his blue eyes were still and glazed over with the intensity of his effort. Amy watched the performance from the balcony, huddled inside her overcoat.

The golden glow... sinks bravely in the West
It lights the sea... it lingers in the sky...

Ike Everett was sitting behind her leaning back in his chair, a cigarette hanging from the corner of his mouth.

'Wallowing in it, aren't they?'

In the dim light he saw her nod. He was encouraged because she took no objection to his presence.

'Joined the overcoat club, I see.'

She turned briefly to look at him. He seized the opportunity to hold her attention. With his hands in his pockets he flapped the panels of his coat. He was pleased when he saw that he had made her smile. On the dance floor the students were joining in the chorus with the college singer.

Though we wander far away
We'll return again . . . some day.

'Pathetic, aren't they?'

Ike had moved his chair so that he could sit alongside Amy and peer over the balcony.

'Apes,' he said.

Amy was watching Mabli and Haydn looking at each other as they sang the soulful chorus. Even Gwenda was singing. She was partnered by an intense young man who was putting all he had into his singing. His eyes were closed, his nostrils flared and his mouth was open as wide as it would go.

'Sedulous apes.'

'There's no need to be so offensive,' Amy said.

'Yes there is. Tell me something. What do you think you are being educated for?'

There was so much going on below, Amy did not take her eyes off the dancers. The song had been a success. There was a mounting call for an encore. The young man with Gwenda was demonstrating his comic enthusiasm by clasping both hands over his heart and singing silent notes. The college singer was having a brief word with the bald-headed band leader. He was willing to go again and clearing his throat and smiling modestly. There was applause and encouragement. Softly the band played the opening bars and the applause subsided.

Sweet home of learning . . . college by the sea
From far and wide . . . we shall return to thee

Amy's lips were moving. She was sorely tempted to sing. But her powerful voice would have drawn attention to herself when she was virtually in hiding, sitting in the most dimly lit part of the balcony.

'Why do you think you're here? If it's biology it should be to double and treble the harvests of the world. Make things grow where they never grew before. Feed the hungry mouths of the world's millions.'

Amy's lips moved with the concluding lines of the college

80

song. She did not appear to have heard anything Ike was saying.

'Just because you're pretty, that doesn't give you a licence to talk nonsense.'

Ike Everett had moved so close to her, she stared at him in frank astonishment.

'But I haven't said anything.'

'Or think nonsense. I can tell quite easily what you're thinking.'

'You certainly cannot.'

Amy was so indignant she forgot the singing going on below.

'Just tell me one thing,' he said. 'Just answer me one little question. What do you think your education is for?'

'Why should I?'

'I want to know if you really know what you are doing.'

'Of course I do.'

'But do you really know? Or are you just another female ape? This Cell business, for example. Do you know what you're talking about? Is it just another spate of Cymric rubbish or is it something more? I've been watching you very closely for some time and I think you've got the makings of a genuine revolutionary. Now that's something a great deal more than just a common or garden rebel.'

'Is it?'

Amy was intent on preserving her composure.

'Well, thank you very much for telling me.'

'Do you know what revolution is?'

He leaned on the railings to stare at her intently, as he screwed the cigarette butt under the sole of his shoe.

'It is the marriage of science and violence. It's the furnace in which the future will be shaped. The invisible source of power. You are interested in power, aren't you?'

'I really don't know what you are talking about.'

'Oh yes you do. Don't give me that innocent girlish stuff. You've spent your fair share of time skivvying, haven't you?'

Amy looked annoyed.

'Now who told you that?'

'Never you mind. I make it my business to know things. Especially about people I'm interested in. Knowledge is part of the apparatus of power.'

81

'What's that supposed to mean?'

'You can't kid me,' he said. 'You know what it's all about. Power. Economic power. Political power. Military power. These are the things that really matter.'

Amy took refuge in silence. He was so authoritative, anything she said would have sounded feeble and even foolish. She turned away from the intensity of his gaze. His metallic voice was threatening her right to be herself. Her lips moved to join in the singing. Gwenda was looking up in her direction. She was showing amused patience with her partner's comic antics. Amy was delighted to give her a wave and a private smile.

'Look.'

His voice was threatening her again.

'I said, look.'

His hands were held out towards her and from his bony fingers dangled a sapphire brooch on a thin gold chain. He jerked it so that the sapphire caught the light.

'It's for you,' he said. 'I want you to wear it. I've been carrying it about in my pocket all day. I want to see it around your neck.'

Amy was frowning.

'I couldn't possibly,' she said.

'Put it on!'

He stood up and turned his back on the balcony rail. He dangled the brooch close in front of her face so that she could not avoid seeing it.

'Put it on.'

He was more urgent and pleading.

'If you don't, I'll stand on the rail and throw myself down.'

Amy looked alarmed. His face was pale and intense. He looked capable of carrying out his threat. She had only to bend her head for him to slip the noose of the gold chain over it. She stared a long time into his eyes before she decided not to be threatened.

'You'd better jump then,' she said. 'I'm not going to wear it.'

His hands began to tremble. He crushed the brooch and chain in his fist and pushed them back in his overcoat pocket.

'You can tread on me as much as you like,' he said. 'As much as you like.'

His head sunk down on his chest. He looked defeated.

'I don't want to tread on you, for goodness' sake. What do you take me for? You do say some silly things. Why don't you try and be more normal? More like everyone else.'

'Is that what you want me to be?'

'It's not a case of what I want...'

He interrupted her desperately.

'Oh yes it is. You've no idea what it's like. It's like a fatal disease. A sort of spiritual T.B. Haven't you noticed my condition?'

Amy was smiling. She was totally at ease now and in a position to enjoy herself.

'I've listened to you before,' she said. 'I've heard you say a lot of interesting things. I think some of them are true.'

He sat down and his head sank still further on his chest. He looked like a caricature of Napoleonic despair.

'Thank you very much,' he said.

'I'm not being sarcastic.'

He pulled out the brooch again to play with the gold chain.

'I bought this thing ten days ago,' he said. 'All I knew was I had to give you something. And it eased the pain a bit. Buying it. Intending to give it you. It's been hanging on the end of my bed for days. My landlady thought I'd gone mad.'

Amy smiled sympathetically and at once he was encouraged. He sat up.

'Oh God. I wish you'd take it,' he said.

'But how can I...'

'No obligation. Honestly. None. It would give me a little peace, that's all.'

'I can't, Ike. I really can't.'

He sat up. His name on her lips had given him renewed strength.

'As a mere gesture of friendship. Of good will. If you refuse to take it, it means you wish I didn't exist. That I was dead.'

'Don't be silly.'

'If you take it, all it signifies is, "Alright, Daniel Isaac Everett, you can go on living". That's all. "Daniel Isaac, carry on breathing".'

Amy shook her head. He was not to be put off.

'Just wear it,' he said eagerly. 'Not even take it. Just look

83

after it for me and put it around your neck whenever you feel like it. Now that's fair enough. I'm in your power. There's nothing you can do to prevent that. You can't stop me loving you. If that's the correct name for the disease. But if it gives me a little easement. If it soothes the damn awful pain for a moment, just imagine the kindness you are doing to an animal in distress. That's all I'm asking. Don't wear it. Just put it in your coat pocket. Just for a few days and then throw it away or give it me back or do whatever you like with it... Come on...'

He held out the brooch and chain for her to take. Her head was still shaking gently when Mabli trod carefully down the steps to where they were sitting. She was still breathless from singing and dancing and her narrow eyes were shining with a happiness she was eager to share as widely as possible.

'Amy,' she said. 'Are you alright? I've been thinking about you.'

At the back of the balcony, Haydn Hughes-Jefferies stood, erect and obedient, like a palace servant who waits to be summoned to the presence. A silver fob chain gleamed on the black material of his evening trousers.

'Haydn wants to apologise,' Mabli said.

She bent low so that she could speak quietly in Amy's ear. She seemed to derive a special excitement from being a messenger and conciliator. Her body was close enough for Amy to hear the thump of her heart beating.

'Be kind to him,' she said as quietly as she could. 'He's very upset.'

Amy was making an effort to remember why it was Haydn should want to apologise to her. The incident came back to her as something that had happened long ago.

'Good heavens,' she said. 'There's nothing to apologise for, is there?'

'You called them "clumsy idiots"...'

There was the ghost of a reproof in Mabli's little smile.

'Did I? Well I was upset about the dress. It wouldn't have mattered so much if it were my own. It was Enid's after all, not mine.'

'I know.'

Mabli showed that she understood every shade of significance in the way Amy felt about the dress and still wanted her to appreciate that there were even wider implications in the unfortunate mishap.

'Tom Arthog was very upset. He went straight home.'

'Did he?'

Amy looked very surprised.

'He was hurt, you see. I know you didn't mean to hurt him. But he was hurt all the same. He's a very sensitive man. I don't know how to put it really. He's only confident and courageous, if that's the proper word, in the pulpit. When he feels that something bigger than himself is speaking through him. Ordinarily he is very timid. I suppose that's really why he's never married. Do you know what I mean?'

Amy looked a little puzzled. While she was lost in thought a hand brushed against her side. She stared down and saw that Ike Everett had dropped the brooch and chain into her coat pocket. When she looked at him reproachfully, he put his hand together in an attitude of mock prayer. There was a fresh cigarette, unlit, in the corner of his mouth and his eyes were wide with pleading.

'This is what I was thinking, Amy.'

Mabli was excited by her own scheme.

'To cheer him up. We could leave before the last dance and call round at his house. Tell him that everything is alright. Have a cup of coffee perhaps. And still get back in Hall in time. What do you think?'

Seeing Amy hesitate she pressed the plan further.

'Frankie said he'll come.'

'Which Frankie?'

'Frankie Yoreth. He's dancing with Gwenda. He's a scream. He would cheer anybody up. And it would give you a chance to explain to Tom Arthog that you didn't really mean he was a clumsy idiot. We could leave now. Haydn would come with us. Poor old Tom Arthog. He must be very lonely in that gloomy old Manse. What do you think?'

'It sounds a good idea,' Amy said.

Mabli nodded, delighted her plan was meeting with considered approval.

'But I must get back.'

Amy uttered her verdict with firm finality.

'I must tell Enid what's happened. And show her the frock. I've just been sitting here plucking up courage to face her, to tell you the truth. Waiting for the thing to dry.'

Mabli was disappointed.

'But Enid's so understanding,' she said.

'That's the trouble.'

Amy showed that her decision to go back to Hall was now made and was irrevocable. She stood up and tightened the belt of her winter coat. Haydn moved forward out of the shadows to remind the girls that he was at their service.

'But you can't go back alone,' Mabli said. 'They say the town rowdies are still lurking on the promenade.'

'The fairy lights are still on! Don't worry.'

Amy was in a lighthearted mood. She smiled at Ike Everett who was lighting a cigarette and touched him playfully on the shoulder.

'The revolution will see me home. Are you coming, Comrade Everett?'

10

In the sitting room on the first floor of the Hall of Residence, the Reverend Tom Arthog Williams used his height to lean on the marble shelf above the fireplace. Close by his elbow the bronze figure of a lightly clad male was taming a rampant stallion that pawed the air above his metal head.

'A good discussion,' he said. 'Very lively.'

Two large, plump girls glanced at each other before nodding their agreement. He was trapped by their devoted attention. Mabli rescued him by holding out a cup of tea for him to accept. It gave him a seemly excuse to break the barrier created by the solemn girls. His eyes roved incessantly around his small audience of women students. Mabli returned to the large teapot on the table ready to fill the cups held out towards her. Carefully the minister shifted towards the side of the room where Amy was talking to Gwenda. He approached them with caution, his teacup in one hand and his saucer in the other.

'Where is Miss Enid Prydderch this afternoon, I wonder?'

He held his head to one side as he addressed Amy and smiled at her ingratiatingly. There was still an element of nervous caution in his approach that showed he had not succeeded yet in expunging from his memory the sight of the spreading ink-stain on her dance frock. He was over-anxious to be friendly. He glanced quickly at Gwenda for some sign of comfort and support.

'A good discussion,' he said. 'Don't you think? Very lively. But I missed her contribution, I must admit.'

Gwenda smiled politely. He was eager for more definite signs of agreement and approval.

'She brought up this point about religious convictions being related to life, last time. How they had to pass through the furnace of experience to prove their value and so on. I was hoping we could have developed that. It would have been a real step forward.'

His teaspoon tinkled in his saucer as he moved to address Amy more directly.

'You were very quiet, Miss Parry, if I may say so.'

Amy directed a faint smile at him. She looked as if she were considering drawing a bow and taking aim.

'Christianity and Socialism for example. I thought you would have a special interest there.'

Gwenda gave a cheerful laugh and for a moment he was encouraged.

'It's an issue, isn't it?' he said. 'We must be fair to Mr. Everett.'

Having uttered the name he plainly began to worry about having said the right thing. Amy was saying nothing and this upset him still further. He looked around towards Mabli. She was too busy to catch his imploring look. Rain poured down the window behind her head. Beyond he could hear the subdued roar of the sea.

'We must be objective and fair,' he said. 'I don't know what you think?'

He smiled at Amy and then looked down quickly into his teacup. She waited until he was taking a sip.

'Most of the time I don't know what you are talking about,' she said. 'The terms you used. I just don't know what they mean.'

Her tone was mild, almost meek. Gwenda was watching

her reactions closely. He relaxed enough to give them both a friendly smile.

'Ah,' he said. '"Terms." What "terms" I wonder?'

'God,' Amy said. 'God, for instance. What is it supposed to mean?'

She was smiling at him politely. His confidence grew.

'Yes, indeed,' he said. 'The unmentionable and so on. That which cannot be named. Try and think of it in anthropomorphic terms sometimes. Our Father which art in Heaven... God the Father and so on.'

He spoke in a very soft voice, evoking old, time-honoured phrases.

'Yes,' Amy said. 'But why not God the Mother? That's what puzzles me. I've often wanted to know the answer to that question.'

He wanted to use his hands. His cup was empty. He waved the cup and saucer around inviting someone to relieve him of them. When Gwenda took them, he glanced reproachfully at Amy and pulled a face of mock rebuke. Out of range of his flickering gaze Gwenda stood where Amy could see her and pushed out her cheek with her tongue.

'Now you are teasing,' the minister said.

Both his hands were free. They began to stray upwards to flutter around his crest of black hair.

'But I like it,' he said. 'And I like plain speaking.'

'I'm serious,' Amy said. 'I'm asking a serious question.'

'Of course you are. Plain speaking is what we need. Our faith must be capable of discussion in terms that are fully intelligible and meaningful to the world of today. My goodness, yes. I conceive of that as a central part of my job, Miss Parry. I most certainly do.'

'So in fact, there is no answer?'

Amy was quiet but relentless.

'Oh, there is. Most certainly there is.'

The minister's desperate gaze settled on the sitting-room door. A maid in uniform had tapped on it boldly as she opened it. She was small with very red cheeks and a pert manner. She stood on tip-toe and called out urgently:

'Miss Parry in here? Miss Amy Parry?'

The minister waved both hands towards Amy and then looked away as if to indicate he was only being helpful and that beyond that he had no special responsibility for her.

'I've been looking all over for you,' the maid said reprovingly.

When she looked up to speak to Amy, her bantam stance implied that she was being prevented from carrying on with more urgent work. She waved a note in her hand.

'I couldn't just leave it in your room.'

She moved as close as she could to Amy, lowered her voice and rolled her eyes.

'There's a man waiting by the back entrance. With a sack of potatoes. He gave me this to give you.'

She handed Amy the note, folded small and bulky inside a used envelope.

'What is it?'

Amy moved closer to Gwenda as though for protection from some unknown hazard.

'It's not Dan Ike, is it?'

Gwenda was trying to guess helpfully.

'At the *back* entrance? That's hardly like him.'

The maid stayed close to them as they both moved towards the door. She enjoyed giving them further information.

'He wouldn't come in. His boots were muddy. He hadn't shaved either.'

She half concealed her mouth with her hand and rolled her eyes again. She seemed to want to show she could be friendly with the women undergraduates if they gave her the chance and showed a proper respect for her innate sense of personal independence.

'Some of his buttons were undone!'

She simpered gaily.

'He could be rich, of course. I've known cases. You can never tell with these country farmers.'

Amy walked away to read the note. Gwenda hesitated before following her. The maid looked piqued, conscious of being ignored.

'What am I to say then?'

She raised her voice, taking refuge in the dignity of the punctilious execution of her paid duties.

'I'm sorry . . .'

Amy waved the note at her. She had moved several yards down the corridor to catch the light.

'Tell him I'll be there in a moment. Listen to this, Gwenda. *"Dear Miss Parry, I am requested by my brother, the Rector of Melyd, to supply you with farm produce in case of need. These to be going on with..."*'

'Who is the Rector of Melyd?'

'You may well ask. Listen... *"These to be going on with. He would like to hear from you when you have time to write. You know his address of course. If you require eggs or butter they are also available on request. Yours faithfully, Amos Philips, Blaencwmbach Isaf, Llanfihangel R.S.O."*'

'It sounds very nice. *"To your feet their tributes bring..."* The more the merrier that's what I say. Let me bask in your reflected glory.'

'Glory, indeed. Blackmail. That's what this is.'

Amy waved the note indignantly under Gwenda's nose.

'And I'm jolly well going to tell him too.'

'Who?'

'The Rector's brother or whoever he is.'

Amy was blushing.

'It's a bit sordid really. The Rector wanted to pay for my education on condition I married him at the end of it.'

'How romantic.'

Gwenda was deeply impressed.

'Not a bit of it. I said sordid and I mean sordid. Don't breathe a word of it, please. Not even to Mabli.'

'Does Enid know?'

'In a way she does.'

Amy looked around for somewhere to sit. Nearby there was a polished bench between a pair of white ornamental urns. She sat down, looking despondent and depressed.

'I don't want to see him. It will just bring back things I want to forget. Oh nothing dark and dramatic. Just the shades of an old prisonhouse. It makes me realise how free and... I don't know what to call it really... how privileged I am here. We all are really.'

Gwenda was eager to show her sympathy.

'Would you like me to go and send him away?'

Amy considered the proposal.

'I could even say I was you. He wouldn't be any the wiser.'

Gwenda's dramatic imagination was being over stimulated. She raised her right hand gravely.

'Hence, Amos! Get back to your Llanfihangel bits and pieces. And tell your brother to keep his silly potatoes!'

They clasped hands. Amy was grateful to her for cheering her up.

'No,' she said. 'I'll have to face him. Nip this in the bud. I shan't be a minute. Go and make it up for me with the Reverend Tom Arthog. I'm sure I was rude, but he does get on my nerves a bit. I don't seem to have any luck with the cloth, do I?'

Gwenda accompanied her part of the way to the back entrance. Then Amy hurried on alone. There was a resolute expression on her face. She seemed intent on rehearsing the most effective words for her encounter with the rector's brother. But when she arrived at the back entrance, there was no one there. Where the visitor may have waited, in the centre of the passageway, stood a sack of potatoes. It was not a full hundredweight. The long neck of the sack drooped to one side like a shy caller declining to speak.

A substantial wooden footbridge led to the outside gate and the rear lane. Stout wooden pillars painted dark green supported the steeply pitched roof that provided a covered way. On the thick wooden planks there were muddy footprints that could have belonged to a caller. There were a few bicycles leaning against the wooden pillars. Amy walked to the end of the covered way to peep out in the lane. There was no sign of the man who brought the potatoes. But at the end of the lane she could make out a familiar figure bending forward as she tilted her umbrella to protect her from the slanting rain. It was Enid Prydderch. When she caught sight of Amy's head looking out, she broke into a run and arrived under the covered way wet and breathless, her eyes shining with delight.

'He's coming back,' she said.

She was assuming that Amy had come out to meet her. 'Who is?'

'Val, of course. It's all been settled. The paper will be called *Dadeni*. Just like that. One word. Do you like it?'

Enid stamped her feet on the planks of the footbridge and the noise echoed in the cavernous basement beneath them. She poked her umbrella over the side of the bridge and shook it vigorously.

'And there'll be the press of course. For pamphlets and even books. Val will be the general editor or the editor general or what have you and he'll have this temporary post in the library as well. Unestablished, I think they call it. Isn't that perfect? I can hardly get over it.'

The happiness she was generating was of such overwhelming strength Amy had no choice but to submit to it.

'You move at such a pace, E.P.,' she said. 'It's hard for us ordinary mortals to keep up with you. You're wet, too. Just look at your feet...'

'Do you know what I've been thinking. On my way back now. Childish dreams I suppose in a way. But I couldn't help it. What the four of us will be able to do together! Cilydd, Val, you and I. Change the course of history.'

'My goodness, that sounds grand.'

'I know it does. But it's perfectly possible!'

Enid made a stern effort to contain her enthusiasm with a more academic exactness.

'In any case there is a sense in which the birth of every single child changes the course of history a little.'

Amy held her arm and pointed at the sack of potatoes.

She handed Enid the note from the Rector of Melyd's brother. She made gestures with her arms to show that she wanted the sack to vanish into thin air.

'I'll have none of it,' she said. 'I may be poor but I have my pride. That's one thing I've learnt from my miserable Uncle Lucas. "Don't take charity from anybody. In any shape or form." I suppose that's one thing about him I should admire. I think I will from now on. I jolly well will. I just won't accept them.'

'Quite right. I tell you what.'

Enid was ready to treat the incident lightheartedly, so that her friend should put it all into a more comfortable perspective.

'*I'll* have them. They were left here for you. You didn't want them. So they were left here again. So I came along and said thank you very much, Santa Claus, I'll have them. Make a wonderful legal case, wouldn't it? I can't wait to tell John Cilydd. Property and possession.'

Amy was still inclined to worry about the sack in front of her.

'Just what are we going to do with them?'

'No problem at all.'

Enid took hold of the end of the sack and began to drag it inside the Hall. Her physical strength matched her cheerfulness.

'We'll take it upstairs. We can carry it between us. Two strong girls. Then we can share them out between us. Or sell them. Potatoes, one farthing a pound! We'll make a fortune.'

With the sack between them they staggered into the Hall. Laughing made the task more difficult. Amy lost her grip of the bottom end and Enid dragged the sack up a short flight of steps.

'Steady on, E.P. You'll bruise them.'

'I didn't know you could bruise potatoes. Just like my thigh, do you mean?'

Everything they said to each other seemed funny. They decided it was easier to carry the sack up the main staircase. Girls coming from the discussion group stopped to watch them. Gwenda hurried to the bottom of the staircase to give them a hand.

'No. Leave it,' Amy said.

Gwenda had tried to take a hold of a corner of the sack.

'I've got a good grip now. I wasn't brought up on a smallholding for nothing. This is a sack, Miss Gethyn, not a cigarette-holder.'

Gwenda put her hand in the small of Amy's back and pushed her up the stairs.

'That's nice,' Amy said. 'Good old Gethy. You are stronger than you look.'

'My great-grandfather was the strongest man in Oswestry,' Gwenda said. 'Believe it or not.'

On the next flight of stairs, when they were overcome with laughter and preparing to take a rest, they encountered the Warden. Her voice boomed above them, commanding attention. She stood imposingly still under a lamp projecting from the wall in the shape of a stylised torch.

'Young women,' she said. 'What do you suppose you are doing?'

Her heavy hair was parted in the centre and dressed in a pre-War style around a velvet headband. She carried a silver propelling pencil and used it for pointing. Her voice was

93

deep and reverberated sonorously down the staircase.

'Be so good as to identify yourselves.'

Her dark eyes gave the impression that she owed her true allegiance to another, higher, world. She focused them with some effort to do service on a lower plane of existence. The three girls were holding on to the sack as if it were some sort of bulwark against any assault from above.

'Miss Gethyn.'

The silver pencil singled out Gwenda.

'You were here last year. You should know how we conduct ourselves. The Golden Mean, Miss Gethyn? An educated female without culture and refinement is an unfired pot without the proper glaze, and so on. I need not quote myself further. What is in that sack?'

'Potatoes, Mrs. Blaize-Rees.'

'Potatoes.'

She lifted the silver pencil to scratch delicately at a perpendicular crease in her narrow forehead.

'And to whom do these potatoes belong?'

'Mine, Mrs. Blaize-Rees.'

Amy and Enid spoke out simultaneously. The noise seemed to pain the Warden.

'I don't know where you two were brought up . . . Haven't I heard you singing duets?'

Enid was smiling cheerfully and nodding.

'Be that as it may, here we do not encourage peasant habits. Was it your intention to hoard the tubers under your bed?'

Enid's unperturbed smile began to irritate the Warden. She became more loftily acerbic.

'Since we are in no immediate danger of famine, would you kindly transport them to the lower regions and have the kitchen staff store them for you until the end of term. If you are overwhelmed with the urge to eat raw potato you will be provided down there with a bowl and a knife.'

With a weary gesture, the Warden indicated that she wished to proceed on her way. Enid dragged the sack aside and then squeezed Amy's arm as a warning to keep her quiet until the Warden had arrived at the broad first landing. They saw her stand for a moment under the great canvas of the Royal Opening in its heavy gilt frame. She was looking up at

94

them with the shadow of a smile on her wide tragedienne mouth.

'She can see a joke.'

Gwenda seemed overwhelmed with relief as she whispered to the others. The Warden had gone on her regal way. Gwenda was prepared to express grudging admiration.

'She was pulling our legs, really. She's not such a bad old stick. Lost her husband in the Boer War. Never been the same since. That's what they say. She doesn't mean to be nasty. And she's down on her luck, you see. By the standards of the family she stems from. They were big landowners in Denbighshire and they became extinct through lack of male heirs. Something like that. But she's not extinct of course. Only on the verge of it. She goes on about the potter's wheel and shaping people and all that rot, but she means well . . .'

'Oh no she doesn't.'

Gwenda looked up alarmed at the vehemence in Amy's voice. Amy was standing above the sack of potatoes. Her arm was outstretched, pointing to where the Warden had stood beneath the painting of the Royal Opening.

'There's the enemy!'

'I say! That sounds just like Dan Ike . . .'

'I can think for myself,' Amy said. 'That woman operates a system! She wants to take your little Welsh girls and turn them into obedient bourgeois imitation English.'

Enid was nodding to show her full agreement with the verdict.

'Yes, but surely that only makes us react against it? What else are we doing? What else is the Cell, for heaven's sake?'

Gwenda put her knee on the sack and made sophisticated gestures with her hands and shoulders as she spoke. Amy shook her head.

'It's so all-pervading,' she said. 'That's what a system means. It's a total atmosphere generated by the apparatus of power. It . . . it controls the whole of our lives in every possible aspect you can think of. Stop grinning, Gwenda. I really mean it.'

'Sorry.'

'If there's ever going to be any change, every one of them must be got rid of.'

'A revolution you mean? A real revolution?'

Gwenda was sobered. Her expression was overcast with doubt and foreboding.

'Of course. It's not at all difficult to see. I'm no genius and I can see it.'

She stared challengingly at Enid, mutely demanding her comment.

'You are right.'

Enid was frowning thoughtfully.

'There's got to be a revolution in a manner of speaking. It can't be avoided. The problem is to find a civilised way of going about it. A Welsh way, if you like.'

'That's the point, surely?'

Gwenda was deeply relieved to hear Enid's words. She stood up. Amy tugged at the neck of the sack.

'You two,' she said in the friendliest fashion. 'You two, you've been brought up soft. You've got to be hard if you want to change things. Me, I'm as hard as a sack of potatoes. Do you want to see me carry these down on my back?'

11

Amy raised her hand to rub her stiff shoulder. The captain of the women's hockey first eleven joined the parade momentarily to deliver her personal congratulations.

'It was a cracker,' she said. 'An absolute cracker. The defence never smelt it. Jolly good work ... I must have a word with Ellis.'

She stepped out of the parade and let it pass her by. The women walked on the left side of the covered quadrangle. It was a cheerful but orderly exercise at eleven o'clock on a Monday morning. The men perambulated on the right and the two trains circled endlessly in opposite directions. The whole area echoed festively with student voices like a railway terminus where the passengers had decided spontaneously to provide all the locomotion themselves: and like seasoned travellers, the young men and women wore coats and gowns and scarves and carried their books like hand luggage. There was some communication between the two lines: there were nods, smiles, greetings, even messages, but the contrary motion never stopped. Those who wished to speak at length fell out and found convenient spots on staircases in doorways or near pillars: or ascended to the narrow stone gallery which surrounded the indoor quad. Gwenda had raised her head to look up surreptitiously in the direction of a Roman style marble bust that stood on a plinth outside the doors of the library on the first floor. She caught a glimpse of the brooding figure of Dan Ike smoking a cigarette.

'He's there.'

She reported her sighting in a whisper to Amy. The four girls walked closely together. Amy had a problem and the other three were loyally prepared to share it. Their walking was in itself an act of solidarity. As a college 'family' they would support each other at all times and managed to do so without intruding indelicately on each other's privacy. As she rubbed her shoulder again, Amy managed to show that she was appreciative of their protection, but ready now to face the problem alone.

'It's got to be done,' she said.

Enid nodded approvingly.

'If I'm not back in five minutes, come and rescue me.'

She broke away from the ranks and hurried up a staircase, her undergraduate gown billowing out behind her. Outside the open doors of the Senior Common Room she was obliged to squeeze through an untidy group of lecturers who had come out to smoke their pipes and watch the parade going on below. They took a lot of room. They stood confidently with their feet apart, their hands in their pockets, their watch chains stretched across their waistcoats and their pipes going in or coming out of their mouths, all ready to laugh loudly at their own remarks as well as their colleagues'. They shifted minimally out of the way without breaking the thread of their complex conversations.

Amy found Dan Ike standing in an alcove near the massive doors of the library. Above his head was a framed reproduction in full size of Holman Hunt's *The Light of the World*. His cigarette was cupped in his hand.

'Where's your bodyguard?' he said.

His eyes glowed conspicuously in the shadowed alcove. He had not shaved for several days.

'You knew we were going on the short tour,' she said. 'I told you. So it's no good you trying to look as if someone had stolen your cheese.'

She was doing her best to be cheerful.

'Why on earth are you lurking in this alcove?' she said. 'Let's go and watch the circus. The hub of the universe.'

'I was afraid you wouldn't want to be seen with me,' he said. 'Thinking of you, I was.'

'Now listen, Ike,' she said. 'I want to talk to you quite seriously.'

'Yes, teacher.'

With her books under her arm she fumbled in her overcoat pocket for a package she wished to hand over to him. The action compelled her to move her sore shoulder and she winced as she drew out the package.

'Hurt yourself?' he said. 'Playing too hard against the wicked English.'

'You've got to take these back now.'

The sapphire brooch and the golden chain were inside a blue paper cash packet. He stared at the packet glumly.

'I'm not going to hold them for you any longer.'

'What do you want me to do with them?'

'I don't care what you do with them. It's nothing to do with me. But you've got to take them, and that's all there is to it.'

She stepped closer to him and stuffed the packet abruptly into his pocket.

'And of course, I can't meet you any more.'

She tried to speak as casually as she could.

'I like to hear you talk. But we can't make a habit of it. It would give an utterly false impression.'

'So he's coming back, is he?'

Ike smiled sarcastically.

'The great man is coming back. He's not to know that you've been keeping bad company. And you're the one that goes on about women's rights. You're just as medieval as the rest of them.'

Amy walked away from the alcove. She found herself a

place to lean against the stone balustrade. Ike followed her. He stared down with some contempt at all the movement on the floor below.

'The prisoners are exercising in the prison yard.'

Amy made no response.

'What makes you think he's so different?'

He was determined to win her attention.

'He's a nice enough chap, I dare say. Good looking in an inane picture-postcard sort of way. But what does he amount to? When you analyse him, as you should do. He's nothing more than a bourgeois nationalist up to his knees in the mud of the past. So what kind of revolutionary action is he capable of? The first act of the true revolutionary is to kick the past hard in the teeth. I thought you understood all this.'

'I do.'

Amy was goaded to speak at last.

'But you are so extreme . . .'

'For God's sake, what else do you expect me to be?'

He turned his back on the view below and pointed at the statue of one of the founders of the college on its solid plinth between where they stood and the library doors.

'If I wanted to remove that statue, could I do it by standing in front of it and putting forward a reasoned argument or by using a stick of dynamite?'

Amy glanced at the statue over her shoulder and then continued to study the parade below.

'You over-simplify,' she said.

She sounded pleased to have seized on a protective formula.

'And what does a statue matter, anyway? What possible harm can a statue do?'

'A lot,' he said.

He was desperately eager to argue. At least an argument would bind her closer to him for as long as he could make it last. Below there was a sudden outburst of boisterous horseplay among the men. The lecturers outside the Senior Common Room moved quickly to the edge of the gallery to watch. Members of the rugby first fifteen walking next to each other started barging. One of them lost hold of the pile of books he was carrying. He fumbled desperately but one by one they tumbled to the ground. A ruck formed quickly around the fallen books. Boots went in to try and heel them out.

'Sons of colliers.'

Ike sounded profoundly angry.

There were ironic cheers. A book slid across the floor and was stopped in its flight by a slim young man in a smart overcoat and spats. He stopped the book with his walking cane.

'The families of some of those men are starving,' Ike said. 'The frivolity of this place makes me sick.'

The young man with a walking cane was amusing the people in the gallery by his antics with the book. At first he treated it as if it were something alive and dangerous. Then he changed his manner and imitated the known eccentricities of the Professor of Botany. He appeared suddenly to have come across a rare specimen on the ground in front of him.

'Prof. Robinson!' Amy said, delightedly. 'Absolutely to the life!'

She joined in the clapping and the ironic cheers.

'Master Spats.'

Ike put as much venom as he could into the nickname.

'Sent here for Welsh atmos and a smattering of your lovely lingo. To help his political career. A bit of spatted capitalist spawn.'

At last the rugby forward had broken free. He charged down the slim young man in spats and sent him sprawling across the floor into the feet of the laughing spectators. Cheers were coming now from every corner. The lecturers were laughing and waving their pipes approvingly and at every vantage point students were scrambling to get a better view of the fun. Here and there singing broke out. A great cheer went up when the big forward eventually held the sum of his books up in the air for all to see. His face was bright pink with exertion. He was so pleased with himself he shook the books above his head like a victorious gladiator until they were in danger of tumbling around him a second time. But this time, he managed to catch them. When he had done so, he glanced all round the gallery with a deliberately clownish smile on his face and bowed gratefully at the clapping.

'Oh dear,' Amy said, as she was still laughing. 'You can't help liking him, can you? Isn't he Tom-Tom's cousin? They're very alike aren't they?'

Ike had sunk into a despondent mood. Nothing he saw seemed to please him.

'I've no idea,' he said.

'I know things are very bad where you come from,' Amy said. 'But we just can't be miserable all the time.'

'We should be marching!'

Ike struck his fist on the cold stone.

'Workers and intellectuals should be together. But this place isn't designed to produce intellectuals. It's a social separator, that's all. Designed to cream off the bright kids of the workers and alienate them from their origins. It deliberately softens their intellectual muscles with a special Welsh Imperial peppermint mish-mash. It stifles their critical faculties for ever with pap from the surface froth of capitalistic culture. My God... Are you listening to me, woman?'

'Don't call me "woman"...'

Amy reacted angrily.

'What else are you? A lady, I suppose. Lady Amy. You are ready and willing to fall in the trap, just like the rest of them.'

'Now look here, Dan Ike. I'm not afraid of you and you know it. I'm willing to put up with a lot, but don't you start trying to treat me like an inferior being. I simply won't have it.'

Ike lapsed back into the depths of his despondency.

'As if I could,' he said. 'An ugly bugger like me. A prisoner inside his own ridiculous appearance. A dwarf. No wonder I know about the sufferings of the proletariat. History screwed me up right from the very start.'

'And don't go sinking into one of your self-pitying sessions,' Amy said. 'I won't have it. I'm sure you are just as attractive to women as any other man. More perhaps than most. You've got very nice eyes.'

Ike's mouth fell open. He pretended to be overwhelmed with the compliment. Then he started laughing in rather a forced manner, turning his back to the stone balustrade and sinking slowly to the ground.

'Ike Everett,' Amy said sharply. 'Get up, will you? And stop making an exhibition of yourself.'

'It's nice down here,' he said. 'I can grovel at your feet. Can you see my nice eyes?'

'Get up, you idiot.'

A fresh commotion broke out on the floor below. The men seemed bent on creating yet another expression of collective exuberance. Out of a newly-formed seething mass of cheerful males, the President of the Students' Representative Council was being hoisted to stand on the ceremonial grid, a narrow iron box frame that covered an unsightly radiator. He looked confident enough. He was enjoying his elevation. He pressed his back against the pale green wall, clutched the lapel of his B.A. gown and extracted a piece of paper from the waistcoat of his brown tweed suit. He was thin and wiry. His wide mouth stretched in a grin that told the student body in view that he was their obedient servant and relied on their friendly co-operation. Two gleaming wings of oiled hair were plastered close to his skull from his white centre parting, while his ears also stuck out in the same direction. They were made more prominent by the thick arms of his horn-rimmed spectacles. The students were everywhere. On the staircases and galleries as well as the floor of the indoor quadrangle. The ritual perambulation had ceased. Enid stepped carefully along the gallery to join Amy. She looked down at Ike on the floor.

'What's the matter,' she said. 'Are you ill?'

He did not welcome her kindly attention. Slowly and untidily he struggled to his feet. In his pocket he found a last Woodbine in a crushed packet. With the nicotined tips of his fingers he tried to restore its shape. He stared malevolently at the President on the grid.

'Millar Morgan,' he said. 'Traitor to the working class. Son of a traitor to the working class.'

'What do you mean by that exactly?' Enid said.

'Morgan Morgan.'

Ike delivered his litany in an almost ecclesiastical monotone.

'Morgan Morgan. Chapel deacon and bosses' stooge. One of oily Mabon's men. A Lib-Lab. Lib when the Liberals are in, Lab when the Labour are in. And there's his offspring for you, already groomed for public office. With a glib tongue to match.'

'Gyfeillion! Friends, comrades, countrymen!'

Millar Morgan judged the correct moment to send his

husky baritone reverberating across the quadrangle. Silence descended on several hundred young people. He was now licensed to speak on their behalf, to shift effortlessly from one language to the other, to display the verbal skills that he knew were to their taste, a peculiar blend of polysyllabic verbosity and deflating colloquialisms. Ike groaned aloud. Amy and Enid were embarrassed at the sound. But no one seemed to have taken notice.

'The auspicious start to the season has been sustained, my friends! The season continues with more resounding successes. Our strongest rugby fifteen for some years has snatched its third successive victory . . .'

His head tilted and froze momentarily in order to indicate he had a toothsome comment to add if they would be kind enough to forbear to cheer until he had made it.

'The backs as usual were outstanding!'

He paused boldly, and sought out the group who would be the recipients of the final accolade.

'But their dashing achievements would never have been possible without the heroic, the titanic, the herculean efforts of the forwards!'

Great cheers and applause broke out and a group of the rugby fifteen gave a hurried but piercing rendering of the college yell. This gave rise to further ironic cheers.

Amy and Enid had joined in the hand clapping and the President was smiling from ear to ear. From now on, anything he said could only express yet another facet of the glowing warmth and limitless virtues of their cherished community life: the gloomy Gothic precinct had been transformed into a temple of youth, alive with spontaneous student cordiality.

'And let us not forget the ladies, God bless them, without whom this illustrious college would be no more than a dull and lacklustre seminary!'

There were more ironic cheers. Amy and Enid glanced at each other quickly with mock apprehension. Amy gave her shoulder a consolatory rub.

'First-class hot air merchant,' Ike said. 'Will do very nicely for the Libs or the Labs.'

He spoke to himself. Amy and Enid had ceased to feel obliged to notice him.

'The women's hockey first eleven crossed Offa's Dyke on a dangerous mission into enemy territory . . .'

The President paused for his meed of applause. It was paid in generous measure.

'That was the tribal touch,' Ike said. 'Always comes in handy.'

The girls leaned further forward over the balustrade. They were eager not to lose a syllable of the President's next words.

'They won in Nottingham on Friday by four goals to three. And then in Birmingham on Saturday they surpassed themselves by a brilliant win of five goals to two. Can we in any sense describe this as deliberate arithmetical progression?'

The final sally was delivered throwaway with a lowered head, and immediately his closest friends groaned to register the peculiar awfulness of his irrepressible sense of humour which was only too familiar to them. This was precisely the effect he desired. He extended a weighty pause to underline further the comic pedantry with which he scrutinised his scribbled notes. A ribald remark was passed about the width of his trouser bottoms: and another about the glossy perfection of his hair. He took the opportunity to look up and grin cheerfully to demonstrate that he was a good sport in or out of the changing rooms. Then he waved his paper urgently for silence.

'Four of those nine goals were scored by a fresher!'

He brought the paper closer to his nose to decipher the name.

'Parry. Miss A. Parry.'

With pontifical benevolence he elevated the paper above his head. He invited Miss A. Parry to identify herself. He had in his gift her moment of glory. Dan Ike began to whistle and wave vigorously to gain the President's attention. Quickly Amy stepped back from the balustrade. She found a place to hide behind the marble bust. In sympathy Enid too withdrew from the edge of the gallery. Dan Ike was left to wave alone. The President could not avoid seeing him. He chose to ignore his inconvenient existence.

'Wherever you are, Miss A. Parry, our heartiest congratulations.'

He passed on smoothly to the next announcement. Dan

Ike turned to look for Amy. At first he only saw Enid.

'Well, my God,' he said. 'Is the man blind or something? Did you ever see such an incompetent idiot?'

He moved closer and saw Amy behind the statue, rubbing her shoulder.

'Blind he is,' he said. 'And deaf in spite of those cloth ears.'

Amy said nothing. She just glared at him.

'Oh dear,' he said. 'I suppose you think I've spoilt your triumph.'

'I dare say that's what you were trying to do.'

'What are you talking about ... ?'

His protest petered out. They ignored Enid's presence. She was embarrassed by the raw hostility confronting her.

'You are a nasty, bitter little man,' Amy said. 'And you won't be happy until you've made the whole world as nasty and as bitter as yourself.'

He tried to smile calmly. His eyes studied her closely like a wrestler who watches for his adversary's next move and the best place to snatch a winning hold.

'I can tell you things about yourself, Miss A. Parry, if you want to hear them.'

Enid moved back to the balustrade. It would have been futile for her to intervene as a peacemaker. Neither wanted peace.

'I don't want to hear anything from you,' Amy said. 'Ever again.'

'Well, of course you don't.'

He was encouraged to cultivate a gravity of manner when he realised how much it infuriated her.

'Nobody ever wants to hear the truth about themselves.'

'The truth! What makes you think you know anything about the truth? Divine Right, I suppose. Just go away and leave me alone. You pushed yourself where you were never wanted. I tried to be nice to you. To treat you decently. And all you want is to take advantage.'

At the balustrade Enid was trying hard not to hear the things they were saying to each other. She watched the crowd below more intently and struggled to give her attention to the announcements. She removed herself as far as she could, but not too far in case Amy should need her. Ike was still tantalising her beyond endurance.

'Of course I can see it,' he said. 'As plain as anything. Nothing more obvious. Can't think why I never saw it before.'

'See what?'

Amy could not resist asking and was immediately angry with herself for doing so.

'Hunger,' he said.

Amy overcame her own curiosity. She moved to join Enid at the balustrade. Ike followed her. He was not to be denied the pleasure of expressing the phrase that had come to him.

'I said hunger. Hunger for success. It's written all over you.'

'Just go away.'

Amy's anger had evaporated. Enid was at hand ready to listen to her.

'I don't know,' she said. 'It's one of those things you can't help noticing. There's nobody in the world more stupid than clever people when they think they're being brilliantly clever.'

She expected Enid to appreciate her remark. Enid acknowledged it quickly and then took her arm to draw her closer and whisper in her ear.

'Amy! Just look. Over there.'

She began to point at someone at the other end of the quadrangle.

'Where?'

Amy tried to restrain her curiosity. She knew that Ike was still watching her. Whatever she did should be in keeping with her mood of rising above the petty annoyance of his presence.

'It's Val!' Enid said excitedly.

Her hand was raised and ready to wave. A bell began to toll. The President had come down from the grid and the concourse of young people was dispersing.

'There,' Enid said. 'By the statue. He's waving. Can't you see?'

Amy recognised at once the thick lock of black hair falling over his white forehead. The collar of his overcoat was turned up higher than his ears. He was as thin as ever and smiling with such obvious pleasure that Amy went suddenly pale and was obliged to make a special effort to smile back.

'He's coming up!'

Enid seemed to be trembling on her behalf.

'He's coming up as if nothing will stop him.'

She clutched Amy's forearm.

'It's amazing,' she said. 'I was just looking around and I suddenly saw him there, standing by the statue.'

They waited for him to appear. They caught a glimpse of him moving cheerfully against the press of people on the narrow gallery. Outside the Senior Common Room he was accosted by a lecturer with a genial manner and a pipe, which he used to tap Val on the chest as he kept him talking.

'Oh bother . . .'

Enid muttered impatiently.

'That one will drag him into the Senior Common Room and hold him there for ages. He's a real old woman for gossip.'

While the lecturer was speaking, Val looked over his head to where the two girls stood waiting for him. Ike moved closer so that he could whisper fiercely in Amy's ear.

'Hail to the chieftain,' he said. ''Ere the conquering 'ero comes. The Welsh White Hope. And I thought you were intelligent.'

Without turning to look at him Amy spoke through her clenched teeth.

'Go away. Just go away. And don't ever bother to speak to me again.'

Val had succeeded in disengaging himself from the importunate lecturer. As he moved towards them he was obviously full of the excitement of discovery. His large eyes were shining and he was speaking before reaching them and offering his hand.

'I went to look for you as soon as I got back,' he said. 'They said you were away. And of course you were. Covering yourself with glory.'

He stopped speaking suddenly. He looked towards the library doors and saw Ike Everett watching them.

'There's so much to say,' he said. 'I don't know where to start.'

He was no longer smiling. He was overcome with a sudden shyness.

'Let's go and have a cup of coffee,' Amy said.

Gratefully he fixed his gaze on her face and smiled as though she had just offered a brilliant solution to a formidable problem. Enid tactfully moved away a little so that he could give all his attention to Amy. His unspoken admiration was concentrated on her like healing sunlight.

'I saw you rub your shoulder,' he said. 'Is it hurting?'

His concern was in itself restorative. He was so consistently polite that politeness governed his charm.

'Oh, it's nothing,' Amy said.

They moved together along the narrow gallery, only just capable of disguising the fact that they were already not fully aware of anything except each other's presence. Val tried hard not to forget Enid walking behind them. His head was lowered as though he were trying to stifle an uncomfortable clamour going on inside his own head.

'So you won,' Val said. 'That was very good. That was very good.'

He was unaware that he was repeating himself. At the bottom of the stairs they met Gwenda and Mabli and Frank Yoreth, Gwenda's dancing partner, who for once was making no effort to draw attention to himself. He was staring at Val like a spectator confronted with a legendary figure for the first time. When the introductions and the pleasantries were over, they moved as a group towards the college entrance. It was their intention to make their way across the square to the Refectory building. Val and Amy were walking ahead of the others. They appeared to be deep in conversation and yet very little was being said.

Under the heavy Gothic portico Enid made a sign to hold the others back. The sun had come out. Val and Amy were walking slowly along the pavement towards the southern end of the college buildings. Their shadows moved along the warm stone wall behind them. Amy's head was raised to listen to what he was saying and a breeze from the sea ruffled her golden hair. Listening gave her an excuse to observe him more closely. A lady on a bicycle wobbled down the deserted street towards them. She was insecure on her seat but even if she had fallen it seemed unlikely they would have seen her.

'They're going the wrong way,' Frankie said.

He pointed with his left arm to the Refectory at the top of the square.

'Shall I give them a shout?'

The two figures had reached the end of the college building. In the distance the broken tower on the castle mound looked less melancholy than usual in the bright morning sunlight.

'Oh no,' Enid said. 'Just leave them be.'

Gwenda was unwilling to be so romantic.

'They did ask us to coffee,' she said. 'They can't just walk away in a trance.'

12

Inside the castle grounds Val and Amy walked together towards the War Memorial. It was in the shape of a Celtic cross. The names of the fallen were freshly inscribed in neat columns around the base.

'Isn't it strange,' he said. 'The last time I walked up here I didn't know you. And yet the world seemed sufficient. And now . . .'

He stopped still to look at her.

'Do you mind if I tell you exactly what I think?'

She smiled and shook her head.

'Well now, when I look around this place, it seems as if you brought it into being. All of it.'

He waved his bony hand to include the entire view of the seaside town lying between the hills and the sea.

'Me? Oh, my goodness.'

Amy laughed happily.

'I used to dislike it all so much. I used to tell myself: this is one place I'll never come back to. And now here I am. And it all looks wonderful.'

They laughed together.

'What made you come back?'

Amy asked the question seriously.

'You, of course.'

She was momentarily embarrassed. She became intent on

demonstrating that she had not been fishing for compliments.

'No. Seriously...'

'I am serious.'

They walked beyond the Memorial. The path led down to a steep street which in turn led through a gateway in the old castle wall down to the harbour.

'I didn't have a photograph of you. I often wished I had. But I carried a medallion around with me.'

He stopped to look at the palm of his hand as if he were studying something held in it.

'A girl with a flag. A golden-haired girl carrying the future in her hands. A very powerful symbol. The standard-bearer of the future.'

Amy determined to be matter of fact and realistic.

'What about America?' she said.

'Ah. America. Now there's a powerful drug.'

'What do you mean?'

'I don't know how much John Cilydd has told you.'

He took off his overcoat with impatient haste and it looked for a moment as though he was going to throw it away. Amy was fascinated by his restlessness. His constant self-discipline was apparent in the way he struggled to harness his energies and at the same time preserve consideration for others in the forefront of his mind. He was wearing a Fair Isle pullover under his double-breasted jacket, but he still looked thin. He had so much to say he seemed to want to walk half in front of her to make talking easier. He hung his overcoat over one shoulder so that it swung between them as they walked under the archway in the castle wall.

'It's in my family. The American drug, we call it. Every generation somebody goes. Off to the Far Paradise. Look!'

He stretched out his open hand towards the south harbour. Hulks of rotting boats were trapped in the silt. There was only a shrunken passage left for the fishing boats. Two small boats were unloading their meagre catches. They could hear the voices of the fishermen complaining. The loudest noise was made by the hungry seagulls hovering just above the heads of the men sorting fish.

'My grandfather came here in 1842 to see his uncle set sail. We still have the wagon that carried their belongings to the ship. And that uncle was going out to join relatives who had gone in 1796. And they're all there. The quick and the dead. In Ohio. Hidden by acres and acres of Indian corn. And look at this place. Derelict.'

'Is that where you wanted to go? Ohio?'

Amy was shyly curious.

'No. Not really. My temptation was academic. Not wealth or land or religious freedom like the others. Just a nice little academic job. I thought a lot about it. It seemed a special sort of chance. I wrote an article about Morgan John Rhys. One of his descendants saw it. He just happened to be President of a university. He offered me a job. I met him in Paris. He made an impression on me. I was flattered that he should think me worth bothering about. And he was charming and cultivated in the way that only rich Americans know how to be. I had a choice to make. Not everyone has a choice. I didn't sleep a wink all night. I was out before six. They were delivering the croissants. Marvellous smell in the early morning. So it was a real French choice I made. Honour. Obligation. Tradition. I could have gone either way. Like my great-great uncle. It took him twenty years to make his mind up. He went. It took me one night. I came back. Am I talking too much about myself?'

He reined himself in so suddenly that Amy laughed aloud.

'You weren't talking about yourself at all. Not really. You were about to deliver a discourse on America and the Meaning of History.'

'Was I? Was I?'

He sounded profoundly displeased with himself.

'For heaven's sake never let me do that. Never. Never. It must be unbearable.'

'No it isn't. I like it. I want to learn.'

He looked at her with open admiration. Whatever she said he treated like a prophetic revelation. He leaned back to survey her in the context of the castle walls as though he was conscious of the privilege of escorting a rare being with magical powers. He spoke with greater haste and then paused suddenly like a votary who fears to impede the oracle by unduly prolonging the grace notes of his devotions. Near the quayside there was a row of ruined warehouses. Alongside them were disused rail tracks. Looking inland they could see the water-logged wasteland around the river that formed the western boundary to the town. It was an unflattering view. Beyond a cramped bridge were the depressing backs of slum dwellings.

'It's a society that's lost its will to live.'

What he was looking at seemed to make him suffer physically. Amy watched everything he did. Every moment she was absorbing something new about a species of male she had never encountered at such close range before.

'Fifty years ago there was growth here of a kind. Some kind of a hope. Some kind of a vision. Now there's nothing. It's worse than provincial. It's dead. It's riddled with a disease of the spirit.'

He stopped suddenly in case she wanted to speak. She shook her head modestly.

'No society can live without a vision. That was something our forefathers had. Now it's gone. The War just blew it up. The War gets blamed for everything of course. In reality it's an even more gigantic upheaval. But for us it's worse. I think so anyway. Perhaps because we are small. Few. And more gullible. We behave well, like well brought up children and we expect our reward. And this is what we get. A nothing country with nothing to offer and nothing to live for. A wasteland.'

His sudden gloom was profound and all embracing. A chill wind blew from the sea. In a characteristic flurry of activity he thrust his arms into his overcoat sleeves and buttoned the coat up.

'That's just what I wanted to ask,' Amy said.

He grew suddenly rigid.

'And I've been ranting on,' he said. 'I'm so sorry.'

She showed that there was no need at all for him to apologise.

'Why did you come back? I mean, what *made* you come? Did something *make* you?'

Once more he was marvelling openly at her ability to pinpoint the crucial question. Whatever she said or did in these precious moments together after his long absence could only serve to increase the depth of his admiration for her.

'Ah, if only I knew that,' he said. 'And yet of course I do know it ... Do we control our own destinies? Is it possible to reconcile free will and predestination? Oh my goodness, you do ask the most fundamental questions.'

'I'm just curious,' Amy said. 'All women are curious. Haven't you noticed?'

He put his hands on his hips, threw back his head and roared with laughter so loudly that Amy looked around her in alarm. The noise he made was disproportionate and incorrect. For all she knew it could have broken by-laws governing behaviour in such a public place.

'Val,' she said. 'I didn't say anything funny.'

He was preparing to laugh out loud again. Suddenly she grabbed his arm and shook it.

'No,' she said. 'Please don't make that noise again.'

Instantly he sobered. They walked to a bench and sat down.

In silence they contemplated the view of the old harbour. Alongside the bench there remained the tall stalks of dead flowers. Nervously he broke one off and passed it through his fingers.

'I want to tell you everything,' he said. 'I want us to understand each other so well that we'll be able to see the world through each other's eyes.'

Her smile was faint and mysterious. He began to break the dried flower stalk into little pieces.

'The old world is finished. And yet out of it we can make something new.'

He watched her face closely for the faintest trace of encouragement. When she smiled at him, his relief was enormous.

'All I had was a medallion.'

He turned out the palm of his hand.

'And now I have the real living thing.'

He held out his hand for her to take. She looked around before shyly giving him her hand. He squeezed it enthusiastically.

'You don't have to ask me,' he said. 'Isn't it obvious? It had to be. You weren't in America. You were here.'

Part Two

1

Amy crouched down in the open doorway to mix the dark blue dye in a cup with a broken handle. Steam from the scullery billowed out over her head. Inside, her aunt was hovering over the brick-built boiler in the corner. The fire under the cauldron was blazing. Esther Parry was poking and stirring a load of bed linen with a spear-like stick while she held the wooden lid of the boiler in her left hand like the circular shield of some antique war goddess. Between them stood the mangle, the uneven wooden rollers still wet from the last wringing. The steam was everywhere in the narrow scullery. It hung like draperies from the ceiling and pushed itself lazily through the small window to disperse slowly in the still summer air. Two full lines of washing stretched across the cobbled yard to the roof of the four outside lavatories that corresponded to the four dwellings in the miniature terrace. On the section of the communal yard that was recognised as belonging to next door, an adolescent boy was painting the frame of an old bicycle. He knelt on a sack and his tongue stuck out as he concentrated on applying the paint evenly.

'Better close the door, Amy.'

Esther Parry replaced the wooden lid on the boiler.

'Your uncle will be complaining of a draught.'

'He's obsessed with draughts.'

Her body, except for her hands and face, was lost in a covering of old clothes. Her hair was hidden by a grey duster. An old mac of her uncle's reached to her feet. She seemed

115

faintly aware of appearing comical: but this in no way lessened the expression of determination on her face. The strength of her cheekbones was more apparent without the softening effect of the golden hair. Her face was flushed with hard work and beads of sweat rested in the delicate hollow above her lip.

'He's got draughts on the brain.'

'So would you, if you worked in the parcel office,' Esther Parry said. 'It's nothing more than a shed dumped down between the chip shop and the petrol pumps. Each draught has a different smell.'

Amy was silent as she struggled to be sympathetic. In a bucket under the mangle were the two petticoats that she wanted to dye.

'It's such a funny time to take as a half-day,' she said. 'A Monday morning.'

She kept her voice down so that her uncle in the living-room should not hear her.

'It's not funny at all. If he's preaching it gives him time to get back.'

'He hasn't changed at all, has he?'

'He doesn't have to.'

Nothing would persuade Esther to be remotely critical of her husband.

'He knows where he stands. That's more than you can say for most people.'

Both women were sweating. Amy put down the bucket. She came close to her aunt and took hold of her hands. They were red and soft from the water. The joints were swollen with arthritis.

'You should give this washing effort up,' Amy said. 'You really should. It's absurd how little they give you anyway.'

'Every little helps,' Esther said. 'I want to keep going as long as I can.'

She tried to take her hands away, but Amy held on to them. She wished to emphasise what she was saying.

'You mustn't do it for me. You really mustn't. I'm getting a normal grant and I've got my Schol. That's enough. Until I get a teaching job. We'll be alright then.'

'Mrs. Thomas is a friend more than anything else.'

There was a pleading note in Esther's voice. Gently Amy released her hands.

'And Mrs. Hughes too, really. But especially Mrs. Thomas.'

'Wants to hear all about Connie Clayton and Cranforth Royal? Adventures on the grouse train. Links with Royalty.'

Esther knew that Amy was teasing her. She lifted the lid of the boiler and steam billowed out.

'It's quite harmless,' she said. 'And she can't help it. It's the way she's been brought up. She doesn't know any better. But she's got a heart of gold. And Mrs. Hughes goes to our chapel. I don't want to let her down if I can help it.'

'Yes, but you mustn't let them make use of you. They're both on the lazy side or they wouldn't be so fat. And Mrs. Thomas is a real old penny-pincher. No wonder she's got a heart of gold.'

'Amy! Please don't criticise. They're my friends. I like going to their houses. They're big and full of life. I wouldn't want to be stuck in this little hutch all day. Are you going to put the saucepan on the fire?'

In the living-room Lucas Parry sat in his high-back wooden chair. Behind him the grandfather clock ticked in the corner. His chair was wedged between the table and the fireplace. The room was crowded with the furniture they had brought with them from Swyn-y-Mynydd. There was little room to move. Amy carried the saucepan carefully to the fire. Lucas Parry lowered his newspaper to see what she was doing. His leg was stretched out and his surgical boot, unlaced, rested on the steel fender. He looked apprehensively at his foot, but did not move it.

'I'm not in your way, am I?'

He spoke to Amy with guarded politeness. She shook her head and smiled. He nodded in the direction of the door she had left open. The steam from the scullery was creeping stealthily along the ceiling of the living-room. As though in immediate response to his unspoken wish, Esther appeared to close the door.

'I see that the Principal of your university has been struck down by a hackney carriage. On a London street. That's most unfortunate.'

Amy stirred the dye from the cup into the water in the saucepan.

'I don't think I've ever seen him,' she said. 'I don't think so, anyway.'

'Oh, I have.'

Lucas looked very pleased with himself. He drew his leg in a little and sat up in the hard chair. He felt his neck with his free hand as though he had only just realised he had no collar on. He was unshaved. His stubbled chin and tousled hair were still black, but his complexion was lined and yellow with middle-age and indifferent physical condition. His sharp features lit up with an opportunity of displaying special knowledge that had unexpectedly been presented to him.

'A strange man. A complex man. A man of strange contrasts. That's what I would call him. Worldly. Very worldly. He had this large motor car, you see. A white motor car. And he was terribly proud of it. You could see that. And he had this coat with a fur collar. And he was proud of that, too. And very expensive gloves.'

Amy looked up from the saucepan. In spite of herself she was interested in what her uncle was saying.

'When did you see him?'

'It was some years ago now. I was preaching at Sardis. A little chapel standing by itself in the middle of nowhere. And this man, Iorthyn, was the leading deacon. His dog used to lie in the vestibule throughout the service. Well now, Iorthyn collected manuscripts. Now isn't that just typical of our people? And your Principal wanted to look at them. So he comes in his big white motor car to pay court to Iorthyn in his isolated cottage under Cefn Collen. "The poor man in his cottage, the rich man at his door..." eh? And I was there, you see. I saw it all. He was very gracious. Very polite. He treated us as equals. As in a sense of course, we were.'

Amy had lost interest in his story. She returned to the scullery closing the door behind her. She lifted a petticoat out of the bucket.

'One at a time is it, auntie?'

Esther was smiling at her fondly. She had heard her husband talking. She showed Amy she was pleased with her for listening to him.

118

'He likes talking to you,' she said. 'You know about the things that interest him. Don't get the dye all over you. It's a job to get it off. I'll close the door.'

By the fire, Amy sat on an old milking-stool while she stirred the petticoat in the bubbling navy-blue dye with a long wooden spoon. Lucas' thin nose twitched suspiciously at the smell.

'Chemicals.'

There was disapproval in his voice. The word seemed to represent one of the numerous undesirable aspects of modern living. Amy poked the Celanese carefully into the dye.

'What are you doing?'

It seemed obvious enough. Amy glanced at her uncle before deciding, for her aunt's sake, not to make a sharp answer.

'Petticoats,' she said. 'Lady Alice's petticoats, from Cranforth Royal. They started off as white and now they're going grey. So I'm dyeing them navy blue. So that I can go on wearing them. I'm saving money.'

She spoke pleasantly enough; but he seemed to take what she was saying as some kind of criticism.

'These are hard times,' he said. 'We are all obliged to do things we don't want to do.'

He retired behind his newspaper. Amy stirred the petticoat in the blue water and then lifted it to examine the degree of saturation in the light from the small window.

'Oh damn,' she said.

The colour was streaking. Blue dye ran down the wooden handle on to her hand.

'Don't swear in this house.'

Lucas' voice sounded more hoarse and sepulchral than usual behind his newspaper. Amy cried out despairingly.

'Auntie! Auntie! What shall I do? It's streaking!'

While she waited for advice, there was a knock at the front door. The Celanese slipped back into the dye. Amy stared in desperation at the coats hanging at the back of the door. Esther appeared in the other doorway accompanied by the customary canopy of steam. Amy was on her feet looking at the dye on her hands and on the long mac she was wearing. She pointed desperately at the front door and then stuck out her arms to invite her aunt to observe her grotesque appearance.

'Well, answer it, one of you.'

Lucas was not even considering going to the door himself. He was wedged safely in his corner and prepared to receive all comers. Amy moved closer to her aunt so that she could speak to her quietly.

'Who on earth ... on a Monday morning ...'

Esther was intent on coaxing a little co-operation from her husband.

'Lucas! Lean back and look through the window.'

Through the lace curtain he could see the low wooden fence painted brown that created a narrow zone of privacy between the pavement and the front door. He behaved as though a dusty geranium on the window sill outside was blocking his view.

'I can't see anything.'

He was treating their delicate panic as an irritating form of female humbug.

'Answer it, for goodness' sake. Why all this fuss? Let the world take us as it finds us. That's always been my view.'

Esther was overcome with timidity. Her eyes pleaded wordlessly with Amy begging her to go to the door. There was little room between the Welsh dresser which touched the low ceiling and the table which took up too much room. As she reached the door the caller knocked again. Amy shook her fist before grasping the latch resolutely and opening the door.

When she saw Val Gwyn, her jaw fell. He was wearing a green bow tie and carried a tweed cap in his hand. He was smiling at her delightedly. She stared back at him as if he were a stranger. Across the street everything was quiet in the derelict timber yard. At the side of the large ironmongers three men were laughing and joking loudly as they loaded a van. Amy pushed the door forward as a screen to protect and conceal herself. Val pushed a lock of hair out of his eyes. Already he was regretting having called.

'I'm so sorry,' he said. 'I should have thought ... I was thoughtless. I'm very sorry.'

As she watched him apologise Amy slowly relented.

'I shouldn't have ...'

She cleared her throat and looked surprised at the calmness of her own voice.

'How did you get here?' she said. 'I thought you were in Ireland.'

'Oh, I was.'

He had begun to smile again, prepared to be overjoyed at being forgiven. Amy pulled the scarf off her head and shook out her golden hair.

'I got off the train,' he said. 'I couldn't just pass through Llanelw without seeing you. How could I?'

One of the men swore loudly as he swung the starting handle of the van and released it just before it kicked. His companion took over. The engine started. The man at the wheel advanced the lever on the steering column and the noise of the engine roared out deafeningly all over the street. The men hurried on board and drove off to leave the street deserted and silent. Amy opened the door a little wider. It was possible now that she would smile and look pleased to see him. The living-room was a few inches lower than the level of the pavement. He seemed too tall to be plucking shyly at his cap. From inside the house Lucas Parry spoke without moving from his chair.

'If you have a visitor, Amy, ask him in. Don't keep him standing on the doorstep.'

It was Amy's turn to look hesitant and apprehensive. She gazed up at Val, mutely begging for sympathy and understanding. His expression was infinitely benevolent. His eyebrows were raised, his eyes shone and he smiled to show that he would meet any challenge on her behalf and easily overcome it. She clutched the old mac about her and retreated into the room. The scullery door shut with a sharp bang. A cloud of steam hung from the ceiling. There was just enough room for Val to stand between the dresser and the table. The street door was still open. The steam crept along the ceiling to escape into the open air. Helpfully Val turned to close the door behind him.

'This is Mr. Val Gwyn, uncle,' Amy said.

Val leaned over the table and used his long reach to offer his hand. Lucas Parry let go of his newspaper and twisted in his chair to take it.

'We have met before.'

121

Amy appeared both incredulous and alarmed. Her uncle was only being jovial.

'In a manner of speaking,' Lucas said. 'In our Welsh press. I used to look out for his letter from Paris. Very original. Always a fresh viewpoint. And of course I read *Dadeni*. Excellent little paper. Something fresh. Something new. I hope I'm not too old to learn. Or keep an open mind. Can you find a seat, Mr. Gwyn? We are a bit cramped as you can see. But we wish to make you welcome.'

Amy drew out a kitchen chair enough to give Val a precarious sitting space. He apologised as he sat down.

'I'm so sorry to have called at such an inconvenient time,' he said.

'"Let the occasion realise itself!" That's what I always say.'

Lucas Parry's spirits had been lifted by the arrival of an unexpected and interesting visitor. His face creased with smiles. He seemed on the verge of bursting into hoarse song.

'"Seize the day, stout heart", and so on.'

Amy opened the scullery door. Once more the steam billowed in. She took firm hold of the saucepan on the fire, preparing to remove it.

'Let me help . . .'

Val found difficulty in standing. His knees were trapped under the table.

'You stay there,' Amy said. 'I'll go and change.'

Out of the mist of the steam Esther appeared briefly to close the door behind Amy. The saucepan was placed under the mangle.

'Who is it, for goodness' sake?'

Esther opened the back door and whispered into the air. They stood close together just outside the door, conversing in whispers. The adolescent boy went on painting his bike, pretending not to listen.

'It's Val,' Amy said. 'Val Gwyn. On his way back from Ireland.'

'But what a time to call. An educated man. You'd think he'd have more sense. Look at the sight of us!'

She expected Amy to join in her indignation: to be at least as angry as herself. Instead her niece was studying the boy painting his bike with an expression of profound and

122

completely uncharacteristic resignation on her face.

'I don't know. He has to see us just as we are. Sooner or later.'

A sudden breeze stirred the washing on the line. Esther's flushed face lost the look of indignation. Her eyes became restless with curiosity. She took Amy's hand and pressed it excitedly between her own.

'Amy...?'

She was uncertain how to phrase the question. The boy's paintbrush was moving steadily enough but there was no telling how much he could hear. She pressed her lips together in a tormented smile and held her head to one side, longing for some sign of affirmation.

'I'll go up and change,' Amy said. 'He can take me somewhere to eat. On the prom perhaps.'

'Bring him back for tea. Please bring him back.'

Amy put her finger to her lips and nodded.

A heavy ladder fixed at an acute angle against the inside wall of the scullery gave access to the two rooms upstairs. It was most easily ascended on hands and knees. At the top, Amy took off her clothes. Esther caught them as she threw them down. She wanted to ask questions. She stood on the stairs until her head was close to Amy's feet. Amy put her finger to her lips again. She knelt down until the distance between their heads was only a few feet.

'I'm sorry to leave you with so much work!'

She mouthed the words without making a sound. For a moment they kept still, smiling at each other, a warmth of understanding passing easily between them. Esther made a gesture of dismissal which told her to get ready as quickly as she could.

Amy slept in the back bedroom but her clothes were kept in a wardrobe at the top of the stairs. As she changed she could hear every word spoken in the living-room. Her uncle was happily holding forth.

'Beggars can't be choosers, Mr. Gwyn. As for me, I'm between Pihahirath and Baalzephon, between the chip shop and the petrol pumps. One lot feeds the passengers and the other lot feeds the buses. And I'm there trapped in my wooden hen coop for ten hours a day, studying the passing show.'

Val could have been murmuring sympathetically. Amy heard little of his voice as she crouched on her aunt's bed in order to see herself in the dressing-table mirror. Lucas Parry's voice rose up with renewed confidence, making Amy wince at her own image.

'I'm not complaining, Mr. Gwyn. In some strange way it does give me some insight, especially in my studies of Socialism. It compels me to overcome certain initial prejudices, you see. People in the mass are not very attractive. But then you pick them out. Faces in the crowd. I study faces in a crowd. And then they become people I know. And slowly the pattern becomes meaningful in a Christian Socialist framework. Because that is where I am now, Mr. Gwyn. That's what I call myself. A Christian Socialist. And it doesn't go down all that well, you know. Not even in my denomination which I regard as pretty liberal and en-lightened by and large.'

In the scullery, Esther turned the handle of the old mangle more slowly than usual, in order to reduce the volume of noise it made. It still squealed and squeaked. The slow speed made the sound more protesting, more human and more ancient. Moving carefully in the confined space Amy tried to get on faster with her dressing. Her uncle was holding forth again. He could have been speaking more loudly in order to diminish the effect of the sound of the mangle working in the scullery.

'As I say, it is draughty and uncomfortable. I'm never without my scarf and coat even in summer. But it does give me more time to think. Now when I was a smallholder I never had time to think. And I am basically a thinking man. The place was strapped to my back day and night. Never any release. And of course no access to a good library. Only the glass case in the vestry. And they were all theological. Not that I'm complaining about that. Best possible grounding and discipline. Queen of the sciences and so on. But a piece of land is with you day and night. Now I know what you think from your articles. Agriculture, the basis of Welsh life and so on. And I agree with you in a way, taking the historical view and so on. But what about my personal experience? What have I lost by becoming a wage slave in Philistia? Incarcerated for ten hours a day in a wooden coop called a parcel office. Do you know, I think my answer will shock you, Mr. Gwyn.'

Lucas Parry paused for dramatic effect. In the scullery the mangle ground on with its ineffective attempt at discretion.

'The answer is, very little. The mountain air perhaps. And the trace of freedom that belongs to it. And on fine days a certain fleeting sense of the beauty of creation. Valuable things in themselves, of course. But they don't mean much to the working man, Mr. Gwyn. And after all, that is what I am obliged to be.'

Amy was dressed and standing in the scullery when she saw there was still dye on her hands. She held them out to show to her aunt with something of the appealing helplessness of a little girl. Esther quickly provided her with a basin of hot soapy water. She placed it outside the open doorway. While Amy washed her hands, Esther bent down to whisper in her ear.

'I want to see him,' she said. 'Shall I peep through the keyhole?'

'No, auntie. Please don't.'

She was so excited she did not realise at first that her aunt was teasing.

'Bring him back for tea.'

Esther handed her a towel to dry her hands.

'I'll have finished by then. And have the place nice and tidy.'

Amy tapped the living-room door before going in. Val struggled in vain to get to his feet. He held on to the table, giving some of his attention still to Lucas who was not to be hindered as he came closer to the vital point he was intent on making.

'The workers should inherit the earth. By now, Mr. Gwyn, I take that to be self-evident. But *how* do they do it in a gentle Christlike manner? To me, you see, as an ordinary worker and as a bit of a lay preacher, this is the central dilemma. How do you take over the means of production, for example, without bloodshed and violence? I would be very interested to know your view, Mr. Gwyn.'

When Val spoke he moved his head to include Amy in what he was saying.

'It's a continuing process of discovery,' Val said.

He sat down again to swivel his knees from under the table. After this manoeuvre, he was able to stand up. He smiled happily at Amy, already cheered by her presence.

'There are no easy simple answers,' he said. 'No instant panaceas. No formulae that can be applied like a manual instruction for repairing a machine. All we are saying, and I know Amy agrees with this, all we are saying is that we have to find our own solutions to our own problems if we are to survive, if Wales is to survive as a nation, as a recognisable part of the great total of European civilisation. And finding a solution for yourself, on your own behalf, is in itself an affirmation. An act of survival.'

Lucas had ceased to concentrate on what Val was saying. He was too taken aback at the fact that the distinguished visitor had referred to his niece as though she were some sort of an authority. This girl for whose upbringing and education he had been responsible was suddenly elevated to an exalted position before his very eyes: even among the furniture that crowded the small room like mute memories of all their struggles in the difficult past.

'Where's your aunt, then?'

He began to mumble defensively. There were mundane social obligations that could easily be overlooked when thinking men were carried away on the wings of speculation. Whoever Amy was now or was about to become, in this household she was still the little girl they had cherished and struggled to bring up as best they knew how.

'I think she ought to meet Mr. Gwyn.'

'She's in the middle of her work,' Amy said.

Val was more than eager to apologise.

'Yes. I know. I do realise I should never have called at such an inconvenient time.'

Lucas Parry straightened himself in his chair.

'There is a great deal to be said for taking people how you find them. And by the same token there is as much to be said for being taken as you are found.'

He stretched out his jaw and gazed challengingly at Val. He sat on his throne before his own hearth, entitled to wield the sceptre and ready to exercise some of the prerogative of domestic majesty.

'I look a mess, I dare say. But does the essential person shine through? That is the point.'

'Of course he does.'

Val was effortlessly friendly and charming.

'Well, bring her in,' Lucas said. 'The woman of the house.'

He smiled to show he was proud of his wife and slammed the surface of the table for emphasis. Amy raised her arm and pushed Val gently towards the street door.

'We'll be back for tea, uncle,' she said. 'That's what auntie wants.'

2

As they walked closer to the centre of the town, the sun burst through the clouds. Val pulled at the peak of his tweed cap until a crest of carefree creases radiated into the crown. His strides were too long for Amy. She tugged his sleeve to slow him down. They turned into a street leading to the promenade. He managed to walk more slowly until he stopped suddenly and plunged his hand into his jacket pocket. He brought out a small box and opened his fist briefly for her to see it.

'Bought it in Dublin,' he said. 'Can't wait to show it you.'

He looked mildly intoxicated by the holiday atmosphere of the place and the fresh smell of the sea. Further up the street a row of empty white charabancs had become suddenly conspicuous in the sunlight.

'No, Val. Not here. Put it away please.'

In the window of a confectioner's shop a slight young woman in a white overall was waving to attract Amy's attention. Her nose was red and there was a small handkerchief in the hand she was waving. Amy waved back without enthusiasm.

'Who was that?'

'A girl I was in school with. I imagine she is just about bursting at this moment wanting to know who you are.'

'Oh, dear.'

Val had begun to recollect the embarrassment of his calling at Number Three, Harris Street, on a Monday morning.

'I must have been mad,' he said. 'It couldn't have been worse if I'd called in the middle of the night. I can't think what possessed me. And I don't know how to apologise.'

Amy was philosophical. The broad promenade opened in front of them like an invitation. They were together and the day and the place were at their disposal.

'You had to see us as we really are. Sooner or later.'

'That's true. That's absolutely true.'

'There's nothing romantic about poverty, is there. It's just shameful. That's all.'

'Well...'

Val snatched off his cap and ran his fingers through his thick black hair.

'Relative poverty... But I think I understand, I'm sure I understand what you mean.'

He was smiling triumphantly. Nothing could suppress the optimism surging up inside him. Only a few more adjustments needed to be made and the miracle would occur; they would see the world through each other's eyes.

'I bought this ring,' he said. 'I know we don't attach much importance to these things. And I don't want in any way to impinge on your freedom, because I know how much you value freedom... It's a part of your being. I understand that. And economic privations or whatever you choose to call them only serve to emphasise the fact...'

He breathed deeply as though he were short of oxygen in spite of the bracing air from the sea.

'But I can tell you this and God knows this is not the way to say it but it's burning inside me and I've got to get it out...'

'Let's go and sit down,' Amy said. 'On the sea wall. Over there. It's not too crowded.'

As they crossed the wide promenade two men from the White Rose Tours kiosk emerged with blackboards on which details of newly-devised trips and mystery tours had been inscribed in coloured chalks. There were also simple sketches in chalk of mountain views like the work of pavement artists.

128

When they reached the low sea wall they saw the tide had gone far out leaving miles of sand streaked with an infinity of shallow pools that reflected the blue sky. Holiday-makers were clustered in the narrow area of dry sand between the pavilion and the pier. In the open-air theatre a children's performance had begun. The croaking voice of the chief comic could be heard clearly as he stalked up and down the footlights in Pierrot dress, inciting the smaller children sitting in deck-chairs or on their parents' knees to react more vocally to what he was doing. Val jumped down on the sand and then turned to face Amy sitting on the wall above him with her ankles crossed. For a moment he took hold of her feet in both his hands and then let them go. He squinted up at her. The sun was in his eyes.

'We went to see Padraig Pearse's mother,' he said. 'And his school.'

Short of taking her in his arms and lifting her down to the sand he had to talk of something else close to his heart.

'Shall we walk?' he said. 'To the edge of the sea.'

Gently Amy shook her head. She realised her power over him but she used it with quiet discretion.

'Come and sit by me,' she said. 'And show me that little box.'

He handed her the box. She opened it to study the ring inside while he climbed back to sit beside her.

'It's a signet ring,' he said.

'I can see that.'

'It's quite old. The jeweller said it belonged to one of the Fitzgeralds. I doubt that myself. But I liked it. I wanted it for you. Better than an engagement ring. Put a seal on our relationship. Put it on.'

At first she was unwilling.

'I've been working. My hands look awful.'

His long fingers hovered above her hands. He took the box and offered her the ring.

'Let me put it on.'

With great tenderness he took her hand and began to stroke it. For a while she was acquiescent. Then she began to look over her shoulder. People were passing. She became self-conscious.

She whispered to him urgently.

129

'Put it on, then.'

It slipped on easily. It was far too big. Amy raised her hand so that the ring rested at the base of her finger.

'O Lord. I've made an awful mess of it again. Lack of discipline. That's what it amounts to. I can see now what they mean when they talk about someone being madly in love. Clichés always mean something. That's what's so infuriating about them. I'm so stupid. I'm so sorry. I'm apologising again.'

'I like it.'

With her raised finger Amy mimed the action of spinning a hoop with a stick.

'I'll keep it. A keepsake. Something Val brought for me from Dublin. The seal of the Fitzgeralds! Just think. It could be valuable. We could sell it to one of your rich American relatives when they come over.'

Ruefully he pressed the palms of his hands into the stone wall they sat on, and watched the ring rising and falling on Amy's third finger.

'I know what I'd like to put on that finger,' he said. 'Permanently.'

'I like this one,' Amy said. 'And I like the way we are.'

'It's a monstrous state to be in love.'

He sounded gloomy and portentous but Amy listened to him as though he were telling her an amusing story.

'It warps the character beyond all recognition. A man in love isn't normal. He is consumed with an unquenchable passion. And all the clichés are true. It feeds on itself. It burns. It eats him up.'

He leaned forward to look at her face.

'Look at you,' he said. 'So calm. So bright. I think that's what I admire most of all in your beauty. The settled calm at the centre of it.'

'I wasn't calm when you called this morning,' Amy said.

'You looked just as beautiful in a totally new way.'

Val was eager to explain. She was not unwilling to listen.

'I'd never seen you with your hair hidden before. Your eyes. Your cheekbones. Your lips. Your chin. I saw them all as separate principalities of individual beauty. And do you know what I was longing to do even when I was standing there mumbling my apologies? I was longing to be a skilled poet in the old style. So that I could devise a great chain of *dyfalu* to decorate you. Great patterns of alliterative praise to every item. A great structure like a cathedral roof...'

Val began to make enthusiastic branching gestures with his arms. Amy again became conscious of passers-by. She placed her hand on his arm. He behaved obediently.

'That's all I am,' he said. 'When you come down to it. A frustrated poet. A poet manqué.'

Amy lowered her hand. She forgot the ring on her finger. Before she could catch it, it had slipped off and fallen into the churned sand beneath their feet.

'Oh no...'

He was preparing to jump down but she restrained him.

'Wait,' she said. 'Wait. Can you see it?'

They both peered downwards.

'I can see banana skins,' he said. 'And bits of paper. Bits of orange peel...'

She shook his arm impatiently.

'Look,' she said. 'Just look.'

They scanned the area of sand beneath their legs with added intensity.

'Once it was too big,' Val said. 'Now it's too small. I'll have to go down.'

He moved several feet to his left before jumping. Then he walked around the area so that he could approach cautiously the spot beneath Amy's feet.

'Don't come too close,' she said. 'It could have flown out a bit. As my hand came down. It wasn't really heavy.'

He sank to his knees and put his nose close to the sand so that he could sniff like a dog.

'Oh Val, look properly! Don't be silly, please.'

'It's only a ring,' he said.

He continued his careful search.

'It doesn't add anything. Not really.'

Amy's sense of loss was growing more urgent.

'Yes. But it was a seal... of something between us.'

He paused in his search to sit back on his heels and look up at her adoringly.

'An agreement. A covenant. That's wonderful. Say it again.'

She shook her hand and pointed impatiently at a spot in the sand where she felt the ring could be.

'Look there,' she said. 'Look properly. Oh dear, I don't want to lose it. It meant so much to me. Help me down. I've got to find it.'

He was disturbed to see that she was becoming tearful. He placed his cap on the spot that they agreed was the most likely place to find it. Amy moved along the wall to a position where the sand was piled high against the wall. He held up his arms to help her. When she landed he was unwilling to let her go.

'It's only an inanimate object,' he said. 'It will be here for centuries after we've gone.'

Her eyes were brimming with tears. By force of habit she was pushing him away at the very moment when she most needed him to hold her. Together on their hands and knees they searched the sand around his cap.

'I can't see.'

Amy wiped the tears away.

'A woman has to be so patient.'

They had stopped looking. He listened to her intently as though the sound of her voice was coming from a distance.

'She has to school herself not to want what she wants until she no longer really knows what she wants.'

'I'll get you another ring,' Val said. 'A much better one. One that will last for ever.'

Amy was looking at him through her tears.

'I used to dream about you,' she said. 'All last summer.'

She raised her arm to point behind her in the direction of a row of boarding houses on the promenade.

'I was washing dishes. Nearly every day. For Mrs. Thomas, Arosfa, and Mrs. Hughes, Bodlondeb.'

She began to smile through her tears.

'I used to think of you. In Paris. Walking up and down the Champs-Elysées. And standing on top of the Eiffel Tower. Is that what you used to do?'

He shook his head. Half-heartedly they continued their search in the sand.

'It was a hard time for me. Very little money. I used to give a few lessons in English and Welsh to get a few extra francs.'

'Meeting lots of important people . . . beautiful women . . . that's what I imagined.'

'No one nearly as beautiful as you.'

'And all the temptations. All those wicked places.'

Amy's tears were gone. Her eyes shone brightly, full of mischief. Val sighed deeply and shook his head.

'It's no fun at all,' he said. 'Being a puritan in Paris. I think we've lost this ring. Don't you? Shall we go and eat?'

3

From a single window in the south wall of the first-floor granary the sunlight poured through the wooden slats. With geometrical precision it cut parallel swathes of vibrating brightness across the shadowed space. The long room was used as a warehouse. Cilydd was in his shirtsleeves shifting sacks of processed maize. He was intent on displaying his capacity for physical labour. He was watched by the sheepdog and by Enid who sat on the threshold of the open door exposing herself to the bright sunlight outside while she weighed on the palm of her right hand and enjoyed studying the movements of the man and the dog. She was a holiday figure, wearing a white dress with a blue collar. Each time Cilydd dragged the hand-truck across the bare board the two wheels squealed from lack of oil, and the dog jerked up his narrow head. His ears twitched before they again registered the jarring sound as mechanical and inanimate: yet another inexplicable accident of human ingenuity. His head thrust forward as though resolved once again to rely on smell rather than sound.

'But look at him... if only he could talk.'

Enid was ready to express her delight in everything she saw.

'He's so anxious to please you. Wouldn't it be a wonderful world if everybody were so anxious to please?'

Cilydd paused briefly to consider the proposition and the sheepdog. The dog gazed back at him, his eyes glowing with mute appeal, his red tongue hanging out its full length between his glistening white fangs. He could have been begging for some special show of ingenuity that would remove all the sacks at once so that he could dart into the darkness and win the approval of a new master by a dazzling attack on the hidden enemy. The pads of his paws thrust down into the old floorboards. The tendons of his legs were trembling like taut wire. His entire existence was devoted to proving his worth and every hair on his body was electrified by the desire to please.

'Stand back, Mot! If that's what your name is.'

Cilydd's command was abrupt and impersonal. It served to keep the dog in his place.

'It could be chaos,' he said. 'Death by suffocation.'

He studied the dog as he spoke to Enid. He was glad of a rest. Sweat hung in a row of small beads above his upper lip. He took off his spectacles to wipe them with a silk handkerchief. Enid waited in case he had more to say. From the workroom at the far end of the row of outbuildings under the warehouse floor came the cheerful tap of a hammer on shoe leather.

'It gives a biological justification for a degree of selfishness,' Cilydd said. 'It is an essential element in the preservation of the balance of nature.'

He smiled at his own mock academic manner, straightened his shoulders and replaced the ends of the spectacles frame over each delicate ear.

'Stand back, dog! I had a dog like this one when I was a boy. He had terrier blood in him. Never saw a dog like him for catching rats.'

Enid could resist her impulsive enthusiasm no longer.

'I love this place,' she said. 'I really do. It's so . . . beautiful. It's like an earthly paradise.'

'Dear me.'

Cilydd leaned on the trolley handle to gaze at her. Together they listened to the tapping of the cobbler's hammer and the patient panting of the dog at Cilydd's heel.

'It's a little world,' Enid said. 'A complete little world. Your grandmother is a remarkable woman.'

Cilydd showed that he could not disagree.

'And the work going on here. The activity! It's more than I ever imagined.'

Downstairs the cobbler began singing a familiar hymn in a tremulous reedy tenor.

'He's such a dear, your Uncle Tryfan. He really is. Always so happy.'

Cilydd smiled at her fondly.

'That could be because he's not very bright.'

'Nanw in the shop. Aunty Bessie keeping house. Uncle Tryfan shoemaking. Then there's the farm. And the post office. The coal business. And curing wild warts. And goodness knows what. It's phenomenal. Your grandmother is a great woman.'

'She's obsessed with work. I know that much.'

'Well, of course. She has to be.'

Enid would allow nothing to diminish her enthusiasm. She jumped when a rustic voice called up from the bottom of the stone stairway.

'Do we have people?'

She caught a glimpse of a man with a face wrinkled like a walnut, gazing up with open admiration of her legs in silk stockings. Shyly she withdrew into the shadow.

'It's Robert Thomas the mole-trapper,' Cilydd explained in a low voice. 'Always prides himself on being early.'

Cilydd emerged to greet the newcomer. He wiped the dust from his face and came outside to stand on the flagstones to the elevated landing surrounded by a protective low wall.

'*Diwc annwyl*, is it you that I see, John Cilydd?'

The mole-trapper displayed exaggerated astonishment. He stretched out a bowed leg to set a foot on the lowest step. He leaned forward to show he was resting after the long steady walk which had brought him early to his destination. He extracted an oval tobacco box made of cow's horn from the pocket of his waistcoat. His sleeves were rolled up to the elbow and he carried a blue linen jacket over his sunburnt arm. When he smiled as he was doing now, the stain of the tobacco juice on his teeth gave a mildly satanic cast to the grimace. Cilydd raised his hand to protect his eyes from the bright sunlight. Enid moved forward to stand half out of sight in the door. She was a figure that could not but arouse the mole-trapper's curiosity.

'You are here before I am ready for you, Robert Thomas. How are you keeping?'

'Very fair indeed, thank you. Leisure is won by early-

135

rising, John Cilydd. My old motto that you may have heard before.'

He twitched his eyebrows and plucked a quid of tobacco with finger and thumb from the oval box to pack it with an adroit movement between gum and cheek on the left side of his mouth. He had won leisure to enjoy a quiet chew and to survey the environment for any significant signs of change. After the girl in the white dress, his attention was taken by a motor car parked on the cobbles outside the main entrance to Glanrafon Stores. A four-seater tourer with the hood up had been freshly polished that morning. The blue bodywork shone even in the sharp-edged shadow cast by the whitewashed stores across the dusty road that separated it from its associated outbuildings. The modernity of the machine was impressive and the mole-trapper was very ready to be impressed. He chewed ruminatively as he absorbed intriguing detail. The spare wheel sunk in the running-board was covered in a mysterious protective material of its own. Alongside it was anchored an oblong petrol can that contained more of the mysterious fluid which made the engine run. Robert Thomas squinted enquiringly at a chromium-plated figurine with outstretched arms that balanced with one foot on the radiator cap. This object, too, had something to do with an abnormal power of motion.

'That is yours, John Cilydd?'

'I suppose so, Robert Thomas.'

In the open air their first exchanges were slow and liturgical. There were tin signs advertising mustard and paraffin oil and cattlefood nailed to some of the half-doors of the extremities of the long white building. All the doors and the woodwork were painted in red ochre. A pony and trap in the shade beyond the motor car looked old-world. Robert Thomas was well acquainted with everything around him except the touring motor car and the girl who stood in the warehouse doorway. Too much direct enquiry would have been indelicate. On the other hand there were things that every respected member of the community was entitled to know.

'That's a very clever car you have there, John Cilydd More.'

'Oh, I don't know that I would go that far, Robert Thomas.'

Their conversation was obliged to flow through recognised channels of politeness. Any information could be gleaned effortlessly without any vulgar display of crude curiosity. Because he was early, the mole-trapper was entitled to use the modes of traditional courtesy and drone on in the sun as a dove would moan in a tree.

'Your success does great honour to the district, John Cilydd More.'

'I wouldn't be sure about that.'

'Have no doubt at all that your father who was drowned at sea, poor man, would be proud of you if he could see you today. And your grandfather too. Noble old man. And your mother, poor soul. And your excellent grandmother who is such a credit to this little parish of ours. Mrs. Lloyd, Glanrafon Stores. People come from a great distance to sample her wisdom and find a cure in her art. A good old family. One of the best in the country, if my opinion were asked. A proper family.'

His peroration gave him the opportunity to shift forward and lean on the wall of the outside stairway. He played with his cap, scratched his head and snatched a surreptitious closer look at the girl in the shadowed granary doorway. He lifted an arm to point at the motor car.

'Goes very fast, I dare say?'

'Not really. Twenty-five miles an hour on a good road. Thirty perhaps, downhill.'

The mole-trapper shook his head sadly.

'Speed,' he said. 'The motto of the age. In all seriousness, John Cilydd, what do you think is to become of us?'

Cilydd gave a sympathetic smile.

'I asked Jones the minister the very same question the other day. That one isn't so sure of his answers as he used to be. This is the Age of Going, I said to him. Quite right, Robert Thomas, he said. Ah, I said. But *where* are we going? He wasn't at all sure of the answer. I'll tell you something, John Cilydd. You may or may not agree with me. Nothing is nearly as good as it used to be. That's my candid opinion.'

'Try not to be too dispirited, Robert Thomas.'

137

'As I said to the wife God has given me, I'm quite relieved that more than half my allotted span is over so that I won't be here to see what's sure to come.'

Attracted by his discourse Enid had emerged more clearly into the light. Robert Thomas looked suddenly cheerful and slapped his horny hand on the sloping wall.

'Where do I start this day? Maybe I should have a word with Mrs. Lloyd, your grandmother, first. Is that what you would say?'

He tilted his head to listen to the tap of the hammer at the end of the building.

'Do I hear a woodpecker making his own boots?'

He waited for John Cilydd to show appreciation of his wit.

'Back at work, I'm glad to hear. Excellent craftsman is Tryfan Lloyd. And verging on the holy in his innocence. I would venture to say that. Maybe, he'll be giving me a hand later to exterminate the rats?'

'Possibly.'

Cilydd could not commit his uncle.

'I judge that you yourself will be otherwise engaged?'

The mole-trapper was smiling almost directly at Enid. He was going as close as he could to asking for an introduction. Cilydd turned to Enid.

'I don't think you have met Robert Thomas, Foryd Bach. This is Miss Prydderch, Robert Thomas, from Llanelw.'

The mole-trapper bowed his head. He was grateful for the information. It was accurate and it had been freely bestowed. This alone was an acknowledgment of his worth as an individual and as a member of the community. It reaffirmed his place in the universe as a small but necessary link in the chain. Enid was intrigued with the mature flavour of Robert Thomas' personality. She murmured enthusiastically and advanced further forward to enjoy more of his conversation. Robert Thomas looked upwards, his mouth open and his eyes twinkling with joyous anticipation.

'So you are here, Robert Thomas!'

From the stores across the lane a squat vigorous woman had emerged. She wore a black felt hat on her head but it failed to trap all her rusty hair. It strayed across her red cheeks and into her piercing blue eyes. In her seventies she was still fiercely energetic. As soon as he heard her the mole-trapper stood to attention and showed by his respectful pose that he was ready for work. While her eye was on him he stopped chewing. Mrs. Lloyd shaded her brow to look up at her grandson.

'John Cilydd,' she said. 'How much more is there to do up there?'

While Cilydd was looking back into the warehouse space to make an estimated answer, his grandmother had already decided on her next course of action.

'We'll do it like this,' she said. 'The same as last year. Start in the stockroom behind the main stores.'

'That would be best, Mrs. Lloyd, in my opinion.'

She barely seemed to hear him. She registered Enid's presence by raising and lowering her eyebrows rapidly. She appeared deeply preoccupied by other matters. Between the outbuildings and the stores she stood like a theatre director who has more ideas circulating in his mind than words to articulate them. She was surrounded by her enterprises and attentive to every one of them. Down the road one of her dray horses was being shod in the smithy at the end of a row of cottages. There was a cart left on the roadside with its shafts in the air while another horse had been taken into the stable to wait its turn. She turned her head and took in a glimpse of Cilydd's sister, Nanw, behind the grill of the post office counter. In that section of the stores there was also a drapery department.

'Mrs. Lloyd,' Robert Thomas said. 'In case I forget to mention it, Mrs. Roberts, Bryn Menyn, asked me to convey a message. She has a wild wart she thinks. On her neck of all places.'

'Tell her to come and see me. I can't say anything without looking at it.'

Robert Thomas was obliged to stride rapidly across the road to reach the door of the stores before it closed on its spring. Mrs. Lloyd had already transferred herself to a fresh field of endeavour and concern.

'She is a wonder!'

Enid was glowing with admiration.

'That is the only way to describe her. A wonder!'

'Of Wales? Or of the World?'

Cilydd wiped the lenses of his spectacles and studied her with short-sighted fondness.

'She doesn't do it all herself,' he said.

Enid was anxious to be accurate.

'Oh, don't misunderstand me,' she said. 'The whole family is wonderful. Your Uncle Gwilym has brilliance. Like you have. He is a real poet. I can't wait to see his office on the Slate Quay. And your Uncle Simon at Ponciau is a model farmer. But she is the *fons et origo* or whatever. She is the phenomenon. Just imagine. If she'd been born a man, Mrs. Lloyd, your grandmother, she would have gone to America or something like that and become a millionaire long, long ago.'

'Dear me.'

Cilydd was mildly surprised by her flight of fancy. He went back into the granary and began to load more sacks on to the trolley to transfer them to the middle of the floor. The dog sniffed delightedly. When a hole in the corner was exposed he began to growl and whine. Enid had to raise her voice as the trolley wheels rumbled over the bare boards.

'She's better than a millionaire,' she said. 'That's what I'm trying to say. She's the dynamic heart of a thriving community. Surely that's close to the ideal? Isn't it what the world needs? What Wales needs?'

Cilydd stopped working. He was breathing heavily from a bout of tossing sacks to the top of the pile.

'Steady on, Miss Prydderch.'

'Surely she is already practising ninety per cent of what we are preaching?'

Cilydd smiled at her.

'If you don't mind me telling you, you are suffering from a mild attack of rose-tinted spectacles.'

The sacks were piled in the centre of the room and all the walls were exposed. The dog seemed disoriented. He stared disappointedly at the walls and continued to sniff the sacks. Somehow his quarry had escaped him. Cilydd rolled down his shirtsleeves and picked up his jacket. Together they went to sit in the sun on the wall outside. An isolated chapel stood on higher ground looking down on Glanrafon Stores and its complex of buildings and on the row of cottages and the smithy. Behind the stores they could see farm buildings partially hidden by well grown beech trees and beyond them the conspicuous corrugated red roof of a new Dutch barn. Cilydd folded his arms and stretched his legs, resting one boot on the other.

'This little principality,' he said. 'Glanrafon. A monument to my grandmother's lifelong activity. Creative activity, you would say. Well, in political terms, it can only be described as a benevolent dictatorship.'

Enid was unwilling to accept the parallel.

'Forgive me,' Cilydd said.

He clearly found it endearing that she should theorise authoritatively about his grandmother after so short an acquaintance with her. He spread his fingers and pressed them modestly against his chest.

'I can speak from experience. I hope I respect my grandmother. I know I do. But I also know that it was to escape from her iron rule that I fled to a solicitor's office.'

'Oh.'

Enid lowered her head. She was disappointed and crestfallen.

'And I also know with the incomparable wisdom of hindsight, that my Uncle Gwilym did the same. He fled to a clerkship in the slate company's office on the Slate Quay at Glaslyn. And there more or less he remains.'

'Ah, but you were both poets . . .'

Enid was already working on the restoration of her original thesis.

'And poets don't like hard work?'

He was teasing her. He began to brush the dust from his waistcoat and trousers. Enid tried to help him.

'I didn't say that.'

'But she did. And I've heard it repeated a thousand times. "Look here, Gwilym, farming and poetry don't mix." So he went off to be a pupil teacher. But he wasn't any good there. Too bad-tempered. Always thrashing the children. So he ended up a clerk in an office. And my history is nothing more than a boring repetition of his.'

He frowned as if he were angry with himself. But when he saw that Enid was perturbed he smiled and slapped the palms of his hands on his knees.

141

'I've never been cruel to children,' he said. 'I never had the chance. But I don't like the sheer grind of physical hard labour. I've got to admit it. I was supposed to have the farm. This one first and then Ponciau after Uncle Simon and Nanw was to have the stores. Or the shop anyway. That was her plan. And I disappointed her. But she's forgiven me.'

Enid's face brightened.

'There you are,' she said.

'I'm not like Val,' Cilydd said. 'I always look for the easy way out. But I try not to deceive myself. Not more than I can help.'

A sudden breeze brought the sound of the anvil from the smithy and voices raised in challenge and laughter.

'You shouldn't run yourself down,' Enid said in a soft voice. 'I'm sure that's wrong.'

'You know what I think?'

She looked attentively at his face as he spoke.

'What it all boils down to. Living, I mean. It boils down to who you can get on with and who you can't get on with. It's as simple as that on the lowest level. And lowest doesn't mean least important.'

Enid gave the deepest consideration to his conclusions. Her enthusiasm had evaporated. She had become wistful and pensive.

'You make me feel so childish sometimes,' she said.

Customers emerged from the shop. A farmer and his wife carrying a basket each. They paused to admire and marvel at the motor car. Even when he had loaded the baskets on the trap, the farmer continued to study the car with profound admiration and envy.

'I want to meet them all,' Enid said. 'Shall we go to Glaslyn this afternoon? Or to Ponciau? Or to both? Uncle Gwilym and Uncle Simon. I want to get to know them both. I want to know them all. Really well.'

Cilydd turned down the corners of his mouth in comic disapproval.

'Why, for goodness' sake?'

'So that I can get to know you better.'

Her frankness seemed too much for him. He hung his head as if to show that he was unworthy of such detailed attention. A bright light of hope was kindling in her eyes, but she restrained herself, aware that they were sitting in a relatively public and exposed position on top of the granary steps. It would have been unseemly for her to be seen talking too much or for them to show any open tenderness towards each other.

'I want to be of real use to you.'

Her lips barely moved as she spoke. They sat as still as two carved figures. Voices came from the shop, shouts from the busy smithy. The cobbler's hammer went on tapping. They were content to listen to it all merging into the ceaseless warm breath of the summer countryside.

4

Mrs. Lloyd sat at the head of the table, nursing a secret joke. Her black felt hat was perched precariously on her head. It seemed to be there to save her wasting time looking for it. The midday meal was a family ritual and she was loyal to family tradition in every respect: but for her, eating was never more than a brief interruption of the far more urgent task of preserving the unbroken flow of labour that kept all the moving parts of her enterprises lubricated and in good order. The joke was to do with Cilydd. He sat at the end of the horsehair sofa with a cushion under him to make it easier for him to address the table. Chatter was no part of the family occasion. Enid sat on the sofa next to Cilydd. Opposite her sat Nanw, Cilydd's only sister. In spite of the weather they were all eating a mutton stew that included turnips, carrots and potatoes. Mrs. Lloyd had finished first. She was twiddling her thumbs and smiling a secret smile. Uncle Tryfan seemed to sense she was in the mood to tell a joke. He looked up expectantly from his plate. Aunty Bessie, too, hesitated to take up a second helping of stew in case her mother should speak. She stood near the fire, her ladle poised above the stewpot.

'Thinking of you, John Cilydd,' Mrs. Lloyd said at last, pointing a piece of bread at her grandson. 'When you were little. You used to hate getting your hands dirty.'

This amused Uncle Tryfan very much. He sat at the other end of the table. He opened his mouth wide in silent mirth and pointed his spoon at Cilydd so that Enid should be in no doubt as to whom his mother was talking about. Although he was bald he retained a certain youthful innocence. In company he was always at pains to show that he wished everyone well, particularly members of his own family.

'I remember that,' he said. 'I remember it as if it were yesterday. You always had a wet flannel ready, Bessie. To wipe his little hands.'

Uncle Tryfan lifted his own hands proudly. He sniffed them and smiled mischievously at Enid.

'Nothing like leather.'

Auntie Bessie was able to help herself to more stew. She was a plump comfortable woman who enjoyed nothing more than eating and talking about the past. A fresh whiff of hot food escaped into the kitchen as she emptied the wooden ladle on her plate.

'He was a very good boy.'

She spoke mainly for Enid's benefit.

'Very sensitive, of course. Which is only natural. And skilled in the *cynganeddion* by the age of twelve. At fourteen he beat his Uncle Gwilym on the subject of "The Garden of Eden" at the Geboah Eisteddfod. His nom-de-plume was "The Eaglet".'

'I never knew that,' Enid said.

Every new item of information seemed to give her special pleasure. The grandmother watched her with wary benevolence. Cilydd's sister, who sat opposite, played with her food and kept everything under close observation.

'And he won twice in the same week once,' Auntie Bessie said. 'At Penygraig on "The Watchman", and Capel Ucha on "The Happy Warrior".'

'*Diawch*, Bess, you have a wonderful power of recollection.'

Uncle Tryfan's chirpy voice was tinged with real envy. His large brow furrowed regularly with the effort of retaining all the fascinating facts that so easily escaped his memory, leaking like gas out of each ear. Auntie Bessie returned to her place. Her eyes narrowed as she gazed into the middle distance above the heads of Cilydd and Enid.

'I think I can remember most of those early wins,' she said. 'Apprentice-work for him. But it meant a lot to me.'

Enid was nodding enthusiastically.

'For heaven's sake!'

Cilydd tried not to sound too exasperated.

'Stop talking about me as if I wasn't here. I'm sitting here listening to you. I'm not dead yet. And it's not exactly music to my ears, if you don't mind me saying so. Now then. The ship will be leaving in exactly twenty minutes. Who is ready to go?'

He looked at his grandmother first and then at his aunt and his sister. Uncle Tryfan was known to be working and did not expect to be included in the invitation. He looked across the table and pointed his spoon respectfully at his mother.

'Go,' he said. 'It will do you the world of good.'

She returned him a practised look of pitying condescension. He was the son who still lived at home. Safe under her protection. When he spoke she listened to him as she would have done to a pet canary in a cage: for sound rather than sense. She valued his boundless good nature but had little use for any of his opinions.

'Sir Fôn is a long way,' she said. 'If we were going, we should have started first thing.'

'Motor!'

Uncle Tryfan whirled his spoon around.

'There and back, toc-tic, tic-toc!'

'Why can't we all go?' Enid said.

Mrs. Lloyd was unmoved by her enthusiasm.

'Well, what is it going to be, Nain?'

Cilydd spoke to his grandmother with a masterful show of independence. Uncle Tryfan was impressed. His eyes switched from one to the other like a spectator privileged with a front seat at an historic encounter.

'It's entirely up to you.'

Cilydd sat back and put his thumb in the armhole of his waistcoat. Above his head there was a coloured aquatint depicting the Broad and Narrow Way. The large Bible, which was read aloud daily before breakfast by each member of the family in turn, lay on a tall narrow desk in the corner of the room between the window and the door leading to the best rooms of the house.

'I would like to see the grave of Mr. Elias,' his grandmother said.

'Well, there we are . . .'

Uncle Tryf was jubilant. Nothing gave him more pleasure than the prospect of other people's enjoyment.

'That's settled then,' he said.

'I don't know why you call him Mr. Elias, Nain,' Cilydd said. 'He was dead before you were born.'

'Mr. Elias he always was in this house. My father thought he was a great man. And he was too. He ordained your great-great uncle Ezra.'

'John Elias it is then.'

Cilydd slapped both his hands on the patterned oilcloth. He leaned with modest daring towards Enid.

'And you can have a look at your Queen Siwan as well. Whatever is left of her grave won't be more than a good stone's throw away.'

'Who was Queen Siwan?'

His grandmother was a little irritated at having to ask the question. She addressed Cilydd's sister.

'Do you know, Nanw? You're a bit of a reader, as we all know.'

'The wife of Llewelyn the Great.'

Nanw looked down modestly at her plate.

'I dare say Miss Prydderch could tell you more than I could about her.'

The grandmother was momentarily inclined to be lighthearted.

'"Queen Siwan",' she said. 'It sounded like the Queen of Sheba to me. And that would be a long way to go.'

She looked shortsightedly at Enid sitting on her right, plainly waiting for more information.

'She was unfaithful,' Enid said. 'So Llewelyn put her in prison and hanged her lover. Although she was the King of England's daughter and her lover was a great Border magnate.'

'Serve her right, I should say.'

Mrs. Lloyd had nothing more to do with eating. She sat

146

back in her chair to deliver judgement. Her arms were
outstretched on the wooden arms of the chair and her fists
clenched: in her mind, passing a sentence seemed to include a
readiness to carry it out. Auntie Bessie looked a little
nervously at Nanw. To her the subject seemed rather
indelicate.

'And him right, of course. There should never be any
shilly-shallying in these matters. Where is she buried, did
you say?'

'In Llanfaes. Across the Straits from the castle where she
was imprisoned. Llewelyn forgave her. When she died he
built a Franciscan house in her memory.'

'What kind of house?'

The grandmother was increasingly annoyed with her own
ignorance. She had lived long enough to have heard of most
historical personages. She could only assume that those who
had escaped her attention were hardly of any consequence.
Therefore the more brightly Enid vouchsafed her information the less palatable she found it.

'A monastery,' Nanw said.

The piercing blue eyes shifted about as she tried to
imagine the kind of institution named by her daughter. It
had small chance of meeting with her approval.

'I'm trying to persuade John Cilydd to think of writing a
play about her,' Enid said.

She smiled at them all. It seemed such an excellent
opportunity to share a confidence with the assembled family,
and perhaps lead them gently to a wider understanding of the
nature of the genius they cherished in their midst.

'He is some kind of poet, is he not?' the grandmother said.
'He doesn't have to go writing for play-acting.'

Enid considered the proposition.

'I think I know what you mean, Mrs. Lloyd. But in the
European tradition, I think it is fair to say that the poetic art
finds its highest fulfilment in the play, in the theatre. For one
thing it allows a richer reflection of the nature of the human
condition by the complex interaction of a variety of
characters caught up in a critical situation.'

Uncle Tryfan's forehead was severely corrugated and his
mouth hung open.

'Would you mind saying that again?' he said.

Everyone burst out laughing. Enid herself joined in. She leaned back against the wall and laughed until her eyes were filled with tears.

'Oh dear . . .'

She gasped for breath and began coughing. She leaned forward and pointed to her back, inviting Cilydd to slap it. He did so too gently.

'Harder,' she said. 'Harder, please.'

When she recovered her breath she was full of apologies.

'Oh dear,' she said. 'I'm so sorry. I don't know what's the matter with me these days. I get so academic and pompous.'

Mrs. Lloyd was listening to her with renewed seriousness. She looked at her grandson closely as though she were making a great effort both to be practical and to see him through Enid's eyes.

'Besides,' she said. 'Where would you put on a thing like that? Poetry or not. A play about an adulterous woman. You couldn't very well put it on in the Vestry, could you?'

Cilydd was smiling, but this time nobody laughed. Mrs. Lloyd addressed him sharply in the way she used to when she was rebuking him as a boy.

'What are you grinning about?'

From force of habit he made a hasty disavowal.

'Nothing in particular.'

This was insufficient to clear him of suspicion of smiling patronisingly at her lack of sophistication.

'I'm not a playwright anyway. I've got no talent for it. It's as much as I can do to manage being a passable poet.'

'Hold on,' Uncle Tryfan said. 'Hold on . . .'

He was loyally opposed to his nephew running himself down.

'After all, you are a national winner.'

'That proves nothing,' Cilydd said. 'You know what Williams-Parry said. Press on from your winnings to your work. Hard work. That's the way I look at it.'

Mrs. Lloyd pushed back her chair and gripped the arms with both hands.

'That's one thing we are agreed about,' she said. 'And that's enough idle talk. I've got much work to attend to.'

Suddenly Cilydd twisted on his cushions, swung his long legs over the curved end of the horsehair sofa and thrust himself over so that he landed on the stone floor and then stamped his feet in triumph. Uncle Tryfan laughed delightedly to see him repeat so accurately one of his boyhood acrobatic tricks.

'How many times do I have to tell you not to do that?'

There was no sting in Mrs. Lloyd rebuke. Just as her grandson had reproduced a piece of their past, she too took up her easily remembered rôle.

'One day you'll do yourself damage. Mark my words.'

'Now then.'

Cilydd used his height to dominate the floor. He was, after all, the favourite of the household. There were privileges that he could exercise.

'Are you or are you not coming?'

Mrs. Lloyd was stretching her arms to reach a small bunch of keys hanging on a nail concealed by the short valance of brown velvet that hung from the high shelf above the kitchen range. Cilydd snatched the keys and held them high above his grandmother's head. She was vexed that he should dare to provoke her. Particularly with his fiancée still little more than a stranger in their midst.

'Coming or not coming?'

'No. I am not. I have too much on hand to go gallivanting in a motor car. Give me those keys and get out of my way.'

Auntie Bessie, quick to follow her mother's example had begun to clear the table. Enid stood up eager to help. She lifted a basin. Auntie Bessie swiftly snatched it from her hands which were left empty, but raised and ready for work.

'Who is coming?' Cilydd said. 'Just tell me that!'

He listened to his grandmother's clogs clattering purposefully down the passage that led to the outhouses at the back of the stores. Uncle Tryfan now rose to his feet and with a regretful sigh placed his chair neatly as far as it would go under the table.

'Who? Just tell me who?'

Nanw's oval spectacles glinted in the light as she lifted her dark head appealingly towards her brother. Her nostrils were pinched white with suppressed excitement.

'I had been rather looking forward to it,' she said.

'That's wonderful!'

She turned her head to examine Enid's enthusiastic

response. She seemed to find it over-rapturous. She would have preferred some word from her brother. He remained silent.

'And what about Auntie Bessie?'

Enid used the familiar mode of address for the first time as easily and as naturally as she could. "Miss Lloyd" would have been too stiff and formal. It drew attention too insistently to her spinster status. Auntie Bessie seemed to like it. Her eyes beamed as benevolently as ever in her plump cheeks. If Nanw had any objection it was not identifiable. There were no means of isolating the exact cause of the mild air of resentment clouding her unsmiling countenance. Auntie Bessie carried dishes to the brown sink under the scullery window.

'No indeed. Not me.'

She could not stop working as she talked.

'I've got too much to get through. And to tell you the truth, I tend to get sick, travelling in a motor car. The smell, I think. It doesn't agree with my stomach.'

'That's just three of us then,' Cilydd said.

There was a note of legalistic finality in his voice.

'Well, I'm not sure...'

Nanw was hesitating.

'Nain might want me to help with the stocktaking...'

If she was expecting him to press her, she was disappointed.

'Make your mind up,' he said. 'Exercise your own judgement, for heaven's sake.'

Enid looked at them both with mute astonishment. Cilydd's manner was so uncharacteristically off-hand and inconsiderate. And yet his sister seemed used to it, almost seemed to be enjoying it.

'If you want me to come...'

It seemed modest and humble. Enid cried out generously.

'Of course we want you to come!'

It wasn't enough. Nanw was staring in front of her with an unyielding self-sufficiency, deaf to the voice of so recent an intruder.

'Don't we, John Cilydd? We want Nanw to come with us, don't we?'

He put both hands in his trouser pockets.

'It's up to her. She's welcome to come if she wants to. Wherever it is we are going. If we ever go.'

5

'Nanw! Did you see that? Did you see it?'

Enid stood in the rough grass her arms raised as she cried out her delight. The hare zig-zagged across the sloping field like a trace of lightning across a placid sky. Enid wanted to share her pleasure. Nanw, further down the field, made no answer. They had left the touring car parked at a careless angle on the rough verge of the road below the field. Cilydd was already far ahead. Above a row of gaunt weather-beaten pines he was making his way rapidly towards an eccentric outcrop of steep rock.

'Isn't it wonderful? Isn't it delicate?'

Enid had discovered the hare's form. She knelt beside it to feel the warmth of the hare's body still lingering in the flattened grass. Nanw reached her side but she continued to watch her brother. She was studying his movements as intently as if she were reading a sequel of expressions on his face. Under a tight-fitting cloche hat with an upturned brim her forehead was creased in frowns. She resembled her brother. The eyes, the mouth, the sensitive flared nostrils were the same. But she was older. There were lines on her face to attribute to ill health or unhappiness. She wore a thick belted coat and gloves. They had kept her warm in the back of the open tourer.

'I shan't go up,' she said. 'I'll wait in the car.'

'Oh, Nanw. Come on. We'll take it in easy stages.'

'It's perfectly obvious.'

She seemed to draw her conclusions from watching her brother's figure in the distance.

'He wants to get rid of me.'

'Nanw!'

'I should have used my common sense.'

'But we wanted you to come. I insisted.'

'That's what I mean.'

In the silence between them, Enid looked hurt. Nanw sat down on the hillside, looking as if she had at least achieved something. She studied the view of the bay while Enid looked forlornly at the hare's form.

'You'd better catch up with him.'

Nanw was able to mutter comfortably.

'Or he'll blame me for keeping you.'

Enid's eyes were watering. She blinked hard and turned her head to follow Cilydd's progress. What she saw alarmed her.

'He's going to climb the rock,' she said.

Nanw did not turn to look.

'Of course,' she said. 'That's why he's come here.'

'But we're going to see the Chapel of Ease, aren't we? And the barn they say was once a banqueting hall. Where Iolo Goch and Dafydd Nanmor must have sung their verses.'

'I shouldn't have come,' Nanw said. 'He doesn't want me on these trips. I should have known it. I haven't been here since the War.'

'Since the War?'

There was too much surprise in Enid's voice. She knelt down as if to show she was capable of being more tactful.

'It's not so long ago. Not quite ten years yet. Every night I used to pray. Make it stop.'

She looked at Enid's youthful face with unconcealed envy.

'I don't suppose you remember a thing about it. Nobody does any more.'

'It was terrible.'

Enid spoke in a reverent hushed tone.

'I was only a child of course. But I knew it was terrible.'

She shifted a little closer to Nanw, eager to be sympathetic.

'You lost someone?' she said.

'We both did.'

A shout echoed from the height above them. Cilydd had conquered the rock. He was insisting on them becoming aware of the fact. He stood on the edge, his hands on his hips, admiring himself and the view. Enid waved her arm to show that she was watching.

'You'd better go,' Nanw said. 'He wants you.'

'Who was it?'

Enid spoke gently. She was determined to know.

'You both lost.'

'Owen,' Nanw said.

She seemed to enjoy uttering the word: whispering an old incantation.

'Owen Guest.'

It was plain that the name meant nothing to Enid. Nanw stared at Enid's face as though there was a world of understanding to be derived from her ignorance.

'You've never heard him mentioned?'

'No. Never.'

'Well then... It's best forgotten.'

Nanw's expression made it clear enough that she would never forget.

'I would like to know.'

Nanw contemplated the girl's simplicity and innocence. She tugged at a blade of new grass and held it in front of her eyes.

'He was killed. November the twenty-second, nineteen seventeen. Three days after his nineteenth birthday.'

'Oh Nanw. How awful. How terrible.'

Nanw took off her glove and passed the blade of grass between her thumb and finger.

'We came here. The last time he was on leave. Four of us. He was in uniform. A second lieutenant. It was a beautiful day. Late September.'

'Oh, Nanw.'

Enid searched urgently for words to express her sympathy. She could not find them.

'Then John Cilydd ran off to join up. He was under age. And his eyesight was poor. But they took him.'

Enid's mouth hung open with surprise.

'You didn't know? He never told you?'

She shook her head. Nanw stood up.

'This grass is damp,' she said.

She tried to give Enid a smile. The effort was too great. The smile looked sour.

'You'd better go,' she said. 'Don't disappoint him.'

Enid hurried up the field as though she had been dispatched on a vital mission. Her head was lowered as she watched where she put her feet. By the pine trees she turned to look back. Nanw was already seated in the back of the Singer tourer, her legs covered with a tartan travelling rug. She sat as still as a graven image. Across the bay the ruined towers of an imposing castle on a rock glistened in the afternoon sun. The expanse of blue water appeared so vast the few sailing boats on it were no more than insignificant dots.

Enid scrambled up towards the outcrop that Cilydd had climbed. She kicked her shoe into a soft rubble of soil and loose stones. His face appeared some thirty feet above her. He was lying down flat on the rock. His face looked different: flushed and threatening.

'Go back!'

Her body was spread against the warm surface of the rock. She appeared determined to follow his exact route and overcome whatever he had overcome. Her shoes were not suitable for climbing. In his acute concern for her well-being he became harsh and overbearing.

'Will you go back! Walk across the scree.'

She stared up at him mutely imploring help. Her legs were not long enough. The expression on his face was hostile. There was no way in which he could help her. She retreated carefully. When she reached his side on the rock she was out of breath after scrambling as fast as she could across the scree. His chin was jutting out. She touched his arm and he responded instantly, looking for her hand to hold. They sat together in silence.

'Nanw has gone back to the car,' she said.

He nodded approvingly. They were alone together. It was obviously what he wanted. She squeezed his hand nervously.

'I never knew you'd been in the War,' she said.

He squinted up at the high clouds in the bright blue sky.

'I was lucky,' he said. 'I stepped off the scaffold before the guillotine fell.'

She held on to his arm feeling it as though to make certain it was there. Cilydd was still staring at the clouds. A ghostly territory, long forgotten, at any moment could drift into sight.

'And to think you lost your best friend.'

Her voice was low and sad. He shaded his eyes with both

154

hands, his elbows on his knees, making out the tiny figure of his sister sitting in the car far below them.

'She's been talking, has she?'

His tone was cold and disapproving. He looked at Enid quickly to see if she had recovered her breath sufficiently for them to go on. He jumped to his feet and offered to pull her up.

'You shouldn't be so hard on her,' she said. 'She thinks the world of you.'

He pulled her to her feet without answering. Impatiently he led the way across the grass slope.

'War should be outlawed.'

Enid stopped to take off her shoes.

'It's barbarous. Uncivilised. Brutal. Savage.'

She was obliged to run to catch up with him. Out of breath, she had more indignation to express.

'It should never ever happen again. Never. Never.'

His mood changed. He smiled at her with affectionate understanding.

'It was so much worse for her,' Enid said.

She seemed to long for him to understand his sister.

'"The wound that never heals
The bitter taste of loss..."'

'They are your words, and it must be exactly what she feels.'

Cilydd walked on. Once again she was saying things he did not want to hear.

'The War,' she said, carrying her shoes and treading carefully behind him. 'For her it will never be over. Never.'

In front of her, he was shaking his head vehemently without turning around.

'People can't go on mourning for ever,' he said.

'I think she will.'

'It's all past history. There may be some mothers who still cry in the night. But I doubt if there are many. They're not people any more. Just rows of names on memorials. And that's the way it's got to be. We have to bury the past. Or the past will bury us.'

He slipped quickly down the slope to reach a cart track. Enid hesitated to follow him. She sat down to put her shoes on again. Cilydd came back up the slope to wait for her.

'Where are we going?' Enid said.

'This is the old road that leads to Llys-y-Foel.'

'Is that where you went last time?'

Cilydd kicked a stone down the slope. It bounced on the cart track.

'It's never any use planning anything,' he said. 'I just wanted to be alone with you, that's all. It didn't seem much to ask.'

'But why here? Why Llys-y-Foel?'

'Why not? You said you wanted to see the places that mean a lot to me. It's a place worth seeing anyway. Or it was.'

They walked up the track together in silence. When they reached the secluded natural shelf of land on the hillside, Cilydd became more cheerful. All around them were traces of human occupation down the centuries. He pointed out the remains of hut circles in the ferns. He began to speak of the safety and seclusion of the stronghold. Behind a green hillock the small thick slates of the ancient chapel of ease were visible and behind it a small plantation of ash trees.

Nearby the farmhouse had been empty for a long time. The outbuildings that were still standing served as rough shelter for animals. The west end of the dwelling was still protected by complete rows of hanging slates that overlapped each other from the roof to the mossy ground. A sapling ash grew like a flagstaff from a crumbling chimney. Enid lifted a loose slate with her finger to examine the state of the wall underneath. The overlap was so complete she could see nothing. Cilydd stood close behind her. He placed his arms around her waist and began to kiss her neck. Enid pressed her finger against the cold slate.

'Who was the fourth person?'

She seemed unable to resist asking questions. He moved away. What was left of the garden was overgrown with brambles. Enid looked through the window into a living-room. The wallpaper was hanging off the damp walls. A heap of old magazines by the rusty fireplace was half eaten by rats and mice. Cilydd came back to her and took her hand. He led her to the sheltered side of the garden where lilac bushes grew in profusion.

'I'll tell you absolutely anything you want to know.'

He found a place for them to sit on a slate bench warmed by the sun. He drew her closer to him so that he could fondle her. She tried to respond with measured restraint. She held his hand tightly as it began to wander up her thigh.

'What was her name? Were you in love with her?'

She looked at him with wide-eyed frankness. They were questions she was entitled to ask. He sighed and hung his head.

'Alice Breeze. Funny name, isn't it?'

'Were you?'

'Alice? She was a snob. And a liar. Our minister's daughter. There you are. Very objective and unbiased.'

He showed relief at having spoken and became more cheerful. He lifted his hand to play with a stray curl that hung over Enid's ear.

'Boyish infatuation. She liked Owen really. She made use of me to get at him.'

He wanted to kiss her again.

'What about Nanw?'

The question seemed to surprise him.

'She was made use of too. Brother and sister were very convenient chaperons.'

Enid frowned hard as if she were trying to estimate the exact amount the brother and sister could have suffered. She seemed to reach a point where the calculation broke down.

'But Owen was killed.'

Cilydd bent over to pick up a stone. From where he sat he threw it at a vague target down the garden.

'So he was.'

'It doesn't mean anything to you any more?'

'I hope not.'

'He was your best friend.'

'He made best use of me. Took the girl. Made me join up. He was mad about winning the War. It was the only thing in life he took seriously. So he gave his life to the War. And the War took it. And the War was won. *Quod erat demonstrandum*. And that's the end of it.'

Enid lifted her head.

'Not for Nanw.'

'I can't speak for her. If she wants to go on deceiving herself for the rest of her life, there's not a damned thing I can do about it. Owen wasn't in the least interested in her. He wasn't even interested in Alice. Women were playthings to him. That's all.'

He was snapping it all out so ill-temperedly, she drew away from him.

'That's what they are for most men,' Enid said.

Cilydd looked so hurt she regretted having spoken. They sat together in silence. From the moor behind the house the cry of a curlew mingled with the forlorn bleat of a lamb looking for its ewe.

'I should never have brought you here,' he said. 'That shows how much of a fool I am. Trust me to make a mess of it.'

Enid jumped to her feet, ready to change the subject.

'Show me the chapel of ease,' she said. 'And the banqueting hall. I'll recite Iolo Goch and we'll use our imaginations. Come on!'

Together they stood in the dusty dung and straw of the previous winter and looked up at the crude wooden gallery where medieval minstrels were supposed to have played.

'This place meant a lot to me when I was young,' Cilydd said.

Enid laughed at him.

'Aren't you young any more?'

She began to recite:

'"... Bright song
Without surfeit, the red music
Of French wine and fresh meat."'

Enid raised her voice to capture some of the echo in the apex of the slate roof.

'"It is the four walls you see
Of the clear fort where men are free ..."'

'I brought you here for one reason. And one reason alone.'

Cilydd was holding her urgently in his arms.

'One thing I wanted to tell you. We ought to get married. That's what I want to say.'

'Of course we will.'

Enid tried to calm him. He was holding her so tightly she could hardly breathe.

'I mean now. Soon.'

'Not in here.'

She forced herself free. She hurried out of the dark stone barn into the sunlight and Cilydd followed her.

'It's like a tomb in there,' she said.

She tidied herself up as they moved away from the buildings.

'Exactly,' he said. 'Exactly.'

He seemed over-anxious to agree with her.

'Boyhood musings about the glories of the past. Lost treasure and sleeping princesses. Totally irrelevant. And I had to bring you here. When will I grow up?'

They walked briskly past the wooden gate that had once stretched across the farm road. It lay rotting in the nettles of the shallow ditch.

'I'm serious,' he said.

The waters of the bay came into view. Cilydd stopped by a grass mound.

'Let's sit here a minute,' he said.

'Nanw will be waiting.'

'Let her wait.'

The house and buildings behind them were almost out of sight. He stretched his long legs on the ground. When she sat beside him he took her hand. He played with her fingers as though he were counting them over and over again.

'I'm earning enough,' he said. 'We could buy a house. I want my life to revolve around you. A new life. With you in the centre. The angel in the house.'

Enid was thinking deeply.

'You find your family too possessive,' she said. 'But they all love you.'

He looked up slowly, a puzzled expression on his face.

'What's that got to do with it?' he said.

'I'm too inadequate. I'm too immature. I'm too afraid. I'm not ready.'

He groaned helplessly and thumped his thigh with his fist.

'Oh my God,' he said. 'I've made such a mess of it.'

'No, you haven't. Don't say that. I had to know all these things anyway sooner or later. They're not important anyway. Between you and me.'

He sat up joyfully.

'There you are then,' he said.

'But I do want to finish my degree.'

'I've got an answer to that one.'

He gripped her shoulders with his hands.

'You despise the place. And what is a degree? You've said so yourself. A rubber stamp. I haven't got one.'

'You don't need one.'

'Well, there you are. That's it exactly. A man, a person, should stand on his own feet. On his own merits. For what he's worth. Down with the Welsh education fetish.'

'But you are a man,' Enid said.

Cilydd was mildly intoxicated with the power of his argument.

'You've said it yourself. The longing for a degree is just another manifestation of the serf mentality. I've heard you say it.'

'Yes, but I'm a woman.'

Enid spoke with desperation in her voice.

'I've got to grow up still. And I've got to prove myself. I need the discipline. I'm too raw. I'm not prepared. For marriage and serious adult living. Really I'm not. I can see that so clearly. Today of all days.'

'Oh... Today.'

Cilydd groaned unhappily and shook his head. Enid was moved by his obvious despair.

'Please don't misunderstand me. I love you as much as ever. More.'

'How can you say, "more"?'

Cilydd stretched out a hand, baffled.

'Most of all I want to be part of your work. And for that I need to be better trained. Better qualified. Better disciplined. You've got a territory to conquer, John Cilydd, and I want to help you conquer it.'

He cried out impatiently.

'Well, then. Why in God's name don't you marry me?'

Enid stared at the sea.

'I don't want to be just a housewife. Not now anyway. I want to be in the middle of the battle. Right at your side. Helping you.'

He looked puzzled and exasperated. She tried harder to make him understand her attitude.

'You can see for yourself now. I'm very childish still. It still frightens me to think of being a wife and a mother. I know it sounds silly. But I want to be *with* you first. Don't you understand?'

She was leaning over him as she pleaded with him. The neck of her blouse was cut low. He touched the taut skin over her breastbone with his dry lips. She ran her fingers through his hair. He drew her down and they lay awkwardly together on the grass. She looked around a little desperately to make certain there was no one watching. He was burying his face in her breasts.

'Just take me for what I am. I could be nothing anyway.'

His voice was muffled and she could barely make out what he was saying. She tried to comfort him.

'For what I am. That's the only way we'll ever find to understand each other.'

'Give me time,' she said. 'Just give me a little more time.'

Part Three

1

Cilydd stood on the boarding-house stairs. The fingers of his right hand just touched the banister as he tapped the polished wood and listened to the drone of conversation in the front parlour. The other lodgers, as they waited for their substantial Sunday midday meal, were taking their ease around a blazing fire. The pleasant sunlight was tinted a deeper gold by the coloured glass that filled the fanlight and the top half of the front door of 'Tadmor'. Across the deserted street the facing stones of two adjacent chapels could have been bathing in an exotic Mediterranean light. A shout of manly laughter from the parlour caused Cilydd to wince. From the kitchen came the clank of the oven door opening and the appetising aroma of the Sunday roast.

'Now along with you, girl, and put more coal on the fire!'

The clear command came from the landlady, Mrs. Perrin, who managed to make her rasping County Antrim voice sound both motherly and kindly. Cilydd looked over the banister and watched the little maid hauling the coal scuttle down the passage. It was too heavy for her. She moved it forward and then turned to look back longingly at the cheerful feminine warmth of the large kitchen. The cook and Mrs. Perrin were bustling back and forth intent on preparation for the meal. More unruly laughter from the front parlour made the girl shiver as though she were standing in a cold draught. Her chapped hand adjusted her white cap which was toppling on her hair. As soon as she had done this she held her hand before her wide eyes and saw coal dust on her finger tips.

The front door opened and Val came striding in. He had come straight from a chapel in another part of the town. His brown overcoat was open and he was humming a hymn tune. He tossed his velour hat on the hall stand. The little maid and John Cilydd were equally pleased to see him.

'Gwyneth.'

His voice was brisk, but the maid looked delighted to hear him speak her name.

'That looks a bit heavy for you. Let me carry it.'

Cilydd moved quietly down the stairs ready to follow Val into the parlour. Rees, the articled clerk, was standing before the fire, his hands behind his back and his feet wide apart. He wore plus-fours and his red hair was immaculately trimmed and oiled in short tight waves. When he saw Val carrying the coal scuttle he wrinkled his flattened nose and displayed gold fillings in his teeth as he smiled.

'Here comes Big Tweeny as opposed to Little Tweeny,' he said. 'Good old Gwyn. Nice to see a spot of practical Christianity on a fine Sunday morning. And here comes the Bard himself. Just dashed off another winning ode, I dare say.'

One plump lodger stood by the window grinning encouragingly at Rees' crisp English remarks. Two others sat side by side on the settee. One held a glass of sherry between finger and thumb and the other flashed the lenses of his spectacles as he polished them. At the same time he twisted his head about determined not to miss a single detail of what was happening or about to happen. Sunday dinner at 'Tadmor' was a pleasurable occasion.

'Good sermon?'

Swiftly he replaced his steel-rimmed spectacles and shot out the question. He seemed barely able to wait for the answer.

Val set down the coal scuttle in its accustomed place alongside the fender. The fire was blazing spectacularly and was in no need of stoking. It was in any case a mild day and Rees seemed the only man who felt a need for the extra heat.

'Long and dry,' Val said. 'And that's the way I like them, Francis.'

164

Francis poked the bridge of his spectacles, opened his mouth wide and exhaled his strangely silent laugh that was more like a cough. The man alongside him sipped his sherry delicately and permitted himself a discreet smile. He was the oldest lodger, but the least assertive. As a grammar-school teacher he did not care to speak without an orderly attentiveness among his hearers. But his lips, wet with sherry, moved fractionally most of the time, as if to imply that there were troops of witty thoughts marking time inside his head ready to advance whenever his younger colleagues acquired enough wisdom to be silent and listen.

'I must say our man wasn't on form at all this morning.'

Francis straightened his back and looked forthright. He was ready to enliven the occasion and expected the others to listen. Rees raised his voice to interrupt him.

'Gwynni-Binnie! Gwyneth-Pen'orth!'

Rees was summoning the little maid just as she was about to make her escape. The plump man by the window grinned delightedly. More free entertainment could still come his way before lunch. Gwyneth moved back into the room, her hands clasped together, still shivering slightly in her thin black dress.

'Hearth!'

Rees enunciated the word with a special clarity.

'Hearth.'

He pointed to make the meaning of the word more apparent.

'Hearth needs a little attention.'

Cilydd muttered disapprovingly under his breath. Val took off his overcoat and went to hang it on the hall stand. Rees moved to occupy a vacant elbow-chair at the fireside. He left room for Gwyneth to sink to her knees and tidy the hearth.

'The chapels must give a lead,' Francis said.

He seized the chance to take the conversational initiative.

'This is a matter of principle,' he said. 'An "absolute" almost. That's my view.'

He cultivated an energetic staccato manner of speech in either language as if to announce that he chose to be honest and forthright at all times. His nose tended to rise and fall as he spoke, like the beak of an aggressive parrot.

'I would regard it as an attempt by outsiders to desecrate the Sabbath day in Wales. Indeed I would.'

'Oh God...'

Rees groaned dramatically and tugged his shirt cuffs into sight.

'Francis, you are getting to sound more like a stuffy little town councillor every day.'

'It's a point of principle. Is it not?'

Francis glanced at the teacher first, obliging him to nod half-heartedly, and then at Cilydd who managed to stare with stony neutrality into the fire.

'Sunday golf is alien to our way of life. It should never be allowed.'

'Oh, for Christ's sake, Francis. Now you sound like a mealy-mouthed Methodist deacon.'

'Don't blaspheme.'

Francis spoke indignantly.

'And don't be personal. It's impossible to have a discussion in this house, Rees, without you getting personal. If you'll allow me to say so, it's a major fault with you.'

Rees' foot was edging towards the hem of Gwyneth's black dress. He stole a glance at the man in the window to make sure he was watching before raising the dress a fraction with the toe-cap of his golfing shoe. Val strode back into the room, his hands in both pockets. He took up a position behind Rees' chair. Rees' shoe crept closer to Gwyneth's thigh. She pretended she was unaware of it and went on brushing the hearth.

'Do you know something, Francis?'

Rees' gold fillings glittered as he smiled at the man in the window.

'I think you and Miss Gwyneth Pen'orth here must be related. There's a distinct resemblance I would say. The same shifty look about the eyes.'

His toe-cap began to raise the skirt higher. Suddenly Val pressed both hands down on the back of Rees' elbow-chair. Rees' legs shot up in the air and there was a splintering sound as the wood around one of the rear castors gave way. Rees glared up angrily at Val who was leaning over him and smiling in a benign and friendly way. He pushed up his left fist with trained speed and landed a hard blow on the side of

Val's mouth. Val let go of the chair and Rees tumbled forward over the maid, who started screaming. Cilydd went to Val to examine the extent of his hurt. The two men on the settee shrank back, looking down at the bodies at their feet, too shocked and embarrassed to move or speak. The man by the window shifted further away, lifting his head to listen apprehensively to shouting from the kitchen. Rees struggled to help the girl to her feet, muttering his apologies. But the girl crawled away not allowing him to touch her.

Mrs. Perrin appeared in the doorway. Her hands were still wet and she held them up with the palms facing inwards.

'Now what in God's name is the matter?' she said. 'Are you trying to murder the poor girl or something?'

A smile hovered on her broad face. She was prepared to keep an open mind until she knew all the facts. She saw the lodgers as her family of young men and her prime concern was their comfort: but in return they were expected to appreciate her efforts and behave towards her in a courtly manner. She was a large woman. Her corseted form and her piled-up hairstyle remained Edwardian, but under her pinafore she wore a purple twin-set and an expanse of long tweed skirt.

'Gwyneth!'

She pronounced the girl's name with explosive emphasis.

'Now get up, girl, do!'

The girl's eyes were rolling nervously in her head. Mrs. Perrin had still not registered the damage to the elbow-chair.

'Now whoever it was, you mustn't play jokes on this poor girl. As you know she doesn't have much of the English but she's very willing. Aren't you, girl?'

Gwyneth managed a nod.

'Sorry, Mrs. P.'

Rees was intent on brushing himself down.

'There's been a bit of an accident.'

Francis leaned over to be the first to draw Mrs. Perrin's attention to the broken chair. But Mrs. Perrin was more concerned with the sight of blood on Val's face.

'Oh Mr. Gwyn! What on earth have you done to yourself?'

'It was my own fault.'

Val tried to smile as he mumbled through his fingers. Rees

stretched out both arms towards Mrs. Perrin, eager to explain.

'It was like this, Mrs. P. I was practising one of my punches. You know the straight left.'

Mrs. Perrin nodded willingly. There were sporting trophies on the mantelpiece and on the sideboard. Mementoes of her late husband's activities and enthusiasms. Mr. Rees was known to excel in amateur boxing. She was always ready to take an intelligent interest in the technique of the craft.

'The straight left. The lightning attack. We were only playing about. And I went too far. That's always my trouble. Very sorry about the rumpus, Mrs. P. Hope you'll forgive us.'

'Will his mouth be alright?' Mrs. Perrin said. 'That is the question. Will he be able to manage his Sunday lunch?'

Val was nodding cheerfully.

'Mrs. Perrin...'

Cilydd addressed her with professional solemnity.

'I think you should know that one of the chairs has been damaged.'

Francis' head was making agitated pecking motions. Cilydd spoke again.

'We all regret this and we hope you will allow us to share out the cost of repair between us.'

Francis' head suddenly stopped. He looked at his companion on the settee, his mouth open with horrified protest.

'That's nothing at all.'

Mrs. Perrin hardly deigned to glance at the broken-off castor.

'So long as the spirit of good will and co-operation prevails among my guests, little things like that will never upset me ... Oh my God, I can smell something burning.'

She turned and rushed headlong out of the room. Gwyneth followed her as fast as she could. Rees offered Val his hand.

'The trouble with all this damn training,' he said. 'It teaches you to be so aggressive.'

'The gentle art of self-defence ...'

Val tried to smile, stretching his tender jaw.

'I'd better go and wash my mouth.'

'I'm so sorry.'

Rees sounded deeply contrite as he screwed his left fist into the palm of his right hand.

'Don't worry about it.'

Val waved his hand gaily as he went through the door.

'... My fault just as much as yours.'

There was an awkward silence in the room. They listened to his footsteps on the stairs.

'Well now,' Francis said. 'Look here. I don't see why Osborn, Davies and I should have to share in the bill for repairs. Or More, for that matter. Although he suggested it. I think Rees should pay, quite frankly.'

Rees had recovered his calm. As Francis spoke he was examining his well-manicured fingernails.

'It's a well known fact that "Tadmor" is the best digs in town. I think it's up to us to maintain a standard of behaviour worthy of the place and worthy of the trust Mrs. Perrin places in us all.'

Francis looked around quickly for general agreement. He froze with fright when a sudden left jab stopped just short of the end of his nose.

'Francis. You little bookworm. I'm short of a punchbag. Your head looks just the right shape.'

Francis pressed back into the settee.

'You are not a man of the law, Rees. You are a thug. A bully. You are the kind of thing the law is supposed to protect us from. And I mean that. On a Sunday morning too.'

He appealed to John Cilydd who was smiling bleakly at them both.

'He's been boasting about this judge they've elected president of the golf club. He was boasting about him before you came in. He'll lead our fight, he said. He'll get us our Sunday golf. The rights and liberties of every free-born Englishman. And every free-born imitation Englishman as well.'

Francis closed his eyes as Rees shaped up to send another practice punch in his direction.

'I don't know, More, what you think,' Francis said.

The presence of the other lodgers gave him courage to go on speaking in defiance of Rees' threats.

'You and all your talk about home rule and self-respect and what have you. But are you prepared to let a handful of the Saxon race and a few renegade Welsh like Rees here change our way of life, and shatter once and for all our sacred Sunday?'

Cilydd put his hands in his pockets. He was in no hurry to answer the indignant challenge. He turned to Rees with a show of mild interest.

'This judge. Is it Lord Afton?'

'No less.'

Rees plucked cheerfully at his shirt cuffs.

'Jolly nice chap, too. No side to him at all.'

Davies at the window lowered his double chin. He looked deeply impressed.

'A great common lawyer,' Cilydd said.

Francis wagged his finger impatiently.

'Yes, More,' he said. 'That's all very well. But where do you stand? You claim to speak for our nation often enough. You and Val Gwyn. We have a right to know where you stand on this issue.'

Cilydd was silent for a while. It seemed a trick he had taught himself: never to be obliged to make too quick an answer. To wait and watch the effect of silence as it settled between him and his questioner. He could hear Val hurrying downstairs from his room on the second floor.

'Neutral,' he said at last. 'I don't like Sunday and I don't like golf.'

2

Francis whistled to himself as he penetrated deeper between the shelves of the stack room in the cellars of the Cymric Library. Large bound collections of periodicals stuck out at different levels, narrowing the space between the shelves. His hand groped nervously for a light switch, but failed to find one.

'Gwyn! Val Gwyn! Can you hear me?'

170

The silence in the long cellars made Francis deeply uneasy. He crept forward, looking back, from time to time, like a man in a labyrinth afraid of getting lost. In the distance a door opened. He could make out a figure in silhouette. There was a sepulchral click as a large switch was pulled. Poor as it was, the yellow light helped to restore Francis' confidence in himself.

'Why on earth do you want to hide yourself in a place like this?'

Val was wearing a grey overall. He was looking at his hands which were black with dust.

'I spend one morning a week down here,' Val said, 'It's easier to come down here and work, than trundle all these tomes up to the cataloguing rooms.'

'It's unhealthy.'

Francis sniffed disapprovingly at the smell of damp and stale air.

'It's not good for books, let alone human beings.'

'I can work faster. That's the important thing.'

Francis showed that he viewed the proposition with great scepticism.

'They'll be here after we're gone,' he said. 'Sometimes I feel like putting a match to them.'

He spoke so feelingly Val laughed aloud. It was an alien inappropriate sound in such dark and drab surroundings. A long volume of an eighteenth-century French periodical was open on the table. It was in poor condition, many pages torn and discoloured. Alongside it was a notebook and a shoe box half filled with reference slips.

'The librarian wants a word with you,' Francis said importantly. He peered closely at Val's face to read any clue he could find that would explain the unexpected summons.

'You sail pretty close to the wind in that magazine of yours sometimes, don't you?'

Val knocked his hands together in an attempt to remove some of the dust. Behind the workroom there was a small w.c. and washbasin. In the dim light Val washed his hands with a bar of cheap soap.

'Tell me something, Francis. I've often meant to ask you. Have you ever read it?'

'I've glanced at it.'

171

Francis sounded indignant.

'There's no law that says I have to read it.'

'I just wondered.'

Val smiled as he dried his hands.

'What are you implying?'

Val switched off the light. They made their way carefully through the stacks. Francis kept as close as he could to Val.

'You think I'm illiterate or something. I read a great deal.'

'I'm sure you do.'

'You know very well I'm a Liberal. A Welsh Liberal.'

'Of course you are.'

'Then why should you expect me to read your magazine, as you call it. When you know very well I don't agree with it. If I read it, it would only upset me.'

'Quite so.'

When they reached the flight of stairs that led to the ground floor, Francis grew more assertive.

'I suppose you look down on me because I haven't got a degree,' he said.

'Good heavens, no.'

Val's laugh seemed to annoy him further.

'Librarianship is my chosen profession. It's not just a refuge from unemployment as it is with some people I could name.'

'Oh dear ... I wish you wouldn't be so touchy.'

'Touchy! Why should you ask me if I read your silly little magazine? I suppose you expect the whole world to read it. I tell you what I would do with it. Even if you gave me a copy. I'd chuck it on the fire.'

Val went to the staff cloakroom to hang up his overall. Francis thought of something else to say and followed him as far as the door. His head jerked up and down as he spoke.

'I'll tell you something else,' he said. 'You've got no real flair for politics, Gwyn. And I tell you this as a friend.'

'Thank you,' Val said.

Francis accepted the expression of gratitude by delaying a fraction before giving his customary headjerk.

'What is the burning issue of the day on this coast? Sunday golf. And there wasn't a word about it in your last number. *Dadeni*, indeed. Just the same old attack against the so-called

English parties. And especially the grand old party that all Wales supports.'

'So you do read it, after all?'

Val checked on his appearance in the mirror.

'I'm jolly glad to hear it. I look forward to your conversion any day now. You be sure to let me know the moment you begin to feel your heart warming.'

Francis pursued Val down the corridor. Val's calm and cheerful demeanour angered and disturbed him.

'I suppose you think you're better than the rest of us,' he said. 'Highly-qualified scholar and all that Sorbonne business. But I'll tell you this much, Gwyn, as far as this work is concerned, you are not a professional. And that's not just my view either.'

Val stood still and Francis retreated a few steps. He seemed to be regretting his outburst already. They were obliged to move to one side to allow the passage of a trolley loaded with books. It was pushed by a cheerful youth who performed a brief pantomime for their benefit, lowering his body until he was almost parallel with the ground.

'Like a bloody coal mine, *myn uffern i*,' he said.

He gave Francis a great wink. Francis jerked his chin to demonstrate that he was a serious man who overlooked childish exhibitions and concentrated throughout his working hours on excellence of service. He marched up to Val to address him in a calmer tone. He had a white index card in his right hand and he held it like a token that proved that he never let up on his labours even if he should appear to be enjoying a quiet gossip with a colleague in the corridor.

'I'm very blunt at times,' he said. 'But I bear no malice. I want you to know that. I speak as a friend.'

He stared hard and challengingly into Val's face.

'Any idea why he wants to see you?'

He struggled to change his tone into a sympathetic mutter. His gaze darted up and down the corridor as though he feared his words being overheard.

'Not the faintest,' Val said.

'You haven't been looking at the old President's Purchase?'

'No.'

173

'Good. He's very touchy about that. He's got Miss Roberts and Warner working on them for him, you see. As you know, he's never bothered to learn our language. He'll bring out a series of diplomatic editions under his name. And there they'll be. The Bellot Papers.'

'I had heard that.'

Val began walking up the stairs to the librarian's room. Francis still followed him. He seemed reluctant to abandon the important rôle of messenger. The librarian himself had allotted him the task of searching for Val Gwyn in the bowels of the establishment. Something of the responsibility remained with him until he saw the summoned man pass through the door of the governing head of the institution: and it would not be inappropriate if the figure seated behind the large desk caught a glimpse of the faithful and obedient messenger before the door was closed.

'He's in line for a knighthood,' Francis said. 'I suppose you've heard that too.'

'Yes, I had.'

'It's the way the world works, of course. The owner of the orchard owns all the apples. Still, it will be a compliment to the profession. That's the way I look at it. We are lacking in status, I feel. Don't you?'

Val breathed deeply before he knocked the librarian's door. Francis watched him with intense interest as he waited to be called in.

He caught a glimpse of the librarian when Val opened the door. He was sitting in a stately pose behind a large mahogany desk, his hand lying on the clean blotting pad, an expanse of starched white cuff showing and his fingers playing with an ebony ruler.

On the wall behind him in a heavy gilt frame, hung a portrait photograph of King George V. It had been placed just above the level of his head when seated, perhaps to draw attention to the happy resemblance between the two. The librarian's beard was a loyal replica of his monarch's and his thinning hair was parted exactly right of centre. By design or by coincidence there was the same worried look in the canine exophthalmic eyes. His desk was clear in order to give him more time to think and plan. He studied the tall figure standing before his desk as an inventor would contemplate a cog in his machine giving unaccountable trouble.

'Mr. Gwyn,' he said,

He sighed deeply as he considered the two sheets of paper on the blotting paper in front of him.

'You are not yet an established member of our staff, I see.'

Val smiled and nodded politely.

'It has been brought to my notice that you edit a monthly publication. A monthly magazine if that is the correct appellation. *Dadeni*, I believe it is called. That means "Rebirth", does it not, or "Renaissance"?'

The librarian paused momentarily as though he were accustomed to be complimented on his knowledge of the language.

'I am given to understand that it is chiefly political in content? Is that the case?'

'It is indeed, Mr. Bellot.'

The librarian stiffened in his throne-like chair. His gaze wandered around the room. Rare books and editions de luxe were safely locked in three handsome glass-doored book cases. On the wall space that was left hung portraits of the first benefactors of the Library.

'Do you not think it would have been advisable and indeed courteous to have sought permission of the Library Council before undertaking such an arduous and possibly question-able extra-mural task?'

Mr. Bellot lowered his eyes to consult the smaller piece of paper on his blotting pad. There in minute black writing was scribbled a list of headings.

'I don't find it arduous,' Val said.

The innocence of the answer made the Librarian suspicious and despondent.

'That is hardly the point, Mr. Gwyn. And it is certainly no answer to my question.'

Val rubbed finger and thumb against his high cheek bones and frowned hard as he gave the question deeper consideration.

'I find it really difficult to answer,' he said at last. 'Part of my difficulty arises from the fact that the magazine was really born in France, so to speak. The first issue preceded my taking up my appointment in the library by a matter of a few days.'

In a manner that jarred on the Librarian's nerves he

175

flicked his long fingers from his jaw before smiling again.

'The dates could be checked of course,' he said.

The librarian looked again at his notes.

'I am aware of the date of your temporary appointment,' he said.

He gave faint but distinct emphasis to the adjective.

'I also have to ask you for a written assurance, Mr. Gwyn.'

The librarian ticked off the points with taps of the ebony ruler.

'That your own work for the library in no way suffers from this additional activity. That you do not take advantage of your position to use the unique facilities of the library to further your political aims. And that you further undertake for the period of your employment not to engage in activities that would tend to tarnish the good name of the library or bring the institution into disrepute.'

'That's very comprehensive.'

Val's attitude was so objective he could have been an amateur player applauding an opponent's virtuoso display.

'It covers a great deal of ground. And of course there are many principles involved. Personal and academic freedom for example. The constitutional rights of the individual. The purpose and aims of the institution itself. It's quite a field really.'

The librarian pushed his piece of paper about as he watched Val with a wary eye.

'Certainly there is a sense in which I do feel I wish I had notified you about my writings when I took up the post.'

Val spoke in such a frank and generous manner, the librarian relaxed a little.

'I think I would even go so far as to apologise about that. To you and to the Council. But as for the letter. The written assurance and so on. I think that needs more thought, quite frankly. I wonder if I could ask you to put the points down on paper so that I could have, say, a day or two, forty-eight hours, to consider the proposal?'

The librarian checked the gold watch in his waistcoat pocket with the clock on the wall.

'The President wants a word with you,' he said.

The look of astonishment on Val's face seemed to give him some satisfaction.

The librarian rose from his chair. The move could have been intended to indicate that he was prepared to unbend a little.

'You're not related by any chance?'

Val was mystified.

'So many people are in this part of the world.'

Mr. Bellot gazed with respectful longing at the photograph of the King Emperor. He seemed to need someone with whom he could share confidences about the problems of order and good government in the less straightforward corners of the Empire.

'He's a very subtle man.'

The librarian was talking about the President of the Library and the Chairman of his governing body.

'Sir Prosser likes to work in mysterious ways. I have to admit I sometimes find him quite unfathomable.'

He moved to the window to take a brief glance at the outside world. What he saw of green hillsides and the roofs of the seaside town did not encourage him.

'One has to expect, of course, with a former cabinet minister that he likes to have his fingers in many pies.'

The librarian drew himself up.

'At least he showed me the courtesy of informing me that he desired to speak with a member of my staff. That's one great thing to be said for Downing Street experience. High office gives a man a proper sense of correct procedure. We can at least be grateful for that. Do you have any idea what Sir Prosser could want with you?'

'None whatsoever.'

The librarian scrutinised Val Gwyn. He seemed to find relief in his blatant incapacity for subtlety.

'Miss Roberts will take you up to his room.'

He moved cautiously to the door of the side office.

'I think you should know that I like my staff to approach me through her,' the librarian said. 'It makes for better order. You might tell Francis that. He seems to have a gift for using the wrong door.'

The librarian gave a slightly crooked smile to indicate he was making a humorous remark.

'In his eagerness to get on, no doubt,' he said.

His hand rested on the doorknob.

177

'I take it, Gwyn, if this interview should in any way touch upon library business, you will keep me informed?'

Val began to pull at his jaw again.

'Of course,' he said. 'Of course.'

The librarian was reasonably satisfied. He opened the door and spoke to his assistant.

'Miss Roberts,' he said. 'Would you be so kind as to escort Mr. . . . er . . . Gwyn to the President's room?'

Miss Roberts smiled willingly. She was fashionably dressed in a knitted suit and her hair tended to hang over one eye. Outside in the corridor she walked with unexpectedly long strides for a woman. She spoke in a shy contralto voice.

'I read *Dadeni* with great pleasure,' she said quietly.

'Do you really?'

Val was surprised and pleased. There were more stairs to climb. The President's room was at the top of the imposing building, next to the Council Chamber. Miss Roberts paused on the stairs, holding on with one hand to a polished oak handrail.

'Perhaps you have more support than you think,' she said. 'When you are being outspoken. I think it's what we need, more than anything else.'

'I'm so glad,' Val said. 'I'm so glad you think so.'

They continued their climb. Val's enthusiasm fired her to further flights of perceptiveness.

'Perhaps we need to fight more against our own natures,' Miss Roberts said. 'We are so eager to be agreeable it must seem like servility to other people.'

It was clear she was thinking of the librarian as she spoke; but Val was more taken with the general validity of what she was saying.

'That's a very good point,' he said. 'An excellent point. It has all sorts of implications. It ought to be developed. Listen, Miss Roberts!'

He stood still on the stairs as though the magic wand of inspiration had reduced him to statuesque rigidity.

'Why don't you write a piece about it? For *Dadeni*?'

Miss Roberts was overcome with shyness. It threatened to develop quickly into an anxiety state.

'Oh no,' she said. 'I couldn't.'

'Why not?'

'He would never approve of it.'

She was appalled by the prospect of the fuss the librarian would make if his assistant contributed an article to what he was inclined to consider a subversive publication.

'You've got a perfect right to,' Val said. 'I'm quite sure about that.'

'I'm not thinking about rights,' Miss Roberts said.

She hurried on up the stairs, clearly regretting having expressed herself so freely.

'You could do it anonymously,' Val said. 'Or under a nom de plume.'

'He'd find out,' she said impatiently. 'He's got his spies everywhere. He'd make my life a misery.'

They stood outside the door of the Council Chamber. They could hear Sir Prosser's sonorous voice booming happily inside. Miss Roberts glanced shyly at Val.

'I've got a widowed mother,' she said. 'We live together. I like my job. It gives me a kind of independence. I don't ask for much.'

She seemed conscious of him observing the dried condition of her skin under the light covering of face powder and the touch of rouge on her cheeks. His obvious sympathy was more than she could bear. She threw the door open with an uncharacteristically bold flourish. She seemed far less in awe of Sir Prosser Ogmore Pierce than of the librarian.

'Sir Prosser,' she said.

Her voice echoed in the empty Council Chamber. All symptoms of shyness had disappeared. She was publicly reciting lines already learned to a fatherly figure she knew would receive them kindly.

'You asked to see Mr. Val Gwyn. Here he is.'

Sir Prosser had a cigarette in his mouth. The smoke was staining his long upper lip and his mouth was turned down in a sardonic grin. When he waved paternally to Miss Roberts it was gratitude as well as dismissal. He was not alone. Beyond the council table stood an imposing figure as well-groomed and as careful of his looks as an ageing actor. He was still frowning at the interruption: but with some restraint as if to avoid introducing too many fresh creases into his high forehead.

'Now then, my Lord Afton ...'

Sir Prosser slapped the palm of his hand down with jovial force on the surface of the table. Immediately with a mild curse he dropped the remains of his cigarette into a large burnished ashtray because it was burning his lip. He spluttered a little but did not lose his good humour.

'You say you want to understand something of the temper of our young people. Here's the very man to keep you informed. Or should I say enlighten you? I'm sure like all great men your lordship is basically humble and of an enquiring turn of mind?'

Sir Prosser's heavy shoulders shook with massive amusement. He slouched back untidily in the ornate uncomfortable chair at the head of the council table. Lord Afton was less amused. He gave a frosty smile and consulted his wristwatch. As he lowered his head highlights flashed along his black hair. It was brushed with glossy precision and the oil he used also darkened it.

'I'm afraid not, Sir Prosser. Not this time anyway. I have another appointment.'

His speech was clipped and precise.

'Oh my goodness . . .'

Sir Prosser struggled awkwardly to his feet. He seemed to have an aversion to walking. His legs were short and he shuffled alongside Lord Afton to the door. Val could not help noticing that the President was wearing carpet slippers.

'You've been much too generous with your time,' Sir Prosser was saying.

His deep voice was vibrant with irresistible sincerity.

'And I'm much at fault taking advantage of you in this way. Much at fault.'

He lowered his voice but it still reverberated in the empty Council Chamber.

'And I can't tell you how grateful I am that you've consented to become a member of our Council. You are just what we need. It's not just your fine legal brain, my dear fellow, but that touch of Anglo-Saxon sang-froid with a dash of sparkling Irish wit to calm down our perfervid and often over-emotional deliberations. Such an asset, my dear man, I don't know how to thank you enough. And I'm sure the Principal will be delighted too. After all the college and the library should work in the closest harmony. And this doesn't always happen of course. But now you are on both councils, how can justice not be done and not be seen to be done? My dear fellow.'

For the moment of farewell, Sir Prosser briefly clasped the judge's right hand in both of his. As soon as the door was closed he turned to shuffle back to the table, chuckling to himself. He glanced slyly at Val.

'Capital fellow,' he said. 'A little stunted emotionally. But many of them are like that. It's the public school that does it. But then you may ask, where would the Empire be without the public school? It's a vexed question. My answer would be, we don't all have to be janissaries.'

His amusement at what he was saying was tempered by his desire for a fresh cigarette. He felt about in the pockets of his untidy double-breasted suit.

'Let's go into my room,' he said. 'I know where I am there.'

He opened the door and led the way into the President's room.

'I close my eyes when I bring anyone new in here.'

He seemed continuously amused by most of what he said or did.

'I'm supposed to be writing my memoirs,' he said. 'Can you imagine a more absurd occupation?'

The room was full of books and documents. Many of the books were open on the floor. There was a fire in the grate. Of two deep armchairs, one was filled by a heap of volumes of a pre-War magazine with green covers. Sir Prosser pushed about among the papers on his desk to find a packet of Gold Flake cigarettes. It was empty. He threw it into the fire and opened a drawer to find a fresh packet.

'I've got the first sentence by heart,' he said. '"What an unnecessary and complicated thing is man!" What do you think of that, Mr. Gwyn?'

He recited the question with a mock-Shakespearean flourish. Val looked incapable of being anything but frank.

'It sounds a bit cynical,' he said.

Sir Prosser was more amused than ever. His heavy shoulders heaved up and down as he held both hands close to his face as though he were lighting his cigarette in a high wind.

'I haven't finished,' he said. '"What an unnecessary and complicated thing is man, without the logic of an earthworm or the sweet obedience of a tree!" Now you must admit that's better, isn't it?'

He motioned Val to sit down in the armchair by the fire. He sat himself behind his desk.

'Mitigated,' Val said, 'I would say that.'

Sir Prosser burst out into wheezy laughter.

'You're an honest man, Mr. Gwyn,' he said. 'That's what I like about you. Now then. To business.'

He scrabbled about among the papers and extracted a copy of the magazine *Dadeni*. He held it up by a corner for Val to see.

'You see I keep abreast with the latest manifestations and manifestos in our dear old language. Now then. This article on Thomas Masaryk. I was most impressed. That's what I wanted to talk to you about. Does that surprise you?'

Val was smiling politely. Sir Prosser did not embarrass him by waiting too long for an answer.

'Tell me, what were your main sources? French, I suppose?'

Val tried to think back.

'Yes. I think they were mainly.'

'A most impressive job. Most impressive. And the parallels drawn with L.G. Extremely effective. Austrian Empire, British Empire, and so on. You have the makings of a great polemical writer, Mr. Gwyn. Have you not thought of what I sometimes please to call "Higher Journalism"? As a profession? No. Of course not. That would mean going to London and writing in English. Which would, of course, be against your principles and policies. All honour to you for them. You see, I am an enlightened man. Not unsympathetic, Mr. Gwyn. Not unsympathetic.'

Sir Prosser stopped talking. The cigarette smouldered in the corner of his mouth as he breathed heavily and became more thoughtful.

'I shall show it to L.G.,' he said in a ruminative voice. 'Just out of curiosity. See what he thinks about it. Of course there's no guarantee he will read it. That's one of his many blemishes. He'll ask some damned secretary to read it and give him an instant opinion. And of course he doesn't listen to me now as much as he used to. Thinks I'm too friendly with the enemy camp. Or the enemy camps to be precise. I'm no longer one of the Inner Circle at the court of the Emperor George. He's still great fun to be with, of course. Especially if you can get him by himself, without all those hangers on and sycophants. I'm not a sycophant, you know, Mr. Gwyn. If I had been I dare say I would have gone a great deal further in politics. Am I boring you?'

'No, indeed.'

Val denied the imputation emphatically.

'I'm just listening.'

'Well now then. I would like to help you. And I have a proposal to make. Are you prepared to listen?'

'Of course I am.'

Val was forthright but respectful. Sir Prosser seemed well pleased with his manner.

'I ... or rather we ... a small group of us ... have been, shall I say, invited – that will do for the time being – to set up an absolutely new kind of small Adult Education College. We already have a fair amount of finance. And we have the promise of the lease of a rather fine country house. Plas Iscoed. You may have heard of it?'

'Of the house?' Val said. 'Yes of course.'

'We have in fact advertised for a Warden and we have already drawn up a short list. I'm talking to you now in the strictest confidence. There are three names on it. You may know some of them. D. I. Everett, J. Macsen Jones, and O. B. Thomas.'

'I know Everett,' Val said.

'I won't embarrass you by discussing them in detail. Let's just say that they don't really impress me very much. Perfectly adequate, I'm sure. But we need something well above the perfectly adequate. Although, alas, the pay could well be less than adequate! We need a leader. We need a man with a sense of mission! Because this is a new venture. A new departure in the field of education. I'm very excited by it. And above all I want it to succeed. It has never been my style to be associated with failure. Now as I see it, Mr. Gwyn, my job ... our job ... is to pick the right man and let him get on with it. Well now ... I'll put all my cards on the table. I've had my eye on you for some time. I see that as part of my function in life. Keeping an eye on people. I've had a word with Prof. Williams and he agreed to let me make an approach. You know he's interested in you too I dare say?'

'No. I didn't know.'

Val looked innocent in his pleasant surprise.

'Well, there we are ...'

Sir Prosser pressed down his chin as if he were dismissing a trifling piece of incompetence on his own part.

'... as usual I've let the cat out of the bag. He has hopes of expansion on the Economic History side. It seems you will have to keep this conversation in the strictest confidence. If that old bearded lady, Bellot, wants to know what we've been talking about, you tell him all about Thomas Masaryk and his mother!'

Val had begun to laugh happily and Sir Prosser did all he could to encourage him. They were cheerful comrades in a harmless innocent conspiracy.

'What it amounts to, my dear chap, is this. Are you interested?'

'Yes.'

Val spoke emphatically.

'Yes. I am.'

'Well there we are then.'

Sir Prosser struggled up from his seat and moved to the window. Val instantly rose politely to his feet. Studying the view seemed a convenient device to conceal his face from the ingenuous young man while he was thinking.

'I have a grandstand seat,' he said.

He could have been humming a tune while his mind was engaged on a deeper level with problems of strategy.

'When I look at this amphitheatre, this delightful little amphitheatre between the hills and the sea, I sometimes think of it as nothing more nor less than a microcosm of our little world of Wales. The stage of many a stirring drama, Mr. Gwyn. Peripheral perhaps and yet so essentially human. You see, in the eyes of an old man, the human predicament barely changes. Even in the exalted cauldron. The Athens of the West as they call it on the Town Council!'

The tide of amusement was returning and his shoulders were beginning to shake again. He turned to smile at Val and raised his hand in a gesture of benediction before clumsily removing the cigarette stump from his mouth and shuffling over to the fireplace to dispose of it. His raised hand touched Val lightly on the shoulder.

'Now I'm going to make a suggestion,' Sir Prosser said. 'I hope you won't think I'm interfering in any way or trying to pre-empt any decision you will want to make for yourself.'

'Of course not.'

'Let me arrange to have you invited to spend a weekend at Plas Iscoed.'

He was scrutinising Val's face carefully for the minutest signs of objection to what he was proposing.

'Now don't think of it in any sense as the aristocratic embrace. The Owens family could hardly be called aristocrats in any case. But it's their property and they will be putting up a good deal of the money. So what I'm proposing is something in the way of a mutual inspection. They can look at you. And you can look at them. I'm quite sure whatever Lord Iscoed, Miss Eirwen and I recommend, the committee will ratify. After all I *am* Chairman of the committee. All very private and informal. You are not committed in any way. And you are not naked, so to speak, of other offers, so you are not without the basic ingredients of negotiating power.'

The greater detail he went into the more rapidly and quietly Sir Prosser spoke. Val listened as closely as he could and when he nodded it was like the fleeting delight of recognition a man shows when he hears the phrases of a familiar melody threatening to emerge from the puzzling complexities of a new symphonic composition.

'At the worst,' Sir Prosser said, 'it could be a very pleasant weekend. We could choose one of those musical occasions so dear to Miss Eirwen's heart. And I could show you projects that could be incorporated in the framework of the new college. At the worst, they might think you too wild, too young, too tactless, too revolutionary, for such a great enterprise. But I don't, Mr. Gwyn. I can tell you that much now. Now it only remains to see how far our minds can grow together. How much your concerns and mine, in the fine old Quaker sense of the word, can be made to cohere and coincide. I believe they can, Mr. Gwyn. I may be a foolish and impulsive old fogey, but I want to do something good for this little country of ours before I cross that frontier from which no traveller returns. I want to pay my debt to the ancestors that made me what I am and gave me what I now honestly believe to be the better part of me. I want to ensure that their values and their vision shall not perish from the earth. That's why your writing interests me so much. We have so much stick-in-the-mud thinking among us, don't we? We have too many jacks-in-office. It's our business to make a working alliance, Mr. Gwyn. To make openings, to make opportunities so that all the appropriate creative juices may flow down all the dried-up channels where they are so much needed. Now then. What do you say? Shall we give it a try?'

Val was smiling hopefully. When Sir Prosser offered his hand, he took it.

3

The new Warden held her head well back as she strolled briskly down the corridor. The shape of a smile played about her lips. She was not to be daunted by the unwieldy bulk of the great mid-Victorian Gothic fortress that was her new domain. Her thick grey curls bounced as merrily as bells on her shapely head. Her figure was still athletic. Her face was scrubbed and youthful. She was conspicuously wholesome. She still moved about the building with the joyous momentum of a reforming power, her wrists twitching intermittently at imagined cobwebs in her path, the enlarged pupils of her blue eyes scanning every corner with search-lights of improvement.

She arrived at the Common Room on a sweeping wave of satisfaction, even of triumph. It had been redecorated and refurnished under her personal direction. Her hands were pressed together with girlish pleasure even before she saw Amy and Enid seated opposite each other near the centre of the room. They were engrossed in a serious consultation and did not see the Warden until she was almost upon them.

'Reform is an atmosphere, don't you think? An opening of windows. An opening of doors.'

Both young women were looking up at her as though they found her resonant enthusiasm a little puzzling. They began to rise to their feet.

'No. Please don't get up. Could I join you for a moment?'

She sat down so that they were also obliged to sit. Her manner was genial. She exercised the easy authority of an older woman who could take her popularity among her senior students for granted.

'Do you like it? Do you approve? Do you like the watercolours?'

The girls nodded dutifully.

'I'm terribly proud of the David Cox and the Innes.'

She leaned back in her chair to point out the two landscapes.

'It's quite a story really.'

'They are beautiful,' Enid said reverently.

'Yes, they are, aren't they?'

Miss Wade was as proud and proprietorial as any mother. She smiled gratefully at Enid for showing so much appreciation.

'An American was after them, you see. A friend of Lord Iscoed's. I think they were at Balliol together. But he was thoroughly confused. He thought David Cox was Kenyon Cox and John Innes was George Inness. Two esses. Or something like that. I pointed out to Miss Eirwen that here was a case where Welsh patriotism had a prior claim and that the university could look after them for her! And I must say, she agreed immediately. She has such a generous nature.'

Both girls were listening to the new Warden of the Hall of Residence with polite passivity. As they took in her confidences they deliberately refrained from glancing at each other. But they need hardly have bothered. Miss Wade was so taken up with her own self-expression, she had little to spare to register the subtleties of their reactions. She clapped her hands together lightly and invited them to join her in smiling at the childlike spontaneity of her enthusiasm.

'We must surround ourselves with every form of excellence. Quite simply a seed bed for the best women's education imaginable. Don't you agree?'

The girls dipped their heads in cautious agreement. Miss Wade leaned forward to become even more confidential.

'Mind you, one has to be careful. There are sacred cows all over the place. It's very easy for a newcomer to tread on their tails.'

Amy found the notion funny. She laughed aloud suddenly. Miss Wade was delighted. She joined in and then Enid laughed too.

'Take that awful room next to the main entrance. The funeral parlour, I call it.'

Miss Wade looked over her shoulder briefly to make sure that there was no one else in the room.

'It was all set out in 1906. By our then Vice-Chancellor's wife. So it now remains as a kind of un-visited shrine to her memory. So I shan't touch it. Not for the time being anyway. But of course there are far more important changes to be made. I want to make this the best women's Hall of Residence in Wales. In the world. Why should we settle for less?'

She smiled confidently at each of the girls in turn.

'It's my view that women must take the lead in the building of a new and better world. I don't know whether you agree?'

Enid showed herself susceptible to so much frankness and applied charm.

'Oh we do. We both do, don't we, Amy?'

Amy was more cautious. She seemed to be still waiting to discover what exactly the Warden wanted with them. Her nod was no more than an interim sign of approval. Imperceptibly, the Warden shifted her body in her chair to direct more of her effort in Amy's direction.

'I know a little of what goes on,' she said. 'But I also know that I still have a great deal to learn. I know that from time to time you were, shall I say, in conflict with my predecessor. Now I don't in any way want to criticise Mrs. Blaize-Rees now she has gone. But what I do want to say is that it does appear quite clear to me that you were at all times impelled by the highest motives. Now I want you to know that I am here to do my best for the education of the women of Wales. That is my avowed aim. And quite simply I want to ask you for your help and co-operation. And I ask it because I am only well aware that in this world nothing of permanent practical value can ever be achieved by one woman working alone, no matter how dedicated and single minded she might be.'

Amy showed more sympathy with this last point. The Warden was encouraged to court her more directly.

'I know you take an interest in politics. There are still people in positions of authority and influence in this university who think this rather forward and unladylike. Well, I don't.'

In spite of themselves the two girls sat up and looked at each other to share the glad tidings.

'Women must learn leadership,' Miss Wade said. 'And after centuries of oppressive conditioning, this is not going to be easy. So I tell you what I have in mind. A small beginning perhaps but I believe a significant one. I'm going to set up a Hall Council. And I want you two to be on it. I want it to govern and inspire every aspect of our communal life. So that the women who come out of this place will be marked with an unmistakable stamp of quality, trained and ready to take up positions of leadership in Wales, in the Empire and in the world! Now will you help me?'

'We'll do what we can,' Amy said.

'Of course we will.'

Enid rolled her handkerchief into a tiny ball and smiled enthusiastically.

'Good.'

Miss Wade looked well pleased with them both.

'Good. That's settled then. That's absolutely splendid.'

She rose to her feet and demonstrated her pleasure with the whole situation by walking briskly up to the Innes water-colour and giving a deep prolonged stare at the sky that dominated the pale landscape.

'Blue,' she said. 'The blueness of blue.'

Her head moved a little to invite Amy and Enid to share a brief moment of aesthetic exultation.

'She's such a sensitive woman, Miss Eirwen. And so shy. I'm devoted to her. Next time the choir sings at Plas Iscoed I'll arrange for you to meet her. And see more of her pictures.

A remarkable collection. But then she's a remarkable woman. I sometimes wonder whether Wales really appreciates her.'

Miss Wade sighed happily, breathing herself out of her aesthetic trance and visibly gathering her strength for a fresh attack on what had to be a mass of unfinished work awaiting her whichever way she decided to turn.

'I'm so glad we had our chat.'

She stood close enough to Amy to embrace her. Then she smiled at them both with equal benevolence before leaving them.

In the doorway, she almost collided with Mabli Herbert. The tall girl stepped back, wringing her hands and apologising but still trying to make contact with her two friends over the Warden's head.

'Ah, Miss Herbert!'

Miss Wade pitched up her voice and it rang like a church bell down the corridor.

'Spare me a moment! I shan't keep you at all.'

She walked briskly down the corridor, assuming that Mabli was following close behind her. Mabli had time to make a series of excited signals to Enid and Amy asking them to wait for her in the Common Room before the Warden could turn and see where she was. She seemed a little alarmed to find Mabli towering above her, pale and breathless, a wild look in her small eyes.

'Have you ever been to Sweden, Miss Herbert?'

Mabli shook her head, nervous and surprised.

'Let's use this charming mausoleum, shall we?'

The office next to the front entrance was rarely used. It had a high ceiling and the view of the sea through a tall, narrow window was obscured by a flourishing aspidistra on a bamboo stand. On another table there were photographs of ancient College ceremonies in elaborate silver frames. Collections of leather bound books were visible behind the locked doors of mahogany bookshelves. The room smelt strongly of furniture polish. It was cold from lack of use.

'I do find this such a depressing little hole. Still we can use it, can't we? Call it neutral ground.'

Mabli gave a weak smile and said nothing. Her head moved about as she tried to avoid the direct scrutiny to which she was being subjected. She stood tall, alone and exposed in the middle of the room.

'Lots of girls in Sweden are over six foot tall. And very good-looking they are too.'

Mabli began to blush.

'We can be friends, can't we? I know you have no inclination to fawn or flatter and I respect you for it.'

Mabli's shoulders sagged a little. It was as ineffective an effort of concealment as a pheasant's in an open field. Miss Wade sat on the edge of the table, informal and yet briskly businesslike.

'Well now,' she said. 'What's all this about an extension on Sunday nights? The record shows you applied last year, and the year before, and each time it was turned down. Now you are applying again. Is that on the assumption that the new regime will be more enlightened?'

Miss Wade folded her arms and stretched her neck to one side to display a wry ironic smile. Mabli cleared her throat, but said nothing.

'Tell me what goes on in these meetings.'

Mabli stared at the rows of books as though she were trying to read the gilt titles. She spoke at last.

'Inter-denominational,' she said.

'Yes. I think I understood that. But what goes on? Enlighten me. I'm a newcomer more or less, remember. So much goes on inevitably, that I know nothing about.'

She smiled winningly and Mabli made a special effort.

'Discussion. Prayer. Hymn singing.'

Miss Wade nodded quickly like a consultant listening to a series of symptoms being inadequately described.

'We must never be afraid to speak,' she said. 'And we must take time to understand each other. I'm quite sure that is right. And speak our minds with frankness and honesty.'

She paused until Mabli had shown signs of agreement with the guidelines for discussion she was laying down.

'You all go to chapel, don't you? Two or three times. Isn't that enough?'

Mabli shook her head.

'This is for young people. Above denominations. Or outside them, I should say. Young people all together. Men and women.'

Miss Wade smiled to emphasise that what she was about to say was a humorous comment rather than a joke.

'There are rather a lot of them, aren't there? Denominations. When I first came here, to be honest I thought I'd arrived in the Middle East. You know. Bozra. Carmel. Shiloh. Joppa. Bethmaca.'

'Those are names of chapels,' Mabli said. 'Not denominations.'

Miss Wade was mildly irritated.

'I am aware of that.'

She stared hard at Mabli.

'But wasn't your father an Anglican rector? Isn't that the case?'

Mabli nodded.

'This is above denominations,' she said.

'Oh dear. It is difficult to understand. You must bear with me. And perhaps you must try and see it a little from my point of view. Surely Sunday is the one night of the week when everyone should be glad to get to an early bed? And then these proposed meetings are over in the College. It's a long distance for first years or any year for that matter to go walking late at night. I've looked into the history of this thing and it is quite clear that the College has always been opposed to meetings on Sunday nights, even for men. That is the precedent. And however good the cause, I honestly can't see why wise precedent should be broken. Don't you agree with me?'

It took Mabli a little time to find the courage to reply.

'No,' she said.

Miss Wade was prepared to be patient and amused. Her arms were already folded, now she entwined her legs as well.

'Very well. State your case, Miss Herbert.'

'Hops and dances. There are always extensions for them.'

'Yes. But never on Sundays.'

Mabli's eyes darted about as she ransacked her mind for substantial facts in support of her argument.

'In any community there are always necessary social occasions,' Miss Wade said. 'There is a pattern of controlled social outlets. Part of the established fabric of university life. Our traditions may be very young compared with the venerable routines of our ancient universities, but they are already time honoured and cherished. I think you would agree.'

Mabli shook her head impatiently.

'That's not what I'm talking about.'

She stopped as if she were momentarily appalled by her own bluntness. Her head swayed about and then the words tumbled headlong out of her mouth.

'Changing the lives of people ... that's what I'm talking about. The life of a whole generation could be changed. That's why young people must come together so that the Spirit can work among them and create something new. Something of their own to give the world. Something the world needs before anything else. A new point of entry for the Holy Spirit.'

Mabli clawed the air with her fingers, willing herself to go on speaking.

'Every generation must rediscover the gospel for itself. That's what the New Testament says. That's what new wine and new bottles means ... It's all there if only we have eyes to read it!'

Miss Wade stretched out a hand to moderate the intensity of Mabli's zeal.

'I do so agree with you. We live in a tired and weary old world that needs changing. Of course it does. No one knows that better than I do. I lost a brother and a person very close to me in the last War. I have dedicated my life and whatever little ability I have towards helping to create a better and a saner world. I don't choose the road you choose. But surely all good roads lead upwards towards the Light?'

Mabli had lapsed into an unblinking sympathetic stare but the last statement made her shake her head.

'Don't misunderstand me. I'm not against Revivalism as such. If that indeed is what it is. Obviously it has had its historic uses. All over the world, not just in Wales. And it has been of enormous social value. I'm not denying that. I suppose it's all in Welsh, is it?'

Mabli's mouth opened and shut before she nodded.

'You are an intelligent young woman. I know that. I don't need to point out to you the dangers and pitfalls of over-easy emotionalism. And I'm not suggesting for one moment that that is what it is. But I do beg you to recognise the guide lines for civilised behaviour that are accepted and supported by the entire university community.'

'Which guide lines?'

Mabli had become cold and sullen. Miss Wade moved from the edge of the table and paced up and down the rectangle of carpet in the centre of the room. She stopped to place both her feet neatly together. She lowered her head, stretching her neck apparently to study her toe-caps intently.

'I'm afraid our little philosophic discussion is not getting us anywhere, is it?'

'No.'

Mabli's voice was firm and bold. She struggled to keep her head still and stare straight in front of her.

'What are you thinking?'

'I'm thinking that if something of vital importance is happening, petty rules and regulations should not be allowed to stand in the way.'

Miss Wade took a deep breath to supplement her self-control.

'You are not easy to talk to, Miss Herbert. It seems such a pity. I am obliged to follow the rules and regulations. You can make a fresh application in writing, stating your case as fully as you wish, and I shall put it before the Senate. I shall also put my point of view, which I hope you have understood is not unsympathetic. Then the Senate will give its ruling. By which we must all abide. And that's as far as we can go for the time being.'

Miss Wade led the way out and Mabli followed. The moment she was sure the Warden could no longer see her, Mabli's long legs sped down the corridor towards the Common Room.

4

'The fact is, Lord Afton, the local people can be very narrow.'

The lawyer who spoke had small feet. From his spats to his wing collar he was dressed in dark Sunday clothes. His feet twinkled forward in a modified dance step and then retreated respectfully when the information had been laid.

'You said it, Tempus, not me!'

The club secretary was lumbering around the room enjoying his authority. He was dressed in plus-fours and a thick green cardigan. From his neck were suspended a heavy pair of German field-glasses. A large bunch of keys jingled in his trouser pocket. The floorboards of the new golf clubhouse echoed his tread as he loped importantly about. He treated the window as though it were an observation post. He placed a large proprietary hand on the bar counter even though the bar was closed. Lord Afton occupied the place of honour before the freshly lit fire, under the obligatory royal photograph. His attitude was pro-consular. Like the architecture of the clubhouse bungalow the theatrical stillness of his stance was cast in an imperial mould.

'Mr. Temple-Bowen is right.'

Rees, the red-haired articled clerk, was in attendance on the head of the firm. Mr. Temple-Bowen had no wish to hear him speak. He had made a considered statement and he deemed it sufficient, needing no further comment. Lord Afton was a man of experience, authority and rare intelligence. A nod to the wise was always sufficient. But Rees seemed too full of self-confidence to observe the unspoken prescriptions of his employer. He pushed a silk handkerchief up his right sleeve and concentrated on the chance to make an impression on the judge.

'There are over thirty nonconformist chapels in the town. At the last count.'

With a bold grin he prepared to give further demonstrations of his charm of manner if given the least encouragement by his superiors. The judge was showing some interest.

'Now then, Lord Afton, can I get you something to drink?'

The club secretary had used one of his numerous keys to open a cupboard.

'Not for me, Major,' the judge said. 'Too early in the day. But pray carry on. Unless there are licensing laws involved. Take no notice of me.'

The Major shook with silent laughter and allowed the bunch of keys to drop back into the capacious pocket of his plus-fours. He stroked his moustache and looked around roguishly at the handful of members who were present, inviting them to note that their club President, Lord Afton, was a man after the heart of their club secretary, Major Lightfoot: a gallant fellow with good humour in his heart and laughter never very far from his lips.

'What school did you go to, young man?'

The judge was giving Rees the opportunity he craved for.

'Christ College, Brecon, sir. Father died when I was sixteen, so I had to leave. War wounds. He was nearly fifty when he joined up. Falsified his age.'

Mr. Temple-Bowen was following the judge's reactions with close attention. Rees' statement was brash and over-eager: and yet it had left him in a stronger position. He had shifted a good two feet closer to the judge. The Major too, had been listening. He moved up to take a renewed friendly interest in the young man.

'You've done an excellent job, young Rees,' he said. 'The essence of a sound operation is good intelligence. Thanks to you we are properly prepared.'

'Tell me . . .'

Lord Afton was at his most judicial.

'What precisely is the Forward Movement? Forward to where? Or to what?'

Major Lightfoot was preparing to burst into boisterous laughter until it bore in upon him that the question was seriously intended. Mr. Temple-Bowen was a little slow with the answer.

'It's religious,' he said.

He was disappointed with the paucity of his own information. Rees was at his side, primed with the missing detail.

'Isn't it a kind of Mission?'

He could be seen by everyone to be asking his employer's consent to elaborate further. Temple-Bowen had no choice but to encourage him to continue.

'Financed by the Welsh Calvinistic Church but conducted mostly in the English language. Intended for the slums and that sort of thing.'

Lord Afton paid close attention to the exposition.

'How interesting,' he said.

Rees beamed as if he had been well rewarded.

'We must get it all right,' Major Lightfoot said. 'An open-air service on the third or fourth green. And by now they're all waiting for the game to begin. Tucked away in the old quarry. Is that correct? As soon as the game starts, out they'll come.'

The Major strode over to the window and lifted the field-glasses to study the grassy ridges along which the golf course was laid.

'Not a soul in sight,' he said.

'Tell me, Mr. Rees,' Lord Afton said. 'How did you come by all this valuable information?'

Mr. Temple-Bowen looked a little worried, but his articled clerk was as confident as ever. Like a subaltern in the mess, he stood with his feet apart and his hands clasped firmly behind his back.

'Something I overheard, sir. In the vernacular.'

For a moment he sounded like a hero who had infiltrated, in robes and turban, the heart of the native quarter.

'Librarian in our digs called Francis. He kept making elaborate jokes about a green hill far away and a pearl hidden in a quarry. I don't think he had any idea how much I understood.'

'Good for you, young Rees, I must say.'

The Major chuckled happily and looked at his watch.

'Quite honestly, I can't stand these Pharisees. I'm a churchman myself, but quite honestly I find them so ignorant and so narrow. Why don't they listen to their own archbishop? Made enough of a fuss trying to get one. Absolutely splendid address he gave at St. Michael's. Only a fortnight ago. "We must find a new harmony in our national life through reconciling the spirit of the gospel with the new

197

world outlook created by modern knowledge.'' Absolutely brilliant. Put his finger right on it.'

When he saw Lord Afton showing signs of willing agreement, the Major got carried away.

'I'm not the chap to beat about the bush. I think they're a pack of ignorant, narrow peasants. The whole blasted lot of them.'

The judge half-raised a warning finger.

'Now, Major Lightfoot. Be guided by me.'

The Major was already apologising and nodding.

'Don't widen the issue. This must remain strictly a legal affair.'

'That's right.'

Mr. Temple-Bowen found the strength to express vigorous agreement.

'Let it be simply this.'

Lord Afton was laying down the law and every man in the clubhouse held his breath and listened.

'The golf links are private property. If the greens are invaded it is quite simply an invasion of private property.'

The judge spoke with such finality that Mr. Temple-Bowen was loath to utter the further gloss he felt professionally obliged to add.

'The area covered by the sixteenth and seventeenth is in dispute, my lord,' he said. 'Certain local smallholders claim they lie across common land.'

'Quite.'

The judge did not altogether welcome the additional detail at this juncture.

'As I said before, let there be no encounters or confrontations on the sixteenth or seventeenth.'

The Major looked again at his watch, and began to pace up and down the club room in a deliberate imitation of a caged lion.

'I just can't wait to teach them a lesson. It'll be a great moment. Let no one attempt to interfere with the liberties of a freeborn Englishman! Where is that fellow, Posnett, do you suppose?'

'His wife.'

Temple-Bowen closed his eyes and frowned hard as he tried to unravel a confused pattern of relationships.

'She is related quite closely to one of the deacons in Arthog Williams' church. And he could well be on the Free Church Council, come to think of it.'

'Cold feet, you mean?'

The Major spoke bluntly like a man of action who has no time to lose.

'I wouldn't put it so crudely.'

'We've got to get out there,' the Major said. 'The sun is shining. We may as well enjoy the test game while we're at it. The First Test, eh? Lord Afton! Why don't you join us? See the fun. From a ringside seat.'

A golfing partnership advanced to the doorway, carrying their own clubs.

'Young Rees would caddy for you, under the circs. Then he could take names and addresses et cetera, et cetera, if the need should arise.'

To show how willing he was, Rees disappeared to the locker room to collect Lord Afton's golf-clubs.

'My place is here.'

Lord Afton made no move from his position under the royal portrait.

'The club does me the honour of making me President, but in a case of this sort it would be wrong for a judge to forfeit the appearance of impartiality.'

He spoke solemnly and not until he angled his head away did the small company realise he was making a sly joke. Major Lightfoot was the last to see it, but when he did he burst out into such a loud roar of laughter that Mr. Temple-Bowen stepped away to protect himself a little from the cloudburst of sound. He saw his articled clerk coming in with a golf bag over his shoulder.

'Rees will make the fourth,' he said.

The Major scraped his lower lip with his teeth before accepting the offer.

'Fair enough,' he said. 'The important thing now is to get started.'

'Let me just say this.'

The bustle of preparation halted while everyone listened to the judge.

'There is an important principle at stake.'

Major Lightfoot leaned forward on his golf bag to pay

zealous attention to every word. Had his knee been bent a little more it would have been the genuflection of prayer before battle.

'One of the glories of our constitution is the way in which it safeguards the rights and privileges of a minority. Now in this context it seems quite clear to me that the golf club is a beleaguered minority. I would like you all to know that I shall make it my business to see that our proper rights are preserved.'

'Hear, hear!'

The Major was on the point of cheering. He was restrained by a spontaneous burst of gentlemanly applause. The Major beamed around approvingly at everyone present.

'Jolly good,' he said. 'We know where we stand and we stand on our rights. No point in delaying the encounter.'

The golfers lingered a moment on the clubhouse verandah, smiling in the sun. It was a bright morning with a stiff breeze blowing cloud shadows over the upland course. The trees behind the clubhouse had long been driven to stretch their branches like despairing arms towards the north-east. Most of the leaves had already been blown off by the prevailing wind. The branches left an intriguing tangle of shadows on the sloping ground.

'Who's that?'

Major Lightfoot raised his field-glasses to train them on the crest of a ridge half a mile away, where in silhouette against the sky a rider sat motionless on a patient horse. Rees placed himself at the Major's elbow.

'Indians,' he said facetiously. 'Or Zulus.'

The Major declined to be amused.

'That's Griffiths,' he said. 'Griffiths, Glygyrog Fawr.'

The consonants exploded under his moustache.

'Dangerous little devil. Very nasty temper. Claims he has grazing rights all over the place. Wonder what he's up to?'

'Could I take a peep, sir?'

The Major handed Rees the binoculars. The young man adjusted them carefully to suit his own eyesight.

'He's dressed for chapel,' Rees said. 'But he's got his dog with him. I like his hat, I must say. Must be sixty years old if it's a day. And look at the way he sits on that cob. Legs straight out, stiff as a poker.'

'What's he up to?'

The Major was impatient and a little nervous.

'Any idea what denomination?'

'What do you mean?'

'What chapel does he go to?'

'Haven't the foggiest. How on earth should I know?'

Rees lowered the field-glasses to give a demonstration of thinking shrewdly.

'He could be a signal man,' he said. 'Ready to tip them off when we make a move.'

The Major was satisfied with the explanation but Rees wasn't.

'There must be more to it than that,' he said. 'I mean anybody could tip them off when we leave the clubhouse. We're visible from all directions. What's he doing all the way up there on his horse?'

Major Lightfoot held out a large hand to receive his field-glasses.

'We shall see,' he said. 'We shall see soon enough.'

He lifted his arm purposefully, relieved to be going into action at last. The foursome made its way down the slope towards the first tee: the Major, two hotel proprietors, and Rees, the articled clerk. It was followed by Mr. Temple-Bowen wearing a raincoat and a bowler hat, and a few members of the golf-club committee.

'There he goes!'

The Major turned around to see what Rees was talking about. Rees was pointing to the far ridge. The farmer on horseback was moving away. The Major looked back at the clubhouse. He was proud of the building. It was a wide expanse of bungalow like something copied from an Indian hill station. The decorative woodwork around the long verandah was distinctly oriental. The Major was pleased to see that Lord Afton had appeared on the verandah. The judge had placed both hands on the wooden rail and was watching the proceedings with close interest.

Major Lightfoot rehearsed his plan as he plodded up the rise to the first tee. Rees listened with a great show of respect.

'If they obstruct or trespass, you take their names and then addresses. Is that quite clear?'

'Perfectly clear.'

'Give your gear to somebody else and concentrate on that job. Names and addresses. We've got to build a cast-iron case. That is of the first importance. And then win it ... Good God. What on earth is that?'

A strange figure had emerged from a clump of gorse between the public footpath and the far end of the first fairway. It was a young woman of exceptional height, wearing a coolie straw hat and a green smock. She was carrying an easel, a folding chair and painting equipment. She half-dragged her cumbersome gear along as she hurried up to the green, her body thrust forward as she struggled against the lie of the land.

'Who on God's good earth is that, do you suppose?'

Major Lightfoot was as mystified as if he had suddenly encountered a family picnic in no man's land in the middle of an offensive.

'She could be lost of course. Looks a bit wild. Artist of some kind. Is there an asylum somewhere around here that I don't know about?'

He put the question to Mr. Temple-Bowen whose small face was also creased with frowns.

'Only the university,' Rees said.

His attempt at humour was ignored except by his golfing partner, a foxy-faced hotel proprietor who seemed to find the occasion more enjoyable when considered as a naughty Sunday prank rather than a campaign to improve the profits of his business. His Adam's apple shot up and down in a suppressed giggle when Rees gave him a surreptitious wink.

'This could be simply awful,' the Major said. 'Some mad female. Simply awful.'

His worry was so great there was no power in his opening drive. Almost out of politeness the other three curtailed their shots. As they trudged together down the fairway the green fell out of sight. The Major addressed his ball and then raised his arm to show that he had been thinking and had come to a decision. The young woman's straw hat could be seen bobbing up and down beyond a bunker as she scrambled towards the green by the shortest possible route.

'This won't do,' Major Lightfoot said crossly.

The others listened to him passively, ready to accept his leadership.

202

'I'll just have to go and have a word with her. There is no other way. You'd better come with me, Tempus. Just in case she's a maniac.'

Mr. Temple-Bowen managed to show distaste for the nickname while agreeing to accompany the Major.

'You come too, Rees,' Mr. Temple-Bowen said. 'To take her name and address.'

Rees was encouraged to be bright and humorous by the ready response of his partner.

'Could we take another shot while we're at it?' Rees said. 'Save us coming back. This is par four after all. Save us a bit of time, wouldn't it?'

'Won't do.'

The Major was adamant.

'We've got to go and see what she's up to right away.'

Members of the golf-club committee were already walking on. Major Lightfoot and Mr. Temple-Bowen made an effort to get in front of them. Rees was making others laugh as well as the hotel proprietor. By the first bunker the Major scrambled ahead to higher ground and turned once more to raise a commanding hand.

'Look here,' he said. 'As Hon. Sec. of this Club it is my job to speak. I would be obliged, therefore, if everyone else kept silent. I won't have this thing degenerate into a miserable shambles. I hope that is very clearly understood.'

Climbing to the level of the green they first caught a glimpse of the straw hat. It was where the flag should have been. She had removed the pin from the hole and pitched her stool over it. Speechless with a certain awe and wonder they watched her set up her easel and open her box of paints. As soon as she heard their approach she flourished a brush in the direction of the canvas although she had not had time to put paint on it. Her thumb gripped the dry palette tightly.

Major Lightfoot tugged hard at his thick cardigan and stepped on to the green. He was an imposing size, broad shouldered, well over six foot. His face was flushed and his pale eyes looked dangerous. With much dignity he advanced towards the obstruction over the first hole. He took a position behind the easel so that Mabli Herbert could not avoid being aware of his accusing presence. He folded his arms and waited with a show of gentlemanly patience for some explanations.

Mabli moved her head so that she could continue to study the view. The coolie hat had tilted back. Her mouth was tight and the base of her nostrils was white with apprehension.

'Young woman.'

Major Lightfoot spoke at last.

'May I enquire what exactly it is that you think you are doing?'

'Painting, of course.'

Mabli's voice, when it emerged was high-pitched and tremulous. The sound seemed to give the Major greater confidence in his ability to handle the situation with ease. He relaxed a little and attempted a friendly smile.

'You've chosen a very strange place to do it, if I may say so.'

'I like the view. My ancestors liked it. All of them.'

'Well now, look...'

Major Lightfoot made a visible effort to be both helpful and agreeable.

'If you cut across the tenth and the seventeenth, there is the most glorious view on the bit of common land beyond our fence. You can see down the coast for miles. It's wonderful.'

'I am perfectly aware of the beauties of my own country.'

Mabli looked annoyed at the wobble she could hear in her own voice, but was resolutely defiant. The Major wagged his head from side to side to show how mystified he was by her unreasonable attitude. Mabli felt she had more to add.

'Just as I am well aware that this is the Sabbath day.'

'Ah!'

Light dawned on the Major's face.

'Painting on the Sabbath is alright. But golf isn't. Is that it?'

'I'm not painting!'

Mabli waved the brush so that the Major could see it was dry.

'I'm protesting.'

'Are you indeed? Well I'll tell you something else, young lady. You are also breaking the law. Mr. Temple-Bowen!'

He summoned the lawyer to his side.

'I would like you to witness that I am now notifying this young woman that she is trespassing on golf-club property, and causing wilful obstruction to our lawful pursuit of the game. Kindly take her name and address.'

Temple-Bowen turned to beckon to his articled clerk. He then addressed Mabli who licked her lips and stared shyly at the blank canvas in front of her.

'Madam,' he said. 'It is now my duty to warn you that you are liable to legal proceedings for trespass and wilful obstruction. Will you kindly provide this young man with your full name, date of birth and present address.'

'Miss Hughes, isn't it?'

Rees tried to be cheerful and chatty.

'Or something like that. Haven't I seen you with Amy Parry and that lot?'

Mr. Temple-Bowen became irritated.

'"Something like that" won't do, Rees. The law requires us to be exact. Now then, young lady, your name and address, please, and don't let's have any bother.'

With a sudden access of strength, Mabli stared at the lawyer with open contempt. She addressed him in Welsh.

'You are a disgrace to your forefathers,' she said. 'You are aiding and abetting outsiders and foreigners to desecrate the Sabbath day in Wales. You are a man who thinks nothing of spitting on the altars of your own people. You have sold your soul to the Mammon of unrighteousness. You are a Judas!'

'What was all that about?'

The Major looked cross and baffled. Rees was smiling secretly at his employer's discomfiture. Temple-Bowen's face turned red and then white in rapid succession.

'Well?'

The Major spoke impatiently.

'She says you are breaking the Sabbath.'

'Was that all?'

Mabli was further roused by the Major's dismissive in-difference. She pointed excitedly with her paintbrush at the Major and continued to address Mr. Temple-Bowen in Welsh.

'Tell your employer he can prosecute me if he wishes. The only law I acknowledge in my own land is the law of Hywel Dda. You tell him that.'

The lawyer was completely taken aback by the fury of Mabli's onslaught.

'Look,' Major Lightfoot said. 'I simply can't have this. She speaks English perfectly well. Rees!'

He turned in soldierly fashion to speak to the articled clerk.

'Why don't you just remove that easel and deposit it safely beyond those bushes? On the public footpath. And then Miss What's-your-name you can kindly push off and we'll say no more about the incident.'

Rees was circling the girl's seated figure while the Major was still speaking. With a quick forward lunge he snatched up the easel and the canvas. He stepped back and held them in triumph high over his head like a matador with a bull's ear. Mabli bent forward as if she had suddenly been left half-naked, seated over the hole in the ground that was the cherished goal of the golfer's endeavours.

'So there we are.'

Major Lightfoot was inclined to relax. He smiled at the girl and waited for her to move.

'Sunday golf must go on, young lady. It's a forward march, you see. Absolutely nothing can stop it, thank God.'

5

People from the town and from the College trudged up the farm lane that wound its way up the hill, parallel with the golf course. Chapel people led the way, many still carrying their hymn books after the morning services. Onlookers mingled with protesters. When the sound of hymn singing was heard from the distant quarry, male undergraduates at the rear surged forward. They scrambled up the grassy banks in a hectic manoeuvre to overtake each other and everyone else.

Amy was also determined to push her way through the straggling groups blocking the rocky cart track. She and Enid, who followed her closely, were wearing college blazers and scarves. Their cheeks were flushed with anxiety and excitement and they seemed impervious to the chill breeze that was blowing which made Gwenda Gethin shiver inside her overcoat, and lag behind. She called to them in a weak voice, but they did not hear her. The dresses the pair wore

206

were very similar, loosely cut with collars that became broad neckties hanging outside their blazers: and they favoured the same hairstyle, a pretty but business-like bob with a neat side parting and a short fringe.

'The poor child will be by herself,' Amy said. 'She'll be terrified.'

'I'm not so sure.'

Enid gathered more breath to expess her reservations at greater length. Amy tapped an elderly man on the elbow. She repeated the action until the man stopped and turned to look at her with an expression of nervous surprise.

'Excuse me,' Amy said. 'Ambulance!'

He shuffled to one side to allow them through. Once they were clear of the crowd of men in Sunday overcoats who were using their breath to talk and make points instead of hurrying forward, Amy was fiercely critical.

'Driftwood,' she said. 'Bobbing along on a current of idle curiosity. Academics don't care about anything except tea and toast.'

Enid hurried forward to keep up with her.

'I want to make a speech,' Amy said.

Enid looked alarmed.

'I'm so annoyed with them for not coming,' Amy said. 'Val and Cilydd.'

'Oh, I expect they will.'

'Yes. When it's all over. And that poor Mabli has been crucified.'

'They're singing again,' Enid said. 'They're singing. Can you hear them?'

'Of course they're singing. They always do that at the slightest excuse. But you can't win a war by singing.'

'Oh I don't know. What about the Halleluja Victory?'

Enid was trying to be lighthearted. Amy's increasingly forceful manner was making her nervous.

'It's a valid issue,' Amy said. 'If handled properly. Val won't accept this, but I'm sure it's true. Underneath the sectarian sabbatarian muddle there lies a solid political issue. I'm convinced of this. It's a chance to harness public support, mass support if you like to the things we believe in. It's a chance, maybe the last chance, to open their eyes. On a popular level. And John Cilydd agrees with me. In his heart of hearts. But he's so much under Val's ideological thumb . . . just like you are.'

Enid was stung by the rebuke to a sharper reply than usual.

'If you made a speech, people would be bound to say, "Since when has this one been concerned about the Welsh Sunday?" It confuses them, Amy. That's the point. And I think Val's right there. It's not a simple issue. It's a confused one. Our first job is to teach people.'

Amy's mouth pouted stubbornly.

'This is the quickest way to do it. Action,' she said. 'You can talk as much as you like. But in the end it's only action that matters.'

There was a fresh burst of activity on the steep bank on their left. Men in college scarves were again scrambling to get ahead of each other. It could have been the sight of the two girls ahead of the straggling procession that spurred them on. Ike Everett was in the lead, his hands in his overcoat pockets and a cigarette stump in the corner of his mouth. By taking rapid short steps, he kept his balance on the narrow crest of the bank. He concentrated on his own progress like an acrobat on the high wire. His concentration became his downfall. He did not notice his two closest rivals catch up by hobbling along the sloping side of the bank. A bulky crop-haired young man in tight trousers gave a hoarse cry of triumph as he charged Ike Everett aside and sent him tumbling down the bank to land in the middle of the cart track. He lay still on his back and the girls ran forward afraid that he could be hurt. The stump was still clamped in the corner of his mouth. His eyes were closed.

'Ike! Are you alright?'

They were undecided whether to kneel down and examine him more closely. He opened his eyes.

'Don't move me,' he said.

When he saw the worried look on both their faces he gave a beatific grin.

'I've arrived! I'm in heaven! This is how I want to spend my life. On my back. Looking up at you. I'm back at your feet. Where I belong.'

'You idiot!'

Amy vacillated between irritation and amusement. She hurried on up the slope. Enid caught up with her. Ike Everett jumped to his feet and chased after them.

'Moral,' he said, panting with the spasm of effort. 'Wear a lot of clothes and you're less likely to get hurt. That's the moral. Overcoats for all!'

'This is serious.'

Amy did not bother to turn around to talk to him.

'It's no time to fool about.'

Ike broke into a trot to keep up with them.

'Where is the great man then? Owain Glyndwr reincarnated?'

Amy was embarrassed by his question.

'Got a nice job coming up,' Ike said. 'Wouldn't want to upset his chances, would he?'

The lane had reached the level of the first fairway. Students had already vaulted a low fence and were running through the gorse in the direction of the first green. Amy wanted to rush on but she could not ignore Ike Everett's questions.

'Since when have you been mad about the Welsh Sunday?' she said.

It was a lame question but it appeared to be all she could think of. Enid was waiting, concerned for Mabli on the green, but ready to support Amy with help if she should need it.

'I'm here for the fun,' Everett said. 'And I wouldn't mind seeing Lord Bloody Afton getting hit over the head with a hymn book. Twenty-three strikers he sent down in 1921. Sentences ranging from six to twelve months. My uncle was one of them.'

A burst of singing from the hidden quarry made the girls rush ahead. The green was hidden by a screen of spectators, just as though a championship match was in progress. The storm centre was so quiet the panting of the students who had just been running could be heard as clearly as the noise of sheep chased into a crowded fold. Amy pushed her way to the front, and Enid found a place by her side. Ike Everett remained on the perimeter of the crowd, a stump in his mouth, his hands in his overcoat pockets. He listened intently to what he could not see.

Mabli was still seated on her stool over the hole. An impasse had been reached. Major Lightfoot was deep in a

muttered consultation with Mr. Temple-Bowen. His lips
were close to the rim of the lawyer's bowler hat. He did not
want even Rees to hear what he was saying. Mabli sat with
her arms folded, her knees together, her feet far apart, and
her face lowered from the scrutiny of the crowd. Major
Lightfoot approached her again, his fists sunk deep into the
waist of his thick cardigan.

'As secretary of the club,' he said, 'I could send for the
police and have you removed. I don't want to do that. And I
would be grateful if you would oblige me by not making me
do that. You've made your protest. Now why not retire
gracefully so that we can carry on with our game in peace?'

The Major spoke in a loud clear voice so that everyone
could bear witness to how reasonable and agreeable he was
being.

'Good old Mabli!'

Amy blushed at the sound of her own voice, but she was
determined to continue.

'You stick it. Don't you give in to them!'

Once she began, more shouts of encouragement came
from the students. The Major turned to glare at them.

'Look here! Every one of you is trespassing. I hope you
realise that. Unless you are club members you are liable to
prosecution. Rees! Where are you? Start taking names and
addresses. That one for a start.'

He pointed at Amy. She stepped forward and he waved
hard and angrily to show she was walking on the green.

'Get back,' he said. 'Keep off the green!'

Rees approached Amy with his note-book and pencil.

'Hello, Miss Parry,' he said. 'I've been rather expecting
you. Where's the noble Val? And the bard of bards, for
goodness' sake?'

Amy ignored his pleasantries. She pointed at Mabli and
then turned to speak to the crowd in their own language.

'We should support this girl. She is sitting there to teach us
all a lesson. Every one of us. Chapelgoers or not.'

She pointed at the Major.

'These people are foreigners. They've taken our country
and they want to impose their will on every inch of it! Every
single inch.'

The students listened. From the back came an ironic

cheer. More of them took it up. They were impressed by Amy's passionate seriousness. Her face was flushed a bright red. She turned her head a little so that the breeze would not snatch her words away.

'Mabli has shown us the way! The time has come to make a stand. If we don't, everything will be taken from us. Everything. Any society that does not show it has the will to live deserves to die.'

She struggled to prevent her voice becoming too shrill. Major Lightfoot found no guidance from Mr. Temple-Bowen who clearly found the whole situation deeply distasteful. The Major strode across the green and laid his hand on her shoulder. Amy shrugged it off.

'Now if you've got something to say, say it in English,' he said.

There was a roar of protest from the male students. More spectators were hurrying across from the farm lane and the public footpath through the heather and the gorse. Amy was encouraged to go on.

'Understand this! If we do not stand up and fight for all the things we hold most dear, they will be taken from us one by one. It's up to us to put a stop to these people.'

She turned to point dramatically at Major Lightfoot and Mr. Temple-Bowen.

'There they are! The enemy! You are face to face with your enemy in broad daylight.'

Her arms lifted as she struggled to contain the flood of emotion that was taking possession of her. She would like to have been a prophetess but she was losing control of her voice. She was sinking in her own weakness, groping for sympathy and support, blinded with salt tears of frustration.

'You must make them turn back!' she said. 'We shan't let them pass.'

The Major had inclined his head forward so that Mr. Temple-Bowen could mutter rapid translations and para-phrases into his right ear. His rheumy eyes swivelled about in his head as he considered what to do next. A stronger sound of hymn-singing wafted towards them from the crest of the hill. The demonstration organised by the Lord's Day Observance Society in association with the Free Church Council, the Forward Movement and the Temperance

Movement was moving down the golf-links towards them.

Men and women in their dark Sunday clothes, instead of straggling down the streets in the direction of their chapels, humble and subdued in their tight family groups, were moving down the hill in a long black line like an army of inexperienced volunteers, led by a short row of ministers who were also having difficulty in keeping in step with each other. Further to the north the farmer on horseback had re-appeared, driving before him a great flock of sheep. His well-trained dog was stalking excitedly about the cob's rear hooves. When they became aware of this dual advance, the students gave voice to an excited cheer. Mabli moved at last like a statue come to life. She shaded her eyes with her hand. She could see Tom Arthog at the head of the advancing hymn singers. He was flanked by two other ministers in solid black with white clerical collars and black hats. Tom Arthog was easy to pick out because he was bare-headed and younger.

'Rees! Rees!'

Urgently the Major called the articled clerk to him.

'Did you get any names and addresses?'

Rees looked ruefully at his notebook.

'Plenty of silly ones,' he said. 'W. Williams, Pantycelyn Farm, Carmarthenshire. H. Harris and family, Trefecca.'

The Major glared at him uncomprehendingly.

'Is that all?'

'Two I know for certain. The girl who spoke. Amy Parry. And her friend, Enid Prydderch.'

'Is that all?'

'One or two more students.'

Rees pointed with his pencil to the line of advancing hymn-singers.

'Those ministers, of course. That one in the middle. I know him. I don't know whether you want to put all those down, do you? And I can see Francis, the librarian. He lives in our digs.'

'Sound the retreat.'

The golfers looked relieved. For some time they had been looking back longingly at the clubhouse.

'Let us retire in an orderly fashion.'

Delightedly Mabli ran across the green to Amy, took both her hands and squeezed them. The Major came up to address them.

'You'll hear from me again, young women,' he said. 'Writs will be issued. I can tell you that much. You are making a great mistake if you imagine a freeborn Englishman will ever submit to mob rule.'

In as dignified a manner as they could manage, the golfing party proceeded down the fairway in the direction of the clubhouse.

The students began to cheer. One dark-eyed young man with a heavy jaw and a hoarse voice rushed up to Mabli and slapped her so enthusiastically on the back she almost lost her balance.

'You've won,' he said. 'Single-handed. You've won the battle of the golf links.'

Waving his arms he ran on to meet the advance guard of the Lord's Day Observance Demonstration. Others followed and they vied with each other to give graphic accounts of Mabli Herbert's victory. The ministers shook hands with each other and then moved forward to congratulate Mabli.

'Well... that's it then.'

One portly minister smiled at his colleague, relief and satisfaction spread all over his face.

'We can go home now...'

He chuckled knowingly.

'With a nice appetite for dinner.'

'It's all over.'

'It hasn't even started.'

Amy's sharply raised voice startled him.

'Do you think they'll give in all that easily? You haven't even begun to make an impression on them. Do you know what I think?'

The minister looked hurt and shocked. He stared resentfully at Amy. Mabli could be openly commended for playing the passive and reasonably mute part of a female martyr to the Chapel cause. But this young woman was something else: vehement, aggressive, dangerously disobedient and undemure. He could see that his colleague Tom Arthog was also eyeing her with practised apprehension.

'We should surround the clubhouse,' Amy said. 'Make them understand the full strength of local feeling. Teach them a lesson they'll never forget.'

Mabli looked towards Tom Arthog, clearly waiting for him to give a lead. While he was making up his mind Ike Everett moved unobtrusively among the students, setting up a cry without taking his stump out of his mouth.

'To the clubhouse! To the clubhouse!'

They began to move away from the green. Tom Arthog still hesitated, blinking into the breeze from the sea. Suddenly an elderly woman among the singers moved forward and swung her handbag into his thigh. He gasped with pain.

'Mrs. Roberts!' he said. 'What have you got in there?'

'A little piece of lead,' she said. 'Just in case. For self-protection. Let's follow these young people then. And finish what we came to do.'

Several hundred people were now moving down the slopes towards the clubhouse. The farmer on horseback could see what was happening. He whistled to his dog and the sheep were slowly driven across the fairways towards the fifteenth green which lay to the north of the clubhouse. Ike Everett turned back to win Amy's attention. As they tramped forward he had difficulty in making her listen.

'I think he should have been here,' he said. 'I don't set myself up as a leader. But I can analyse a situation. And there are parallels you see. Clear parallels. Between a national struggle and a class struggle. But I ask you? Where is he, on a day like this?'

Amy walked so quickly he had to break into a trot to keep up with her.

'You were very good, you know,' he said. 'I'd say you've got better qualities of leadership than he has, quite frankly.'

'Oh, just shut up, Dan Ike.'

He was so pleased with having made her react and use his name he took his thin hands out of his pockets and waved them towards the clubhouse. In the flourish of malevolent conjuration his long fingers stretched out like the bare writhing branches of the trees bent by the prevailing winds.

'Oh God,' he said. 'I tell you what would be marvellous. Set the bloody place on fire.'

214

Amy shook her head.

'It's mostly wood anyway. It would burn beautiful. And roast the rats inside it.'

He chuckled to himself when she looked at him in real alarm. She looked around for Enid. There was a press of excited girls around Mabli, who was shaking her head like a runner exhausted by a long race. The crowd stood expectantly at some yards below the clubhouse. The verandah was deserted. The shadowy figures of members could be seen looking out through the windows. Amy pushed her way towards Tom Arthog.

'Don't lose the initiative!'

She was so emphatic it made him nervous. He waited for further advice, staring over her head. Then he turned first to one minister and then to the other, who seemed to be speaking without saying anything. Francis, the librarian, thrust himself forward, the light glinting on his slanted spectacles as he held back his head.

'What I want to know is, what are we going to do next?'

He demanded an answer as a man who had an immediate right to know.

'Sing,' Amy said fiercely. 'Sing, for goodness' sake! And then one of you speak. State your case. That judge is in there. Make him hear you. This is your chance to convince him.'

When Mabli came to her support, the ministers were more inclined to follow the suggestion. One of them decorously opened his hymn book and the sea breeze fluttered the India paper under his fingers.

'Let us sing together hymn number two hundred and thirty in the Congregational Hymnal, number three hundred and seven in the Hymns of Praise and two hundred and seventy-eight in the Methodist Psalter. "Be silent, cruel foe, / Give way, my hour is near / You shall not bend my knee / Before the Throne of Fear / I have my own my gracious Lord / Whom this life long I have adored..." On the old Welsh air, "Canan".'

The crowd was very ready to sing. It was both a form of creative activity and an expression of consensus that came easily to them. It was also a convenient substitute for action. Each individual was prepared to give himself wholeheartedly to the virtuous exercise. For once Amy and Enid were not

215

inclined to sing. Amy prowled about, watching the pale faces beyond the windowpanes of the clubhouse. Enid followed her, plainly nervous at her friend's overwrought state.

'I think we could leave now,' she said. 'I honestly don't see what else we can do.'

They both saw Rees press his face close to the window to wave the tips of his fingers and blow them a cheeky kiss.

'I can't stand that man,' Amy said. 'I just can't stand him. He's the embodiment of everything I despise. He really is.'

'We may as well go,' Enid said. 'I don't want to listen to their speeches.'

'I suppose that's Lord Afton. The one with the glossy hair. Look at him smirking. You can just hear his remarks. You can just hear them, can't you?'

Amy stamped her foot with futile force on the soft grass. The hymn singing was also getting on her nerves. She saw Ike Everett standing between the trees, smiling sardonically at the scene. At the side of the clubhouse was a rubbish heap with a mound of broken bricks left behind by the builders.

'Why don't they stop?' Amy said. 'Can't they see they're just entertaining the people inside? The authentic noise of the slave. Black or white. What's the difference?'

Unable to stand still she moved closer to the rubble heap. Enid called her back. Ike Everett waved his fist at her in a gesture of mock defiance. Quickly Amy bent down and picked up a lump of hardened mortar. She was near enough to a side window of the clubhouse not to miss her aim. The crash of splintered glass coincided with the end of a verse. The singers looked at each other in alarm and then at the figure of Amy standing alone by the rubble heap. There were tears of anger in her eyes.

'If you want to win,' she said, 'you've got to fight for what you've got.'

Enid rushed up the slope to her side. Mabli and several other women students followed. While the ministers were appealing for calm and someone was suggesting another hymn, the clubhouse door opened. The Major appeared on the verandah, quivering with rage. Lord Afton was not far behind him in the shadow of the half-opened door.

'You mealy-mouthed bunch of hypocrites,' the Major said. 'You see where your miserable protest leads you! Right into the paths of lawlessness, vandalism, disorder, chaos. Is that what your Christianity and Welsh Sabbath mean? Is it? Is it?'

The ministers and their supporters were uneasy and dismayed. Amy was still ready to speak, but Enid and her other friends were pressing her to leave. They took her arms and led her through the trees towards a path that led to the hill that overlooked the town. They pushed her forward as she continued to argue.

'You've got to stand up for yourself,' she was saying.

The others were nodding and making comforting noises. No one disagreed with her.

'If you don't win, you lose. It's as simple as that. Can't you see? I mean what else does history teach us, for goodness' sake? We can't go on losing for ever.'

At the top of the hill they could see far down the rocky coast while the town still remained hidden. When they looked back they saw that the crowd around the clubhouse had already begun to disperse.

6

Sir Prosser was dressed in a black cloak that reached to his ankles. He shuffled along inside it as if he were giving a humorous imitation of an elderly bishop going about his business encumbered with too heavy a crust of vestments. He carried a stick and used it to point out features of the landscaped garden that took his fancy. On his white head he wore a flat black hat which added to the ecclesiastical effect. And Lord Iscoed, so much taller, walked at his side with the restrained respect of a recently ordained priest with his mind already dwelling on the tortuous upward path of preferment. Lord Iscoed was bare-headed. His hands were clutched tightly behind his back. He was losing his hair prematurely but what was left was brushed close to his head in precise military fashion. He cultivated a neat black moustache under his sharp nose. His eyes studied the landscape with a

217

restlessness that spoke of either obsessive concern or profound distrust.

They reached the ornamental bridge at the end of the lake and Sir Prosser leaned on the parapet, ready to give himself to the enchantment of the view confronting him. The afternoon sun was glittering through the tall tree trunks of the wood at the far end of the lake. The ducks swimming hopefully towards them drew ripples of crimson sunlight on the still face of the water.

'Well,' Sir Prosser said. 'So far, what do you think of him?'

Lord Iscoed's thick lips hung open some time before he spoke.

'He's alright I suppose,' he said at last.

Sir Prosser raised his ebony walking stick to indicate his unspoken admiration for a boathouse on the side of the lake disguised by the white glimmer of the façade of a Greek temple.

'Reservations?' he said.

Lord Iscoed waited cautiously again before speaking.

'I don't like nationalism,' he said.

Sir Prosser chuckled happily. Lord Iscoed looked mildly irritated by the sound. He seemed to accept it as part of the price he had to pay for a close alliance with a man with greater power and influence than he had so far been able to acquire himself.

'That's rather like saying I don't like rain, my dear chap. I don't like it any more than you do. But it's a bit like sex. You just have to live with it.'

He narrowed his eyes against the dazzle of the sunlight through the trees. He was ready to give the younger man a master class in political art.

'There are always two elements to bear in mind,' he said. 'The man, and the ideas he thinks he cherishes. The ideas in isolation may sound unacceptably extreme. But if the man's nature is mild and moderate, as time goes on that inherent mildness and moderation will moderate the extreme ideas.'

Lord Iscoed stood up straight and looked suddenly bright.

'My dear P.O.P.,' he said. 'Surely the absolute opposite could also be the case? Extreme ideas turning a mild man into an extremist. Surely? Surely?'

He was content to have adjusted a balance of intellectual

power between them. They were able to walk on towards the great house, taking a path through the sheltered shrubbery that led towards the trim hedges of the Dutch garden. At one end of the house a Gothic campanile in granite was prominent among the tree tops. At intervals elaborate clusters of chimneys were dark against the sky. At the southern end a hexagon was crowned with an unexpectedly oriental cupola.

'He has no affection for England.'

Lord Iscoed voiced the indelicate suspicion as though he were referring to a physical defect. Sir Prosser was pleased to start chuckling again.

'Oh dear,' he said. 'Is that such a terrible sin?'

'He seems to take the French point of view about everything,' Lord Iscoed said. 'It's all very well to pretend to be objective but I don't think we should ever be disloyal to the senior partner. For a very good reason. It would tend to undermine the unity of spirit of our Empire at the very moment when it seems to me it could be transformed into a major force for the proper settlement of the problems of the modern world.'

Sir Prosser paused to poke at a dead thistle in the grass verge with the point of his stick.

'So you don't want him.'

Lord Iscoed appeared content to have penetrated the thick folds of Sir Prosser Ogmore Pierce's sacerdotal complacency. He raised a pacifying hand.

'I wouldn't go that far,' he said. 'And this is Eirwen's house, after all. And the college idea is hers. Or rather hers and yours. I am only a well-wisher. I wouldn't want to impose any veto on whatever you two decide. On the other hand I take it you want me to speak my mind.'

Sir Prosser gave a deep sigh. Iscoed was ready to accept the noise as a major concession.

'My dear David,' Sir Prosser said. 'We need your advice. We lean on it. We would do nothing without your complete approval.'

'Well, let me put it this way.'

As they approached the house Lord Iscoed was in the mood to be agreeable.

'He seems an excellent fellow in many ways. Very straight.

219

I like that about him. A considerable scholar. An able gifted writer, as you have pointed out. Well mannered and all that. He would seem to justify your choice in all sorts of ways. But I do find him lacking in one particular. And of course it happens to be the particular in which I have the closest interest. That's always the case, isn't it?'

Sir Prosser was scraping his boots carefully outside the main door. Lord Iscoed stood on the large mat, his hands clasped behind his back watching Sir Prosser's inexpert efforts with a tolerant smile on his face.

'And what particular is that?'

Sir Prosser listened carefully for the answer which was a little slow in coming.

'I would say he is rather lacking in idealism.'

Sir Prosser looked at him, his mouth hanging open with genuine surprise.

'Would you?' he said. 'Would you really?'

A welcome fire was burning in the lofty panelled hall. A wide staircase led to upper rooms. There was an oak chest of great antiquity under the window and in the corner under the staircase alongside the long sofa stood a large bust of the first Lord Iscoed crowning a solid plinth of black marble.

'I found him luke-warm on the League of Nations Union,' Lord Iscoed said.

'Not against the League, surely?'

Sir Prosser stood gazing appreciatively at the wood fire.

'Lacking in enthusiasm.'

Lord Iscoed closed his fist and shook it in a miniature demonstration of the enthusiasm he was after. As he opened his overcoat they heard the sound of a motor car arriving on the drive outside. It put an end to their discussion of the merits and defects of the character of Val Gwyn. While they were looking at each other, Miss Wade walked in. When she saw them she hurried up to them with a girlish cry of relief and pleasure. She pulled off a woollen cap and ran her hand through her grey curls.

'No choir, I'm afraid.'

She looked to them for support and comfort.

'I do hope Eirwen won't be too disappointed. You haven't heard about our troubles?'

Lord Iscoed had rung a bell, and already a servant had

appeared. He stood by, ready to set domestic machinery in motion.

'It's all rather fearful, really. The Principal is very ill. His doctor won't allow him to be disturbed. The Registrar is quite unable to make his mind up about anything. So is the Senate Sub-committee on Discipline. So all I can do really is to confine them to barracks, so to speak. The Sub-committee agreed to that. My first inclination was to recommend suspension. Lord Afton of course is furious. He would have them sent down. And I can't say I really blame him. But what worries me now most of all, of course, is disappointing Eirwen.'

Miss Wade looked around.

'Is she about? Shall I go and tell her straight away? The quartet has arrived, I hope?'

Lord Iscoed persisted in making a series of calming gestures. Miss Wade stopped talking at last and gave him all her attention.

'You mustn't worry,' he said. 'And I speak as Vice-President of the College Council and College Treasurer.'

He gave a toothy smile as though he had just made a joke.

'Eirwen and Mr. Galt are showing Mr. Gwyn the pictures and so on. So why not join us in the library in ten minutes or so and we'll have tea and discuss all the problems.'

'I suppose I'm being a bit hysterical, am I?'

Miss Wade smiled a little wistfully.

'It has all been rather frantic and unexpected, I must admit. The sort of thing I never dreamt would happen.'

Sir Prosser held his head to one side and smiled sympathetically as though Miss Wade were a favourite niece complaining with dove-like innocence at her first encounter with the harshness of the outside world.

'Anyway, it is good to get away,' she said. 'If only to see things in perspective.'

'So true,' Sir Prosser said. 'So very true. I was telling David when he took me out to exercise my legs, the life of a country house must be the most civilised ever devised by the ingenuity of man. And I speak as a boy who was brought up over a shop.'

Sir Prosser put everyone at their ease, even the servant standing by, who was obliged to overhear their conversation.

Miss Wade was already happier as she climbed the imposing staircase, followed by one of the maids carrying her cases.

Lord Iscoed and Sir Prosser wandered down the corridor at a leisurely pace. They had more to say to each other and were not inclined to sit down. From the music room came the sound of the quartet at practice. The harassed accuracy of the sound was a convenient cover for a further exchange of views and discreet confidences.

'Afton sound?'

Lord Iscoed's eyebrows lifted apologetically as he put this question. Sir Prosser flicked the pile of the carpet with the tip of his walking stick and shook his head, already saddened by the judge's shortcomings.

'It so often happens,' he said. 'Proof if proof were needed of the profound wisdom of the separation of powers. The judiciary are not fitted to govern. Obviously he has a taste for confrontation. That just isn't the way to go about it.'

Lord Iscoed nodded sagely. Then he ventured to raise a qualifying finger.

'At the same time, students, undergraduates, should never be allowed to get out of hand. I've never felt, *entre nous*, that the Principal was ever really sound on discipline. Even when he was one hundred per cent fit.'

Sir Prosser was not inclined to agree. Through an open door they saw Miss Eirwen, her artistic adviser and Val Gwyn looking at a selection of woodcuts and engravings on a table in the white drawing-room.

'It's virtually axiomatic,' Sir Prosser said. 'Student escapades should be treated lightly. But if there are principles involved then the escapades are best ignored. I mean what did this poor girl do? Pitch an easel over a hole.'

Sir Prosser had begun to chuckle. He seemed openly grateful to the girl for helping to dispel what had threatened to be a prolonged and unwelcome interval of gloom.

'A window was smashed,' Lord Iscoed said. 'That has to be borne in mind, surely. Violence and vandalism and so on.'

Sir Prosser made a despairing gesture with the hand that held the walking stick.

'A little broken glass,' he said. 'A little broken tea cup ... The man mustn't make a fuss. He'll get his Sunday golf just as surely as night follows day. But the good people must be allowed their little protest. What else are safety valves for? Really Afton doesn't know the first principles of good government.'

Lord Iscoed was listening intently to his mentor.

'So you think, "drop it"?'

'Of course drop it. Such a trivial thing. Send the girls down or even suspend them and you'd have the whole College up in arms. The student body rampant. The denominations on the barricades! And the advent of Sunday golf postponed for at least another five years.'

Sir Prosser raised his voice. He was so pleased with the sequence of fancies that were presenting themselves to him, he wanted the largest available audience to hear them. Miss Eirwen looked at them expectantly. The tortoise-shell slide in her straight hair slipped down towards her ear. She was a pale, shy, thin figure unfashionably dressed in brown woollens. By contrast her artistic adviser looked crudely robust. The fingers of one hand fondled his luxuriant beard as the other dealt gently with the proof of a woodcut. The stout calves of his legs swelled robustly inside his claret-coloured woollen stockings. Val was absorbed in what he was being shown but ready enough to show a polite interest in the noise made by the men in the doorway without having the least idea what they were talking about. He wore a bow tie with his well-cut grey worsted suit and looked perfectly at his ease in unfamiliar surroundings. He pushed back a lock of black hair that had fallen over his forehead.

'Eirwen.'

Lord Iscoed addressed his sister.

'The choir's not coming. Miss Wade just arrived. She brought the bad news.'

He seemed to be encouraging her to take the disappointment in her stride, but she was much less inclined to take the matter lightly.

'How annoying,' she said. 'How very annoying.'

She moved away from the men so that they should not see the disappointment on her drawn, intense face. Through the window she stared at black cattle making their way through the brown world of the ancient forest of oaks on the slope opposite.

'I must confess I'm disappointed,' Sir Prosser said.

He entered the room in his most avuncular manner. He was aware that he was an unusual sight in his long cloak. He used his flat hat to sketch an imaginary prospect before his own eyes.

'Such an enchanting sight,' he said. 'Those pretty sopranos in the front row.'

Miss Eirwen showed no inclination to respond to his jocularity. Sir Prosser was not put out. He put his hat on his heart and sang a silent note.

'And they sing so well, into the bargain. All from my valley of course, Mr. Galt. You realise that?'

He wagged his hat under the nose of the artistic adviser.

'Relatives, Sir Prosser?'

Mr. Galt had a playful understanding with Sir Prosser. They enjoyed being genial together.

'Ah, Mr. Galt! You have to live a long time in this little country of ours before you can grope your way with any degree of confidence through the labyrinth. Isn't that so, Mr. Gwyn?'

'Alas, yes,' Val said.

He struggled to accommodate himself to the jocular atmosphere Galt and Sir Prosser were generating between them.

'Alas! Why "alas"?'

Sir Prosser exaggerated his offence at the sound of the word.

'We are not ordinary common or garden English like our friend Galt here. We are a metaphysical people, understand. That is why we produce metaphysical poets.'

Galt laughed delightedly, lifted a stockinged leg and rubbed strands of his beard between finger and thumb. He was about to indulge in a further piece of repartee when he heard Miss Eirwen speak. He fell respectfully silent on the instant.

'Mr. Gwyn approves of my idea, David.'

She was addressing her brother across the room. The light from the window showed an expression of timid defiance on her pale face. She seemed conscious of her own plainness, taking grim satisfaction in her lack of adornment.

'Which one, I wonder?'

Lord Iscoed had been absorbing solace from a fine

Pissarro winter scene on the wall. His attitude to his sister was benevolent but wary: aware that she cherished her independence most when asking for his advice.

'A series of concerts in aid of the distressed areas. Alternately here and in the university Hall. He thinks it's a very good idea.'

Lord Iscoed refrained from comment.

'Art should be harnessed for the benefit of social good causes,' Miss Eirwen said.

Her voice was inclined to be soft and plaintive but stiffened with all her conscious aspirations to goodness and worthwhile works.

'Mr. Gwyn agrees with that. And so does Mr. Galt, of course.'

Sir Prosser beamed happily at what he was hearing.

'Splendid,' he said. 'Splendid. What is more creative in this world, when all is said and done, than a true meeting of minds?'

Miss Eirwen did not take kindly to the loudness of Sir Prosser's voice. She seemed to find both his assertive benevolence and his ageing masculinity oppressive. The large white drawing-room had become too full of men and she shrank away from them fastidiously.

'I'd better go and see Miss Wade,' she said.

She looked at her brother hesitantly as though she were asking for his advice and approval. Behind his back he smacked a fist into the palm of his hand and strode masterfully towards the white marble fireplace.

'I've asked for tea in the library,' he said. 'Is that alright?'

'Of course,' she said. 'Of course.'

She hesitated to leave only because her brother could have been wanting her to stay. An awkward silence began to gather in the room. Val had examined the woodcuts. Mr. Galt unobtrusively fingered his beard. Lord Iscoed stared across the room at a glowing Bonnard still-life as though he were testing his eyesight. Sir Prosser found a drawing-room chair and sat on it. He placed his hands on the top of his ebony stick. Both his short arms were fully extended as he took up a deliberately Johnsonian posture. He determined to take the occasion in hand, making his voice more nasal and resonant than ever.

'Tell me, Mr. Galt. How does Mr. Gwyn's concept of a Folk High School on Danish lines strike you?'

'Interesting.'

Mr. Galt tugged at his beard.

'Very interesting. I sympathise with it very much.'

Sir Prosser nodded encouragingly. He wanted Galt to enlarge on the theme.

'There wouldn't be any place in it for me, though.'

Galt was being both modest and tactfully frank. He smiled happily to show the full measure of his objectivity and lack of self-interest.

'I don't have the Welsh.'

Val was moved to intervene. He was acutely anxious to show that he would never want to overlook Mr. Galt's special gifts or the great value of his contribution.

'That wouldn't be so important. Initially. In the case of the plastic arts, that is. Sympathy and standpoint come first I think. My main point is the attack on what I called conditioned helplessness.'

Lord Iscoed frowned with a fruitless effort of recall.

'Tell me again,' he said. 'What did you mean by that exactly?'

'The basis of the experiment,' Val said. 'Adult education based on co-operative living.'

'Yes. We agree upon that I think,' Lord Iscoed said.

He was more aware than Val that the others were watching and listening closely; and perhaps more concerned not to appear insufficiently informed or shaky in judgement.

'But what's this about "conditioned helplessness"?'

Val struggled to express himself clearly.

'It could be an exercise to restore people's confidence in themselves and their own origins. Of course we want to enrich their lives with everything the arts can bring to them. Music, painting, the fine arts. Everything that can be decently done within the period of six months to a year that a student spends in the college. But the core of the teaching must be the restoration of confidence in their own roots. So that by repossessing the fullness of their own culture, they also find the door to the whole of the European inheritance. And this will give them the spirit and strength to face the awful problems of the world outside and the spirit and strength to do something about it on a basis of creative co-operation. That's what I'm saying.'

Sir Prosser struck the end of his stick against the carpet in muffled applause.

'That sounds very good,' he said. 'What do you think, Eirwen?'

Miss Eirwen murmured to herself. It was clear she resented being questioned. She looked longingly at the open door and seemed to measure the distance across the room. Mr. Galt glanced respectfully from Val to Lord Iscoed, indicating he would like to say something.

'I think I understand what Mr. Gwyn is saying. And I sympathise. But of course art *is* international.'

His eyes closed momentarily as he intoned the axiom.

'Of course it is.'

Lord Iscoed was pleased to deliver his imprimatur. He waved a hand to take in the pictures on the walls.

'And so it should be.'

He was taken aback when Val showed an inclination to argue.

'I don't doubt it,' Val said. 'I freely acknowledge I am no expert in this field. But on a philosophic basis, so to speak, is not art by definition proceeding from the particular to the universal? Therefore, is not the artist under a primary obligation to master the particular? And is not his particular in almost every case that particular society that gave him birth, in all its strengths and weaknesses?'

'Well put, Gwyn. Very well put.'

Sir Prosser was very ready with his approval. Lord Iscoed was not pleased. He seemed to have lost the thread in the middle of Val's rapidly-delivered discourse.

'We have to face these things.'

Iscoed rescued himself with a sudden burst of categorical emphasis.

'The world is rapidly becoming one village. And I look forward to the day when the place will be kept in order by the one village policeman – and by that I mean, an international police force.'

By some swift but inscrutable course he had arrived at his favourite topic, upon which he felt free to make pronouncements with unqualified authority and fervour.

'Tea!'

Sir Prosser made a noise like a genial umpire.

'How can I take in all this high thinking without the cup that cheers?'

The word was also a signal of release for Miss Eirwen. She crossed the room with her head down, doing her best to disguise the slight limp from which she suffered. Mr. Galt seemed at a loss for a moment. He touched the woodcuts.

'I'd better put these away.'

Val smiled at him. He was ready to continue a friendly discussion on the nature of art, but he was summoned by Sir Prosser.

'Mr. Gwyn,' he said. 'I meant to ask you this before. It's a personal question, of course. But in view of all the exciting plans ahead, it is extremely relevant. Do you mind if I ask you a personal question?'

There was an urchin-like grin on his face. Weighing on his stick he rose to his feet and beckoned with his head in Lord Iscoed's direction. Whatever was said, he wanted him to hear. Lord Iscoed approached them slowly, his neck stretched out as if to take whatever he was required to know without being obliged to share the whispered air in too uncomfortable proximity.

'National and international,' Sir Prosser said. 'Formulae. Words. Are they so inherently in conflict? I don't think so. Why can't we have the best of both worlds? That's always been my policy. Ah well, I can see nobody agrees with me. Old Prosser Pierce, as usual in a minority of one.'

He was inviting them to share his mood. Lord Iscoed held back. Val was trying to give a willing smile.

'Now then,' Sir Prosser said. 'My personal question. You are sure you don't mind?'

'Of course not.'

'In the strictest confidence, as they say. Is there, in the immediate future, or indeed the less immediate future, any prospect of a *Mrs.* Gwyn? Forgive me for asking. Please don't consider yourself bound to answer. But in a venture of this kind . . . you will appreciate . . . the more we know . . . the more complete our information.'

'Of course.'

Val seemed happy to discuss the subject.

'As a matter of fact there is.'

'Good. Good. Excellent.'

Sir Prosser was assuming a rôle of episcopal benignancy.

'Engaged?'

Val's smile was almost nostalgic.

'Yes. But we've lost the ring.'

Sir Prosser was grateful for the opportunity to laugh.

'Ah the young,' he said. 'What a blissful condition it is.'

He was ready for the walk to the library and tea.

'Would we know the young lady, do you suppose? Or does she come from some foreign clime? Some beauteous daughter of France or even Italy. Pretty as a southern sky.'

'She's reading for her degree.'

'That's good. A modern educated young woman.'

Val's face began to redden suddenly.

'You may have read about her. Over the golf-club affair.'

'My goodness.'

Sir Prosser held his stick in the air like an exclamation mark.

'Not the girl caught painting on the first green?'

He suppressed his amusement while he waited for an answer. Lord Iscoed's eyebrows were raised, an expression of dawning disapproval on his face.

'No. One of the others. Her name is Amy Parry.'

They were in the corridor. Val was able to derive some ease from the motion of walking.

'Isn't that the one that broke the glass?'

Lord Iscoed put the question bluntly.

'I'm afraid so. Yes. Of course I would say they were greatly provoked.'

Lord Iscoed walked on more rapidly. Before they reached the library he managed to take Sir Prosser to one side.

'Look here, P.O.P. We couldn't possibly have a girl in here who goes in for breaking windows. Be fair. Could we now? I have to think of Eirwen, you know. I made a solemn promise when my father died.'

7

Mrs. Perrin's knees creaked as she bent inside her corsets to
pick up the poker. The gaslight was turned down but the
room looked warm and inviting. It was at the back of the
house on the first floor and the wind outside was comfortably
distant. On the sideboard and on the mantelpiece rows of
silver cups glowed and glimmered when the flames shot up
from the broken coal. Amy remained on the landing outside.
Her cheeks were flushed and she still breathed heavily after
running against the wind. Quietly she went as far as to
unwind the long college scarf around her neck, but she did
not unbutton her short overcoat. While still bending Mrs.
Perrin turned to look at her and beckoned her in with the
poker in her hand.

'Will you come in, for God's sake,' she said.

'I don't want to disturb you, Mrs. Perrin . . .'

Amy murmured her apologies as she stepped diffidently
into the room.

'How am I supposed to know College rules?' Mrs. Perrin
said. 'I never keep students. Wouldn't have them near the
place. So I make my own rules. Number one, keep a good
fire!'

Her brogue and her bronchial condition both lent
additional charm to a generous expansive manner. Once
again she thrust the poker aggressively into a black clump of
coal so that it burst apart and sent a spectacular flame roaring
up the chimney.

'Now isn't that better?'

She had straightened her back and to save herself bending
down again she dropped the poker with a noisy clatter inside
the brass fender.

'Come closer, won't you, and take off your coat.'

She dusted the palms of her hands and watched Amy
appreciatively as she took off her coat. A blouse, a cardigan
and freshly-pleated skirt set off the grace of her figure.

'You've got things to say to each other,' Mrs. Perrin said. 'Of course you have. So you can say them in here. In the privacy of my little room.'

'You are very kind, Mrs. Perrin.'

'And he's my favourite, as you know.'

She made Amy sink into the comfort of the deep armchair.

'Do you smoke, Miss Parry? I know many young women do these days. You can smoke in here if you want to.'

'No, thank you,' Amy said. 'I don't smoke.'

Mrs. Perrin rested her hand on the marble mantelpiece and gazed down at Amy with open admiration.

'Life's very short,' she said. 'So why can't we all be a little more free and easy? That's what I say.'

She read the inscription on a large silver cup on the mantelpiece.

'"In memory of Kate, mother of champions and the best bitch I ever had." Named the bitch after me, if you please.'

Mrs. Perrin stared nostalgically into the fire. Her large chest rose and fell.

'That's the kind of man he was. I can only hope they have dogs in heaven.'

Amy watched her carefully until she was sure that she was going to laugh rather than cry. The laugh grew slowly. A rasping sound that ended with a red face, a spasm of coughing and the back of her fat fist striking the lace crest of her modesty vest. Mrs. Perrin looked around to note the exact location of a tub-chair before venturing to sit in it. She sat with her knees apart, her mouth open and the firelight glittering cosily on all the rings of her plaited fingers.

'He is my favourite, I can tell you that much. Not that he'd ever notice. He's so lost in his notions, isn't he?'

Amy clasped her knees together with both hands to avoid sinking back too far into the luxurious comfort of the low armchair.

'Not that I have much idea what they are. There's a lot of arguing that goes on in this place and I don't follow half of it. But it's within bounds, you see. There's never a gun around here and that's a blessing. Mind you, I know he's handsome and brave is Mr. Gwyn. And you can't ask more of man than that. When all's said and done. And he's such a gentleman. Now there's the difference, you see. Mr. Rees, bless him, longs to be a gentleman but never will be. Mr. Gwyn is a gentleman and doesn't know it. Oh dear . . .'

Mrs. Perrin was threatened again with a spasm of laughter.

'Am I the foolish old woman to make him my white-headed boy?'

'Oh no.'

Mrs. Perrin raised her arm to the mantelpiece to stem the engulfing tide of levity. The warmth of the sitting-room was a forcing ground for friendly curiosity.

'Tell me something, my dear. Have you ever met his mother?'

'Yes.'

Mrs. Perrin waited for more information. Amy was beginning to blush.

'Doesn't encourage you much, does she?'

'Well, I haven't really seen all that much of her.'

It was difficult for Amy to fend off the landlady's curiosity without appearing ungrateful for her special hospitality.

'I may as well be frank with you,' Mrs. Perrin said. 'She's not what I would describe as a loving mother. That's why the boy's so thin. When he's home I don't think he ever gets enough to eat. And it's not as if they're lacking in means or anything of that sort. You take a look at her. Why is she thin? There's only one answer. She's just too mean to eat. And all that strict religion. It's a wonder to me the boy is as good as he is. It's what I would call a miracle. And of course she doesn't approve of me at all. Thinks I'm much too free and easy. I think the truth is she is a teeny-weeny bit jealous.'

Amy was slipping back in the armchair. She made an effort to keep her back straight. Mrs. Perrin inclined her heavy torso forward to address Amy with even greater confidentiality.

'And what about your family, my dear?'

Amy's cheeks were bright red.

'I'm an orphan,' she said.

'Are you really?'

Mrs. Perrin's lips rounded sympathetically while her bloodshot eyes seemed to continue with a process of shrewd calculation.

'Now isn't that always sad? On the other hand it's modern and romantic. Have you noticed whenever you go to the pictures the heroine is nearly always an orphan? At least every time I go.'

Her large body began to shake with a mild earth tremor. She took herself firmly in hand. Her voice sank to a confidential murmur.

'I must be getting on every nerve you've got in your body,' she said.

'Oh no. No indeed.'

Mrs. Perrin's sudden change of approach took Amy by surprise. She hastened to plug the gaps in her defences.

'You must think me an unholy terror,' Mrs. Perrin said.

'Oh no. No indeed.'

Mrs. Perrin made a fresh bid for good will and approval.

'I'm so pleased for Mr. Gwyn. I can honestly tell you. When all is said and done. What a man needs most of all in this wicked world is the comfort that only a loving woman can give. An orphan. And so beautiful. What was the story I wonder?'

'My mother died five weeks after I was born,' Amy said. 'My father was killed in the War. At Vimy Ridge. I was brought up by my mother's sister and her husband. On a little farm in the country. Swyn-y-Mynydd it was called.'

Amy licked her lips. She was running out of facts she could easily reveal and she could see that Mrs. Perrin's appetite was far from satisfied.

'They live in Llanelw now. My uncle's health has given way. They're sort of retired.'

Mrs. Perrin's head lifted sharply as she heard the front door open and shut.

'Is that Val?'

Amy looked overwhelmed with relief and joyous antici-pation. Mrs. Perrin watched her fondly. She moved suddenly. In no time she was out of the room and leaning over the banisters.

'Mr. Gwyn! Is that you? Could you come to my room for a moment, please?'

'Certainly, Mrs. Perrin.'

Mrs. Perrin turned to smile roguishly at Amy standing by the fire.

'I have a visitor for you.'

She spoke to him in a low seductive voice as he climbed

the stairs with his customary nervous energy, three steps at a time. He looked cold. His long nose was red. He stood in the door, confused, pleased and uncertain what to say. Amy looked ill at ease in Mrs. Perrin's private sitting-room as though she had begun to regret having placed herself in such a vulnerable position. Mrs. Perrin looked from one to the other with arch expectancy.

'Now I am going to leave you both,' she said. 'So that you can have a nice little chat. Rules or no rules there's not a soul in the wide world to disturb you for the next twenty minutes or so. I can promise you that.'

She closed the door with soft care. They listened to the stairs creaking in response to her heavy progress. In the deep silence of the room the two gas mantles hissed excitedly. Amy was shy and uncomfortable.

'I shouldn't have come here,' she said. 'But I wanted to apologise.'

The sound of her voice was enough to make Val react as though he were listening to unexpected music.

'Cilydd told me,' Amy said.

She stared with distaste at the row of silver cups bulging on the sideboard.

'What did he tell you?'

'I lost you the job.'

'He shouldn't have said that. That's absolute rubbish.'

'Oh no, it isn't.'

She showed him that the patient sympathetic smile on his face was no comfort to her at all.

'I was wrong all along the line. I could kill myself.'

'Oh now, don't be absurd.'

Amy seemed relieved to be able to get angry.

'I'm not being absurd,' she said. 'I can see it quite clearly now. Much ado about absolutely nothing. I must have known it even when I picked up that piece of brick or whatever it was. Frustration, no doubt. The story of my life. The whole thing has made me absolutely miserable. And if you want to . . . throw me over . . . give me up or whatever the expression is . . . I would perfectly understand.'

'Amy. Please.'

He crossed the room to put his hands on her shoulders.

For a moment, she looked as if she were inclined to shrug them off.

'This place is a trap,' she said. 'A spider's web or whatever.'

'You followed your heart, not your head.'

She seemed to have difficulty in hearing what he was saying. She stared into the hot centre of the fire.

'I hate this place,' she said. 'They will always win and we shall always lose. One more year and their stupid Sunday golf will be here to stay. Not that it matters. But it's a symbol. Just think of it. Cilydd persuades that awful golf club not to prosecute, and the awful Free Church Council treats it as a great victory!'

Val had begun to laugh. Amy took the excuse to shrug his hand away from her shoulder.

'It's not funny,' she said. 'It's tragic. You should know that better than anybody. "We have no power to control our own destiny." You said it yourself. And I believe you. It's true. It's not just the stupid Sunday golf business. It's everything from the smallest to the greatest. Do you think you are ever going to get a decent job here? Ever?'

'Plas Iscoed was a bad idea,' Val said. 'You see, I was just as wrong as you were. Just as muddle-headed.'

He took hold of her hands and squeezed them gratefully. Amy did not look pleased at being called muddle-headed.

'Shall we try and be absolutely honest?' he said.

'That's what I always want to be,' Amy said. 'You know that.'

'You never really believed in the golf protest. Not like Mabli Herbert with her religious convictions. You just wanted to use it. For a political purpose.'

Amy tried to take her hands away. He held on to them.

'Now then, Miss Parry. By the same token, I never believed in the Plas Iscoed offer. Not in my heart of hearts. But I wanted to use it. For purposes both private and political. I had all sorts of foolish dreams. And they all seemed to revolve around you and I living in a great big country house.'

Val was laughing. Amy was not amused.

'What's so wrong about that?' she said.

'The struggle ahead,' Val said. 'We can't avoid it.'

He let go of her hands and began to pace restlessly about the room.

'It's ourselves alone,' he said. 'We've got to accept that. And we've got to get used to thinking in terms of years and decades, and not hours and days.'

Amy sat down in Mrs. Perrin's tub-chair. Her shoulders bent as though Val's words were placing a heavy yoke on them.

'You just have to use your reason,' Val said. 'If you want to change the course of history – and that's what we are talking about in terms of our own country . . . our own people – what force do you need? The kind of will that changes the courses of rivers. That moves mountains. That's what we are talking about. And that's the only kind of force that's going to save a nation that's dying on its feet.'

Amy muttered to herself so quietly, Val could barely hear her.

'Why can't we let it die?'

He knelt on the hearthrug so that he could look into her face. He was as concerned as if she were physically ill.

'What's the point of fighting all the way if you can never win?'

He touched her cheek gently and consolingly with the outside of his fingers.

'What's the point of being alive if you can never ever have what you want?'

He seemed unable to answer the questions she was asking principally because it had never occurred to him to ask them before. He stared at her face with loving concern, absorbing every detail like a traveller who memorises the map of a crucial journey that has to be made.

'Shall I tell you what I've been thinking?' Amy said.

'Of course.'

He found her hands in her lap and fondled them comfortingly.

'A silly dream I suppose. You won't think me childish if I tell you?'

He lifted her hands to his lips and she was encouraged to go on.

'I dreamt it really. I dreamt you had forgiven me.'

'That's silly,' Val said. 'There was absolutely nothing to forgive.'

'We were in America together. In a great big wooden house. By a large river. And everything was alright. The sun was shining and there were men working in the cornfields under a bright blue sky. And we were together.'

She took his face between both her hands. They kept so silent the beating of their hearts was louder than the wind outside or the distant sounds that came from the rest of the house. Val drew her forward and together they lay down on the rug in front of the fire. For each of them the embrace was a passionate reconciliation, the sudden all-absorbing centre of living. Amy's pleated skirt rode up. She tried in vain to push it down. The low armchair slipped back as Val weighed upon her. A loud burst of sound from downstairs made Amy sit up. She was already angry and embarrassed.

'This place,' she said.

'It's Rees and Francis at it,' Val said.

She was in no way comforted by his tolerant smile.

'We simply never have a chance to be alone,' Amy said. 'How can we ever learn to understand each other?'

She looked around Mrs. Perrin's sitting-room with open distaste.

'We shouldn't be in here anyway,' she said. 'How can I . . . ?'

She struggled to her feet. He looked up at her trying to fathom her sudden change of mood. She was looking for her overcoat and scarf. He wanted her to stay.

'Amy. Listen.'

He managed to take her in his arms.

'Never mind about this room. Never mind about this house. We love each other. That's wonderful. That gives us such enormous strength. Shall I tell you something?'

In spite of her discontent she became conscious of the strength of emotion that was sweeping through him. She allowed her body to lie as close as it could to his as she absorbed the mystery that was possessing him.

'You,' Val was saying. 'You are the source, the centre . . . Do you know what I mean? It's you . . . you . . . you.'

He held her so tightly, she gasped for breath.

'Together we have great strength, Amy,' he said. 'That should give us patience.'

As they were kissing, they heard Cilydd's voice calling downstairs. Amy stroked Val's hair affectionately. She seemed to want to show she was learning to be patient. With the tip of his finger he gently traced the shell-like contour of her ear, before opening the door and calling Cilydd upstairs. He arrived in the doorway with a bundle under his arm tied in string. He wore a blue belted mackintosh. There was a mischievous smile on his face. He showed no surprise at seeing Amy. He held up the bundle as a pleasant gift he wanted them to share.

'Propaganda,' he said.

He enjoyed the sound of the word. He held the bundle up so that he could read the headlines of the first leaflet.

'*Simple facts that every Cymro should know.* I like that,' he said. 'It's like a line of poetry. The typeface is a bit old fashioned but it's the message that counts. Powerful stuff. "There are more unemployed in Wales than anywhere else in the United Kingdom. More people die of consumption in Wales than in any other country in Europe"... and so on. Rhythmically expressed in strong, simple language.'

Val was laughing at him affectionately.

'Cilydd,' he said. 'You sound positively optimistic.'

Cilydd showed that he himself was mildly surprised at his own condition.

'Well, in a funny way I am. It's been one of those days, you know. Something terribly simple started it off. A ridiculous little calculation. Do you know that there isn't a single poet or writer in our language – of any importance I mean now, and not addled old relics from the last century – who is not part of the New Movement. Now I find that very encouraging.'

'It is,' Val said. 'Of course it is. Very significant and encouraging.'

'And these leaflets. Leaflets are leaves. And leaves herald a new spring. Branches are spreading all over the country. It could happen. There is a possibility of a great awakening.'

'Of course there is,' Val said.

In spite of herself Amy was beginning to share in the men's

enthusiasm. Shyly she let her hand touch Val's even though Cilydd was looking.

'The thing is,' Cilydd said. 'The exciting thing is, we are not alone. Do you know what I mean?'

'Give me some of those,' Amy said. 'They've got to be distributed.'

Cilydd was unable to stop talking.

'We live in stirring times,' he said. 'I've been thinking about it all day. In a sense the armed struggle has begun. And these are the most powerful weapons. Tiny little words.'

He held up the bundle with both hands.

8

The students struggled cheerfully up the broad footpath high above the coastline. The women were in front, bending forward to take advantage of the protection of the slope in order to continue talking to each other against the wind. The men were inclined to make a more leisurely progress. Haydn Hughes-Jefferies was conspicuous because he continued to smoke a pipe, turning his back to the wind to do so. He stopped frequently to emphasise the point he wished to make with the stem of his pipe and there were always enough men glad to take a brief rest and listen to the contest between his senatorial discourse and the wind from the sea.

Frank Yoreth detached himself from the men and raced against the wind to catch up with the women. He performed a series of antics on the path to attract their attention, but the wind swept the sound of his efforts away. The women heard nothing. Gwenda was distinctively dressed in a blue cloak. The hood slipped back as she brought her face closer to Enid's to make herself heard.

'I'm not denying the importance of the language issue,' she said. 'You know that. But there must be a measure of popular support, mustn't there? That's the point I'm making.'

Mabli moved closer to catch whatever Gwenda and Enid were saying. She wore a new woollen cap. It was red with a white bobble on the top. The cap was a visible symbol of her freshly-won self-assurance and it was pleasing to her fellow students.

'You can't wait for ever for popular support!'

Mabli raised her voice to a shout to make herself heard. Gwenda and Enid smiled at her understandingly.

'You have to give a lead,' she said. 'It's the same in every sphere of life, I think. But I don't want to generalise.'

With a wild yell, Frank Yoreth plunged through the group of girls. Some were so startled they ran off the path into the heather. With surprising skill, Frankie spun on his heel to turn his back on the wind and pretend to float up the hill. He tacked upwards on tip-toe holding down his hair with both hands while the strengthening wind thrust out his wide trousers into barrels of fluttering cloth.

'Frankie, you clown!'

Gwenda shouted after him and he tilted his head to one side to show his gratitude for the compliment. The attention of the girls stimulated him to greater exertion. He began to make a cackling noise, advancing and retreating as the girls walked towards him.

'What is he?' Mabli cried. 'Mother Goose? Or Father Gander?'

The girls who heard her applauded. Gwenda concentrated her attention on Frankie. He bowed and scraped in front of them all to begin with and then gave Gwenda his particular attention before dancing backwards up the path.

'Frankie,' Mabli said. 'Mind you don't go over the edge!'

He floated down again to Gwenda.

'You clown,' she said. 'You silly clown.'

There was affection as well as rebuke in her voice.

'That's what we all are,' Enid said.

'What?'

Mabli frowned and leaned closer to Enid to show she had not heard.

'What did you say?'

'Clowns on the edge of the world.'

Enid squinted up at the clouds as they tumbled into each other, fleeing before the wind. The path spread up before

them, parallel with the edge of the cliff above the rocky shore.
A vast expanse of shifting sea stretched to the horizon.

Because they had stopped to watch Frankie, the men
caught up with them. Haydn Hughes-Jefferies stood behind
Gwenda and inclined his long torso forward to speak in her
ear. Even his confidences were deliberate and statesmanlike.

'This is all for your benefit, Miss Gethin. I do hope you
realise that?'

He had to smile broadly to underline the fact that he was
being particularly friendly. He turned to Enid to seek
information.

'I wanted to ask you,' he said. 'Where is Amy Parry this
afternoon? I would have thought she would have been
interested. As a noted reformer.'

He smiled again to indicate that the sarcasm was
humorously intended. Enid ignored his question. She
continued to watch Frankie. He had let go the cherished
waves of his hair to stretch out his arms and lean further back
against the wind in order to perform a grotesque dance,
displaying as much as he could of his soles and heels to the
audience below him.

'We've been discussing this business,' Haydn said.

He was confident his deep voice was audible to all the
women.

'And the general feeling was that we ask for an emergency
meeting and put forward a motion of no confidence in the
Pres. of S.R.C. That was the general feeling.'

He shaped his utterance with care to sound fair-minded,
reasonable, modest and statesmanlike.

'I don't know whether you ladies agree?'

He waited for an answer. Some of the girls were already
glancing at each other and nodding approvingly. It was
enough that he should seek their approbation for them to
give it him.

'It's all so trivial,' Enid said.

'I beg your pardon?'

Haydn looked surprised and shocked. He stared at Mabli
as though expecting some sign of support from her. Mabli
grinned happily and left him to defend himself.

'What can it possibly matter?'

There seemed no limit to the depths of Enid's gloom.

241

'It does matter. It does matter. It certainly does matter.'

Haydn repeated himself to fan the embers of righteous indignation and gather support from the men standing behind him.

'It has been established beyond dispute that the Pres. of S.R.C. claimed expenses for attending a conference that he never in fact attended! Now apart from the questions of elementary morality, the point we are making surely is that the President should respond responsibly to the high office he holds. Isn't that so, men?'

'High office.'

Enid repeated the two words with open contempt.

'Well, of course it is.'

Haydn stood high above Enid, his eyebrows and the stem of his pipe raised.

'It's our Representative Council and he is our President. He should behave at all times with strict constitutional propriety. We knew he was inclined to be a dictator. We now know that he is dishonest as well. It's up to us to put things right, Miss Prydderch. As senior students. And it is our democratic duty.'

Enid turned to face him, stepping up the path so that he should not use his height to tower above her. The wind blew the ends of her scarf like battle pennons on either side of her head.

'Your nation is bleeding to death,' she said. 'Don't you ever think about that?'

'Oh, come now . . .'

Haydn used the deepest tone of his fine voice and smiled at her tolerantly.

'That's putting it a bit melodramatically, don't you think?'

He glanced behind him for friendly support.

'Not by any means. You listen to me. The young people are leaving the valleys at the rate of hundreds a week . . .'

'According to your leaflets.'

Haydn underlined his interjection with an understanding smile.

'According to published statistics! People going away is a social haemorrhage.'

'Didn't I read that phrase in *Dadeni*?'

'That doesn't make it any less true.'

Frankie stopped his dance. He fluttered down the path to get close enough to hear the argument. All the students were glad of a diversion and ready to listen.

'Examine yourself.'

Enid was full of confidence in the strength of her convictions.

'You want to impeach our smirking self-satisfied, self-seeking, self-infatuated President of S.R.C. Am I right?'

'Impeach.'

Haydn showed that he found the word outlandish and exaggerated.

'Now let me tell you why. So that you can be elected in his place and become the self-satisfied, self-seeking, self-infatuated President of S.R.C. yourself.'

There were murmurs of protest from some of the men.

Haydn looked dumbfounded and hurt.

'A personal attack,' he said. 'That's not an argument. That's a personal attack.'

Enid was in no way deterred by the growing sympathy the men were showing for Haydn.

'I'm using you as an example,' she said. 'This is what we are reduced to. The dregs of a dying nation is a breeding ground for self-seeking, self-infatuated, ambitious men. And that's why I say this college is decadent. Absolutely decadent. Because it's full of them.'

A roar of protest went up from the men.

'That's disloyal. That's disloyal if anything is.'

Haydn seized on the accusation and turned around to seek more support.

'Go on, Haydn boy! You give it to her!'

'Disloyal to the student body,' Haydn said. 'The finest society of young men and women that I know of.'

'Hear! Hear!'

'Disloyal to the Col. spirit. Disloyal to S.R.C. Disloyal to all sorts of things.'

He swelled his chest in triumph. Enid was walking away. She looked defeated. Mabli hurried after her to give her some comfort and Gwenda followed them. When he saw Gwenda move, Frankie swept up the hill again intent on drawing attention to himself. He held out his arms when he reached high enough ground and prepared to repeat his dance.

'Watch me, my dears!'

He called out in a mock-effeminate voice.

'I'm going to be self-indulgent and decadent.'

He found their laughter enough reward. Even Enid was smiling. He angled his body back, made his peculiar cackling noise and prepared to excel himself. In the middle of his performance there was a fractional lull in the wind. He collapsed on his back in the heather, his heels kicking in the air. Hooting and yelling with pretended fear and helplessness he rolled down the slope towards the cliff edge. Some of the women screamed. He came to rest in a patch of bracken already brown in its exposed position. Male students on the path waved large gestures of farewell and encouraged him to roll right over the cliff. They cupped their hands around their mouths and shouted against the wind like supporters at a football match.

'Go on, Frankie boy! Finish it off! Roll over the edge!'

Frankie's white arms shot up out of his sleeves as he graphically mimed the clutching of an invisible rope. There were cheers from the path as he struggled dramatically back up the slope.

'Should we help him do you think?' Mabli said.

Gwenda laughed and shook her head.

'He can look after himself,' she said. 'He's not such a fool as he looks. Come on, girls. I'm cold enough in this cloak. You must be perishing.'

They struggled on, kept warm by their exertions. When they reached the summit they could no longer talk or sing. They were buffeted by a wind that seemed to have taken charge of the world. Gasping for breath Gwenda pointed at the great clouds massing on the western horizon. She spoke but they didn't hear her. There was a black mouth to the clouds that looked large enough to swallow all the waters of the bay, and the light that moved on the water seemed an expression of foreboding in itself. Immediately below them the seaside town looked brave but vulnerable. A shaft of pale sunlight touched the end of the fragile curve of promenade and the brief shelving of pebble beach. The girls moved down the path to regain their breath. Mabli swallowed hard and drew their attention to the Hall of Residence, the last building at the north end of the promenade below them.

244

'Look!'

There were tiny figures of men sandbagging the front entrance and boarding up the ground floor windows. Already the waves were riding full tilt against the first defence of rocks, their energy exploding in wild fountains of white spray. Gwenda was moved to use her blue cloak and make dramatic gestures towards the sea. She recited Seithenyn's speech at the top of her voice.

'"The walls are ready, let the tempest roar
Let the sea send its insane spray to the gates of heaven
I shall not fear . . ."'

While she was still reciting they were swept aside by the men who had suddenly taken it into their heads to race back to College. As they shot past, the faces of the front runners were already set in expressions of childish determination. There were others a little more relaxed. But all were transfixed with delight at the prospect of complete physical exertion. Frankie brought up the rear. Because he had no hope of winning he concentrated on a fresh exhibition of eccentric movement, hopping and skipping, zig-zagging from one side of the path to the other as he descended. The runners soon spread out. The three girls hurried down to follow the race. They saw the leaders leap like deer across a narrow chasm in order to take the shortest and most direct route to the promenade.

'Children,' Mabli said. 'That's all they are.'

There was a note of maternal fondness in her voice. Her face glowed with sympathy and understanding.

'It brings my dream back,' Enid said.

They both looked expectantly at her.

'There were green waves rolling over and over full of seaweed. They kept rising and coming closer. Then I saw the water was full of dead men, rolling over and over. And the waves kept growing bigger and bigger, threatening to engulf the whole world.'

'Um . . .'

Gwenda nodded understandingly.

'That ghastly War film, I expect. I don't know that we should have gone to see it. I had bad dreams too.'

'I'm glad I went,' Mabli said. 'I tell you what effect it had on me. It reinforced my pacifism. Absolutely.'

"You and your "isms".'

Gwenda nudged her playfully.

'I do think films are bad though, in a way,' she said. 'I mean, it's not a true picture of the world as it is. It's all distortion surely. And trickery. I mean it's the fashion to think it is the coming art form. I'm not so sure. Theo certainly doesn't think so.'

The runners were sprinting across the promenade. The men sandbagging the Hall of Residence stopped work to watch them.

'They just love a bit of notice,' Mabli said. 'Children. That's all they are.'

'They're men too.'

Enid was unrelentingly gloomy.

'Old enough to die in a war if there was another war. If the Imperial trumpet blew this minute they would be off. Every jack one of them. And yet not one of them would lift a finger for their own nation. Not one of them.'

9

Gwenda's study bedroom was crowded with young women. Most of them were in dressing-gowns. They made themselves as comfortable as they could. They sipped hot milk and tried to talk but it was no longer a party. The ominous roar outside brought them together for comfort. When one of them began to talk about the sinking of the *Titanic* she was told to shut up by those sitting next to her. One short girl with spectacles and her hair in curlers had perched herself on top of the heavy wardrobe. She had a book in one hand and a tin mug in the other. The mug was empty but she went on sipping it as she listened to the sea. Amy tried to draw her attention. The girl refused to take her eyes off her book. Amy was wearing an overcoat and her scarf lay doubled over her right shoulder. A nervous girl in pigtails held a cup with both hands and spoke loudly into Amy's face.

'What I'd like to know, Amy Parry, is just why does everything in this place have to be politics all the time.'

The effort was too much for her. She sank back to her knees and crawled towards Gwenda who was crouched down heating more milk over her little fire. The girl in pigtails tapped her on the backside with her cup.

'Haven't you already had some?'

The girl held out her cup without answering.

'Oh, never mind.'

Sipping the milk restored the girl's strength. She tackled Amy again.

'What a time to organise a protest,' she said. 'Putting all our lives in danger. Refusing to do fire drill because it's organised in English. It's mad!'

'Why did you take part then?'

'Because everybody else was doing it.'

The girl sank back to the floor on the verge of tears.

'The waves were thirty feet high at least!'

Mabli stretched her long arms to illustrate the height of the waves. The girl on top of the wardrobe glanced at her briefly, shuddered and returned her attention to her book.

'The men brought us home to the back entrance. The sea was coming down the side streets. It was terrible.'

The talking stopped suddenly as they all listened to a rumbling boom that seemed different from what they had heard before. Gwenda's room was at the rear of the building on the second floor. All the front rooms had been evacuated. The granite face of the building and half its width was their protection from the raging sea. More of them sank to the floor facing the attack of sound as though it was no longer practicable to stand. Their eyes widened as they listened and strained to interpret the significance of the smallest variation in the endless concatenation of thunderous noise. A large girl squatting on the floor rolled her eyes and whispered her question.

'What time's high tide? That's what I'd like to know.'

She was glared at for asking what they all wanted to know. The girl in pigtails resumed her attack on Amy.

'You know what I think?'

Mabli bent down in her kindly way to see if she could help.

'What's the matter, Ella?'

'I think she's mad.'

The girl had found the strength to look defiantly at Amy.

'Talking about building a spiritual dyke to keep out the language of the machine. That's what I call it. Mad.'

Mabli patted her comfortingly on the back. It only made her more incensed.

'How is that ever going to be done? In the modern world. Just tell me that?'

'Have some more milk,' Mabli said in a soothing voice.

'What time's high tide? Doesn't anybody know.'

There was a note of desperate pleading in the voice from the floor. Amy looked down.

'Now,' she said.

'Now?'

The girl crawled on her hands and knees closer to the door.

'You've got to wait.'

The others vied with each other to keep her in order.

'When the bell goes, that's the evacuation – like the fire drill.'

'At high tide the prom will collapse. It happened before.'

The girl was in near panic.

'And if the prom collapses, this place will collapse.'

As they looked at the trembling girl by the door a cascade of sea water came plunging down the chimney blotting out Gwenda's fire. The girls nearest the fireplace jumped back screaming. A pool of black water spread out, sweeping hissing cinders into the room. Several girls rushed into the corridor, talking and shouting. Amy pushed her way through them.

She found the front corridor in darkness. She began to call out Enid's name before she reached her door. The roar of the waves was so great Amy could barely hear her own voice. She found Enid sitting on the floor with her back against the inside wall. She was wearing her overcoat with a scarf tied tightly around her head. Her knees were gathered in her arms as she listened intently to the awesome noise of the storm. To speak to her Amy herself sat by her side, placing her lips close to Enid's ear.

'Are you trying to hear the bells? *Cantre'r Gwaelod?*'

Enid smiled.

'You've got to come away from here. It's dangerous.'

Enid placed her arm over Amy's shoulder. Together they listened with hypnotised fascination to the pounding of the waves against the narrow bastion of promenade. She moved her head closer to Amy's so that she could speak to her.

'This is my protest,' Enid said. 'I'm not leaving.'

'Oh no ... But listen ...'

As Amy tried to speak the whole building shook and the single centre light went out. In the dark they felt for each other's hands and grasped them tightly. Together they bent forward in a posture that was almost embryonic. The pounding of the waves was the earth turning. They could still live if they remained still and passive, rolling over and over, like winged seeds wrapped in the centre of a whirlwind. Outside they must have known the giant breakers were tearing hungrily at the sea wall. A cosmic appetite let loose the sea would consume villages and cities. Nothing could resist it. Great coping stones and rocks like pyramids would be picked up and hurled like childish missiles at all the habitations of man. Only when all the fortress was down would the exhausted sea lap its tongue lazily among the rubble: and if they preserved their stillness they could still be washed up alive on another shore ... Their trance was broken by the strident ringing of the firebell in the empty corridor. Amy jumped to her feet.

'Come on! They are evacuating the building.'

She bent down to hear what Enid was saying in the darkness.

'You go,' she said.

'Go! How can I go without you?'

'I've said I'm staying here until I get instructions in my own language.'

'Enid. Come on. Don't be unreasonable. It's dangerous. They're evacuating the whole building. It must be very dangerous or they wouldn't do it.'

'You go. I've made up my mind.'

Amy found herself alone in the dark corridor. With her arms outstretched she moved forward carefully towards the main staircase. At the top of the stairs she turned to look back into the darkness, as though she hoped that Enid was following her. She called out her name. Her cry was drowned in the implacable roar of the sea.

On the lower floors there was light from the storm lamps that had been placed at intervals to make movement towards the rear of the building possible. The matron, the bursar and other members of the staff of the Hall of Residence were moving up and down the rows of young women, providing them with red blankets and ground sheets. Further down Miss Wade could be heard calmly issuing her orders. She stood in a raised position and looked impressive in the flickering light.

'The roll call will be taken as you file through the covered way. Is that clear?'

Her voice rang out with the clarity of a bell. When she spoke the young women stopped whispering and listened to her with rapt attention.

'The first-year students leave first, proceeding in an orderly fashion to the Church Hall where Miss Hughes and Miss Buller are already prepared to receive them. Protect yourselves with your hoods and your groundsheets like the Tommies did on the Western Front. And try to keep your blankets dry.'

Amy waited impatiently for the Warden to finish speaking. She was standing on a crate to get a better view of the first year girls lined up on the left side of the corridor.

'Yes, Miss Parry. What is it?'

'Enid Prydderch is still in her room. On B corridor.'

'For heaven's sake ... That was evacuated two hours ago! Get her down here at once.'

Amy was embarrassed.

'She won't move until she gets instructions in her native language.'

The Warden stepped down from the crate. She stared angrily at Amy's face.

'This is too ridiculous,' she said. 'At a time like this.'

Her voice was lowered. As few persons as possible should be aware of her dilemma.

'Miss Hughes is already at the Church Hall.'

She brought her face closer to Amy's and whispered fiercely.

'Your friend is a very stupid, selfish girl. I hope you realise that.'

Amy licked her lips. Her throat seemed too dry for speech.

Miss Wade left her for a moment to confer with the bursar and the matron. The evacuation was set in motion. The first-year women began to file out into the covered way.

'Come with me.'

Miss Wade had a bicycle battery torch stuck on her belt. In her hand she carried a storm lantern. Amy hurried after her. Together they ran up the stairway and down the dark deserted corridors.

'I don't know what you think about this, Miss Parry.'

The Warden could have been talking to herself. Amy made no attempt to speak.

'I thought you and I had come to some understanding ... I thought you appreciated my position. I am literally responsible for over two hundred lives ... Where is she?'

Amy pointed down B corridor to the door of Enid's room. Communication was difficult. They ran down the corridor and burst into Enid's room. The lamplight fell on her pale face. She still sat on the floor with her back to the inside wall. Beyond the shuttered windows the wind howled above the crashing boom of the raging tide. It seemed as though the sea wall and the promenade could not hold out much longer. Then nothing would stand between the sea and the building that would remain the unprotected target of its concentrated destructive power.

'Get up! This minute!'

Miss Wade was obliged to scream to make herself heard.

'You heard the bell. The building is being evacuated.'

Enid stared in front of her. She was refusing to understand.

'I am concerned with the safety and well-being of every single one of my students. I am ...'

Enid raised her arm suddenly and pointed accusingly at the Warden. She spoke but her voice was inaudible against the noise of the storm. Amy knelt down on one knee to hear what Enid was saying.

'Tell her I am quite prepared to die for what I believe in. Tell her I am prepared to die for my identity.'

'Enid ... don't be so extreme.'

Amy tried to speak to her friend in confidence. The noise outside allowed no such subtlety. Enid's eyes were glittering with fierce determination in the lamplight.

'Tell her she can kill me if she likes. I don't care.'

Amy rose to her feet and moved closer to the Warden.

'She won't move,' Amy said. 'Not until she gets the order in Welsh.'

'But Miss Hughes is in the Church Hall,' the Warden said. 'I've already explained that.'

Miss Wade looked down at Enid with desperate distaste.

'I wish to goodness I could leave her here. It's what she deserves.'

Enid was speaking again, her arm stretched out to indicate it was the Warden she was talking about. Whatever she was saying was too elaborate and detailed for Amy to follow. She did not kneel down this time to listen. Instead she spoke to the Warden.

'Give me the order,' she said. 'And I shall translate it.'

'Good heavens, Parry. This is too ridiculous. I've never met anything so absurd in my whole life.'

'Give me the order. Kneel down so that she can hear you.'

Together they knelt on either side of the girl sitting on the floor with her back to the wall. Solemnly the Warden issued her orders. As quickly as she could Amy translated them. When she was satisfied, Enid allowed them both to help her to her feet.

10

Val and Amy were walking side by side when she stopped to stare into a ditch filled with water. It glistened in the sunlight and mirrored the straggling hedgerow above it. Amy could make out her own blurred reflection.

'I let her down,' she said.

Val waited patiently for her to say more. After the great storm the grass was greener and the sky was blue, embellished with a flourish of high white cloud. A robin no more than a few yards away, balanced on a trembling briar, was ready to sing. Val looked admiringly into the blue of her troubled eyes.

'I was the one that wanted to leave, and she's the one that's gone,' Amy said. 'Isn't that ironic?'

'I don't think she will be sent down,' Val said. 'Suspended. Not sent down.'

'She'll never come back.'

Amy seemed to take gloomy satisfaction in the finality of her pronouncement.

'She'll get married.'

'Good Lord!'

Val sounded shocked and surprised. They walked on. He was anxious to hear more.

'All that fuss and bother.'

Amy was cross and discontented.

'The buildings were never in any real danger. The damage looks much worse than it really is. And to think I've got to go back and put up with it all. She looked as happy as anything going off in the train.'

'Does John Cilydd know?'

Amy cheered up a little.

'I shouldn't think so,' she said. 'She'll probably write him one of her long letters.'

Val looked a little confused.

'I've always been impressed by Enid's moderation,' he said. 'She has a very good mind.'

'It really is ironic,' Amy said. 'She more or less ordered me to stay put. "Think of your uncle and aunt," she said. "You simply must get your degree." I mean that's absolutely typical. I don't know why I should feel so guilty. All I did was give way to common sense. We can't all afford to be relentlessly logical.'

'You'll miss her.'

Val stated the obvious apologetically. In the bright sunlight everything appeared more visible than it had ever been before. The tops of the stones in the lane were bleached and dry while their sides were wet in the mud. They both gave close attention to where they put their feet.

'The librarian has turned nasty,' Val said. 'Wants me to go at the end of the month.'

'Oh no.'

Amy stood still, balanced on a dry stone, her face white with outrage.

'The swine,' she said. 'The nasty swine. And what about that mighty gnome? Your great protector. Sir P.O.P. Oh they can't do it! Surely they can't. Can they, Val?'

From her position on the stone Amy was confronted with a patch of water and mud. She became more helpless than usual. Glad to take action Val picked her up. He was wearing heavy farm boots and not over-troubled where he put his feet. He was happy to carry her. He snatched a kiss against her cold cheek. He put her down at the opening of the farm road that led to Glygyrog Fawr. The name had been painted in crude white letters on a boulder alongside the tilted slate gatepost. A narrow ridge of green turf down the centre of the lane offered them a pleasant path to walk on between the reed filled ditches and the dry stone walls.

'I'll go to the settlement,' Val said quietly.

'What settlement?'

Amy was instantly prickly.

'Anyway the key to the future is the south-east,' Val said. 'We've got to face that. The coalfield in particular.'

'What settlement?'

'I'm not a Quaker, but that doesn't matter. I can keep body and soul together lecturing for the W.E.A.'

'It's all settled,' Amy said. 'You've worked it all out, I see.'

'It's the place to be,' Val said. 'I'm certain of it. It's where the struggle will be won or lost. I've believed that for some time. Of course in a stable society agriculture should be on the main basis of an economy. But we are not living in stable times or in a stable economy. We have to deal with the situation as we find it.'

He had been speaking for some time before he became aware of Amy's profound silence. He waited for her to speak. She said nothing. The gurgle of water in the ditch seemed unnaturally loud. She was biting her lower lip. In the absence of any comment he could only continue.

'John Cilydd calls it a conspiracy.'

Val laughed half-heartedly.

'I don't take that view myself. He says Iscoed has got it in for me since I published that bit about him having more in his pocket than in his head. Funny isn't he? People often don't mind being called evil or wicked. But you call them stupid and they get hopping mad.'

He paused hopefully for her to show she shared his appreciation of the vagaries of human nature. She stared stonily ahead of her.

'I suppose it is possible that he could have got at Professor Williams in some way. Cilydd says Williams has a secret daily bulletin on the state of the Principal's health. He reckons that's why Williams has changed his tune with me. He still has hopes of succession. Which is absurd because the man is not far from retiring age. Cilydd says the flame of a lifelong ambition is still burning in the old boy's breast. It is possible of course. Although I must say I do find it difficult to accept that grown men can behave so childishly.'

Val began to laugh but he restrained himself when he saw how unhappy Amy looked.

'What's the matter?'

'Oh nothing. Absolutely nothing. Nothing at all.'

She began running as though she could not bear to be near him another second. He stood still for a while too puzzled to move. Then he hurried up the lane to catch up with her. He was confronted by a wide patch of mud and water. It was even bigger than the one that confronted them earlier, but this time Amy had fled across and vanished out of sight. There were stones here and there that she must have used, but no trace of her passing. She had gone with the speed and sure-footed grace of a gazelle. Val plunged forward, clearly determined to catch her and careless of where he put his feet. Mud splashed over his trousers. Nothing seemed to matter except her pursuit and capture. She had looked at him with such clear-eyed coolness before she left his side it was as if his entire existence had suddenly been called into question.

The hedge on his right came to an end in a series of stony mounds. In the field beyond stood a well-constructed stone barn. From the distance it could have been mistaken for a stern, ancient, isolated place of worship. The long slate roof had dried after the storm and was shining in the morning sunlight. It was surrounded on the west side by an irregular semi-circle of trees. The largest tree had been blown over by the storm. The great root ends, and the stony soil they had snatched up with them, clawed upwards at the open sky. Black cattle stood near like spectators unable to leave the scene of a disaster, awestruck by the strangeness of the sight.

The massive trunk lay across the approach to the main door of the barn. The topmost branches had fallen within inches of the gable end. Both halves of the door were open at different angles. It was obvious that Amy had gone inside. Val ran forward until he reached the hole in the ground created by the uprooted tree. It was several feet deep and almost full of water after the storm. His attention was taken by a slithery track from the edge of the water to the hard surface where he stood. The sunlight was glittering on strands of metal sticking out of the mud. One piece curved like the arm of a spectacle frame where it goes over the ear. He was torn between his desire to investigate and his concern for Amy. He stood still and called out her name. There was no reply.

Inside the barn he stood on the flagstones of the threshing floor. Opposite the door he had entered was another oak door, both halves firmly closed with heavy oak latches. To his left straw was piled as high as the rafters. To his right, the hay had settled to a lower level. A wooden partition created a narrow passage past the hay to a cattle stall used only in the depth of winter. The yearlings and young store cattle, entering by a gable door, could feed from wooden racks easily filled with hay.

'Amy!'

He called her name again. He climbed the hay ladder to discover where she was hiding. He found her looking down into a nook that had been formed between the hay and the wooden partition. There was a clear impression of where a body had lain in sleep. Near the sleeping hole, there was a pair of shoes without laces, a blue jacket and a white muffler and a turnip watch with a chain all neatly laid out on old newspaper.

'There's someone living here.'

Amy whispered as if she were afraid of being overheard. She turned on her side in the hay to look at Val, her eyes wide with wonder.

'Is it a tramp, do you think?'

She sounded a little afraid. He smiled at her comfortingly. His smile seemed to remind her that she was cross with him. She rolled away from him.

'Somebody out of work,' Val said. 'A miner I think.'

His loud voice would betray their hiding place. She frowned her disapproval.

'How can you possibly tell?'

'I could be wrong. But they do favour white mufflers.'

Amy stretched herself forward to study the hole again.

'And he's made this his home,' she said. 'It doesn't look too bad.'

She placed her fists under her chin.

'People don't need all that much,' she said. 'When you come down to it. To be warm and dry. And have somewhere to sleep. And a little bit of something to eat. We make our lives too complicated.'

He did not venture to disagree with her.

'I wouldn't mind changing places with him,' Amy said.

She tried to show she was being defiantly realistic rather than fanciful or romantic.

'Better than spending another year in that miserable prison. And no one with me. No one at all.'

She was suddenly overwhelmed with pity for herself.

'I don't think I can face it.'

Val shifted along the hay to be nearer to her. He stretched out his hand to touch her hair. Amy was ready to be comforted. He came closer to her.

'It's unnatural to worry about money as much as we have to. It's utterly unnatural. And it's so unfair. I seem to have been doing it all my life. Why can't we forget all these problems we worry about sometimes and just be ourselves?'

Her appeal was irresistible. She was closing her eyes.

'I'm so tired,' she said. 'We hardly slept at all last night. All the hubbub and fuss. It was like the end of the world.'

Her eyes opened and she saw his face was close to hers.

'And that's just what it's turning out to be!'

She spoke in a fresh spurt of anger. It was the flame of a dying fire quickly put out by a rise in the level of self-pity.

'The end of my world anyway,' she said. 'Enid has gone. Just disappeared. And now you're going. And I'm the only one left. All by myself. It's too bad. Really it is.'

She closed her eyes again. With great tenderness he kissed her on the lips.

'Listen, Amy.'

He spoke softly in her ear.

'We've chosen each other. We've made our design. We must trust each other and everything will be alright. I'm sure of it.'

'You're not in love with me.'

She spoke so softly he could barely hear her.

'You're in love with a ghost country that you imagine exists behind this one. I remember Enid saying that a long time ago. Trying to explain to her stupid friend that you were a man with a mission. The man with a single voice.'

'Amy. Listen.'

He paused while he considered what exactly he should say.

'I'm listening.'

There was a note of mock-patience in her voice.

'I thought we understood each other. It's not easy. The task that lies ahead.'

'It would be a lot easier if we were together. I'm quite sure about that.'

It was warm in the hay. Amy unbuttoned her overcoat. Val was leaning over her respectfully. She raised her hands and passed them around his neck.

'Together. Like we are now.'

She opened her eyes to look into his.

'Lie on me,' she said.

He lay on her with great care as if he were afraid to crush her with his weight.

'I'm not made of glass,' she said. 'I won't break, Val Gwyn. I won't break at all.'

He struggled out of his overcoat. She held her hands about his neck as though she were unwilling ever to let go of him. She was making a conscious effort to overcome her own shyness and modesty.

'New life.'

She murmured with her eyes closed.

'New life begins like this. I don't care if you take me. It's what I want. It really is.'

His hands were already touching the soft warmth of her naked skin, when he pulled himself up, his head bent under the pressure of her hands still clasped tightly around his neck. He was moaning as if in pain and muttering her name. When she heard the noise he was making, her hands fell away from his neck. Her arms spread out on the hay and she stared at him with cold curiosity, not caring about the partial nakedness of the lower half of her own body.

'If you want to be so good,' she said, 'you shouldn't have anything to do with women.'

'Don't.'

He put his hand in front of his face as though he were trying to ward off a blow.

'You should be some kind of monk and dedicate yourself to the service of your country. Found settlements all over the place. That's what you should do.'

'Amy...'

He was begging her to spare him.

'If that's what you care about so much, that's what you should do.'

He bent his head submissively as if he were inviting her to rain blows on it: whatever punishment she meted out he would accept.

'Amy... I'm twenty-seven years old and I've got nothing. I've got no right... no right to...'

'You worry too much.'

She pushed him aside so that she could dress herself. She was angry with herself and with him.

'And you want too much.'

'What do you mean?'

His face was pale and his breath was short like a man running away from some nameless threat in a dream.

'For instance if you want to enjoy the luxury of regularly offending all the important people, why don't you settle at home on the farm? Of course I know your mother wouldn't want me there. But then perhaps you don't want me anywhere.'

She sat up and began to brush her sleeves. Awkwardly he shifted around on his knees so that he could touch her head and stroke her hair. She tossed her head petulantly but he continued to remove bits of hay from her golden curls.

'I don't know what it is that drives me,' he said.

He spoke more freely because he had moved behind her and she could not see his face.

'Some kind of honour I suppose. I know it's honour that forces me to respect you. To suppress my natural impulses. Because I believe our lives have a purpose.'

259

'That's nice.'

He overlooked her irony.

'I'm not selfish. I mean, I try not to be selfish. But I have this sense of mission. I thought you understood that.'

'Oh yes, I do. Indeed I do. What I didn't understand was that there was no part for me in it.'

'Amy! That's unfair. And it's cruel. How could I take you down there to live on nothing? What would they say if I made you leave the university without a degree?'

'They? Who are "they"?'

Val sank down with a groan to lie helplessly in the hay.

'I want to make you happy. I want to be responsible,' he said. 'And all I've got is some kind of mental paralysis.'

He lay still and quiet like a man on a sick bed. At last Amy began to show him some sympathy. She moved to sit nearer to him. She drew up her knees and rubbed them thoughtfully with her chin.

'I don't know,' she said. 'We think we know what's right. We want to control our lives. But we never seem to do what we want to do. Why is that, Val?'

She was encouraged by his inability to answer.

'You know, sometimes I feel that every little thing I do just helps to drive me in the direction I really don't want to go. I saw a monkey once in the Marine Lake. They laid out tit-bits for him. So whatever way he went he always ended up back in his cage. Is that what we are, do you think? A couple of monkeys?'

Amy was laughing, pleased with her notion. She drew out a length of dried grass and used it to tickle Val under his ear.

'That's all you are, Mr. Gwyn. A political monkey. And I'm tickling your body politic. And you've just got to put up with it.'

Val sat up. He smiled and shook his head with bewildered admiration.

'You mustn't tease me,' he said.

'I shouldn't, should I? You are even more innocent than I am.'

'I'm still not on an even keel. I could suddenly go berserk and then goodness knows what would happen.'

He took her in his arms and she giggled gratefully as she snuggled against him.

'Perhaps you are right,' he said. 'Perhaps we should give way, and follow our natural impulses. And take the consequences.'

'Too late now,' Amy said. 'I've woken up. You've lost your chance, old man.'

Fondly they began to kiss each other and sank back comfortably into the hay.

'I trust you, Val Gwyn.'

Amy was whispering to him.

'That's what love is, I think. That's what it's got to be. Patience and trust. Learning to wait. We could lie still like this for ever. For a hundred years. Under a coverlet of cobwebs.'

They were content to lie in a silence that excluded the whole world. They spread their hands so that all their finger tips touched in ten guarantees of peace and passivity. Amy's eyes closed. Her breathing drifted into sleep and he was content to watch her with the fondness of a parent who watches a child sleeping peacefully after the crisis of an illness. Quietly he moved his face close enough so that his lips could touch her eyelids without forcing them to open. She murmured comfortably. The barn was so silent he could hear the feet of mice scuttling across the threshing floor.

Their private peace was disturbed by the squeak and rattle of a farm wagon and voices approaching the barn. Amy's eyes opened in sudden panic.

'Oh my goodness . . . We're caught!'

Her face was already red with embarrassment and shame. Val was less concerned. He held his head to one side and listened intently to the voices. The wagon stopped on the hard surface some distance away. The voices of two men approaching the barn grew louder.

'Oh my goodness . . . Val . . . they're coming in here.'

Amy's whole instinct was to hide. She burrowed more deeply into the hay. Val stayed still and watched the figure of the little farmer enter the barn. He wore a hard hat on his head and a tweed overcoat with a short cape. His legs were bowed like a jockey's and he carried a short riding stick in his hand. He was followed by a stout police sergeant who dragged his heavy boots along the threshing floor and sighed deeply to himself at regular intervals.

'I let him sleep in here,' the farmer said.

His voice was high-pitched and querulous.

'Fair play to you,' the police sergeant said.

'As I told you he did odd jobs. As much as he could with that chest of his. We gave him something to eat every day and he made himself comfortable out here every night.'

The farmer and the police sergeant squeezed down the narrow passage that led to the cattle stall. The farmer pointed with his riding stick at the neat lair between the hay and the wooden partition.

'*Duw, duw, go dda . . .*'

The sergeant was lost in admiration of what he saw.

'Neat as a hare's form,' he said. 'Comfy as a bird's nest. Well, I never.'

'There's his things.'

The policeman did not seem over-eager to pick them up.

'Poor fellow,' he said. 'Didn't have much in this world, did he? Reader he was, too. Out of work for three years, you said.'

The farmer was immediately on the defensive.

'As I said, he had some supper in our kitchen last night. Left a bit late because of the storm. It was darker than inside a cow's belly. But he would go. And out he went. He couldn't have seen that the tree was down. He must have walked straight into that hole full of water. And too weak to get out. And he must have died of exhaustion. I dragged him out at half-past seven this morning. It was a shock, I can tell you. He was as cold as a fish. Been dead for hours. Aren't you going to collect his things?'

'Aye, aye. Aye, aye.'

The police sergeant appeared to believe that he was showing some respect for the dead man by being slow and philosophical.

'It comes to us all in the end, Mr. Griffiths. Rich and poor alike. Down we go to the last long home.'

Val moved in the hay to try and catch a glimpse of the two men below. Amy pressed the back of her hand against her mouth and sank even further out of sight.

'He's having his last ride in your cart, Mr. Griffiths, the poor dab. Stiff as a board under your soft blanket.'

'I don't see any liability on me, Jones. Do you?'

The farmer was making an unusual effort to soften his normal combative tone and be agreeable to the police sergeant.

'From the Rhondda Fach. Well, well. Well, well.'

Jones talked to himself as he entered the hole on hands and knees to collect the ex-miner's belongings.

'I've got a brother that works on the coal-face at Clydach Vale. The Cambrian. It's the dust that gets them you see. It's not a healthy job. There's quite a bit of dust here too, Griffiths bach. Should have made him feel at home, poor dab. Who cares about them in the end? That's what I say to myself. Who cares?'

'I'm not responsible, Jones. I hope you've made a note of that. I didn't ask him to come and sleep in the barn. I didn't give him permission. All I did was give him food when he came to ask for it. He didn't work for me. Not at any time. Whatever he did, he did out of gratitude for the food I gave him. And for me turning a blind eye to him sleeping in here. That's my legal position.'

The farmer was reaffirming a summary of his position. He would make it many times again.

'Nothing else here, is there?'

Griffiths was a little put out by the police sergeant's unexpected question.

'What do you mean, nothing else?'

'I don't know. Tidy fellow, wasn't he?'

Griffiths led the way down the narrow passage to the threshing floor.

'He was quite intelligent. Wouldn't go to Chapel because he didn't have the clothes. A respectable fellow. Quite bright in his Bible.'

'Dear me. Dear me.'

The police sergeant had lapsed again into philosophic sadness.

'I tell you one thing he told me.'

Griffiths stood in the doorway, his stick and his eyebrows raised as if he were about to impart a surprising confidence.

'He liked being here. Because it was as far away from the pit as he could go. He said that quite often.'

The farmer tapped his chest significantly with the riding stick and made a rasping sound.

'Do you want to close it?'

The policeman's hand was on the latch of the half-door. Val crawled forward on top of the hay to catch a last glimpse of them.

'Better do that.'

Griffiths raised his voice in the open air.

'I was in a state, Jones, when I found him in there. I couldn't believe it had happened. On my land. Do you know what I mean?'

Val struggled to his feet and moved along the hay to be able to see outside through a ventilation opening in the wall. The farmer had the reins in his hands. The police sergeant had one foot on the shaft ready to climb up and sit alongside him.

'What's the matter? What's happening?'

Amy whispered urgently, reluctant to emerge from her hiding. The wagon wheels squealed as they began to turn. Val saw the body lying under a blanket. The sergeant's bicycle was tied to the tailpiece of the wagon.

'The dead miner,' Val said. 'They're taking the body down to the town.'

Part Four

1

Val and two other men were walking briskly along the uneven slope of moorland above the terraced housing, when he took it into his head to start running. At once the short man in mended spectacles protested. He wanted to call Val back but his throat was sore and his croaking voice did not carry.

'Pen!'

He tried to shout at his companion who was shifting further up the mountainside.

'Call him back, will you? Call him back.'

Instead of shouting, Pen stopped to look down into the narrow valley. His face was unshaven as though he wished to demonstrate that he held his good looks to be of little account. But the red neckcloth tied neatly under his left ear was bright and clean. It was his style to appear cool, imperturbable, even enigmatic. He watched a train drawing a plume of grey smoke behind it as it travelled southwards between the slag heaps and the shining slate roofs of the endless terraces. White cloud was drifting pleasantly across the blue sky high above Pen's handsome head. The sky looked abnormally clean compared to the dark valley.

'Call him back, Pen. Do you hear me?'

The small man's jaw was jutting out angrily. He pushed back his cap and a bunch of springy yellow hair came into view.

'God damn it, Pen man! Can't you see what he's up to?'

Pen laughed out loud when he saw Val leap into the air to

clear a derelict hen-coop first and then skip up to avoid a broken bedstead sticking out of a hole in the ground.

'A bloody kangaroo,' Pen said. 'That's all he is. An overgrown schoolboy. Let the bugger run, if he wants to run. Makes no difference. Don't wear yourself out, Wes.'

The small man was reduced to setting an example. He made an effort to run but his boots were too big for him and each step seemed a painful effort. He turned back to lift his fist towards Pen in a gesture of passionate exhortation. Val was now running downhill. He was making for the last of the short rows of houses that thrust up the hillside from a long terrace. These abortive streets were unpaved and the cinder tracks were scored with the dried wheelmarks of vehicles. Outside the last house a large brown furniture van was parked. It had been reversed up the short street and the cavernous rear doors were open. It looked big enough to swallow all the cottages and their contents. Val leapt over the dry wall at the top of the small garden. To reach the back of the house he avoided the small potato patch and a wooden bathtub left on the path. He knocked the back door and went in.

In the passage he discovered a woman nursing a baby in a cloth shawl and holding a half-naked small child by the hand. Both the baby and the toddler had dummies in their mouths. The woman was sobbing and her cheeks were stained with tears. The infant, rubbing his bare foot on the worn linoleum and sucking his dummy, stared with wide-eyed fascination at his mother's distorted face. She was talking to two men in green aprons who were struggling to manoeuvre a wardrobe down the narrow stairs. The front door was already half open, but she blocked their way.

'You can't take that,' she was saying. 'Dick made it himself. With his own hands. You can't take it. You can't.'

Another woman emerged briefly from the middle room. She was holding a small frying pan in both hands, containing uncooked liver and onions. She seemed to view the proceedings with the stolid and indifferent impartiality of a lodger who has paid her rent for her room and refuses to be involved in any disturbances in the rest of the house. Her curiosity had brought her out. When she had satisfied it by

266

staring at the latest intruder struggling to regain his breath, she withdrew, slamming the door.

'What is it?'

Val managed three words as he looked up the stairs.

'What are your reasons?'

The bailiff set his feet on the passage floor and held out one hand with the palm upwards. With his bowler hat perched on the back of his head, he was ready to speak to anyone who would be reasonable, especially a man with a white open-necked cricket shirt who was clearly not a miner, unemployed or employed.

'Two counts,' he said. 'One, he hasn't paid the fine and two, he hasn't paid the rates. So there we are. That's life, isn't it? I've got my orders.'

'What was it? The fine?'

Val was plunging his hands excitedly into the pockets of his grey flannels.

'Two pound, I heard. But that's nothing to do with me, is it?'

Val waved two pound notes in the bailiff's face.

'Well consider that paid. Right? Right?'

The bailiff screwed up his face undecided what to think. He glanced at his assistant but found no help in the pale adenoidal expression on that face. The youth was listening intently to a sound approaching in the long street below them; it was like the relentless hob-nailed rhythm of crowds of men on their way to a football match, in support of their team and determined not to be late for the kick-off. Men signing on for the dole had got word of a pending eviction. Already the first sympathisers were drifting up the side road to the removal van outside the threatened house.

'What about the rates?' Val said.

The woman with the baby reacted as if she had been stuck with a pin.

'I've told them,' she said. 'Dick's paid them. I keep telling them. He has, I tell you.'

Her hot anger dried the tears on her cheeks. She was infuriated by the look of disbelief on the bailiff's face.

'Maybe he has, maybe he hasn't, Mrs. Jenkins.'

The bailiff offered the remark as a concession. It only

angered the woman more. She was becoming conscious too, of the support gathering in the street.

'Don't you call me a liar, Moses Harris,' she said. 'Don't you dare. I tell you plain enough. He paid them.'

Wes pushed his way through the sympathetic crowd to get to the front door. Pen followed him, a cheerful smile on his face. If there was any enjoyment to be extracted from the unhappy occasion he was the man to find it. Wes raised both his hands to adjust his spectacles after pushing his way forward. They had been repaired with bright beads of solder. The loss of his voice made him gesture aggressively. He glared sternly at Val Gwyn through his twisted spectacles.

'This is no concern of yours, Gwyn,' he said. 'You keep out of this.'

Pen leaned on the front door post, a thumb stuck under his waistcoat, grinning happily at everyone in the house and Val Gwyn in particular.

'It's got to be stopped,' Val was saying. 'We're agreed about that at least.'

Wes ignored him, satisfied that he had put him in his place. He turned to address the bailiff.

'Wes Hicks, Vice Chairman, Cwm Du Unemployed Miners' Movement. I want a word with you.'

Moses Harris was obliged to lean forward to catch the whispered words, bending his knee as he did so and supporting the wardrobe with his shoulder. Wes Hicks accepted the movement as a sign of respect to the elected representative of the people. Squaring his broad shoulders he took decisive charge of the situation.

'In here.'

After a brief glance at the woman of the house, Hicks opened the door of the room on his left. The bailiff abandoned the wardrobe to his assistant and followed him in. Hicks sat on a corner of the table and motioned him to close the door. The bailiff obeyed. Mrs. Jenkins shifted the baby in its shawl and looked apprehensively at Pen who moved into the house as though to bring her reassurance and comfort. She was staring at the closed door.

'Will he be alright, Pen?'

Pen ruffled the little boy's hair with his hand. He exuded strength and confidence.

'Nothing to worry about, Nell. Nothing at all. Wes will take care of it.'

'They're going to take it all away. I was down the garden with Tommy and they rushed the front door. I forgot to lock it. And she didn't give me any warning. None at all.'

She nodded towards the middle room where the liver and onions were now being fried. The little boy caught the smell and began to whimper hungrily.

'She's no help,' Nell Jenkins said. 'No help at all. Thinks of nobody but herself.'

'Nothing to worry about, Nell. We've got a butty for each wheel. If they try to move it there'll be a knife in each tyre.'

He smiled indulgently at the bailiff's assistant who was showing signs of trembling.

'Don't worry, lad. If you behave yourself, it may never happen.'

Val was concerned with the woman cooking in the middle room.

'Is she a relative, Mrs. Jenkins?' he said. 'Does she pay you any rent?'

The woman stared at Val, considering whether or not to answer his questions. Pen saw her difficulty and was quick to speak on her behalf.

'Don't worry, Nell. You don't have to answer if you don't want to. He's a do-gooder, see. From the settlement. Not a bad lad when you get to know him. Very highly educated. Very polished. M.A. and all that. He'd like us to talk Welsh all the time. Bit limited, see. But he means well.'

Pen was shaking with silent laughter, delighted with the opportunity of exercising his own brand of ironic wit. Nell Jenkins looked confused. She had still not made her mind up about answering Val's questions when the front room door opened and Wes Hicks emerged followed by the bailiff.

'Right,' Wes said in a hoarse whisper. 'The furniture stays. That's settled anyway.'

The bailiff cleared his throat and raised his hand as though he were asking permission to speak. Wes ignored him.

'The bailiff has asked for certain safeguards, I have agreed.'

He thrust out his head in the direction of the bailiff's assistant.

'What union do you belong to, brother?'

With his mouth open the assistant swallowed nervously and shook his head. He seemed acutely aware of the noise growing in the street.

'Never mind.'

Wes pressed his hand on his neck. His eyes rolled as he tried to clear his throat.

'You are deputised for action. Remove your apron. You come with me to telephone the Council Office. It's been agreed.'

Val supported the wardrobe while the assistant squeezed his way past it and advanced reluctantly towards the front door. The bailiff took his apron while Pen slapped him heartily on the back in a broad gesture of congratulation.

'You'll go down in history, boy,' he said. '"How they brought the good news from Ghent to Aix."'

Wes Hicks stood in the front door and raised his arm. He was ready to address the crowd. But the voice came out in a desperate croak. With an exasperated frown he turned to Pen Lewis and invited him to speak. A kitchen chair stood on the pavement on its way to the furniture van. Pen set it outside the door and stood on it to address the crowd. His powerful figure inspired confidence and respect. Small boys thrust their way to the front door and kneeled down to listen, looking up at his bold chin.

'Now then, lads!'

His voice was sonorous and powerful. Within a matter of seconds the crowd was giving him a respectful hearing.

'Wes is going to settle this one in no time at all. We can promise you this ... there will be no eviction and no victimisation!'

The cheer that went up was a sign of relief as well as approval of Wes Hicks' characteristically swift action. His name was passed down through the crowd with something like tenderness as well as admiration: it was the name of a man who shared their suffering, a man prepared to fight at any time or at any place on their behalf.

'Dick Jenkins is working fifteen miles away. He sought employment and by some miracle he found it. But what do they do? They want to penalise him because he's got a job. Before, they penalised him because he *hadn't* got a job.

Bloody hard lot to please, aren't they? But there is an explanation. Oh yes, there is an explanation. He belongs to the wrong party. He belongs to a party that believes in action and wants to get something done. So what do they do? They penalise him. They try to evict his little family from their little home. Well, now then, comrades, you know, and I know, that just isn't going to happen!'

Pen waved his arm triumphantly and a great cheer went up from the crowd. A piping voice called out.

'What about the van, Pen? Shall we tip it over?'

Someone else shouted.

'Aye! And pitch the bailiff in the river!'

Wes tugged impatiently at Pen Lewis' trousers. It was a message for him to curb his eloquence. There was a complete strategy taking shape in Wes' mind but he had no voice to put it into words. He half turned his back on the crowd and struggled once again to clear his throat. Pen raised both his arms in the air, completely confident of his ability to keep the whole occasion firmly under control.

'Listen, lads! Wes gives these guidelines and it's up to us to follow them. You know and I know from long experience that Wes is usually right in these matters. Whatever you do, don't touch that van. Not on any account. We're going to play this straight down the legal line. They make the laws and it's up to us to see they apply them! We pledge to you now, Dick Jenkins and his little family will not be evicted. Our comrade Dick Jenkins will not be victimised!'

The crowd found relief for its feelings in another rousing cheer. Once again Wes plucked at the material of Pen's patched trousers.

'Just be patient a few minutes! Give Wes Hicks room to negotiate. And then you'll have the pleasure of watching this thing drive away empty!'

Pen came down from his perch. Wes pushed the bailiff's assistant straight into the crowd, following him closely one hand on his arm the other waving in the air, his face intense with responsibility and authority. He confronted two large men with stones in their hands. He was unable to muster his voice to deliver the sharp reproof he wanted to make. Like a diminutive schoolteacher dealing with overgrown pupils he knocked the stones out of their pliant hands. With a voice no more than a whispered croak he muttered short inaudible answers to the dozens of questions put to him, all the time pushing forward and looking first to one side and then to the other of the bailiff's assistant's nervous body like a pilot navigating a crippled ship through a narrow channel. Pen was at a loss for a moment. He hitched up his leather belt and strode manfully back into the house. He sniffed hungrily at the smell of liver and onions seeping under the door of the middle room.

'Could you do with some of that?' he said.

He leaned against the wall to take a long look at Val.

'You know what your trouble is, basically.'

He smiled in the friendliest manner possible.

'You're not one of us.'

Val leaned the wardrobe carefully against the inside wall. He stared with compassion at the dirty brown wallpaper.

'I would have done just exactly what you have done,' he said. 'Or more precisely what Wes Hicks is doing.'

They faced each other in the narrow corridor.

'Except that I wouldn't have made party capital out of it.'

Pen grinned happily.

'Wouldn't you now? Well, that's self-deception pure and simple, isn't it?'

'I wouldn't say so.'

'The very fact that you can kid yourself that you were not going to make political capital out of it proves that you are a bloody amateur.'

Val's face turned white with the effort of restraining his anger.

'You don't begin to deal in reality, see. I can't read your funny little magazine, but I can catch the drift, and I can read you. Take away the cultural trimmings, and sentimentality and soft soap and what have you left? Petit-bourgeois nationalism. That was out of date in 1848. You want to identify with the Welsh workers. And the irony is, mun, the irony is you are even more foreign than those do-gooding English Quakers. And that's a pretty bitter bloody pill for you to swallow, isn't it?'

In spite of the vehemence of his utterance Pen was still smiling. The little boy's lips parted and the dummy fell on the dirty floor. Immediately he began to whimper. The two men towering above him had become frightening, threatening shapes. His mother bent down to pick up the dummy. She wiped it on the woven cloth of the baby's shawl and stuck it back in the little boy's mouth.

'Don't argue, Pen.'

There was pleading in her tired voice.

'It upsets him, see. It always upsets him.'

Pen moved outside. With an inclination of his head he invited Val to follow him. Val managed to squeeze his way past the wardrobe. He touched the little boy on the shoulder, but the child shrank back from the contact. On the pavement Pen was in the mood to conduct a public debate. There were idle men watching and willing to listen.

'While we are waiting I'll give you a lesson if you like in scientific thought.'

His manner was jovial and relaxed.

'Look around you, Mr. Gwyn. And what do you see?'

He waited patiently for Val to answer.

'Poverty and misery,' Val said. 'The suffering of our own people.'

Men pushed forward to listen to them, looking from one to the other like spectators at a prize fight. Pen's smile had become a hungry grin. He was a seasoned and trained debater, poised to demolish his opponent.

'You see a black valley,' he said. 'That's what you should see. And that black valley is a black crucible that contains the stark essentials of the class war. Now if your mind had the correct scientific training that's what you should see. That's the only way forward, my friend. Winning that war. That's the only foundation on which we can build a new society. A new civilisation. A new world.'

Pen's eloquence was fed by noises of approval from the men behind him.

'So when I look around me, see, I don't see despair. I don't see hopelessness. I don't even see misery. I see hope for the future. I see heroic possibilities. Even poverty can be a cloak of hope. I see the darkest hour before a glorious red dawn.'

'That's it, Pen. Give it him, lad. You tell him, boy. We're behind you, boy. Every inch of the way.'

273

The men looked expectantly at Val. As an opponent he was disappointing, lacking in fire, lacking in vision, without any spark of enthusiasm.

'Fantasies,' he said. 'Fantasies. Not facts.'

Val was sighing deeply and shaking his head as though he found it difficult to know where to begin. Pen seemed to be taking pity on him.

'What's the Welsh for "victimisation"?' he said. 'What's the Welsh for "dialectical materialism"? What's the Welsh for "bicycle" for God's sake?'

He was encouraged by the laughter of the men standing behind him. Val pointed at him suddenly.

'What's your name?' he said. 'What's your first name? What's your full name anyway, if it comes to that.'

'Pen Lewis, man. What's the matter with you? Don't be so childish.'

'Penry Aneurin Lewis.'

Val spoke the name with a kind of possessive confidence that annoyed his opponent.

'This is ridiculous,' Pen said. 'It's like children in standard two. Sticking names on each other.'

'It's your proper name,' Val said. 'You have every right to it.'

Pen drew his flat hand backwards and forward under his chin.

'You are up to here in it,' he said. 'Medieval mumbo-jumbo. You're irrelevant, man. You're in the wrong century.'

A disturbance in the crowd reached them. Three open vehicles filled with policemen were converging on the side of the road from three different directions. To clear a way the driver of the nearest was working energetically at his klaxon horn. The concourse of men began to move. The more nervous were already dispersing up the hillside.

'It's the Pats, mun. Coming in at the double. They're coming from all over. With their truncheons out. Look out for the buggers.'

Pen jumped on the chair and raised his hands to restore calm.

'We've done nothing! Just keep calm and hold your ground. Let the inspector through there, please.'

The police inspector's eyes were bloodshot and protruding. They swivelled about suspiciously. He was too hot in his uniform. When he stood by the chair, Val could smell his apprehensive sweat. He wore a flat cap and a strap which reached just under his first chin. He had a smudge of black moustache under his long fleshy nose. Val's presence seemed to displease and perplex him. He looked up at Pen Lewis on his chair. He spoke in a slow ponderous manner that was the fruit of a strange amalgam of experience and instruction.

'Agitation, is it?' he said.

Smiling cheerfully Pen Lewis came down from his chair.

'Everything is in order, Inspector Davies. A little misunderstanding. It's being cleared up. I was just telling the lads here about a meeting to be held in the Miners' Welfare this afternoon. Very interesting lecture. "Why Lenin dedicated 'Left Wing Communism' to Mr. Lloyd George."'

Inspector Davies's eyes shifted about restlessly. The title of the lecture sounded improbable. And yet it was unlikely that Pen Lewis would risk making up lies in public just for the pleasure of making a senior police officer look a fool. The bailiff quickly assumed a stance that implied he had been engaged in prolonged and thoughtful discussion with Mrs. Jenkins. The small child shrank away from the shadow of the policeman to suck his dummy, with his face to the wall. Inspector Davies frowned as he stared at the child's bare bottom. He was thinking hard. A cloud of cunning settled on his thick eyebrows. A course of action presented itself to him. He considered it and found it good. He came out of the house more lightheartedly than he went in.

'Where's your sparring partner?'

The question he put to Pen Lewis was almost jovial.

'In communication with the Council Offices,' Pen said. 'On the telephone. Everything is in order.'

'What about the fine?'

'Paid. First thing this morning.'

The Inspector gave a slow nod that could have been interpreted as being approval. His whole manner seemed to grow less ominous and threatening.

'Better tell them to disperse.'

He muttered his advice in a manner that was almost

informal: a hint from a referee well in control of the match.

'We don't want this to look like an Unlawful Assembly now, do we? Or incitement. Or defiance of Law and Order. Et cetera, et cetera.'

'All right, lads! We can all go home. Now don't forget the lecture this afternoon. "Lenin and Lloyd George." Under the auspices of the N.C.L.C.'

While Pen was speaking the Inspector touched Val lightly on the elbow. He spoke to him in Welsh.

'What are you doing with a lot like this? I've seen you in Chapel, haven't I? Let me give you a word of advice.'

Val looked away. His cheeks were flushed with embarrassment and anger.

'Maybe you don't know the conditions around here as well as you should.'

Inspector Davies made an effort to show he was being helpful and kindly.

'These two men are Moscow trained,' he said. 'And of course there are others. We know who they are. Every single one of them. And they're Moscow paid as well. They've got no respect for anything. You come down to the station and I'll show you their records. Aggressive and dangerous. And these two are the worst of the lot. So take my advice, brother. Don't associate with them. And I mean that. If you do it will only land you in trouble.'

Wes and the bailiff's assistant were pushing their way through the dispersing crowd. The pale young man looked relieved, his head swinging loosely on his long neck as he watched the men moving away. Alive with triumph, Wes' small features radiated puckish delight.

'You're too late, Inspector Davies!'

He was no longer annoyed by his own croaking whisper. 'Unless you want to tell the bailiff to go home.'

He gave the bailiff's assistant a push into the house.

'Go on, tell him,' Wes said. 'Pass on the message.'

Inspector Davies put his hands behind his back. He gazed innocently at Val and then at Wes.

'One or two with stones in their hands, I think you saw?'

'Certainly not.'

Wes Hicks hotly denied the allegation. Inspector Davies

looked at Val again with the stern benevolence of a Sunday School Superintendent.

'One or two I'm sure. One or two wouldn't you say now? *Yn enw'r gwir.*'

Val breathed deeply and shook his head.

'No rough stuff, Inspector.'

Pen was grinning provocatively.

'No rough stuff at all. Pure justice it was and lovely to watch. Wasn't it, Mr. Gwyn?'

'You haven't given me much of a chance to say anything,' Val said.

'Well here's your chance, man. You can tell the Inspector how you enjoyed every minute.'

'We can do something about the rates,' Val said. 'There should be a reduction.'

'There you are, Inspector,' Pen said. 'A big-hearted bourgeois who wants to help the working class. Not many of them left. Even in chapel these days.'

The inspector did not enjoy being teased.

'You watch your tongue, Lewis,' he said. 'It's funny how there's always trouble when you're around.'

Pen made a face of childlike innocence.

'This isn't trouble, Inspector. This is a spontaneous celebration of the joy of living by the working people of Cwm Du. They've got so much to be thankful for.'

Val burst out laughing. He was awarded with a glare of intense disapproval from Inspector Davies.

2

Laughter and voices in the garden induced John Cilydd to open his eyes. He lay as still as a stick in the centre of the wide double bed, his head resting on a tumulus of white pillows. The hotel room smelt of furniture polish. It was ostentatiously clean. On the bedside table a bottle of medicine and a box of pills had pride of place alongside a glass vase loaded with moss roses arranged to nestle in their own green leaves. His dressing-gown hung over the bottom rail of the brass bedstead. His right hand emerged slowly from under the sheet. He examined it at a distance of two feet from his nose as if it could have been a subtle and unique machine he barely expected ever to work again. He exercised the long sensitive fingers. The voices in the garden rose and fell. At last he was encouraged to get out of bed. When his bare feet touched the cool floor he clutched his stomach with his hand and leaned forward pointing his head in the direction of the section of the large room that had been converted into a bathroom. He held this position as long as a model posing for a picture. A barrel-organ began to play in a distant street. The sound was pleasingly muffled by the cool green trees in the hotel garden.

John Cilydd swayed on his feet. He tried to stand still, apparently intent on listening to the workings of his own intestines. He moved carefully around the bed to take hold of the medicine bottle and consider once again the mysteries of the exotic label. What could have been a Frenchman, complete with moustache and imperial beard, was posed before the golden dome of a mosque dressed in a turban and Turkish trousers swigging from a bottle marked with an identical label. For some time Cilydd studied the picture and the French instructions with obtuse concentration. A tablespoon by the hour. The bottle smelt of liquorice and paregoric. He shook it listlessly before applying the bottle to his lips in the manner demonstrated by the man in the turban.

The half-door to the balcony was open. The morning light filtered in through a thin yellow curtain that sometimes trembled from top to bottom in the occasional breeze. John Cilydd made the effort to put on his new dressing-gown. He tied the knot of the green sash as though he were unpractised in such subtle art. Enid's voice talking with lighthearted animation in the garden gave him a spurt of energy. He lifted the curtain and stood among the geraniums on the balcony blinking hard in the bright sunlight.

Enid was sitting at a table set under the trees. A book she had been reading lay face downwards on the table. From the branch of a tree nearby hung the long ropes of a children's swing. A fair-haired young man stood balanced on one foot on the low seat of the swing. His outstretched arms extended the distance between the ropes. The toe of his left boot was anchored in the dust and restrained the taut swing from too much movement. His striped blazer hung over his arm. His white shirt was open at the neck and his trousers were held up by a college tie. He seemed totally unaware of his own charm and good looks. Cilydd stared down at the young pair with miserable fascination. He looked longingly at Enid and then at the young man's handsome head and close-cropped golden hair. As he gazed with critical intensity from one to the other, he could have been making an adjudication as to whom was the more beautiful. He gripped the ornamental railings of the narrow balcony and leaned forward to listen more closely to their conversation.

'I was so surprised,' the young man was saying. 'I've got to admit it. I had no idea.'

He was American. Like a pretty child he was articulate, guileless and used to being listened to: but this in no way impaired his innocent charm. He seemed to find the words constantly astonishing. He was happy to laugh at himself and frankly admit his own naïvety and innocence.

'I'm sure he's a poet,' he said. 'I can quite believe that. And a very good one too. But writing in Welsh. That's what astonishes me. I've certainly got to go and see that country some time. I certainly have.'

Enid tapped the table with a schoolmistressy fingernail.

'In the Middle Ages, it was one of the three great literatures of Europe,' she said.

'Is that so?'

He was respectful and mildly surprised.

'And it still flourishes,' Enid said. 'As a matter of fact you could say we were in the middle of a sort of renaissance even now. A sort of twentieth-century renaissance. Does that surprise you?'

'Oh yes. Indeed it does.'

His gaze strayed up to the balcony. He smiled at Cilydd with his customary winning frankness. He raised his voice to reach the second floor of the building.

'Hello, Mr. More! Your wife is kindly trying to educate me! It's an uphill task, I guess. Are you feeling better?'

Cilydd nodded with fragile care. Enid jumped to her feet, pressing her hands together, delighted to see him. Her face was freckled by the sunlight through the leaves. The mauve dress she wore was made of shot-silk.

'Do you feel like eating something?'

She did not use terms of endearment but her affection was expressed in her eager face and tone of voice.

'Some toast perhaps? And Vichy water.'

Cilydd smiled weakly. It implied that had he a little more strength he would have made a joke about it.

'*Raie au beurre noir!*'

Playfully the American raised an admonishing finger.

'The kitchen still stinks of it. I wouldn't come down for luncheon if I were you. I tell you what! If you feel strong enough why don't I go off and hire you a car? And then you can still make Turenne Beaulieu before you leave. How's that for an idea? It's no trouble.'

Enid looked quickly from Cilydd to the young American and back again to Cilydd.

'Thank you, Mr. Jensen,' she said.

'Harry, for goodness' sake. Or I won't know myself. It would be no trouble.'

He abandoned the swing and went to stand under the balcony, his hands on his hips and his short hair glistening in the sun as he held back his head to look directly up at Cilydd.

'Go through the hills of Correze,' he said. 'I liked that best of all. The smell of gorse and wood burning. Nothing better to settle the stomach. Eat a good tea at Collonges.'

Enid was watching Cilydd with eager expectancy.

'Maybe this afternoon,' he said, 'I shall feel a little stronger.'

'That's the man!'

Harry Jensen was ready to be enthusiastic on their behalf.

'I'll go downtown and get old Alphonse and his limousine. It's slow but comfortable. And comfort you need in your condition. Don't I know it. Down with *raie au beurre noir*! Will you excuse me, Mrs. More?'

Enid and Cilydd looked at each other and waited until he had gone before speaking in subdued voices in their own language.

'What have you been telling him?'

'Only that you were a poet, that's all.'

Cilydd turned down his lips in a grimace of self-disparagement.

'He doesn't know much,' Enid said. 'But he's very nice.'

Cilydd clutched at his stomach.

'Are you alright, John?'

Enid was alarmed.

'Do you want me to come up?'

Cilydd shuffled back into the bedroom without answering. In the dining-room Enid collected a bottle of Vichy water and some dry toast. The lift was out of order. She trotted briskly up the stairs to their room on the second floor. Cilydd had returned to bed. His green dressing-gown lay on the floor. Enid picked it up and stood watching him sympathetically. His eyes were closed.

'You poor darling,' she said. 'I do hate to see you suffer.'

'What a honeymoon.'

He spoke so softly she could barely hear him. He seemed to be apologising.

'You can't help it, dear. Anyway I'm enjoying myself, I really am. I've seen so much I always wanted to see. Thanks to you.'

She moved around the bed to pick up the bottle of medicine. Cilydd opened his eyes to look at her.

'Is this doing you any good?' she said.

'Lock the door.'

She hesitated as though she had not understood what he was saying. He did not repeat himself. She followed his instructions, turning the ornamental key in the lock.

'Will you come to bed?'

She was standing at the foot of the bed, looking surprised.

'John . . . It's the middle of the morning.'

He smiled faintly.

'I know the time.'

Enid was suddenly possessed with a panic of embarrassment. She glanced wildly around the room. The bathroom door was ajar. The half-window was open. The curtain stirred in the gentle breeze. She seemed acutely aware that the whole world could be watching her.

'I left my book in the garden,' she said. 'I ought to go and get it.'

She held her head to one side, listening for sounds in the hotel and in the garden.

'I'm jealous.'

He spoke as though he were describing his physical condition.

'That American is so handsome. He looked so innocent and beautiful standing on the swing.'

Enid smiled understandingly.

'He is rather like a child,' she said. 'And he's so glad to have someone to talk to. He's lonely really. Homesick for Red Wing, Minnesota.'

'You sounded so happy. Your voice in the garden.'

She went to get a glass from the small bathroom. He opened his eyes to watch her movements. She stood close to the bed to offer him a glass of Vichy water.

'Drink this,' she said. 'It's sure to make you feel better.'

His hand stretched towards her and plucked at her dress.

'You know the picture we saw...'

She was tender and sympathetic as she held his head and he sipped the water in the glass.

'Which one, Sionyn,' she said. 'We've seen so many.'

'The naked woman bathing in the stream,' he said. 'I've been thinking of her as you. Will you come to bed?'

'Someone could come.'

Enid was blushing in spite of her smile.

'It's the middle of the morning. The maid or something. Or Harry Jensen. Anybody.'

He was pale with self-pity.

'Of course. "I'm very weak on female anatomy"...'

'Darling...'

She stroked his cheek.

'I was only joking.'

'I can see that picture. Like a symbol of the immortality of the flesh. I've been lying here thinking about it. It's the only way back. I want to make a poem about it. A man is lost in a dark wood. He finds a beautiful woman bathing naked by a small waterfall. She takes him back to the Earthly Paradise. Where there is no guilt or shame.'

Enid sat on the edge of the bed and squeezed his hand.

'That sounds good,' she said.

His eyes were large with doubt.

'Does it? It could be rubbish. How can I soar without wings?'

She was anxious to be helpful.

'Do you want to make notes? Shall I get a pad? Do you feel strong enough?'

His voice rose mournfully from the pillow.

'I'm a failure,' he said. 'I'm no good.'

'That's not true.'

'What is this longing for sensuous release? I can tell you. It's another form of the fear of death. Did you know that?'

He closed his eyes wearily. Enid leaned towards him.

'It never leaves me. There are days, beautiful days in this beautiful season, when I can see nothing but Death.'

'Oh, my darling.'

Enid was filled with concern for him. She began to undress. Her mauve frock fell to the floor.

'It's not the War. I don't think so. It's worse in a way. Adolescent fears dominating the life of a grown man. It's a fear of nothingness. A fear of nothingness inside me. Does that mean the fear of failure?'

The whiteness of her bare skin glimmered in the subdued light. She obliged herself to stand still so that John Cilydd could look at her. When he spoke he had regained some of his confidence.

'Nakedness is important,' he said. 'The naked truth. Truth is beauty.'

His head lay back on the pillow. Only his eyes moved as he studied her body.

'If we have no life of the flesh,' he said, 'we have nothing. That's what I was thinking.'

'I wish I were beautiful,' Enid said. 'I wish I were beautiful for you.'

His hand moved out to touch her thigh. Her skin trembled as though it knew a fear of its own. His hand travelled more boldly across her belly to touch her pubic hair.

'This makes me better,' he said. 'I know it does.'

She reached forward to touch his forehead with her hand. Her firm breasts were suspended above his face. He thrust out his lips to touch her nipples. His arms drew her into the spotless white bed alongside him. He murmured his pleasure as he kissed her body. She listened to him. Her eyes were wide open.

'This is the source of power. This is our marriage. There are no ghosts here. No witches.'

She listened intently to his fevered whispering.

'You're not a witch are you? You won't eat me. You. You. You.'

She placed her fingers on his mouth when he became incoherent with the repetition of phrases. Then she held his head gently with both hands and soothed him like a mother nursing a child through a fever.

'Never mind,' she said. 'Never mind.'

'There's no shame ... in the garden ... is there?'

'Never mind.'

She murmured comfortingly.

'Never mind.'

Her whole concern seemed to give him whatever he longed for. She was both nurse and doctor and he was the patient tossing on his sick bed. Still inexperienced she moved her arms and her legs according to any pressure that suggested it was what he wanted. It was difficult for her to distinguish between expressions of agony and of joy. His strength was still limited because of his condition. But inside these limits a passion seemed to be raging that she had never seen before. He was willing himself to transports of bliss and she was obliged to will herself to share in his desiring. The heat of the white bed became unbearable. The clothes were thrown off. When he began to shiver in his sweat, she covered him gently with her body and reached over to drag up a sheet to cover them again. He lay still on the bed, gasping like a man exhausted and wounded at the end of a fight. Her concern for him became even more tender. She found the glass of Vichy water and brought it to his lips. He drank it greedily, his eyes searching out hers for approval. Both their bodies were covered in sweat. He became concerned because her back was wet and her buttocks were cold. She brought towels from the bathroom and began to dry his thin body. He laughed as she did so and said she was tickling him. He drew her inside the bed again and made her lie alongside him, to listen to him whispering.

'We shall learn,' he said. 'Won't we, Enid? We've got all our lives to learn together. That's why I need you so much. Without you I am utterly lost. Do you hear me? Can you hear me admit it? But it's true. Every word I am saying is true.'

He was growing agitated again. She pressed her hand on his bare chest to restrain him, anxious as ever for his welfare.

'You give me so much, Enid. In myself I'm so empty. So negative. So meaningless. You bring me to life. That's why I owe you so much. That's why I can't live without you.'

'Try and rest, darling. Try and rest.'

She stiffened suddenly when she heard Harry Jensen's confident American voice calling from the garden. Cilydd was amused by her consternation. With a grin of triumph he lifted himself from the bed and struggled alone to put on his dressing-gown. Enid hid herself under the sheet. He moved with unsteady speed to the balcony. Jensen was by the table under the trees. Enid's book lay face downwards near him. The swing was still.

'You've got the car,' Jensen said. 'Alphonse is willing!'

'I feel much better.'

Cilydd leaned over the balcony, smiling happily. Each seemed to find the other's accent intriguing and agreeable.

'That's great. I'm delighted to hear it.'

'Look. Jensen. Harry. Why don't you come with us this afternoon? Show us the marvels. That fine castle on the mountaintop. Turenne. Collonges. Beaulieu. Aubazine. The lot. The blooming lot.'

Jensen was obviously delighted with the prospect: but he struggled manfully to be polite and not impose himself on new-found friends.

'Oh well,' he said. 'That's really kind of you. I wouldn't want to intrude. I would love to come of course, but don't feel obliged to ... I mean, I wouldn't want to be a gooseberry.'

'Gooseberry?'

Cilydd enunciated the word in his own peculiar way.

'What's that I wonder? I must say you don't look like one.'

They laughed together with unconcealed pleasure. For each of them there was a twilight zone of communication that seemed to lend enchantment to the effort of reaching some understanding.

'We'll go together,' Cilydd said. 'Like a Sunday school trip. I'm sure Enid will be delighted.'

3

The train was very late. It sniffed and shuffled its way deeper into the valley. The steam hissed in the drizzle. The winding gear at the pithead came into view. It stuck out of the mist as threatening as a giant gibbet. Amy gazed apprehensively through the window. Black slag heaps dominated the funereal procession of terrace dwellings called to a permanent halt in the narrow valley. The mountains above them were hidden in cloud. In the far corner of the compartment a woman with a thyroid condition protected a seven-year-old boy who lay stretched on the seat, his school cap on his head which lay in her lap. He was sleeping with his mouth open and her arm lay across his chest. She had difficulty in keeping her arm still. Her hand with the thick wedding ring on her sensitive finger twitched with the desire to feel her son's hot forehead and move the limp lock of hair. She studied the view on her side of the carriage as intently as Amy studied the view on hers. Talking would disturb the boy. Distaste for the view through the dirty window mingled with concern for a son who could be ill.

The train jerked forward again. The engine seemed confused by a sequence of contradictory signals. The mother clutched the boy too tightly. He stirred and opened his eyes. Without moving his head he catechised his mother in a parched babyish voice.

'Are we there, then? Are we there yet, Mam?'

She bent her head to whisper to him soothingly, keeping a calculating eye on the world outside. A row of ruined miners' cottages came into sight. They had been abandoned when the coal waste reached the back doors. She seemed to consider drawing the boy's attention to the sight and then to think better of it: even the ominous cocoon of mild fever was preferable to the grim reality outside the window. Above the ruined cottages a row of unemployed men and boys were on their knees turning over the slag and picking out coal to put into sacks. The woman shifted in her seat. She found the sight of the ragged men on the side of the tip too embarrassing to watch. She looked at Amy as though to register her reaction. The boy was awake. She could break the silence in the compartment. A little talk might soften the stark surroundings. She seemed ready to snatch at anything that would bring a little warmth and comfort.

'People don't know,' she said. 'People don't realise. Not until they come here. The sheer misery. They don't understand.'

The boy began to complain again. His throat was burning. He pressed his hand against it and seemed to consider crying. The mother bent over him, whispering urgently, begging him to be patient. They were almost in sight of the station. Once again the train ground to a halt. The woman looked at the drizzle outside and began to whisper explosively.

'I never wanted to come here,' she said. 'Never. I told my husband. It's not fair to the boy, I said, and it's not fair to you. One minister for two circuits. And most of the members unemployed. It's ridiculous, I said. Absolutely ridiculous.'

Amy nodded understandingly. There was nothing else she could do. The journey had to come to an end; but they were still bound together like two strangers trapped in a tunnel sharing the same pocket of air.

'The day we arrived it was terrible. The sun was shining and you think that would have helped but there was coal dust all over the street. And the girl had left the front door open and the dust had blown inside. It was all over everything. And to crown it all a dog from the street had wandered upstairs and left his paw marks all over the white bed. I can tell you. I just sat down and cried.'

Amy was doing her best to look sympathetic. The boy had begun to mumble disgruntledly. He wanted all his mother's attention. He made her bend down to catch his murmuring complaint. She smiled apologetically at Amy and brought her face as close as she could to his. When the train suddenly jolted forward, their noses touched. The boy broke out into delighted laughter. Her expression was instantly transformed.

'You're better, aren't you?' she said. 'My little boy is feeling better.'

He jumped to his feet, tottering about drunkenly as the train moved forward in fits and starts. They were coming into the station. He shouted out the name on the signal box.

'Cwm Du Signal Box!'

And he caught the first glimpse of his father waiting for them in the shelter of the waiting-room door. He was a conspicuously neat figure in clerical grey and a trilby hat. He walked briskly alongside the moving train, his white hands raised ready to open the compartment door.

'Now then, Dad! Catch me! Catch me!'

Amy moved aside to allow the boy to jump out into his father's arms. While he still held his son the minister enquired in muted tones about his condition. Amy hurried down the platform to the luggage van at the end of the train. The guard was scratching his head as he looked at two large bales of old clothing.

'I don't know how you're going to manage,' he said. 'They're heavy, you know. They're heavier than you think.'

The only luggage truck available was parked under the station canopy. Two children were sitting on it. It was a pleasant place to sit while they watched the train. One of the boys sat with his back to the track and studied it over his shoulder. When Amy bent down to pick up the long handle she saw that the boy's feet were bare. His companion wiped his nose on his sleeve and grinned at Amy encouragingly. When the truck was gone they scampered across the entrance to take up perches on the seat outside the waiting-room.

'Isn't there anybody here to meet you?' the guard said.

'They must have given up.'

Amy looked determined to be cheerful.

'The train was so late.'

The guard raised his eyebrows loftily, ignoring any implied criticism. With Amy's help he struggled to deposit the two bales on the truck. With both hands she dragged the load under the wooden canopy. The drizzle had stopped for the moment but the clouds were low. The rain could fall again at any time. The minister and his wife watched her with mild interest. He plucked out his watch from his waistcoat pocket and studied it carefully.

'Would you believe a train could be almost three quarters of an hour late? It's symptomatic, you see. We don't count. A decaying community. Left to one side and forgotten.'

He put his watch back and pointed hesitantly at the bales on the truck.

'What will you do with them?' he said. 'I suppose there is somewhere here where they could be locked up overnight. Unless you've made arrangements, that is.'

'They are for Val Gwyn,' Amy said. 'At the settlement. Clothes we've collected for distribution among the unemployed.'

The minister's wife pulled a face.

'Our front room is full of them,' she said.

She was about to burst out into prolonged complaint but a sharp glance from her husband restrained her. A gesture from his left hand indicated the extreme delicacy of the subject. He drew his son closer to his side.

'I think it's our first duty to get this young man nicely tucked up in bed, as soon as possible.'

Amy was left alone on the platform. As the train drew out the door of the waiting-room opened and two ageing figures emerged, displaying playful caution as soon as they knew that Amy was watching them. They wore cloth caps, mufflers and old coats that were too big for them. The smaller man had no teeth. They both had difficulty in breathing. They nodded pleasantly at Amy who smiled back at them. She adorned the drab platform like a visitor from a brighter world. The larger man hummed delicately through his wide nostrils. He had a limited amount of wind but he wanted to show he could use what he had with virtuoso skill.

'Bus,' he said.

His voice was resonant and rich, like that of an itinerant player preparing to give a more strenuous performance than usual.

'Be along in a minute.'

His smaller companion was ready with the tenor part. Although one was large and fat and the other small and thin, their lungs appeared to be in equally bad shape.

'Thank you.'

They both enjoyed the pretty way in which Amy showed

gratitude for the information. The large one deepened his voice.

'Evans gone?'

He was referring to the minister. He waited for a reply, his eyebrows like pulleys, drawing up the rest of his flabby features. He was the less mobile and therefore entitled to the services of his smaller friend as outriding observer. The entrance and the ticket office were deserted. The minister and his little family had hurried off on their homeward journey.

'We must make allowances.'

The rich voice was pitched so that Amy was invited to listen.

'It's not easy for him, is it? Do you know how many members he's got in Moriah? Moriah North Street. And that's his biggest, mind you. One hundred and twenty-four.'

The smaller man came closer to express his admiration.

'You are hot on facts, Emmanuel, I'll say that for you.'

'Yes, but do you know how many of them are in work?'

Emmanuel asked the question so forcefully his large lips quivered. With a glance at Amy to make sure she was listening he raised two stubby fingers into the air.

'Two,' Emmanuel said.

His lips minimised the sum, drawing full attention to the absurdity of its size.

'A teacher and a night watchman. Out of a congregation of one hundred and twenty-four adults. Of course I'm not counting the children.'

Emmanuel lifted his face and screwed up his eyes with an extra effort of thought. His small companion stole a quiet glance at Amy and then ventured to smile. He wanted her to note the richness of his friend's character, his unique combination of knowledge, wisdom and entertainment value. Emmanuel raised his arm with prophetic deliberation and pointed towards a mountaintop hidden by the low cloud. His public mode of address was modified by a courteous concern for Amy as a newcomer in their midst.

'Up there,' he said. 'We have a perfect example of a "mesa" or a "tabular hill". A protective cap of hard sandstone on a base of shales. It's a great pity you can't see it.'

His friend was delighted with Emmanuel's scholarly

display. He looked expectantly at Amy, the small blue scars visible in the shiny pallor of his skin.

'You are interested in geology?' Amy said.

She took care not to sound too surprised.

'We are interested in everything, aren't we, Watty? You might say we have ample leisure for intellectual pursuits. That would be a way of putting it.'

Watty moved nearer to Amy. The moment was approaching when he would be able to exercise friendly curiosity. A bus drove noisily into the station square. Watty pointed helpfully at the bales of clothing.

'He could take those on top,' he said.

The bus was parked by the drinking fountain in the centre of the square. Emmanuel was annoyed that the driver had taken the vehicle so far from the pavement outside the station.

'What does he want to go over there for? Always the same with him.'

Emmanuel had called out but the driver ignored him. He climbed down the steps with the bow-legged importance of a captain leaving his ship. The coin bag and ticket punch dangled like chains of office around his neck. He had something to say to a group of idle men who were waiting for him on the opposite corner.

'The transport system of this valley is going to rack and ruin,' Emmanuel said. 'How would it be now if we had an urgent appointment?'

Watty laughed wheezily and ended up by coughing. Emmanuel was not so amused.

'This young lady is in need of the best that we can offer by way of transport. And just look at it. And him. The ineffective dregs of an inefficient system.'

Emmanuel was pleased with the last sentence. His companion was showing appreciation and Emmanuel was clearly considering repeating it when his attention was taken by a young man on a bicycle who rode up-hill into the square standing on the pedals as flamboyantly as a picador practising his entrance into a bull-ring.

'Pen Lewis coming on a bike!' Watty said. 'Now what's happened? Always something if Pen's around.'

'It's a new bike,' Emmanuel said.

He spoke shrewdly and opened his mouth ready to be fed with the information he craved.

'With what did you buy that bike, Pen?' he said. 'Moscow gold?'

Pen laughed as he jumped off the bike, landing in front of Amy.

'You Miss Parry?'

His chin was raised as he asked the question, the shadow of a confident smile on his solidly handsome face. He had shaved and his dark blue eyes glowed with excitement and exertion. He was wearing a red shirt without a tie.

'Val is in Cardiff jail.'

'What?'

Amy was so taken aback she shouted out the word. Emmanuel and Watty moved closer to listen.

'It was two pounds or fourteen days. They took them down on the train last night. Wes Hicks, Dick Jenkins, four of the women's committee and your friend, Val Gwyn.'

'What for?'

Amy was still confused and puzzled.

'They lay across the street on Empire Day and obstructed the procession. Very wicked, they were. Where's your stuff?'

'The bales for the settlement are in the station.'

Pen set the bicycle against the pavement. He went into the station to look at the bales. Amy was too upset to follow him. Watty whispered to her in a confidential voice.

'He's a Communist.'

'You can't hold that against him,' Emmanuel said. 'He does his best for the lads.'

'I'm not saying he doesn't.'

Watty seemed to resent the implication that he was lacking in impartiality.

'Point of information, that's all. Nice to know where you are, I always think.'

He fell quickly silent as Pen returned from his inspection.

'They're no problem. I'll get them seen to. Do you think you could sit on the crossbar and hang on to your case?'

Amy stared at the bicycle and then at the bus, unable to decide what to do.

'It's alright,' Pen said. 'It's Val's bike. I've only borrowed it. If we hurry now, we can take part in the procession.'

'What procession?' Amy said.

The word captured Emmanuel's interest immediately.

'Did I hear you say "procession", comrade?'

He spoke in his deepest voice, anxious to be noticed and to be agreeable.

'Down one side and up the other,' Pen said. 'Could you get those chaps over there to come? Fill that bus. There'll be a protest meeting at the end of it. In the Welfare Hall. There was police provocation. Restricting the activities of militant leaders. And harassing the friends of the working class. You know what it's like. They've got a real down on the Right to Work Movement. Pass the word round, boys, and come yourselves if you can.'

He turned to Amy. His manner was brisk and forthright.

'Are you coming? It's downhill all the way.'

He spoke as if sitting on the crossbar of a bicycle was the only reasonable action she could take. He mounted the saddle himself and tilted the bike towards her to make it easier for her to settle on the bar. When they were moving, Amy leaned forward over the handlebars to hold her head away as far as she could from his.

Through half-closed eyes she saw people on the pavements stop to look at them. Pen was enjoying the ride. He swerved to avoid a grimy sheep straying across the street and Amy bunched herself more apprehensively over the handlebars.

'Would you like to speak?'

He brought his mouth close to her ear.

'Me?'

Amy concentrated on maintaining her self-control.

'Could be very effective.'

He was calling out boldly behind her head. He could not see her frown of displeasure.

'I could introduce you as the victim's fiancée. She turns up on a visit and finds the poor fellow has been dragged off to jail.'

'No.'

Amy shook her head.

'It's no use being half-hearted down here,' he said. 'You can't win anything by being half-hearted.'

For the first time it seemed as if what he was saying was

beginning to reach her. He turned right down a steep street where men sat on the windowsills of their terrace houses. She closed her eyes and did not open them until they had reached the bottom. They turned left into a street with tram lines. Pen stopped suddenly and dismounted. He held the bike firmly while Amy got off the bar. With a large smile he showed how much he admired her fortitude.

'Give me your case,' he said. 'The settlement is behind this chapel. I'll dump your bag in the vestry. We haven't any time to lose.'

Amy waited for him on the pavement. She looked up at the blackened façade of the chapel. A stone tablet above the gallery windows said it was Noddfa Baptist built in 1869 and extended and rebuilt in 1898. People were emerging from the terrace houses across the street to show neighbourly interest in her presence. A young mother nursing her baby in a long shawl moved from her open doorway to the pavement. Pen called out to them when he emerged from the vestry.

'Come on now,' he said in a loud commanding voice. 'Get your coats on and come and join the procession. Men, women, children and dogs.'

'And sheep!'

They shouted back at him. He laughed and waved. The young mother stepped back apprehensively into the protection of her own doorway. Amy listened with some amazement at the banter. In the long drab hopeless looking street where every other shop was closed, some with their windows boarded up, so much brightness and human warmth shone like isolated sunlight. She looked around her with the fresh eye of someone arrived unexpectedly in a strange land.

'What's the matter with you, then?'

Pen Lewis was laughing at her confusion. He waited with one foot on the pavement for her to place herself on the crossbar.

'Is it true you've been to Russia?'

Amy could not prevent herself sounding impressed.

'It is and it isn't. In the spirit, see. Wes has been. I'll be going. That's for certain.'

He was looking so pleased with himself she clearly regretted asking the question.

'Sometimes I think that's what I like most of all about women.'

'What do you mean?'

Amy was blushing.

'Their curiosity. It's lovely.'

He spoke as if he were admiring a physical attribute.

'Not at all,' Amy said. 'I just wanted to know.'

His laughter annoyed her so much she was reluctant to sit on the cross-bar.

'Come on,' he said. 'We can't keep history waiting.'

She was obliged to ride with him. He tried to get her to enter into the spirit of the occasion.

'Talked about me, did he?'

He spoke up loudly as he steered the bike over the tramlines.

'Just in passing.'

'He's gone up in my estimation,' he said.

'Has he?'

Both Amy's hands were free to grasp the chrome handle-bars. She held on as though she were taking part in the steering. The bicycle bumping up and down brought a smile to her face.

'Old father Gwyn,' Pen said. 'I had no idea he had such good taste.'

'He's not old!'

They turned a corner and suddenly the road was full of people. Amy pushed herself back as though she were applying brakes. Behind her, Pen was laughing delightedly.

'Look at that,' he said. 'Just look at that. It's taking time, but we're teaching the people to march!'

Amy's eyes were wide open. The shabby clothes the people wore as they marched past were like ill-fitting uniforms. They moved forward in a great tide and their talking was like the monotonous rustle of waves among pebbles and the occasional laughter of the less responsible young like the calling of small sea birds.

'Can you feel it?'

Pen's voice was trembling with suppressed excitement. They had dismounted. She did not turn her head to look at him.

'The strength of the proletariat. The true source of power.'

At the head of the procession home-made banners were being carried aloft like ikons. Amy could only see the back of them. They squeezed into the street and moved forward with the human tide. Amy was soon separated from Pen. She found herself walking side by side with a group of middle-aged women. Many of them had no teeth. She could see this because their mouths were open as they laughed happily, obviously enjoying themselves. Even the tramp of feet on the hard street seemed to give them pleasure. They looked from one to the other and their lips moved as if they were being exercised in readiness of learning a new song. Accidentally Amy kicked the heels of the woman immediately in front of her. The woman turned around. Her face was creased and unwashed. She heard Amy apologise. Her mouth opened in a broad smile. She had one single tooth in her mouth. But her face was a mirror of happiness.

'That's all right, my little love,' she said. 'We got to tread on each other sometimes. When we're all in it together.'

4

Mrs. Lloyd was treating a patient. Through the frosted glass of the door marked 'Dispensary' the thick shape of a woman seated with her head held back in the swivel chair in front of the roll-top desk was a sculpture of patient suffering. A small boy carrying a paraffin can stared over the counter at the fascinating sight. Auntie Bessie leaned over to prise the tin handle out of the boy's tight grip.

'Leave go, Owie,' she said. 'There's a good lad.'

Owie let go but did not take his eyes off the shapes moving beyond the glass. Auntie Bessie trudged to the back of the shop to fill the can. Owie put his finger in his nose and leaned further over the counter. He was in this position when the shop door bell rang and Uncle Gwilym came in.

'What do you think you're doing, boy?'

Owie stared at him in mute alarm. Uncle Gwilym wore a straw hat and a grey alpaca jacket as a concession to summer.

The rest of his suit was a rusty black. His stiff winged collar rode high under his sharp chin. He cultivated a moustache that once had waxed ends. It was now more indecisive. Through his gold pince-nez he was eyeing the boy with active distaste. He carried two recently-published magazines under his arm. He roamed about the shop with a certain confidence; a son on one of his regular visits to his old home. In the Post Office section Nanw was serving Robert Thomas, the mole-catcher.

'Gwilym Glaslyn!'

Robert Thomas was launched on an instant flow of flattery. He stood with his feet apart as if preparing to conduct an invisible choir. The sound made Uncle Gwilym look distinctly happier and more at ease.

'First thing I turn to in *The Weekly Herald* when I've been through the column of death – and maybe births and marriages. Gwilym Glaslyn's Diary. Always very tasty.'

'I'm very glad to hear it.'

The first flush of flattery quickly faded. More specific references were needed to reinforce the pleasing effect.

'Haven't seen this week's yet.'

Robert Thomas adroitly evaded the secondary obligation.

'That's what happens with a working man. After the long day. Falls asleep over the paper. Tastier over the weekend. After Sunday tea.'

'Here's your change, Robert Thomas,' Nanw said.

The hours of business were coming to an end and she had already begun to close her accounts.

'Many thanks, Miss Lloyd.'

The material of his trousers was so stiff he pocketed the coins with difficulty.

'A noble old family, the family of Glanrafon.'

Robert Thomas bowed ingratiatingly towards Uncle Gwilym as the most illustrious member of the family within his immediate ken.

'Very pleasant to know that John Cilydd has brought his young wife back to the old district. Buying a nice house in Pendraw, I hear. Not far from the beach. He was too far away before. Now with the aid of a motor car he'll be to and fro with the ease of a homing pigeon, so to speak. To be able to stay in the old home while the new nest is being got ready ...

297

"It is a fair thing to look homeward"...'

Uncle Gwilym looked trapped: the brief prelude of flattery had left him in the mute pose of willing listener. Robert Thomas was capable of talking for a long time. Nanw was too busy with accounts to rescue him. He dared not disturb his mother in the dispensary. A new customer had come in and handed a list to Auntie Bessie, scribbled in pencilled abbreviations on a fragment of a dark blue sugar bag. She was finding it difficult to read. Robert Thomas shifted his bow legs closer to Uncle Gwilym for a more intimate conversation. He lowered his voice and his fingers played excitedly with the oval tobacco box in his waistcoat pocket.

'I'm a man without education, as you well know, Gwilym Lloyd,' he said. 'But I take an interest in "The Things" as they say. This business about withholding the Chair. What did the judges have in mind, do you think?'

Uncle Gwilym jerked up a finger to draw Robert Thomas' attention to the magazines he was carrying.

'It's all in there if you want to read it, Robert Thomas. All very plainly set out.'

'That's where it is, you see,' Robert Thomas said. 'It's getting difficult for the layman. Now you take my father now. He learnt to read in Sunday school and he got into the habit of devouring newspapers and magazines and books and it seemed no effort to him. Now in my case, interested as I am, there's so much of this new college stuff that I find hard to swallow. Tell me in a nutshell, Gwilym Lloyd. What was the trouble?'

Uncle Gwilym breathed deeply as though he wanted to demonstrate that he was not afraid to face the truth.

'The work was too daring,' he said. 'Or in the words of one distinguished adjudicator, "a heap of filth".'

'Duw. Duw!'

Although he had almost certainly heard of the condemnation before, Robert Thomas reacted with an attitude of petrified astonishment.

'Is that what it was, do you think?'

Robert Thomas put the question in the voice of an innocent inquirer.

'How should I know?'

The answer was a sharp rebuke.

'I haven't read the work.'

Robert Thomas was not too put out.

'There was talk, you see, around the village that John Cilydd was going to be a Winner again. That was the expectation. That's how we are, isn't it? Always living in hope. And of course as we all know, in these matters, he is your pupil. He learnt his craft as they say in the workshop of a master of the strict metres.'

Uncle Gwilym was plainly torn between pleasure at the public recognition of his skill and annoyance at being associated even indirectly with a composition already popularly dubbed a heap of filth. He took refuge in an adamantine silence. Like a priest who closes the gates of the shrine to show ignorant worshippers that the oracle has departed, he moved solemnly to the main shop. He lifted his head and studied the rows of new buckets hanging from the ceiling. Robert Thomas followed him, looking up to locate the object of the master-poet's concentrated attention. He began to recite.

'"Matches and sago, snuff and tobacco
Sapolio tablets and sauces galore
Buckets, cornflour, scythe blades, cocoa
Tin tacks, saltpetre and mints by the score."

. . . I could go on for quite a bit you know. Of course it's easier to remember if you sing it.'

Robert Thomas cleared his throat to indicate he was prepared to sing if given a little encouragement. Uncle Gwilym glanced towards the dispensary door and gave his head a brief minatory shake. Nanw emerged from the post office section and prepared the shop door for closing. The woman at the grocery counter eyed her with an aggressive nervousness as if she were afraid of being locked in. There was the noise of a motor car outside. Nanw opened the door again because her brother was arriving. He was alone. She gave him a smile of welcome that lit up her tired face. He looked stern and preoccupied. He carried an attaché case as he came into the shop. Robert Thomas watched everything that was happening with the keenest appreciation: not the smallest expression or gesture would escape him so that on his long walk back to his cottage on the foreshore he could ruminate and reconsider all that he had witnessed while quietly chewing tobacco and spitting at regular intervals into the hedgerow.

'Where's Enid?'

It was Cilydd's first greeting to his sister. Her smile faded.

'I've no idea,' she said. 'I've been working right up to this minute. Have you had any tea?'

Cilydd ignored the question. Uncle Gwilym was silently demanding his attention.

'You are coming through?'

Uncle Gwilym muttered the words. He began to turn his back on Robert Thomas, ready to begin the brief journey to the big kitchen behind the shop. Robert Thomas made a last modest bid for notice.

'I was reciting, John Cilydd,' he said. 'Just before you came in.'

'Were you really?'

He was much encouraged when Cilydd showed polite and friendly interest.

'I don't know whether you know it. Word for word. I expect you do. It was your grandfather wrote it. In praise of this place. I learnt it when I was a lad.

'"The shop at Glanrafon, a notable haven
Is more than a warehouse we hope you'll agree
The prices are low but the quality fancy
Nothing is missing and the welcome is free!"'

A muscle under Uncle Gwilym's left eye twitched.

'Now then,' he said.

At last Robert Thomas took the hint. He picked up his small bag of shopping and prepared to depart. Uncle Gwilym led the way down the dark passage reasonably secure that his nephew was following. The small window was open. The bees were humming in the honeysuckle outside. At the same time the necessary fire burned in the great chimney and a heavy black kettle hung on its chain. The familiar warmth and smell of the room seemed to give Uncle Gwilym fresh confidence in himself.

'Well, now then,' he said. 'What about the Chair?'

Cilydd was calm and casual. He sat on the edge of the table with his hands in his pockets and swung his legs to and fro. His uncle took up an authoritative stance in front of the fire.

'I know no more than you do,' Cilydd said. 'I didn't go to the eisteddfod. Went to Cardiff instead. I had a friend there in trouble.'

'Val Gwyn, I suppose?'

Uncle Gwilym brought up the name as though he were alluding to a forbidden drug. Cilydd grinned.

'In prison,' he said. 'For refusing to pay a fine. He doesn't know yet, but I paid it. I don't know how he'll take it quite, if he finds out.'

Uncle Gwilym stretched out his arm and shook it with a gesture of indeterminate censure.

'There you are, you see. I told you long ago. That man has got no sense. He doesn't know how to go about things so all he can do is be extreme.'

Cilydd's smile increased his uncle's annoyance.

'Of course I know you'll never listen to me. I'm old-fashioned. I've got my legs stuck in the dried jam of the last century, haven't I?'

Belatedly Cilydd began to placate his uncle.

'Now don't start picking at old sores, uncle,' he said. 'Nobody respects you more than I do.'

Uncle Gwilym advanced from the fireplace to throw down the magazines like gauntlets on the table.

'What about those?' he said. 'The Chair was withheld because the best poem in the competition was "a heap of filth". And the nom de plume was "Glanrafon"!'

'I was in a bit of a hurry,' Cilydd said. 'I just put it down because I couldn't think of anything else.'

'Do the others know?'

Uncle Gwilym appeared overwhelmed with delicate anxiety.

'Know what?'

Cilydd took his hands out of his pockets and folded his arms.

'That you've lost the Chair by writing "a heap of filth". And used the name of your old home as a nom de plume. Is that all you think of it?'

'Don't jump to conclusions, uncle. This is how you always

are. I would have thought you'd learned your lesson with Lloyd George and the Great War. You were the chief Jingo in the district. Remember?'

Uncle Gwilym was embarrassed and hurt. He sat down in his mother's large wooden chair, his chin sunk in his hand. It took him some time to regain his composure. At last he spoke in measured reasonable tones.

'The subject set was "The Lady of the Fountain". An excellent subject that could be taken in many ways. I started myself on the woman of Samaria. "There cometh a woman of Samaria to draw water . . ." and so on. But it was too much for me. I don't mind admitting it. But what have you done? Painted some picture of two naked women by some spring in the rocks. Two, not one! And what are you talking about? Sexual lust as the source of life. And praising it to the skies. And calling the women the dark goddess and the fair goddess and so on and so on. "A hymn to lust", one of the judges called it!'

'Can I ask you something?'

Uncle Gwilym looked nervously at his nephew as a man who had been fully revealed now as capable of asking anything.

'Have you read it?'

'I read the adjudications. They upset me, I can tell you. No one likes to see a member of his family accused of having a depraved and dirty mind.'

Cilydd laughed aloud.

'I just don't understand it,' Uncle Gwilym said. 'How you can laugh about a thing like that. I ask myself sometimes. What's happening to the world?'

'You're running in front of the hounds,' Cilydd said. 'You haven't even read it. So how can you judge?'

'Those men,' Uncle Gwilym said. 'Those three judges. They are men for whom I have the greatest respect.'

'Idol worship.'

Cilydd's condemnation was brief and immediate.

'What do you mean?'

'A weakness of your generation. An appetite for idols. An inability to think for yourselves. I have a theory that it's something to do with the decay of religion.'

'Decay?'

Uncle Gwilym found the word deeply offensive. He repeated it.

'Decay?'

'Anyway...'

Cilydd pressed both his hands on the table and jumped to his feet.

'You'll soon have a chance to judge for yourself.'

He walked into the front hall of the house and shouted up the stairs.

'Enid! Are you there?'

He waited until he was certain that there was no one upstairs and then returned to the kitchen with more time for his uncle.

'I'm going to publish it. With a modest little foreword. I'm thinking of using "A Heap of Filth" as a title. Be a bit catchpenny that, though, wouldn't it?'

Uncle Gwilym was shaking his head in horrified unbelief.

'I don't know what it is,' he said. 'It's a spirit of madness and misrule that's taking possession of the world. That's how it seems to me ...'

'Put it down to the War,' Cilydd said. 'Nearly everybody does.'

'Where are they, I ask myself. Where are they? All the old values?'

'Buried in the trenches,' Cilydd said. 'That's the general view.'

Nanw came in. Without speaking she began to prepare tea. Uncle Gwilym watched her movements with gloomy appreciation.

'I think the least you could do,' he said, 'would be to ask your family. If it's your intention to drag our name in the mud, we should at least be consulted.'

Nanw was listening intently to what they were saying without slackening the pace of her movements. The tinkle of crockery brought a promise of relief to Uncle Gwilym's sharp and worried features.

'Just ask yourself how it will affect your grandmother. I shouldn't have to say this to a man who's supposed to be gifted with imagination, but imagine her having to face people, in the shop, in chapel!'

Whatever answer formed itself in Cilydd's mind, he did

not allow himself to speak it. The shop was closed and the family was foregathering. Uncle Gwilym's chin jutted out hopefully as each member came in. Auntie Bessie supplemented Nanw's efforts. Her actions meshed in without speech. She produced pickled herrings from the larder. When they arrived at the table Uncle Tryfan was there in time to mime his appreciation by sniffing audibly through his narrow nose and rubbing the hard palms of his hands together with a rustling noise.

'A place for everything,' he said in his melodious happy way. 'And everything in its place.'

He sat down in his customary chair and then uttered his own sprightly variant on the adage.

'A place for everybody and everybody in his place!'

Mrs. Lloyd bustled in pressing her felt hat down on her springy hair with one hand and taking in the presence of the different members of her family as she did so. Uncle Gwilym quickly stood up. He could not willingly continue to sit in his mother's chair when there was any likelihood that she might want to sit in it herself. She made no demonstration of pleasure at seeing him.

'Who was the patient you had in there?'

He spoke with a nervous attempt at easy affability. His mother's blue eyes seemed to make him uncomfortable: they stared through the accoutrements of middle age to see more than a man would wish to be seen of the remnants of the expectations of youth.

'I don't know that you would know her,' Mrs. Lloyd said. 'A woman from Amlwch.'

Uncle Gwilym was impressed in spite of himself.

'They come from all parts,' he said. 'On the pilgrimage of health.'

Mrs. Lloyd was suddenly tired. She sat in her chair, her arms stretched out and her fists closed.

'If that's what you want to call it,' she said.

She smiled grimly.

'I must say it's a bit of responsibility to have two poets in the kitchen at once. I'm not sure that we are worthy of the honour. How is Annie?'

She managed to make the enquiry after the health of his wife sound mildly accusing.

'She's not too well,' Gwilym said. 'I wouldn't have come today, to tell you the truth, except for concern. About a certain matter.'

He picked up the mazagine so that his mother could see it. 'I'm worried about John Cilydd,' he said.

Cilydd sat on the end of the horsehair sofa, his arms folded.

'Thank you very much,' he said.

Uncle Gwilym ignored the sarcasm. With the zeal of a prosecutor he pointed his arm at his nephew as he appealed to his mother.

'He's threatening to publish the unchaired poem,' he said.

He watched her closely to register the effect of his bombshell. Momentarily Nanw and Auntie Bessie held up their complicated warp and woof of movement. Uncle Tryfan frowned hard, clearly incompletely informed about the case in hand.

'A strange thing,' Mrs. Lloyd said. 'To put a crown on the head of your own lack of success.'

It was an impersonal comment. It displeased Cilydd and gave Uncle Gwilym no satisfaction.

'Did you see what the adjudicators said about it? That's what worried me. "A heap of filth" . . .'

Auntie Bessie was so shocked she was unable to stop herself speaking.

'Oh, God help us,' she said.

Nanw darted out of the room to the scullery where she held her breath to hear what her grandmother would say. The ticking of the grandfather clock loomed loud in the expectant silence.

'There are things that worry me more,' Mrs. Lloyd said. 'How long is it, John Cilydd, since you were in chapel?'

John Cilydd tried to take the question lightly.

'Oh, we've moved to the chapel now, have we?' he said.

'Effusions are one thing,' Mrs. Lloyd said. 'The means of grace are another. And I know which is the more important.'

She could have been rebuking her nephew and her son simultaneously. Uncle Tryfan listened to her with undisguised admiration. Like an unpractised juggler Uncle Gwilym struggled to hold on both to his dignity and to the initiative.

'What are we going to look like, as a family, if this thing is published?'

He was trying to compel them all to consider deeply the consequences of such a rash action.

'He's got to be told,' Uncle Gwilym said. 'For his own good. He's starting a new legal practice in Pendraw to all intents and purposes. Well now, who will want to go to a lawyer that the adjudicators accused of having a depraved and dirty mind: of having composed a heap of filth?'

'Not to attend the means of grace is to put your immortal soul in peril,' Mrs. Lloyd said. 'That's more important.'

'I'm not saying it isn't,' Uncle Gwilym said.

His voice was sharp and relentless. He was suddenly full of confidence.

'But here we are confronted with an immediate problem. And in my view it's a family problem. A family affair.'

'Oh, be quiet, will you?'

Cilydd was on his feet, quivering with anger.

'You are driving me mad with your stupid noise. What do you think I am? A child still?'

He stumbled around the kitchen looking for his attaché case.

'Don't you understand I'm a grown man? A married man. Don't you understand that I'm free to do as I like? What do you think this place is? A prison? A dungeon? A grave for the living?'

He found the case and rushed up the stairs to the bedroom he occupied with Enid while their house in Pendraw was being prepared. They listened to the thud of his footsteps as he walked heavily down the upstairs passage.

'There is such a thing as the family's good name.'

Uncle Gwilym's effort to justify himself was ignored. Uncle Tryfan began to whistle a hymn tune under his breath, beating time on the edge of the table with an index finger.

'Food is ready,' Auntie Bessie said.

Mrs. Lloyd pushed on the arms of her chair to help herself to her feet. She looked more tired than usual.

'To the table,' she said.

It was partly a signal and partly an invitation. Uncle Gwilym became hesitant and finicky.

'I ought to go,' he said.

'Sit down and eat.'

Meekly he did as he was told. Plates had also been laid for John Cilydd and Enid; but they were conspicuous in their absence. The meal was eaten in silence.

5

Amy's footsteps echoed in the empty hall as she hurried from the kitchen at the back of the stage to the green baize table near the entrance where the money was being counted. The small schoolteacher was enjoying the job. Val stood by watching him. The schoolteacher's head was lowered close to the table. He had startlingly blue eyes and thick black eyebrows. Altogether his head seemed to need a longer body. His lank black hair was brushed carefully across his head in a vain attempt to conceal his premature baldness.

'How much have we made, I wonder? How much, Mr. Roberts?'

Amy was eager and curious. Val placed a restraining hand affectionately on her shoulder.

'"Iorrie" for goodness' sake, or I won't know who you're talking to,' the schoolteacher said.

He flashed her a smile like a personal gift. He was proud of his long white teeth. His manner was mildly effeminate.

'I sometimes think I should have worked in a bank,' he said. 'There's nothing I enjoy more than counting money. Isn't that a dreadful confession? Four pounds, twelve shillings and fourpence.'

'Very good,' Val said.

His tired benevolence seemed so general and other-worldly, he would have said the same had the count been either half or twice as much. His head lifted as he heard the bright note of a cornet being played in the dressing-room behind the stage. The chairs had been stacked against the walls and a haze of dust still filled the hall.

'What is that tune?'

Val spoke as though the name might be the clue to a mystery it would be interesting to solve.

'"The Carnival of Venice",' Mr. Roberts said. 'Personally I must say I can't stand it.'

'It's haunting though, isn't it?'

Val showed respect for Iorrie Roberts' opinion. He was a conductor of children's choirs, a figure of some significance in the musical life of the valley.

'He is a strange fellow.'

Val was even more fascinated by the player than the tune he played.

'Maddening, more like. He's been drinking.'

Amy was determinedly realistic.

'Even the cornet is a piece of propaganda.'

Iorrie Roberts gave Amy a shrewd glance.

'You could well be right,' he said. 'That's the difference between them and everybody else. They know exactly what they want and they go all out to get it. I've got an uncle, a miner's agent. He says there's no stopping them. You have to watch them every inch of the way.'

Amy looked knowingly at Val.

'There you are,' she said.

Val was obliged to defend himself.

'We can co-operate on the cultural front surely?' he said. 'We've got to keep things going. This is a land that's being left to become derelict and desolate. "Sioni is dying." Any movement for life has got to be welcomed.'

The other two were uneasy but unable to disagree with him. Iorrie Roberts put the money carefully into paper bags, keeping the silver and copper apart. Val yawned and stretched his arms.

'I'm so tired,' he said. 'I've got to admit it. I can't wait to get to bed.'

Iorrie Roberts showed serious concern.

'You've got to look after your health,' he said. 'That's all important. It's not my business to say this, Miss Parry ...'

'"Amy",' Amy said.

Iorrie smiled gratefully.

'It's not my business, but he does work much too hard. And I doubt very much, just between you and me, whether he eats enough either.'

'Who does these days?'

Val was uncharacteristically abrupt. Iorrie did not give up.

'You can't live on a perpetual diet of bread and cocoa,' he said.

Val smiled wearily.

'We had fish and chips tonight,' he said. 'It made a nice change.'

Iorrie had not finished. He wagged a finger at Val.

'You must eat,' he said. '*You* are not unemployed. You are working every hour God sends.'

Pen Lewis appeared at the back of the stage. Val took the excuse to stop listening to Iorrie's lecture. Pen had a cap with a small bright peak perched on the back of his head and a Ukrainian shirt with loose sleeves and a flowered front that buttoned high on the side of his neck. He was still in concert mood, ready to perform and be observed. He half closed his eyes as he blew his cornet. The belted trousers he wore did not quite suit the upper half of his costume, but he was happy to be looked at. The light glinted on the three buttons of his shirt collar. He jumped down from a rostrum with the theatrical flamboyance of an athletic film star.

'Dougie Fairbanks!'

He shouted out gaily. His face was flushed.

'All next week at the Grand. Great double feature. "When Love grows Cold" and "Love 'em and leave 'em". Opium for the masses.'

With some stiff miming, he began to play his own mocking version of 'The Indian Love Call' on the cornet. Tired as he was Val exerted himself to show some admiration for the performance. He seemed to offer himself as a bridge between the smouldering hostility of Iorrie Roberts and Amy and the aggressive challenge Pen was making as he pranced around the centre of the hall, kicking up the dust and blowing his cornet. And in the end the dust was too much for him. His solo ended in a bout of choking and coughing. He staggered towards them and offered his broad back for slapping. Amy was nearest, but she drew back from the task even as he was pointing in rough gestures to his own back. Laughingly Val moved forward to oblige. His thumping was too gentle.

'Harder, for God's sake.'

Pen gasped with exaggerated desperation.

309

'I may be wilting but I'm not a lily.'

He recovered his breath and smiled boldly at Amy, inviting her to share the joke. Iorrie was annoyed. Pen began coughing again.

'I'm not silicotic, either.'

As he spluttered, Pen stretched his neck to look at the treasurer's note-book.

'How much did we make?' he said.

'Four pounds, twelve shillings and fourpence.'

Iorrie Roberts spoke with extreme precision. The effort made him sound more effeminate. Pen held the mouthpiece of the cornet to one eye.

'I still think Barry Island would be better,' he said. 'That would be for all the kids and not just a small group of pubescent female élite.'

'The decision has been taken,' Iorrie said. 'There's not much point in discussing it any further.'

'"Preference will be given to girls who can speak Welsh."'

Pen recited the imaginary condition in the prim and over-pious manner of a spinster talking to a Sunday school class.

'That's not true,' Amy said. 'And you know it.'

She could not resist intervening. Pen looked at her, obviously pleased that she had risen to the bait.

'They are not an élite in any sense,' she said. 'Unless of course you can call the sick an élite.'

'Sherbet and buns,' Pen said. 'And a ride on the figure-eight for all. Better bargain. And the donkeys. Of both sexes.'

It was only then that Amy saw that he was teasing her. She made a dismissive gesture, but he was enjoying himself too much to stop.

'And apart from that,' Pen said. 'What are you doing? Putting salve on the sore conscience of the rich. Making a coal-owner's sensitive sister feel good. They've got three mansions, for God's sake. At least one of them should be a home for miners with dust on the lung.'

'You're not saying anything I haven't said already,' Amy said. 'Many times.'

'Go on. You've told her that already, have you? To her face?'

Val stretched his arms and yawned. A childish note had

entered the argument. Amy and Pen could have been facing each other in the corner of the playground.

'A chance was offered and we're taking it,' Amy said. 'Thirty girls at Iscoed Hall. Some camping, some indoors.'

'Aye. Aye. So long as the lady of the manor doesn't change her mind.'

'What on earth makes you think she would do that?'

'You don't know much about the rich, do you?'

'Do you?'

'I know one thing. They find it very easy to change their minds. Doesn't cost them anything, see.'

Pen blew two notes on his cornet to illustrate a quick change of mind. He followed it with a brassy snort of contempt.

'That's why they've got to be swept away.'

'I suppose you want to shoot the poor old thing?'

'No I don't. But I would if I had to.'

'Poor old Miss Eirwen.'

'Poor old nothing. The lines are drawn up. In the class war she's one of the enemy. You get them or they get you. That's what war is all about.'

'What about us?'

Amy indicated Val, Iorrie and herself.

'Will you shoot us as well?'

'Depends which side you're on,' Pen said. 'That's logic, Miss Parry. Didn't they teach you that in College.'

While they were still arguing the caretaker of the Welfare Hall emerged from the shadows. He was singing gently to himself in a high tenor. He wore a bow tie in honour of the musical evening, but now his jacket was removed and his shirtsleeves were rolled up to the elbow to reveal the tighter sleeves of the woollen vest that clung to his wrists. He carried a brush like a ceremonial halberd. One leg was stiff at the knee and he rose and fell as he walked. His manner was totally affable.

'Lovely it was.'

He spoke as he advanced. Amy and Pen stopped arguing.

'A real treat. Lovely. Lovely. Tell me, Mr. Gwyn. I've been meaning to ask you. Did you ever hear of Madame Sarah Gwyn?'

311

He leaned on his brush as he waited for an answer, his head tilted back to one side and his lips curved in a musical smile that revealed the tips of his upper dentures like the ivories of a partially concealed keyboard.

'I'm afraid not.'

Val was apologetic.

'An outstanding soprano. Thought she could have been related. Sang in America I don't know how many times. Once she sang "Abide with Me" to a man condemned to the electric chair. A unique experience.'

Pen burst out laughing. The caretaker looked at him challengingly.

'Sorry,' Pen said as he recovered. 'Which was the unique experience? The song or the electric chair?'

The caretaker was offended.

'It was his last request, man. A Welsh singer. And Madame Sarah Gwyn was selected. It's an interesting fact. I thought Mr. Gwyn would like to know.'

'Yes,' Val said.

He stirred himself to soothe the caretaker a little.

'Very interesting. It's very kind of you to tell me.'

The caretaker shifted about as though he was about to begin work. Then he returned to speak to Val again.

'And I'll tell you something else. She nearly went down on the *Titanic*. Her train was late and she was transferred to another boat. She always used to mention this fact before rendering "Ocean, thou mighty monster".'

The caretaker sang an illustrative line and looked at Iorrie Roberts for confirmation and approval. Pen lifted his cornet to his lips and tried to blow an accompaniment. They were in different keys. The caretaker pulled a face. It gave Pen a more acceptable excuse for laughing. In the end they were all able to join in a brief outburst of comradely merriment. They stood looking at each other in the empty hall like an operatic quintet attempting a first rehearsal.

'God, I'm hungry,' Pen said. 'How about some chips?'

They stood together on top of the steps of the Welfare Hall. Outside it had been raining. The water gurgled in the gutters. The poor street lights only served to draw attention to the quiet desolation of the deserted streets. A breeze blew from the mountain and they shivered after the warmth of the Welfare Hall.

'Everything's closed already,' Pen said. 'What a bloody dump. You look up the street and you look down the street and you see bugger all except misery and slag heaps.'

'Come in for a cup of tea or cocoa or something.'

Val had woken up in the cold night air. His natural generosity was reasserting itself.

'Me?'

Pen pointed to his chest with his cornet.

'In there? Isn't Holy Ned down on a visit?' he said. 'He'd go barmy if he saw me in there.'

It was obvious how much he wanted to accept Val's invitation to the settlement house in spite of what he was saying.

'They sleep at the top,' Val said. 'If we don't make too much noise they won't know who's inside.'

Like a naughty child Pen hid the cornet behind his back. All four walked up the lane alongside Noddfa Chapel. Pen took the opportunity to speak to Amy in a more friendly and understanding fashion.

'He turned me out, see,' he said. 'I was just having a little theoretical discussion and he got all white in the face and stormy. You can't turn this settlement into a propaganda den, he said. Alright, I said. Keep your hair on, Rev. He took real offence at that because, as you know, he's as bald as a berry.'

He had succeeded in making Amy laugh. He wrinkled his blunt-edged nose and she laughed even more. Val looked back over Iorrie's head which was lowered as he made one more calculation of profit and loss over the evening's proceedings. He was pleased to see that they were getting along better.

'We'll have to give Mrs. Stephens something,' Iorrie said, demanding Val's attention. 'I don't know ... half a crown perhaps? What do you think? Or is that too much?'

'Whatever you think best, Iorrie.'

Pen slowed his step. He spoke in a low confidential tone words meant for Amy alone.

'Three things concern me,' he said.

Amy was obliged to slow down and listen. He stopped as though expecting her to give him a fair and sympathetic hearing.

'Now they all mesh into each other, see? I'd like you to understand.'

He held out his hand to tick off the points on his fingers. The cornet hung from his thumb.

'Power at the Lodge level. The day to day struggle.'

'But you're out of work,' Amy said.

'Don't interrupt, love. While the spirits move me. There's a good girl.'

Pen drew a deep breath and went on.

'Power in the Trade Union movement. Now you know what I call that? The Drive to Militancy. That's crucial. Absolutely crucial. Linked to organising the unemployed in an effective right to work movement. And then of course there's the great International of Red Labour Unions. And it's all linked you see. All linked.'

'You said three things,' Amy said. 'You've named at least four.'

After a moment's pause he chuckled to himself.

'Sharp, aren't you?'

Amy walked faster to catch up with Val and Iorrie.

'Hang on,' Pen said. 'Hang on, girl. I haven't finished yet.'

Val did not switch on any light until he found his way to the kitchen. He put his finger to his lips and beckoned them all in. He closed the corridor doors. Iorrie filled the kettle and lit the gas. Amy reached down four enamel mugs from the row of hooks inside the large wooden cupboard. The kitchen was clean but very bare. Pen was full of things he wanted to say.

'You want to watch out for philanthropic noises,' he said. 'She's got a chapel name I know, Eirwen Owens, but scratch the surface and what you'll find underneath is Salome dressed as Marie Antoinette.'

Val laughed obligingly. In the small larder a can of milk stood in an enamel bowl filled with water. Amy smelt the milk before pouring it into the jug. Pen raised his voice to make sure she could hear him.

'When you're at the bottom of the pit, boy, you know that those three mansions have been built right on top of you.

And all you are good for in this world is for them to make use of you.'

'He doesn't have to tell us anything about that, does he, Val?' Amy said.

She was eager to speak.

'Val had a great idea for a Welsh Folk High School on the Danish model. They were all for it. It was all going to happen. And then suddenly they dropped it like a hot brick.'

Only when she had spoken did she see Val's distaste for the subject. She moved to the stove to help Iorrie with the tea. She poured milk into the four mugs. Pen sat on the table, pushed back his cap and grinned sardonically at Val.

'Oh, so you've been peddling that idea before, have you?'

Val looked too tired to argue. Pen picked up his cornet and placed it to his lips. His cheeks expanded and contracted in silence as he threatened to blow it and waited for Val to reply to his challenge.

'A good idea is a good idea,' Val said. 'This year. Last year. Next year. Good ideas don't wear out that quickly.'

'Ah, but is it a good idea? That is the vital question.'

Pen was alive with the desire to argue.

'Or is it just one more palliative?'

'That's a big word,' Iorrie said.

Pen turned on him in a flash.

'Want me to tell you what it means, Mr. Roberts?'

Val suppressed a yawn. He looked around for a chair to sit on and rubbed his cheeks with his fingers. Pen's confidence seemed to make him more tired.

'Look around you, for God's sake,' Pen said. 'You can see for yourself the capitalist system is finished. Kaputt. And the simple logic of the situation is, it's got to be replaced by something better. That's all there is to it.'

'Communism, I suppose?'

Iorrie handed Val a welcome cup of tea.

'That's it, comrade.'

Pen grinned cheerfully.

'How did you guess?'

'I tell you what I think,' Iorrie said.

He spoke as though he were standing in for Val whom he knew to be almost too tired to speak.

315

'I think a healthy society is a society that has a proper respect for the past.'

'"Comrades, we must shake off the dead hand of the past" V.I. Lenin.'

Iorrie made his dark cheeks dimple with an ironic smile.

'Good preacher, was he?'

Pen ignored Iorrie's frivolity. He lifted his mug to point at Val.

'He knows in his heart of hearts,' he said. 'That's why he's so quiet. He's bright is Mr. Val Gwyn. The trouble is he belongs to the wrong class. That's what it amounts to on the level of historical analysis. I tell you I've been seriously thinking of writing a song about it. "The future belongs to the working class." Would you like to hear it?'

Val pointed to the ceiling to remind him of the people sleeping at the top of the house.

'The first line goes, "The future belongs to the working class and I belong to the working class, so the future belongs to me". Good, isn't it?'

He spread out his arms as though waiting for a measure of applause.

'Think it will catch on?'

'So do I,' Amy said. 'I belong to the working class.'

'Well it's your lucky day, girlie.'

Pen was carried away with his own eloquence.

'We're taking them on! And we are going to win. All over the world.'

He threw out his chest as though he were exhibiting the details of the flowered front on his shirt.

'That's why I can be confident and optimistic and full of energy in the middle of all this misery, while all you lot are moaning and groaning and fiddling about. I belong to the party that is the spearhead of a great world-wide movement. And I have my little place in the struggle. And it doesn't matter what happens to me. I don't give a tuppeny damn. Because we are going to win. And if you lot had the least bit of bloody sense you'd stop being *twp* and come in and join us. And that's a bit of the best advice I can give you.'

'Thank you very much,' Iorrie said.

He sipped his tea and waited for Val to provide a better and more conclusive reply. Val looked pale and tired.

'All aboard the great salvation train. Heaven is just round the corner.'

This was all Val was prepared to say. He put his mug down on the sideboard.

'I'm off to bed,' he said. 'Tomorrow . . .'

He closed his eyes wearily and decided against reciting the catalogue of work in hand for the following day.

'Tomorrow is just another day. Not the Red Dawn.'

Pen was plainly disappointed to forgo what he had wanted to become a vigorous debate. He pushed his hands under his thighs and swung his legs.

'Can I finish my tea?' he said. 'Before I go to the home I haven't got to go to?'

Val raised an arm in a gesture of deep apology.

'Amy will see you both out,' he said. 'Good night and thank you both for all your help.'

When Val had gone, Amy sat at the table turning her mug around slowly with both hands. It seemed for a while that all three were at a loss to know what to say to each other. Iorrie sipped cautiously at his mug, his eyes shifting discreetly from Pen to Amy and guarding a frontier of silence along the rim of the mug.

'Tell you something I wanted to ask you.'

Pen leaned down the table so that he could put his question to Amy. He did not seem to worry that by so doing he was obscuring her from Iorrie's view.

'This Head of Hall business. At College, like. And this camp committee business. Were you appointed or elected?'

Amy's cheeks began to redden.

'As a matter of fact I was elected,' she said. 'Why?'

'Just interested,' he said. 'I like to know how things work. Always analyse to find the source of power.'

Iorrie got up to rinse his cup under the single brass tap.

'I think it's time to go home,' he said.

Pen looked at him thoughtfully as though he had made an odd and unusual proposal.

'Educational systems reflect economic systems,' Pen said. 'God Bless the Prince of Wales in the infants. God save the King in the college. It's all the same thing.'

Iorrie stood by the table. Amy was listening to Pen but he insisted quietly on her attention.

317

'I'll say good night then, Amy,' he said.

Amy pushed back her chair and stood up apologetically.

'Of course,' she said. 'I'll see you both out and lock the door.'

Pen was reluctant to leave.

'Pity,' he said. 'I was about to learn a little more about our vaunted education system.'

In the corridor he looked towards the uncarpeted stairs.

'Where do you sleep?'

He put the question to Amy and waited for an answer, ignoring Iorrie's look of disapproval. Amy raised an arm and then lowered it.

'Why do you ask?'

'Got to know which window to play my serenade under.'

Pen gave a roguish smile and put the cornet to his lips.

'What would you like me to play? I've got a vast repertoire.'

He blew a brief note. Amy grasped his arm and shook it, anxious to stop him but laughing in spite of herself.

'For goodness' sake, don't wake them,' she said.

'Aye.'

Pen appeared contented to have evoked so much response from her.

'You've got a point there. Let sleeping friends lie. Free cocoa for ever!'

In the lane, Pen waited until he heard the door being locked. Iorrie had already reached the side of the chapel. He stood with his hands in his mac pockets, as if it were part of his duty to see an irresponsible element off the premises. A gust of wind blew a greasy paper bag up to their feet like a pale miniature ghost. Pen rubbed the palm of his hand against the uneven surface of one of the foundation stones of the tall chapel.

'You think I'm a barbarian,' Pen said. 'A Philistine. Well I'm not, see. I used to like going to this chapel when I was a kid. Even though I couldn't understand a word of it. Boy soprano, I was. Outstanding. In a way you could say I've got nothing against the place. It's just that it's peddling the wrong medicine. Look at it like this. Would you go on employing a witch-doctor when you knew for certain that all he was doing was spreading death and disease?'

Pen sank down on his heels, his back to the chapel. He peered up at the Settlement House and saw a light going on in the room on the first floor where Amy slept. For a moment she appeared in the window to draw the thin curtains.

Iorrie was looking down at Pen squatting in the shadow of the chapel like the caricature of a collier ignoring the difference between day and night.

'You don't have to be here,' he said. 'You could get a job anywhere you liked.'

He was plainly steeling himself against taking too sympathetic an interest in Pen's fluent discourse: determined not to be caught by any gift of the gab.

'You had a job in London,' Iorrie said. 'Everybody knows that.'

Pen grinned up at him.

'True enough, comrade. Squat down here and I'll tell you all about it.'

'It's late,' Iorrie said suspiciously.

'The night is young, comrade. In Paris, Rome, Berlin, the talking hasn't started yet.'

'This is Cwm Du,' Iorrie said. 'Not Paris or Berlin. And it's getting late.'

'It's later than you think!'

Pen flourished his cornet at the schoolteacher.

'I tell you one thing, Mr. Roberts. And I've noticed this often with teachers. Elementary or otherwise. I find them lacking in intellectual stamina.'

'I don't know about you, but I'm going home,' Iorrie said.

'Are you now? Well, I fancy sitting here for a bit. Imagine King Canute as old King Coal the collier. That's me. Telling the waves of hunger and depression to roll back. To the bottom of the street, back into the river and down to the bloody sea.'

Pen touched the mouthpiece of his cornet with his tongue.

'That's one thing a Marxist has to have, Mr. Roberts,' he said. 'Patience. Patience to watch the great patterns of history unfolding. If you don't do that, see, you'll never know just where to give that little extra shove in the right place at the right time.'

With an ironic display of force, Pen pushed his back against the stone wall behind him. He watched Iorrie passing

319

through the weak light of the bracket lamp at the end of the chapel wall. When his footsteps had faded in the distance, Pen moved quickly to the rear of the chapel. He was familiar with the dark territory. He felt under a long slate shelf for a ladder lying on its side against the wall. He put the cornet down carefully on the shelf, knelt down and eased the ladder out. When it was free he set it on his shoulder and walked steadily up the lane to the settlement. Without apparent effort or haste he settled the ladder down alongside a drainpipe. Whistling under his breath he climbed up to the window of Amy's room. Her light had gone out. He tapped lightly on the windowpane and waited. The crescent moon appeared out of the clouds. He saluted it before rapping the window again a little louder. When Amy moved the curtain aside she had a heavy hairbrush in her hand. Pen smiled at her winningly as if he were paying a social call. The top half of the window was open a few inches.

'What on earth do you want?'

Amy made an effort to stop her voice trembling. Pen was peering through the glass into the room.

'Got a room to yourself then,' he said. 'Guest room, as they say. I thought you'd be on a straw mattress on the floor. Where's Val then?'

'What do you want?'

Amy was forcing herself to sound angry.

'There's a lot of things I'm dying to talk about,' he said. 'Can I come in?'

'Indeed you can't.'

'Fair enough.'

Pen nodded understandingly.

'That's what old Wes Hicks keeps on telling me. I'm weak on the respectability front. Tell you what, let me just ease this window down a little. To facilitate communication.'

With some show of strength and skill he pressed the top half of the window down without making too much noise. He placed both arms on the frame and leaned into the room – a black shape against the pale moonlight.

'That's better,' he said. 'It's not as good as being inside of course, but one must be thankful for little mercies. If you came a little closer I could touch you. I don't suppose you've got much on under that.'

Amy moved away into the shadows.

'It's a funny old world, isn't it? I want to touch you more than anything else I can think of and yet the conventions of middle-class morality demand that I should never mention it. Shall I tell you what I think? A fine woman responds to touch. The gentle touch of really strong hands. What I mean to say is, why can't we just be frank and honest and open about it?'

'You're drunk.'

Amy tried to whisper fiercely.

'Somebody's sure to hear you.'

'Feel like screaming, do you? Well, go on then. Let's see what you can do.'

Pen shook with amusement and the ladder wobbled alarmingly under him.

'Oops.'

He held on to the window frame and pretended to be frightened. Amy walked determinedly to the window. She lifted her hairbrush threateningly.

'I could push you over,' she said. 'And then you'd break your silly neck.'

Pen managed to remain calm and innocent.

'That's it,' he said. 'My life is in your hands.'

'You're drunk,' Amy said. 'You must be.'

'Only on you, my lovely. Only on you. You are a marvellous creation.'

'Go away. Please. Just go away.'

Pen nodded philosophically.

'Okay,' he said. 'Okay. Fair enough. You're Val's girl, after all. Fair enough. But let me ask you just one thing. Why aren't you sleeping with him?'

'That's none of your business.'

'Of course it isn't. Of course it isn't. He's a man of many virtues and if I wasn't committed to the Party like, I could well be inclined to admire him. He's bright and he's good of course, by the best Chapel standards, but you know, there are times when I think he doesn't understand anything at all.'

He listened hard in an attempt to gauge Amy's reaction to what he was saying. She stood clutching her hairbrush in the deepest shadow so that he should not be able to see her face.

'Now he doesn't understand that a man's job is to lead his

woman into a magical world – another level of existence that she wouldn't otherwise ever know about. Do you know what I mean?'

'Why don't you go? You've heard me ask you.'

'I've watched you pretty closely when you're together,' he said. 'I know it's rude but I can't help it. I'm a pretty observant sort of fellow. Well ahead of my time and my level of education, if the truth were told. The conclusion I've come to is he doesn't touch you enough. It's as simple as that really. He doesn't understand women. He just doesn't know how to bring that special light into their eyes.'

'Get out. I'm telling you to get out!'

'I've read a bit about these things. And I expect you have, too. But it wouldn't do to get it all out of books. You can't become a virtuoso without plenty of practice.'

'Just go away.'

The words came out in a suppressed scream.

'Fair enough,' he said. 'I'm on my way. But you've got to let me do my little bit of boasting. What's wrong with sexual enjoyment? You just ask yourself that? What's wrong with physical ecstasy? Don't worry, now. I'm going. Shall I close the window?'

'Leave it,' Amy said. 'Just go.'

Pen looked down the ladder. The moonlight showed more of his face. He looked as though he were beginning to regret his adventure.

'I've made a mess of it, I can see,' he said. 'I know I've got the name for being a bit of a philanderer. I have played around a bit, there's no use me denying it. But this is what I want to say. You are something special. And I'll come any distance if you ever want me. It's ironic really. I'm supposed to have given myself to the Party, and of course I have. After all we are the élite, the spearhead, the officer corps if you like, of the world-wide working-class movement. But if it was between you and the Party, my God it would be a hell of a struggle.'

He began to climb down the ladder, testing each rung as he descended. While Amy was struggling to lift the top half of the window, he looked up at her, able at last to see her face in the moonlight. He leaned back from the ladder to call up at her in a loud whisper.

'Next time we talk about politics not sex. Right?'

Amy pushed out her head.

'Pig!' she said. 'Pig!'

It seemed to be all she could think of saying. She could see his teeth as he grinned. Her anger gave her the strength to close the window. For some time she paced up and down the room swinging the hairbrush at an imaginary adversary. Then she went to the window to stare at the dim roofs of the terrace houses and the movement of the clouds in the moonlit sky. Pen had disappeared.

In the narrow bed she sat up with her arms wound tightly across her knees. She was too disturbed to sleep. She lay down with her head on the pillow but her eyes were wide open, staring at the window. Suddenly she threw off the bed clothes and made for the door. Barefoot, she tip-toed across the landing to the small room where Val was sleeping. With two hands she turned the brass door knob and entered. At the side of the iron bed she whispered his name. He was fast asleep. She stood in her pyjamas, indecisive and nervous until she began to shiver. Resolutely she lifted the edge of the bed clothes. She would slip in without waking him up. Her hand pressed on the pillow. She withdrew it quickly. Her palm was wet and sticky. She began to tremble.

'Val,' she said. 'Val. Wake up.'

'Um?'

She could hear his tongue clicking against his palate.

'My mouth feels full of salt,' he said. 'Amy. Is it you? What's the matter?'

He sat up and pressed his hand to his mouth. Amy stumbled to the door and switched on the light. Val's white pillow was soaked with blood. He blinked wearily and moved his hand from his mouth. It was covered in blood.

'Look at that,' he said.

He was still confused and bewildered with sleep.

'Just look at that,' he said.

6

A high wind shook the leaves and swayed the branches of the trees that covered the slope on the east side of the drive. On the west side, between the shrubbery and the open parkland, a stalwart line of oaks was less affected. Black cattle sheltering from the gusts of rain moved their heavy heads to stare at Amy as she trudged along the drive. The trees dwarfed her solitary figure. Her hat was pulled low over her face. A long macintosh reached down over gumboots that made walking more tedious. Her hands were plunged deep in her pockets and she leaned forward looking at the ground as she marched towards the distant house. In spite of the weather, red squirrels were active on the lower branches of the trees. Absorbed in her own thoughts Amy took little notice of them.

She was roused by the sound of a motor horn. Without looking up she moved to the mown grass verge to allow the vehicle to pass. A woman driver was hunched over the steering wheel of the Austin saloon. She applied the brakes suddenly. The skidding of the wheels on the wet surface made Amy look up with alarm.

'Miss Parry!'

The driver's door opened and Miss Wade leaned out. She was smiling rather desperately.

'I'm sorry I didn't recognise you. Let me give you a lift.'

Amy opened the passenger door and then hesitated with one rubber boot on the running board.

'I'm wet,' she said.

'Oh my goodness, that doesn't matter.'

Miss Wade clutched the vibrating steering wheel and smiled at her most affably. Her teeth were almost clenched as the car moved forward. She thrust her face as close as she could to the windscreen.

'How's it going?' she said.

'I've been to the post,' Amy said.

Miss Wade nodded understandingly. She snatched a wondering glance at Amy's wet face and the car swerved in response to the jerky movement.

'Everything would be fine if the weather was fine,' Miss Wade said. 'That's always the case with camping. Still, happy healthy fellowship. That's what keeps things going.'

A front wheel hit a puddle and water cascaded over the windscreen. Miss Wade narrowly avoided driving into a ditch on the right of the drive.

'I suppose it could be worse.'

She laughed bravely.

'Snow. Ice. Floods. We have to be ready for absolutely anything. Much as I hate motoring in this weather, I had to come. Eirwen is expecting me. And I was longing to see how the camp was getting on, of course. Are the younger girls behaving?'

'Oh yes.'

They reached the second lodge, a low building half hidden with rambling roses. The long white gate was already open. A gardener with a sack over his head and shoulders was poking a drain with a long-handled shovel. He paused in his work to turn to raise his right hand to touch the peak of the sack as if it were a cap. He seemed eager to be recognised as a useful and respectful worker. Miss Wade jerked her head without taking her eyes off the slow curve in the drive. The trees stood further apart to present the first glimpse of Plas Iscoed standing in splendid isolation among its several gardens.

'It's always a little thrill,' Miss Wade said. 'The first glimpse of the house.'

It was obvious that she wished Amy to share the nuances of the aesthetic pleasure that still visited her in spite of the responsibilities of driving the saloon.

'Where shall I drop you?' Miss Wade said. 'Where are the tents?'

'I expect most of the girls will be in the outbuildings,' Amy said. 'That's where they go when it's raining.'

'Oh dear ... But we can't legislate for the weather, can we? They say this is the wettest summer since the War. Oh dear ...'

The front wheel of the Austin went over the edge of the lawn. Miss Wade over-compensated, swerved to the right, and then back to the left before eventually establishing the car back in the middle of the drive. She forked right to take the rougher road that led to the stables and the outhouses behind the house. The car bumped and jerked over the cobbles. Girls appeared in the open doorway of the coachhouse. They looked cold, hungry and bored.

'Oh dear,' Miss Wade said. 'We must find them something to do, mustn't we? I suppose they sing, do they?'

'We need a table tennis of some kind,' Amy said. 'There is a shuttlecock but there's only one racket. And the strings are nearly all broken. We need games really, more than anything.'

'Look,' Miss Wade said.

Now the car was stationary she sounded more confident and resourceful.

'As soon as I've had a word with Eirwen we'll have a conference. What do you say? An emergency meeting. What do you say?'

More girls appeared in the tall doorway. They were mildly diverted by the spectacle of Miss Wade reversing her car in a space where there would have been room for her to turn in a comfortable circle. When she had driven off, an eager girl carrying a bald tennis ball ran up to Amy.

'Miss Parry. There's a young lady waiting for you in your tent. She said she'd rather wait for you there.'

A second smaller girl followed her to repeat the message.

'She's wearing a ring, miss. She's married. I noticed that.'

They began to follow Amy as she started walking towards the field gate. She turned to stop them.

'No,' she said. 'You stay here. It's too wet in the field.'

The camping area was hidden from the great house by a shoulder of tree-covered hill. There were seven bell tents, and a small marquee. Hurdles covered with sacking hid a latrine area in a corner of the field sheltered by tall hedges.

Amy lifted the canvas flap. In the grey light of the interior she saw Enid seated on a camp stool. She was reading. She wore a thick woollen cardigan for warmth. Her knees were pressed close together and she sat as patiently as a mute statue of fidelity. Amy looked down at her wet wellingtons. When she lifted her head her eyes were filled with tears. Like a mother greeting a child late arriving home, Enid put down

her book and quietly embraced her. She helped Amy remove
her mac and her boots, lifted her legs and made her lie down
on the camp bed. So much kind attention was too much for
Amy. She turned her face into her pillow. Her whole body
shook with unrestrained weeping. She held out her hand.
Enid took it. When Amy spoke her voice was muffled by the
pillow.

'Why?' she said. 'Why?'

'He's going to get better,' Enid said. 'I'm sure of it. He's
strong. He's a strong man in every way.'

Amy sat up and groped about for a handkerchief. Enid
gave her hers.

'It's like a sentence of death,' Amy said. 'You know that as
well as I do.'

Enid was ready to disagree vigorously.

'No it isn't,' she said. 'That's not true any more. When it's
caught in time, there are all sorts of cures.'

Amy wiped her eyes and stared at Enid.

'I saw his pillow,' she said. 'It was soaked in blood.'

She rubbed her fingers together nervously and gave back
the handkerchief.

'I can't sleep,' she said. 'I just lie here thinking about him
and listening to the rain, waiting for it to seep through the
canvas. I keep seeing his pillow all the time, soaking with
blood.'

Enid leaned forward to touch Amy's face.

'I would have come sooner,' she said. 'We didn't know. I
mean we didn't realise it was so bad.'

'When I couldn't sleep, I tried to pray. Can you imagine
that?'

'Of course I can.'

Amy struck herself on the chest with her open hand.

'Yes, but I mean me. Of all people. Then I began to believe
it was all my fault. I was so certain of it I could prove it like
working out a theorem. Q.E.D. I write every day. But I don't
say anything new. Hopeless letters. Just "I love you" over
and over again.'

'You mustn't start blaming yourself,' Enid said. 'That is
ridiculous. And it would be wrong too. Quite wrong.'

'I'm so miserable,' Amy said. 'I thought this camp
business would help. I try to do it as best I can. I just go

through the motions. That's all I am good for. Two of the girls have gone home. One was homesick and the other was coughing all the time. I couldn't stand the sound of it.'

Together they stared in silence through the slit entrance. All they could see was wet grass and clouds that seemed to be touching the hedges. The outlook was so depressing even thistles stood out as welcome relief. Amy turned on the narrow camp bed to look longingly at Enid.

'I'm afraid to kiss him,' she said.

Enid moved her camp stool closer.

'Can you imagine anything more shameful? Last time I met his mother in the corridor when I was leaving. She stood as still as a graven image looking at me and saying absolutely nothing. I could just see her white hair in the shadows. I followed her back to the door of Val's room. I watched her kiss him. And then I just ran away. I ran like a little weasel. Can you imagine that?'

Enid rubbed a knuckle against her lips as she searched for the right words to use.

'Look here, Amy,' she said. 'You've just got to realise that you are suffering from a form of shock. In a sense you are just as much of a patient as Val is.'

'Of course I'm not.'

'You should be looked after. There's really no sense in you being here, taking on this huge job all by yourself.'

'It's not a huge job,' Amy said. 'It's purely mechanical. Any fool could do it.'

'Well ... any normal fool.'

Enid ventured a smile.

'The weather's awful anyway,' she said. 'Sitting in a wet tent like this is enough to give anyone the blues. Give the order ... abandon ship! And come and stay with us. John Cilydd said that was an order. We've got a house of our own with lots of rooms. All of them empty. I know you don't like the idea of teaching. You could stay with us while you make your mind up what to do next.'

Amy considered what Enid was saying.

'I'm responsible for these girls,' she said. 'You should see the poverty they come from. It was our idea. Val's and mine. I've simply got to see it through. They've got to have a proper holiday. This awful weather can't go on for ever ... But it is nice of you both to ask me.'

'When we moved in it was the first thing we thought about,' Enid said. 'We were in a bit of a state about the eisteddfod poem. The poor old "heap of filth".'

'Oh yes.'

Amy made the effort to show that she knew what Enid was talking about.

'A minor family crisis. But it could have been a major one. You know. A large-scale family quarrel where people don't speak to each other for years and years and all that sort of thing. But I persuaded him not to publish it. I just convinced him it wasn't good enough.'

Amy smiled at her admiringly.

'You clever old thing,' she said.

'And of course when we heard about Val everything fell into perspective. The first thing we thought when we moved in was, Val and Amy could live here as well. We arranged it all. We could nurse him in turns, you and I. There are good cheap printers in Pendraw. We could publish *Dadeni* ... you know ... I'm ashamed to say we were both of us boiling over with ideas about how to make use of you.'

The flow of Enid's enthusiasm dried up when she was aware that Amy's attention had wandered. In silence they sat together and listened to the wind like waves on a distant shore rustling through the tall trees that surrounded the site of the great house.

'I can tell you what I've been thinking,' Amy said.

Her voice sounded remote and forlorn.

'It must be all these hymns we've been singing in the rain. I think God and Death are two different words for exactly the same thing.'

She gazed challengingly at her best friend in the weak light of the tent interior.

'I know you don't agree with me,' Amy said. 'I know you think I'm confused and all over the place. Well I'm not, you know. I do know what I'm talking about.'

Enid's hands began to flutter in the air as she made a series of rapid adjustments in an invisible scale of justice.

'All those dreadful hymns in the minor key,' Amy said.

'All that Chapel noise. Why can't we stand up and fight back? All that whining and snivelling. Did we ever ask to get born?'

Enid swayed rhythmically to and fro on the camp stool.

'I think I understand what you mean,' she said. 'But there are basic facts that we all have to accept.'

Amy stood up and stretched herself to look up at the ventilators in the canvas at the top of the pole.

'This tent pole is a fact,' she said. 'But does that mean I've got to worship it?'

Enid also got to her feet. The tent pole was between them.

'Alright,' she said. 'If you're staying I'm staying. I'll have that empty bed.'

Amy took her hands and squeezed them in gratitude.

'It's marvellous to see you,' she said. 'You wise old thing. I feel better already.'

A girl put her head in the tent. Her eyes were large with self-importance and eager for attention to her message.

'Miss Parry,' she said. 'There's Miss Wade by the house, she says she wants you.'

Amy looked at the girl understandingly.

'Thank you, Menna,' she said. 'Tell her I'll be along in a moment, will you?'

The girl hesitated for a moment at the mercy of a bout of inquisitive interest in the figure of Enid. She seemed to have to wind herself up before she smiled, nodded and shot off.

'Want to come and meet her?'

Amy was talking about Miss Wade.

'Your old friend. She said she had a great respect for you. She said she didn't agree with our politics, et cetera, but respected us for standing up for them.'

Enid made no comment. Amy began to take the Warden more lightly.

'Tinker Bell. That's her nickname believe it or not. Frankie Yoreth, I need hardly add.'

Amy searched in her canvas washbag for a wet flannel with which to wipe the tear stains from her face. She struggled to comb her hair, holding a small shiny metal mirror in her other hand.

'The joys of camping,' she said. 'High tea in the stables at five o'clock! I expect old Tinker Bell will keep herself cosy in the house with the lady of the manor. She's not so bad, though. I must say she's gone out of her way to be decent to me.'

Amy paused before pulling on her wellingtons.

'I suppose it all seems very far away to you now, does it?' she said. 'Hall of Residence and all that . . . Battles long ago.'

Enid smiled shyly.

'You won't believe me,' she said. 'If anything I'm more extreme than ever. More political anyway. I've spoken at public meetings.'

Amy's eyes opened wide.

'And in the open air. And from the top of a cart once. Uncle Gwilym saw me. Reported me to the family. He was quite upset.'

They began to laugh together. Amy kissed Enid fondly on the cheek.

'You're wonderful,' she said. 'My old E.P. Mrs. More and all. As wonderful as ever.'

Amy ran awkwardly across the wet field. Miss Wade was waiting by the gate. Amy lifted her arm to wave. Enthusiastically Miss Wade encouraged her to hurry.

'It's rather exciting.'

She spoke as soon as Amy reached the gate.

'I shouldn't say anything, shouldn't anticipate and indeed I won't, but Eirwen is most anxious to have a little word with you.'

As they walked together towards the outbuildings the girls emerged and came to meet them. Miss Wade pressed her hands together and tossed her grey curls.

'Well now then,' she said. 'The glass is going up. The rain has stopped. The carpenter is on his way with his assistants and we are going to make two tables for table tennis right away! Isn't that nice?'

One of the girls began to cheer and then clapped her hand nervously over her mouth. Menna ran about with her neck stretched well forward to spread the good news. In no time Amy and Miss Wade were surrounded by girls all anxious to take part in the preparations and promised activities. Miss Wade touched Amy's arm and pushed her gently towards the house.

'You can leave them to me, my dear,' she said. 'The main

door is open. Leo Galt is about. He'll take you up. Just walk in.'

The presence of the girls made it difficult for Amy to ask questions. She crossed a courtyard and began to climb a shallow stone stair between a mass of shrubs and the wall of the west end of the house. As if to give herself time to think she paused to move her face closer to a rose bush laden with raindrops to take in the smell. She turned her head and saw Miss Eirwen watching from an open window on the second floor.

Amy smiled back politely and made for the front door which was wide open. She stood on the broad mat and considered her wet wellingtons. She pulled them off and walked into the hall in her bare feet quieter than if she had been entering some exclusive archiepiscopal chapel. She raised her head to admire the fine panelling and the great sweep of the staircase. She walked around the massive table in the centre of the floor and stood in front of the bust of the first Lord Iscoed on its plinth of black marble. Leo Galt leaned over the banisters above her head to watch her studying the statue.

'It's carved from coal,' he said.

His voice startled her. Her reaction was instant counter attack.

'Of course it isn't.'

She glared at him so hard he stopped fondling his beard and held up his fingers as though to protect his face. In contrast to the crinkly luxury of hair they were white and thin and ineffective concealment.

'"Could have been!" That's what I should have said.'

He smiled at her ingratiatingly. She observed the calves of his stockinged legs passing the wrought iron banister rails as he descended the remainder of the stairs.

'I've been listening to the singing,' he said. 'Sweet and melancholy. Made me think of all sorts of theories. Not really my cup of tea, but Miss E. just loves it. Suits her temperament I suppose. Would you like to see some treasures on our way up?'

With just a little more confidence he could have carried out the rôle of genial host. His fingers were spread out in a gesture of open invitation. His beard was trimmed so as not to conceal a full expressive mouth which was now stretched in a coaxing smile.

'Just as you like.'

Amy's manner was guardedly non-committal. Leo Galt halted at the top of the stairs to consider a long pre-Raphaelite panel of angelic young women singing on an unnaturally precipitous spiral staircase.

'I don't quite know what we can do with this one ...'

He fingered his beard judiciously.

'The old man liked it you see. The first Lord Iscoed. And he had this bee in his bonnet about the pre-Raphaelites being Welsh-inspired and Arthurian or what have you. Because of those Welsh sounding names of course. William Morris, Burne-Jones, Arthur Hughes. I don't quite know how he managed with Rossetti.'

He bent his knee and shook his leg a little to emphasise the fact that he was being playful. Amy shrugged her shoulders.

'It looks hideous to me,' she said. 'But I don't know anything about painting.'

Leo Galt clapped his hands, apparently delighted with such a forthright answer. He led the way boldly down the corridor, the toe-caps of his boots conspicuous in a sweeping busy walk. He paused in front of a picture hung opposite a window facing north.

'Now here is something really worth looking at,' he said. 'What does this mean to you, Miss Parry?'

Amy stared intently at the white farm buildings, the horse and cart and the shadows of tall leafless trees falling across the wide perspective of a French farm road. She bent closer to read the artist's signature.

'Pissarro,' she said.

'What do you think of it?'

Leo Galt sounded possessive and his eyes were twinkling as if he were a magician about to perform a trick.

'Very nice,' Amy said. 'It really is.'

'Ah, Leo Galt said. 'But what's so special about it?'

Amy stood back ready to walk on. She spoke coldly.

'Is this some kind of examination?'

'Oh, by no means. Oh no.'

Sorrowfully he enlarged his glowing brown eyes and tilted his head like a faithful spaniel unjustly reproached.

'Winter light. That's all I was going to say. He was forty when he discovered it. So there's hope for us yet.'

Interpreting what he took to be Amy's wishes he led the way at an increased speed to the room Miss Eirwen used as a studio. There were more pictures on the walls including a series of neatly-framed pen and ink drawings but Leo Galt did not stop to comment on any of them. Amy's gaze was fixed on the pale bald patch on the crown of his head. She studied it so closely she could have been estimating the age of a tree by counting the rings.

'Do you like skiing?'

He stopped unexpectedly on the next flight of stairs to look down and ask the question. Amy had become more relaxed.

'I don't know,' she said. 'I've never tried it.'

'I try to go every winter,' he said. 'It's a little bit of freedom I treasure. The French Alps. It's another world. Heaven in fact. Perhaps you might like to try it?'

He was so eager to please. Amy smiled at him quite warmly.

'Perhaps,' she said. 'You never know.'

He seemed reasonably contented with her answer. He knocked politely on the studio door and ushered Amy in, leaving her with Miss Eirwen, who came to meet her wiping her hands with a rag. One leg dragged slightly as she made the effort to approach her briskly across the long room. The muscles of her thin face were tight with visible determination to set aside an inhibiting shyness.

'Miss Parry... I am so grateful you could spare me a moment.'

She looked around the bare room as if it would provide her with inspiration about what to say next. Her searching gaze rested on the door to a comfortable sitting-room. The door was ajar. Amy could see a large black cat on a red cushion sleeping before the fire. The brightness of the flames was enhanced by a highly-polished brass fender.

'Would you mind if we went in there?'

Miss Eirwen pointed at the sitting-room.

'It's more comfortable. It could be too hot of course. I have an arthritic hip. I have to be careful. Especially in this damp weather. It's such a pity about the weather. I would have liked to come out and perhaps help you a little.'

'It hasn't been too bad,' Amy said. 'It is very kind of you to allow us to be here.'

Miss Eirwen rubbed hard at a smudge of blue paint on her hand. She spoke without looking up.

'I was so terribly sorry to hear about Mr. Gwyn. I liked him very much. He was so transparently honest and good. I want to tell you that I think we treated him rather shabbily.'

She took a quick glance at Amy and found the strength to continue.

'I'm quite convinced that Sir Prosser went much too far in raising his expectations. I know from personal experience that that is one of the little ways he has of manipulating people. Not that I'm entitled to lay all the blame on him. I think I was weak. I didn't have the resources to act alone. But that is not the point. I feel guilty and I want to say so.'

She had begun to stare at Amy's feet.

'Really I shouldn't keep you standing in your bare feet. Let's go and sit down, shall we?'

In the sitting-room the basket armchair creaked as Amy sat down in it. Miss Eirwen stood in the doorway looking at her.

'I'm quite sure you have every reason to disapprove of me and my family and whatever you think we stand for. Before I say any more I want you to believe that as far as I am concerned my one remaining desire in this life is to use whatever wealth I have for doing good.'

Still rubbing her hands with the duster she sat in her customary chair and gazed at Amy with humble expectation.

'Will you believe that, Miss Parry?'

Amy tried to shift in the chair without making it squeak.

'Yes of course I will,' she said.

Miss Eirwen was immensely relieved. Her wan features were transformed with the bright strength of her smile.

'I've watched with great interest the wonderful work you've been doing with the girls,' Miss Eirwen said.

'I'm afraid I haven't done much.'

Amy was frank rather than modest. Miss Eirwen was clearly delighted with her response. In the seclusion of her own private sitting-room she was able to talk so much more freely.

'Would you mind very much if I talked to you about some

of my plans? Or my "problems" as my brother calls them.'

'Of course not.'

'To begin with, let me make a confession. I'm not very orthodox.'

They smiled at each other conscious of the easier atmosphere that was growing between them.

'Neither am I,' Amy said.

'You've probably noticed I'm excessively shy. I don't like going to chapel.'

'Neither do I.'

Amy agreed enthusiastically.

'But I struggle to put in an appearance for the sake of my father and my grandfather. Family piety you could call it. But I don't really believe in denominations. What does it matter what denomination one belongs to? It's doing good that matters. And cultivating the life of the spirit. In every possible way. I think to myself sometimes, why should people always divide up and separate and take different roads? Why can't we unite more often and co-operate to achieve great things and do some good in the world?'

Amy stretched out a bare foot towards the fire. Her cheeks were flushed with the warmth of the room and her eyes sparkled. She began to bask also in the rays of Miss Eirwen's open admiration.

'Miss Wade has such a high regard for your character and ability,' Miss Eirwen said. 'She has talked so much about you. I was delighted when I realised you were to be in charge of the camp. And I did so long to get to know you better. But I realised that you could very well dislike and despise everything to do with this place and this family... and of course I am so stupidly, so painfully shy. At my age it's too ridiculous. Now I really must come to the point, mustn't I?'

She smiled at Amy as if she had succeeded in sweeping aside all the obstacles that lay between them and they were looking at each other for the first time in the full bright and totally congenial light of complete honesty and frankness.

'I need a secretary. That's putting the position at its lowest. What I really need is a strong young friend who can help me realise some of the plans that I am longing to carry out. But I want to be realistic, and I want to talk in realistic terms. It is so important to get these things right in the very beginning. Salary, terms of employment and so on. Now, Miss Parry, would you consider accepting the position? If the terms were right?'

Both Miss Eirwen's hands were raised, in an attitude of polite supplication, traces of paint still on her fingers. She prevented herself from speaking and concentrated with obvious patience on waiting for Amy to consider her proposal and make up her mind.

'I am on a short list,' Amy said speaking very slowly. 'For a school not very far from the sanatorium.'

Miss Eirwen was instantly sympathetic.

'Of course,' she said. 'Of course.'

'Not that I'm keen on teaching,' Amy said. 'I don't honestly feel any vocation for it. But there isn't much else a girl in my position can do.'

Miss Eirwen understood at once that Amy was referring obliquely to the poverty of her background. She made an effort to look stern and businesslike.

'What salary are they offering? What would you earn? Have you any idea?'

'I think it's one hundred and forty pounds per annum to begin with,' Amy said.

Miss Eirwen considered the figure for a moment.

'Well I think we can do better than that,' she said. 'Then of course you would have your quarters. And as regards visiting the sanatorium I'm sure there would be no difficulty in getting you there... By car for example. Griffiths could drive you. It's not so very far across country. And it would give me particular pleasure if Mr. Gwyn and yourself could think of me as a friend.'

'Oh I do. I really do...'

Amy was suddenly anxious to show her gratitude.

'But you need time to think it over. Of course you do.'

Miss Eirwen showed how stern she was prepared to be with herself.

'People with so-called wealth should not take it upon themselves to order other people's lives. I think that is a lesson I can claim to have learned. I've sprung this on you without any preparation at all. I can see now I was impulsive and selfish, even when I was trying my hardest not to be.'

'Oh no,' Amy said. 'Not at all. I am very grateful. I really

337

am. And of course it appeals to me enormously. It really does. I honestly am aware of your kindness ... but I would like a little time to think.'

Miss Eirwen was nodding to show complete understanding.

'We have laid the foundations,' she said. 'The foundations of friendship. That is the first and probably the most important step.'

'Oh yes,' Amy said. 'I'm sure it is.'

Miss Eirwen dropped her duster and did not bother to pick it up. She stared sadly into the fire.

'My life is dry,' she said. 'It was never so much in need of renewal and hope. What I need is strength in myself and help to put myself and whatever possessions I have to better and higher use. My brother thinks I am a hopeless idealist as well as a weak woman who could never stand on her own feet. It might be very wicked of me, but I would love to prove him wrong.'

She stood up and Amy jumped to her feet.

'I expect you want to get back to your camp. What comes next?'

'High tea,' Amy said. 'And then more hymns, I'm afraid. But Miss Wade is working hard at the games programme. And I think the weather is looking up.'

Miss Eirwen offered her hand and Amy took it.

'I'm so glad we've had our first real chat,' Miss Eirwen said. 'It's the most difficult thing in the world for me ... We've broken the ice, haven't we?'

Amy was eager to agree.

'And you can take your time. And let me know the minute you have made up your mind.'

'Oh, I will,' Amy said. 'Of course I will.'

'And then we can get down to serious planning. But I must restrain myself.'

They stood in the studio and Miss Eirwen looked at her easel.

'I'm no good at all,' she said. 'But it soothes me. "Therapeutic" is the word nowadays.'

She turned to Amy.

'When I looked through the window you were smelling a rose,' she said. 'And it was on the very bush I was trying to

338

paint. And I thought to myself then, my goodness. That's a good omen.'

7

'Something must be done.'

As he spoke the lecturer in Hebrew stamped his heavy boot. It was like the action of a wily old ram caught in a corner of the fold. He clicked his dentures and then extended a gnarled hand to the gas fire. It was not lit but the hand was familiar with the area where the warmth would have been. He sat on the low chair he always favoured when visiting his neighbour's room. His bony knees jutted towards his long hard nose.

'I was coming out of an Examination Board meeting in Shrewsbury when I heard,' he said. 'I must admit I was very upset. This young fellow, a pattern of unselfishness, giving up everything for this little country of ours, struck down in the flower of his days.'

His frankness and sincerity made his colleagues uncomfortable. There were six academics in the room, smoking and drinking tea. The younger men had chosen suitably obscure positions, their backs pressed against bookshelves as they listened in respectful silence. John Cilydd occupied a compact position under the window, a privileged visitor to the room in the tower that belonged to the independent lecturer in Celtic Philology. His host sat now in the centre of the room, sprawled in his worn chair, his dark narrow head apparently sticking out of the folds of his tweed waistcoat.

'I agree entirely with John Cilydd More,' the lecturer in Hebrew said. 'Not that he has said it in so many words. He's too polite for that. It is our duty to do something.'

He avoided looking at Cilydd. Instead, he studied the crooked clay columns of the gas appliance as though the solution to their problem could be abstracted from their curiously angled relationships.

'A man needs help,' he said. 'One of our own kind. Only

339

better than most of us. Braver and more brilliant. Help isn't the precise word possibly, but it will have to suffice. Val Gwyn needs our support. We all agree there. As friends. As admirers. As sympathisers. As well-wishers.'

The host in the central chair grunted his agreement. He sat as he liked, but he was a genial host, pleased, whenever his great labours permitted, to entertain his closest colleagues in his legendary lair. Every table in the room was laden with books. They lay like heaps of slate-waste quarried from the shelves that covered every available wall space in the high ceilinged room. The pile on the table immediately confronting John Cilydd looked the highest and most precariously balanced. Sunlight from the high window above his head created a pool of light on the threadbare carpet. It just missed the books. Cilydd cocked his head as if he were considering how a book could be extracted or even touched without the whole heap falling to the floor: and if they should fall, how could the exact balance of disorder, with so many volumes open and so many faced downwards, ever be restored?

'If this little country of ours can afford to lose a young man of such uncommon qualities, such strength of character, such honesty, such courage ...'

Once again the lecturer stamped his heavy boot.

'... then all I can say is it is much further on the road to apotheosis than even our respected archdruid would have us believe!'

The younger men glanced across at each other and ventured to chuckle. The host looked around him with a benevolent smile. It was to savour such sallies that he encouraged their presence. And there was a man standing by the window who still had said nothing. From his central position the Independent Lecturer silently indicated they could expect some pungent contribution from that direction at any moment. This distinguished figure was not wearing a gown but its ghost seemed to lie in outline over his bent shoulders. There was a frown on his handsome ravaged face as he studied the view and watched the cloud shadows shift on the dark sea. At any moment he would say something and whatever he said would be memorable.

'I am what you might term a survivor.'

He spoke without turning to face his colleagues. He was

the oldest man in the room. Out of his pale face his fierce blue eyes continued to scrutinise the view.

'Consumption, the white plague, that was the enemy within as far as my family was concerned. I lost both my parents when I was still at school.'

His friend and debating opponent by the gas fire straightened his back and opened his mouth to receive details from a distant past now being divulged for the first time.

'My grandmother brought me up in the heart of the country. She was a most intelligent woman. Far ahead of her time. My bedroom window was open all around the year. She used to watch me through the corner of her eye when she thought I wasn't looking. Watching out for those first tell-tale signs. The flush high on the cheeks. Eyes too bright. Little beads of sweat without exertion. A waxy pallor of the visage. She knew them all. I never coughed in her hearing if I could possibly help it. I knew it upset her.'

He drew himself up, delicately staunching the flow of reminiscence. In the silence they could hear the distant noise of the sea.

'Long ago,' he said.

He lifted his pipe to peer at the crumbling bowl in the light from the window.

'A case like this brings it all back.'

He stuck his pipe in his mouth to show his contribution, so unexpectedly personal, was finished. The lecturer in Hebrew pulled faces. The grimaces suggested he was torn between the desire to hear more reminiscence from his friend and the urge to come to some positive decision about the case of Val Gwyn. The Independent Lecturer was moved to speak. He did so without lifting his chin off his chest.

'Williams let him down,' he said. 'There can be no question about that.'

He grunted his complete agreement with himself.

'Led him on. Gave him grounds for expectations. And then dropped him. Just because of an article in a magazine.'

'That's true enough, but where does it leave us?'

The brown boots creaked as the lecturer in Hebrew bent forward to examine the carpet. They seemed to demonstrate that their owner would have liked to have seen himself as a countryman rather than an academic.

341

'We lack power you see. That's what it amounts to.'

The younger men were becoming restless. A pale spark of revolt seemed to leap from one to the other. The smallest from his corner burst into speech. Heads were turned to look at him.

'That man Bellot! He treated him so badly.'

'Bellot . . . Bellot . . . Bellot.'

The name was repeated with increasing sounds of disgust and condemnation. The small man gave way to a second outburst.

'The harm he has done. It's incalculable!'

The man at the window raised his pipe. He was ready to speak again. There was a bitter smile on his face.

'From a newspaper-kiosk on Watford Junction to the head of our precious new institution on the hill – there's a jump for you! There's been nothing like it since the cow jumped over the moon.'

Indignation turned into mirth and stifled laughter until once more, under the haze of tobacco smoke, a morose and awkward silence descended on the room. Cilydd looked into his empty cup and studied the tea leaves. Like a man obliged to leave a place of worship before the service was ended, he tip-toed with bent back to the corner of the largest table where room had been cleared to put down the battered tea tray. He hesitated above it, selecting a spot to put down his cup without upsetting the balance of a tray that protruded dangerously over the edge of the table. The Independent Lecturer was speaking again. It was his room. Like an hereditary precentor, he had the right to strike the note for the repetition of a familiar litany.

'We lack the power,' he said. 'As Val Gwyn often put it, we are captives in our own country. Serfs. Easily imposed upon. Without the will to resist. The edge of resolve eaten away. That's what it amounts to.'

The boot stamped by the gas fire.

'That's all very well,' the lecturer in Hebrew said. 'But something must be done. The question is, what? That is the question.'

A younger man plucked up courage to speak. He had a moustache but his voice was as reedy and as shy as a girl's.

'Why not a Fellowship?' he said.

Cilydd and the younger men were instantly elated.

'That sounds a good idea,' Cilydd said.

The young man was much encouraged.

'There are Fellowships,' he said. 'They do exist. Research Fellows for example. Suppose a letter was sent to the Principal in the first place, setting out Val's merits, and signed by as many senior people as can be persuaded to sign it...'

The young man was put off by the sound of the Independent Lecturer in Celtic Philology tapping his teeth with the stem of his pipe. There was a pained restlessness in the man's brooding eyes that suggested he was dredging the remoter recesses of his mind for buried obstacles and hidden snags.

'You would need to watch out for Williams,' he said.

The dark warning ushered in a further interval of melancholy and sober thought. During the profound silence, the door opened. A man with twinkling eyes, a crooked nose and military bearing stood boldly on the threshold, prepared, even before he entered, to be forcefully jovial. With a freshly-printed pamphlet he briefly mimed the action of cutting his way through the haze of tobacco before he made his way to the aluminium teapot and poured himself a cup. He caught sight of Cilydd as he stirred his tea and his bushy eyebrows shot up in a joyful signal of welcome.

'John Cilydd More!'

He accentuated his nasal delivery.

'How nice to see you. How is the heap of filth? Growing, I trust?'

His hair was prematurely grey and clipped short in the Prussian style. His skin was strikingly smooth and youthful. To safeguard his smart suit he held his cup away and stretched his neck to sip it. He was disappointed when no one smiled. He pulled a face to indicate that he found his tea stewed and cold. He moved about among the tables, nodding briskly.

'What's the trouble? End of the world been announced? I've been to funerals that were more lively, I can tell you.'

'Have you, indeed?'

The lecturer was heavily ironic.

'With all due respect to the Independent Department of Celtic Philology, this tea is dreadful.'

'We are concerned about Val Gwyn, Powell.'

The lecturer in Hebrew's fingers twitched impatiently as they dangled before the gas fire.

'In the Quaker sense?' Powell said. 'Hence the profound silence.'

He was still determinedly jovial.

'He's in a sanatorium.'

'Yes, of course he is.'

At last Powell seemed to take in the significance of John Cilydd's presence.

'Poor chap. Such rotten luck.'

The Independent Lecturer was eyeing Powell from the depth of his chair.

'Powell,' he said, 'you may be able to help us.'

'Anything I can do,' Powell said. 'My dear fellow, absolutely anything.'

He stood above his chair and dropped the pamphlet neatly on the tweed waistcoat, a passing gift to be examined later. The Independent Lecturer let it lie untouched in his lap and finished what he had to say.

'It has been suggested this college could, and should, award Val Gwyn a Fellowship of some sort. You are a committee man. What do you think of the idea?'

'Poor old Gwyn.'

Powell demonstrated infinite sympathy.

'Such rotten luck. And such a nice chap. Very able. Very, very able. Although I must say he did seem to have a peculiar gift for getting on the wrong side of the right people, if you know what I mean. I never saw anything quite like it.'

The lecturer in Hebrew creased the leather of his boots.

'It does happen,' he said. 'Especially to people who are attached to the truth.'

He spoke as though from bitter experience. There were murmurs of support from the younger men.

'Off hand, I could name at least nine influential persons and organisations in this fascinating little country of ours that Val Gwyn has managed to offend or insult in a variety of ways during the last eighteen months or so. I look out for

344

these things. It amuses me. Now I reckon that is an outstanding score by any standard.'

'Good for him,' the lecturer in Hebrew said.

'Oh quite. Quite.'

Powell had the attention of everyone in the room.

'But alas, there is a price to be paid. A man acquires the reputation of biting the hand that feeds him.'

'Bellot!'

The small man in the corner gave explosive vent to the name.

'That would be Bellot. It's incredible the harm that man has done!'

This time the chorus of support was not forthcoming. Powell stood in the centre of the room, holding everyone's attention.

'Let's put it in a narrower academic focus. Quite apart from treading on important toes, I would say Val Gwyn – excellent chap though he is, with all his flashes of brilliance – has gained the reputation for a certain unscholarly wandering all over the shop.'

'Look here,' the lecturer in Hebrew said. 'The man is quite brilliant. There's no question about that.'

'Yes, but what is he?'

Powell persisted in his argument.

'What would you call him? An historian? A philosopher? An economist? A specialist in eighteenth-century French literature? A social worker? An editor? A polemicist? And so on.'

He paused to wait for dissenting comment to the argument he was building up. It was obvious that he considered it to be irrefutable.

'I've nothing against the man personally. Understand that. As a matter of fact I've always been on the most friendly terms with him. John Cilydd can vouch for that. But you've asked my advice and I'm giving it to you. Abandon the idea. In this place, a Fellowship for Gwyn is quite simply a nonstarter. Furthermore it would be very wrong in my view to raise a man's hopes when he's lying on his sick bed, when you know perfectly well that there isn't an earthly chance they can be fulfilled. I'm sorry . . . But you asked me. And as you know, I'm a realist. And I say what I think.'

He was staring defiantly at the lecturer in Hebrew who had resumed his study of the crooked columns in the gas fire. Out of the unhappy silence he began to mutter almost as though he were talking to himself.

'What about some sort of testimonial?' he said. 'What do you think of that? A really substantial testimonial from friends and admirers in the academic field. That could bring a few blushes to the cheeks of people in authority and committee people.'

His spirits seemed to lift as he went on thinking aloud. He began to smile and look around for support.

'What if every single man subscribed a percentage of his salary for the next two or three years? We could make a start ourselves. Say five per cent. You would only need twenty to thirty people to subscribe and there you'd have a very decent sum to present him with!'

He looked around eagerly for support. Some young men were nodding but no one broke the uneasy silence. The Independent Lecturer in Celtic Philology picked up the pamphlet Powell had dropped in his lap and took a surreptitious glance at it. Interest kindled in his eyes. It was a paper on the place names of West Herefordshire.

'I must be off.'

Cilydd was by the door when he spoke. They looked at him with some surprise as if they had forgotten he was there. The Independent Lecturer dropped the pamphlet and stretched out the hand that held his pipe delicately between finger and thumb towards Cilydd. It seemed that he had something important he wished to say. Cilydd waited. The pipe sank slowly like a flag being lowered.

'We must think of something,' he said. 'We really must.'

Cilydd was unable to compose an appropriate reply. His head bobbed briefly before he left the room. At the top of the tower staircase he was overtaken by Powell.

'They're a hopeless lot,' Powell said. 'Good enough in their own fields, you see, but hopelessly impractical.'

His smile was warm and friendly. Cilydd said nothing. He began to descend the winding stone stair.

'Just a moment.'

Powell hurried after him.

'I don't like to see you go off like this. I really don't. They won't face facts. That's their trouble. A breed of spiritual ostriches. And tinged with disappointment of course. You've got to remember that. Most of them know they will never reach the top flight. In cases of this sort it does no good at all to get sentimental. That's no way to help him.'

Powell passed the palm of his hand carefully over his short hair.

'What do you suggest?' Cilydd said.

He stared up at the elegant figure with smouldering hostility.

'Shouldn't he get well first?'

Powell made an extra effort to sound agreeable.

'There is in fact a medical contingency fund. They didn't even know about that. They take so little interest in administration. Ostriches you see.'

'It isn't money he needs,' Cilydd said. 'It's support and encouragement. That's more important in his condition.'

'Of course it is.'

Powell showed his respect for Cilydd's opinion.

'Let me think about it, will you? Leave it with me. I understand how these things work.'

Cilydd said nothing. But he showed he was aware how little choice he had in the matter.

'I wanted to ask you about your poem.'

Powell was ready to display some enthusiasm.

'I'm a great admirer of yours, John Cilydd. I'm one of those people who want to see new ideas. A real breath of fresh air. Why haven't you published it? It sounds fascinating, I must say. And what would sell better than a heap of filth? Eh? You know what the English say. Where there's muck there's brass.'

Powell was greatly amused.

'Seriously, though. Why not? Why don't you publish? It would do an enormous amount of good. If only to see the fuddy-duddies dancing with rage.'

'My wife doesn't think it's good enough.'

Powell was slow to accept the simple answer. He began to laugh, incredulous and yet charmed at so much naïvety.

'No... Really? Well I must say... On what grounds I wonder? Or shouldn't I ask?'

Powell's eyebrows went up and down suggestively.

'Of course, women are not always as modern as they look, are they? It's always a problem, isn't it? What degree of freedom can be exercised in what is virtually a closed society dominated by nonconformist chapels.'

Powell grew more confidential. He brought himself closer to Cilydd and lowered his voice.

'This is the real problem we are faced with, you see. Can you have a viable culture in the twentieth century dominated by non-conformist ministers? I doubt it. I very much doubt it. I tell you what I think with complete frankness. The age of pulpit eloquence is over.'

Cilydd considered seriously what he was saying.

'And it's you the artists, that have to face this problem. You are the ones to give a lead. And my sort are the ones that should back your sort up. It's all got to change. We agree about that. But not by revolution so much as by change of emphasis. Do you know what I mean?'

Powell's eyebrows were raised and his face wore an expression of total frankness and sincerity.

'We must allow room for manoeuvre. So that men of good will and creative men can get together, pool their talents and make the whole thing work. A new cultural pattern, you see. That's what I'm after. If I had a little more time I'd write a book about it. It's a subject very close to my heart. We have to reconcile what we believe with what we want to achieve. Don't you agree?'

Cilydd frowned hard as he considered the proposition. Powell made a nimble adjustment of his feet on the stairs.

'We've got to go into this you know. It's got to be faced.'

For a moment he sounded stern and urgent. Then he smiled again, stretching out his arms until his fingers almost touched Cilydd's shoulders.

'Look here,' he said. 'Let me know next time you'll be coming up. We'll have dinner together. And a really searching talk. Threshing-floor stuff, eh? What do you say?'

348

8

'Trams,' the chauffeur said.

Crossly he drummed the steering wheel with his gloved fingers. There was not enough space between the double-deck tramcar and the fruiterer's van to make a safe passage for the black limousine.

'I know what I'd do with them.'

Amy could not be sure that he was addressing her. He was a taciturn man. What little he spoke resembled thin steam escaping from a geyser of masculine aggression insufficiently smothered. She rode in the back in solitary state and comfort, keeping a calm eye on the unframed paintings in her charge. There was ample room for them to lean against the tip-up seat behind the chauffeur. Amy was smartly dressed in a pale blue and white jumper suit with a hat to match.

'Time they did away with the lot of them,' the chauffeur said.

The rattle and the clanging of the tramcars reverberated further down the important street. Amy sat up straight, grasping her hands together tightly in her lap as if she were struggling to contain a childlike zest. It was her business to take a more cool and critical view of the main streets of the busy city. She placed her face as close as her hat would allow to the side window to squint up at the point of contact between the tram's traction pole and the overhead cable.

'Don't do no more than ten miles an hour.'

The chauffeur's voice was dark with contempt. He stared balefully at the back of the tram in front of him. The top half was cream, the lower half maroon. Above the single cold lamp gleaming back at him a thick figure ninety-six was painted in gold. There could be no question now that he intended Amy to hear when he spoke.

'And the noise is something awful.'

While they were stationary he tugged off his glove and popped a white digestive tablet into his mouth.

'Oh, I don't know.'

Amy sounded sophisticated.

'I'd say they looked quite pretty.'

'Pretty.'

The chauffeur could not conceal his contempt for the word.

'Blocking up the streets. Holding up the traffic. That's all they're good for.'

The car was unable to move forward. They were committed to talking. Amy ran a finger down the inverted pleat in the centre of her skirt.

'So you believe in progress, Griffiths,' she said.

She made an effort to speak lightheartedly. She used the chauffeur's surname as Miss Eirwen would have done; but with less emphasis. Her tone reflected with delicate precision their respective distance from the centre of power. Amy was a passenger sitting in the place of their mutual patron and employer. She was to some unspecified degree Miss Eirwen's surrogate or at the least her confidante, with whom she would discuss private and even intimate matters. But the black limousine was Griffiths' responsibility. His dark grey uniform and the matching cap, worn with correct flatness so that the glossy peak shaded his bloodshot eyes, emphasised his close relationship with the machine. The cyclic motion they created together was potentially a state of perfection. The clutter and incoherence of the city street interrupted the flow of spirit and understanding circulating between his covered hands and feet and the hidden murmur of the smooth running engine.

'Progress?'

Griffiths considered the implications of the word.

'Everybody does.'

He was grimly satisfied with the stark conclusion. If such determinism existed he was well placed to collect some fringe benefits. The tram was moving. The car surged forward, elated with the promise of release.

'We've got to, haven't we? We don't have any choice.'

Amy took hold of the side strap and pulled herself up to study an assembly of pianos in a large shop window. In the department store next to it, furniture was displayed in a crowded succession of three-piece suites. A card on an armchair read, '£13.19.6 buys this superb Jacobean set in Rexine with velour cushions'. The sun came out and penetrated the cavernous interior of the shop, showing up rows of bedroom suites. A succession of tramcars clattered cheerfully past each other down the centre of the street. Amy looked up and saw flags flying from the larger buildings. Once again the car was brought to a halt. There were many more people in the street. Amy was restless with curiosity.

'Griffiths,' she said. 'Why are there so many people about?'

He seemed to resent being asked a question he couldn't answer. He looked from one side of the road to the other, clearly concerned about the well-being of his motor car. There were policemen about, but there was not enough order. Young men who should have known better were running about the street like schoolchildren given an unexpected holiday. They were helping to generate an atmosphere of dangerous excitement. He frowned hard under his peaked cap. Irresponsible pedestrians kept spilling off the pavement into the street. Someone could easily scratch the high polish on the bodywork.

'Shall we get through, do you think?'

Griffiths said nothing. His passenger was being infected by the festive air beginning to surround his limousine.

'There must be something on. Don't you think?'

Amy leaned well forward and spoke as sweetly as she could.

'Griffiths, why don't you ask?'

He was most reluctant to take up her proposal. Another tram was blocking his way. His criticism sounded urgent.

'Every time they meet they have to reset the points,' he said. 'It's ridiculous.'

'There must be something. Look at all those policemen!'

The chauffeur glared at the trams.

'They're like something since before the Flood.'

Amy wound down her window and beckoned faintly with a bent finger at a man who stood on the edge of the pavement as though he had been waiting for a long time for someone to speak to him. He dropped his cigarette stump, crushed it under his heel and touched his brand new trilby hat worn at a rakish angle, before Amy actually spoke.

'Excuse me ... Excuse me ... But can you tell me what's happening?'

'Freedom of the City,' he said. 'For Mr. Stanley Baldwin.' His new hat signalled his approval.

'Could be coming this way. Could be.'

The limousine began to move while the window was still open. Somewhere ahead, louder than the traffic, human voices were chanting in unison. The words were unclear and broken by unruly shouts and sudden screams. The source of all the sound was in a side street. It became powerful enough as they advanced to alarm passers by. Women shoppers scattered indiscriminately like ants in a disturbed nest. Some ran into the road and held up the traffic. Men stood between the tramlines, smoking calmly, as if it were the safest place to view the clash between the demonstrators and the police, until the clanging of a tram forced them to move. The car came to a halt. Griffiths now seemed possessed with as much curiosity as Amy. A solid cordon of bulky policemen blocked the junction of the side street with the main thoroughfare. Above the police helmets a red banner was visible, tilting drunkenly from one side to the other as the demonstration heaved forward. The words 'Right' and 'Work' were written in crude white letters on the red background.

From the car, Amy saw the police cordon open briefly to allow the passage of a struggling figure in a brown suit. Four policemen dragged him forward with his face close to the pavement. As they dumped him in front of the department store window his head struck the edge of the long ornamental metal name plate under the window. One policeman knelt on his shoulder while another delivered a kick towards his back. As he slumped forward Amy recognised Pen Lewis.

'Griffiths!'

She shouted urgently as she opened the car door.

'Griffiths! Wait!'

She knelt on the pavement to examine Pen's condition. He was groaning angrily between clenched teeth. Blood was seeping through his hair. His forehead too was scratched and bleeding. His neat collar and tie were twisted halfway around his neck. There was a fresh surge from the demonstrators. The two policemen abandoned him for a moment to reinforce the cordon. Like a wounded animal that scents rather than sees a last avenue of escape, Pen crawled towards the open door of the car. Without hesitating Amy helped him in. A policeman who was not part of the cordon placed a heavy hand on her shoulder. He was on traffic duty but a smartly dressed girl helping a dishevelled demonstrator into an expensive limousine could not be ignored.

'What's this then?' he said.

'A relative. He's hurt.'

Amy's quick answer was an effective simulation of unpremeditated truth. She was looking up at the policeman, her blue eyes imploring and innocent. He was a large thick-set man who clearly disliked being hurried. He was about to bend down and examine the man lying on the floor of the car when two drivers near by blew their horns, disputing the right of way. The noise took the policeman's attention. He unbuttoned his breast pocket and felt about, preparing for the ceremony of opening his notebook. The case of the shouting drivers appeared more urgently in need of resolution.

'You wait here then.'

He squeezed Amy's shoulder before releasing it. As soon as he was in the road, Amy closed the car door. She sat on the back seat as primly as if she were Miss Eirwen herself. Pen Lewis remained on the floor at her feet.

'Drive on, Griffiths,' she said.

He hesitated. Amy peered from the corner of her eye through the rear window. The policeman was deeply engaged with a driver who was waving his arms accusingly at his opponent who was almost standing over the wheel of his open car to shout back. The police cordon was regaining control over the demonstration. One of their number was gazing suspiciously at the spot on the pavement where the dangerous agitator had been safely deposited.

'There's a way through now.'

Amy's voice was urgent and authoritative.

'You can drive on.'

The habit of obedience overwhelmed the chauffeur's suspicious hesitations. The car glided forward. Amy lifted her chin imperiously, impersonating a lady of wealth and importance. As she did so, she used her foot to keep Pen Lewis down and out of sight. He groaned with pain as she pressed his shoulder. Amy's lips moved in an apology that was almost silent. He began to mutter as he stared at the tight grey cloth stretched across the chauffeur's back. The sight of yet another uniform could have made him uneasy. He tilted his head to see from his low angle of vision Griffiths' fierce eyes in the driving mirror. He closed his eyelids and sank back apparently willing to abandon himself to his fate.

The car turned left. Amy relaxed a little. She peered through the rear window to satisfy herself that they were not being pursued. The car entered a quieter and more elegant street. The long imposing black body drew up outside a shoe shop. Above the window in gold lettering was printed 'THE GOLDEN SLIPPER – PREMIER FOOTWEAR'. Pen was recovering. He leaned on an elbow and read out the name of the shop.

'So that's it,' he said.

He was trying to smile even though talking was an effort. 'You're playing Cinderella.'

Amy had extracted a bunch of keys from her small travelling case. The chauffeur and Pen were watching her. She was brisk and businesslike.

'You had better drive straight on, Griffiths, and pick up Mr. Galt at Dyffryn Abbey. I shall stay here and start measuring. I suppose we may as well leave these pictures in the car. So that you can get away quickly. In case they recognise the car. I'm fairly sure no one took the number, though.'

Griffiths had retired inside the fortress of his own taciturnity. He craned his neck over to look down at Pen Lewis who was struggling to sit up.

'Just look at it, for God's sake.'

Pen was examining the state of his brown suit with unconcealed dismay.

'They've got no respect for anything. Bloody police. And I've signed for it an' all.'

'Don't worry, Griffiths.'

Amy spoke to the chauffeur as she helped Pen from the car. He swayed dangerously as he stood on the pavement.

'I take full responsibility.'

As if from force of habit the chauffeur touched his cap and showed that he was happy and relieved to drive off: both he and the machine would be better off driving smoothly and unimpeded by riot or by dubious cargo to a destination that was an address above reproach.

'Are you feeling better, Mr. Lewis?'

Pen was grinning at her with a touch of his old bravado.

'If I tried to run,' he said, 'they wouldn't have much trouble catching me.'

Without hesitation she unlocked the door and helped him inside the shop. The interior was hot and stuffy. There was old stock left on the shelves and piles of empty shoe boxes stacked in the corners. On the plum coloured walls hung a series of tinted photographs of a variety of ladies' shoes and slippers set like precious gems on folds of rich velvet. The photographs were mounted in heavy gilded frames. Amy stood by the glass door uncertain what to do next: to hide Pen Lewis effectively the blinds would need to be kept down. Already there were two ragged children loitering on the pavement, ready to ask inquisitive questions. Pen had found a feather duster. With the bamboo handle he struck the plum-coloured upholstery and watched the dust floating up the diagonal stripes of sunlight let in by the faded blinds. The effort at gaiety was too much for him. He slumped into a customer's chair and rested his legs on a shoe fitting stool.

'Do you think we should get a doctor?'

Amy was eager to be practical. He shook his head and then tried to bring it forward to hang between his knees.

'I'll be alright,' he said. 'I'm used to it.'

Amy moved closer to examine his condition.

'You need attention,' she said. 'You really do.'

He struggled in the chair to make his position more comfortable.

'You saw for yourself,' he said. 'Naked force. That's all it is. To keep us down. It's a war, see. That's what it amounts to. Have you read Clausewitz?'

He opened one eye to register the shake of her head.

'"War is a continuation of politics by other means." That's Clausewitz. No mention of him in that little college of yours, then?'

She seemed touched that he was still trying to tease her even in his battered condition.

'I saw a chemist's shop on the corner,' she said. 'I'll get

some first-aid stuff. Cotton wool. Lint. Bandages. And boil some water. There's a flat on the top floor. Belonged to the manageress. You could hide there until you get your strength back.'

His face creased with a spasm of pain from an unexpected quarter. He felt his back as he spoke to her.

'You're a marvel,' he said. 'I always knew it. A true daughter of the working class. You know there's a war on, don't you? That's what it's got to be in the end. An armed struggle.'

Amy pulled off her hat and threw it on a chair. Pen folded his hands patiently and fixed his benevolent attention on the hat as if it would represent Amy during her short absence. As she hurried along the pavement she glanced at her reflection in an opaque shop window and shook out her fair hair.

The chemist shop she entered was a small establishment. It was dark inside and the numerous glass display cabinets left little standing room for the customers. By the brass weighing machine a tall man in a bowler hat was waiting for his prescription to be made up. The chemists looked like father and son. Both wore black overalls and both frowned below receding hair lines as if they had just turned away from some nice calculation above the balances in the dispensary. The customer in the bowler hat scraped the point of his unfurled umbrella on the uncovered floorboards.

'There it is,' he said. 'Twenty-seven thousand pounds worth of Moscow gold. It's all in the *Mail*, Matthews. I suppose you've read it?'

The older chemist barely had time to answer.

'I'm afraid not. I'm afraid I've been too busy.'

'That's how it works, you see. While society sleeps, the rats are gnawing at the foundations.'

Amy had the attention of the son. He stood frowning gloomily in the gap between tall cabinets.

'A first-aid kit, please,' Amy said.

The younger chemist jerked his head sideways to encourage her to be more specific.

'What size?'

'Where does it all go?' the customer was saying. 'It's quite obvious. Into the pockets of paid agitators. And what for? To cause disturbances. We've just seen a prime example.'

Amy's eyes looked quickly over a display cabinet.

'One of those,' she said.

She pointed at a blue tin with the words 'Motorists' First Aid' stamped in white on the lid, and in smaller letters, 'recommended by the R.A.C.'.

'They are a shilling each.'

The younger chemist spoke as though he were giving her fair warning of a high price.

'There's a booklet to go with it, if you want it.'

Amy nodded hurriedly.

'And I'll have some cotton wool, please,' she said. 'And some lint.'

The other customer was beginning to take an interest in her.

'Been an accident, has there?'

He had a way of holding out his lower lip that suggested he was in the habit of asking questions and receiving answers.

'Not really.'

Amy fumbled in her purse for her money. The scraping of the metal point of the umbrella was getting on her nerves.

'Motoring,' she said. 'And so on.'

'I'm an ex-policeman,' the man in the bowler hat said. 'If you want any help.'

'No. No thank you.'

He was still staring at her with open curiosity as she hurried out of the shop. The sharp eyes of the older chemist suggested that he could comprehend in a glance a good deal more than the openly inquisitive ex-policeman. She clutched her parcels close and looked over her shoulder before turning abruptly into the entrance of the shoe shop. As she locked the door, she saw through the tinted glass that the two ragged children were still watching the shop from across the street. One wore the cap of a school he obviously did not attend. A panel of the material had torn free and hung over his ear. With his hands in his pockets he seemed capable of watching anything for any length of time.

Pen Lewis was not in the shop. Her hat still lay on the chair where she had left it. She paused as though she were about to call out his name. She decided instead on a brief exploration of the premises. The rear of the shop was dirty and deserted. An unpleasant smell came from the row of three water closet latrines in the small enclosed yard. With determined disapproval, Amy pulled each short chain in turn. In the back room where the shop assistants had eaten their sandwiches, there was still a long table and two benches. She turned on the tap at the sink and let it run until it ran clear. Opposite her head faded fragments of a calendar for 1927 were still stuck to the dirty green wall. Under the table there were magazines and newspapers left there since the shop closed down. Briskly Amy returned to the front of the premises. She ran up a curved staircase with a sign suspended above it saying 'Children's Department'. The next stairs were narrow and the word 'Private' had been printed in black letters on the wall above the dado. The door to the flat was open. Amy smiled with relief. It was clear where Pen had gone.

She found him lying on the mattress of the manageress' single bed. He had taken off his brown suit. The jacket and the waistcoat were hung over the back of a chair and the trousers folded neatly over them. Next to the chair a large teddy-bear with only one beady eye leaned sadly against the wall. Fragments of straw peeped out of his worn stomach. The room smelt of mothballs. The wooden bedstead had been painted a crude pink. The marks of the brush were still visible. Above the headboard cheap pink material had been gathered into a coronet and pinned against the wall. The late manageress must have wished to brighten her nightly solitude. There were coloured reproductions from magazines still stuck to the wall with drawing pins. Two lightly draped females bathing two naked babies in a stone fountain was called 'The Bloom of Youth', and two similar figures wearing more diaphanous draperies danced under decorative trees on a carpet of flowers. This was called 'The Awakening' by the same artist, with letters after his name.

Pen's eyes were closed. Amy was tempted to tip-toe forward into the room to take a closer look at him. The blood on his forehead emphasised the whiteness of his face. Bruises were appearing. There were scratches on his arms and on his long legs. The socks on his feet were not a pair but both had holes in them. His masculine body seemed absurdly strong on the narrow bed with its pink decorations. While she watched him he opened one eye and smiled at her with the bruised charm of a naughty boy.

'I'm dreaming about you,' he said.

'I'll put a kettle on,' Amy said quickly. 'We need boiling water.'

'You are on the barricades. Like one of those passionate French females half naked and half wrapped in a red flag.'

She worked in the kitchen across the small landing. She filled a kettle and placed it on the gas ring. She could hear Pen calling her from the bedroom. She took her time before she appeared in the doorway. He had a hand under his head and he was smoking a cigarette.

'What's it all about, then?'

He smiled at her knowingly. Amy looked around the bedroom. On the dressing-table with a cracked mirror there was a row of four female dolls in peasant wedding costumes.

'Some poor working spinster's fantasy,' she said. 'People are strange, aren't they? When you see beneath the surface.'

'No. This place.'

Pen showed he was more urgently concerned with the general set-up and Amy's exact function in it.

'It's going to be an art centre,' Amy said. 'An art gallery I suppose you could call it, in the first place. "Art for All." I'm here to measure it up and take notes. It will be a new kind of art gallery. Concentrating on modern work. And maybe we'll have a series of chamber concerts. Admissions free, we hope.'

'Who's "we"?'

'Miss Eirwen Owens I should say. It's her money and her idea.'

Amy had begun to blush before he raised his eyebrows and stretched down his mouth in a grimace of mock admiration.

'Very nice too,' he said.

'What do you mean by that?'

Her voice was sharp and defensive. He smiled and with the cigarette still between his fingers felt his teeth tenderly with finger and thumb to make sure none of them was loose.

'Nothing like a spot of fiddling while Rome is burning,' he said. 'Cheers you up no end.'

Amy's hands were on her hips. He grinned at her cheerfully.

'We shall be bringing new colour into working people's lives,' she said. 'Just tell me what is wrong with that?'

He continued to stare at her with open admiration.

'Nothing I can think of at the moment,' he said.

The kettle whistled shrilly in the kitchen. He shouted from the bedroom.

'Nice domestic touch that,' he said. 'If a kettle whistles there's always a good woman ready to come and pay attention. Homely, I'd call it. All mod. cons. and the freedom of the city thrown in.'

He gave up when it appeared that she couldn't hear what he was saying. When she returned with a bowl of water steaming in the centre of a black lacquered tea tray, she found him in a more sober mood. He was leaning on his elbow contemplating the brown suit on the chair. He barely glanced at the cotton wool and dressings on the tray.

'If you want to demonstrate or march, never do it in your best suit,' he said. 'Especially if it belongs to the Party. I've signed for that thing.'

Amy brought the tray on a bedroom chair to the top of the bed.

'Sit up,' she said. 'I'll start on your head.'

Her nearness and her ministrations raised his spirits. He began to talk with greater animation.

'You won't believe this,' he said, 'but it was none of my business. It was a seamen's protest to start with. And then the word got around that Baldwin was on his way to City Hall, to collect the Freedom of the City. And it all grew from there.'

'Keep still,' Amy said. 'I want to clean this. For all I know it ought to be stitched.'

'I'm doing a course at the Technical Institute. Mining engineering. Do I look like a mining engineer?'

Carefully Amy cleaned the superficial cuts on his face. He stared at her admiringly.

'Florence Nightingale is it? Or Joan of Arc? Did I tell you I was dreaming about you?'

'Yes. You did.'

Once more he considered the brown suit on the chair across the room.

'I was so worried about that bloody suit, I had no business

to be there, understand? You've got to have discipline in a movement. You can't have comrades charging around and getting mixed up in every damned thing that comes along. That way chaos lies. You've got to have order. But I was so damned curious to find out how the police got the wind of it. Deputy Chief Constable and all. In the twinkling of an eye. Where did they all come from? Who tipped them the wink?'

Amy was so pleased with her first-aid work she allowed herself to become more playful.

'Don't look at me,' she said. 'I was just passing.'

He laughed out loud as though she had made a brilliant joke.

'Isn't that right? Historical determinism if I ever saw it. Proved one thing, you know. What I've been telling you all the time. We were meant for each other.'

Amy stood up to attend to the back of his neck. He bent his head forward like a man in a barber's chair. With cotton wool she cleaned the scratches on his neck.

'How's old Val anyway? Still waiting for a personal message from Owain Glyndwr?'

Amy bit her lip and said nothing.

'Where is the old faggot? I miss him on the street corners. Him and his little red dragon on one side, me with my hammer and sickle on the other and the Salvation Army banging away in the middle. He's not a bad lad. Heart of gold, as they say. Only soft gold, see. That's his trouble.'

He became aware of her silence. He looked up and saw that her eyes were filled with tears.

'What's up?' he said.

'Val is in a sanatorium.'

'T.B., you mean? Oh no ... The poor bugger ... I am sorry.'

Amy was too blinded by her tears to see what she was doing. Pen took the cotton wool and moved the tray. He stood up to fold her in his arms and comfort her.

'Now then,' he said. 'Now then.'

He stroked her back and spoke softly into her hair. She was ready to absorb his sympathy and shelter in his strength.

'Now then ... Let's take this pretty suit off then, shall we? ... So that it won't spoil ... Now then ...'

Amy made a token resistance as he unhooked her skirt.

She stepped out of it as it fell to the floor, her tears still falling.

'He's so brave,' she said. 'So uncomplaining.'

'Of course he is.'

He bent down and deftly picked up her skirt with one finger.

'He makes me feel ashamed.'

'Of course he does.'

Pen's understanding and sympathy were total. He wiped away her tears with the tips of his fingers and fondly began to kiss her cheeks.

'It's cruel,' he said. 'That's why we have a right to comfort each other.'

He whispered continually as he stroked her hair and her body. Amy's protests were feeble and disjointed.

'We mustn't,' she said. 'We shouldn't . . .'

Even as she spoke she was relaxing in the great comfort of his muscular grasp. His voice and his hands wove a web of sympathy that could not be resisted or broken. He helped her remove the top half of her jumper suit. While he laid her clothes neatly on the chair with his own she stood trembling with nervousness in her petticoat.

'Working-class people got to be careful with their clothes,' he said.

She barely heard him, looking at him with sudden fright in her eyes. He was quick to reassure her with steady patient embraces. Although his lips were close to her ear, she listened to his voice as if it had travelled across some great distance to reach her.

'You mustn't be afraid,' he was saying. 'Nobody can be free if they are afraid.'

With gentle persistence he brought her to lie on the narrow bed. When she was prone she stared at him with numb apprehension.

'I can't,' she said. 'I said I'd wait for him. I must keep my word.'

'Of course you must.'

As he fondled her, Pen agreed with everything she said. Concentrating all his attention on her seemed to heal up all his own bruises and injuries. Nothing could be allowed to come between him and his chosen goal.

'We should be undressed.'

His head found room to lie next to hers on the uncovered pillow.

'If you feel shy I could pull this pink stuff down to cover us.'

She shook her head to discourage his whispering.

'I should undress you. I really should. We should never be afraid. Revolutionaries should never be afraid. You can't change the world if you can't take your clothes off, girl.'

He was trying to make her smile through her tears. He kissed her with an infinite and expert gentleness. She still sighed from time to time, but the tears ceased to well up so easily into her large eyes. She was listening to what he had to say with a fresh intentness.

'I told you,' he said. 'Determinism. You made a choice when you stopped that big car. Or history made the choice for you. Like it did for me. We've got to accept it. There's nothing else we can do. Your body was calling for my body before you even knew it. That's historical materialism. Can you imagine it?'

He gave her body a gentle squeeze with his powerful arms.

'Well you don't have to imagine any more, Miss Parry. All we have to do now is to go gently forward together. Accept it. Because that's what love is. That's what life is. A voyage of discovery. A voyage together.'

Abruptly Amy put both her hands against his cheeks. Her eyes stared urgently into his.

'Do you love me, Pen? Do you really love me?'

He smiled as if to welcome the pressure of her palms on his cheeks. She was so careful to avoid his cuts and bruises.

'What else could I do?' he said. 'What else was I made for?'

She seemed completely satisfied, but in a short while she had more questions to ask.

'You've been with many women, Pen? Married women. That's what they said about you in Cwm Du.'

He sat up, wincing slightly with pain as he did so. She stretched a hand to touch his cheek apologetically.

'I know how to make a woman happy,' he said. 'I admit that. Married or virgin. I know how to do it. And with complete safety. No awkward after effects. It's right that you should know this.'

363

Amy smiled at him.

'I can't understand it,' she said. 'My conscience has fallen into a deep sleep. It's terrible. I'm so relaxed. I don't seem to care about anything any more. Not anything at all.'

His hands were exploring her body, removing more clothing. He spoke to her soothingly.

'You have to help me to make you happy,' he said. 'By trusting me. That's all. Just trust in me.'

'I do trust you. I do.'

For the first time she began shyly to return his kisses.

'All I want to do is to go on asking you if you love me.'

He scrambled off the bed and made a comic inspection of his physical condition. Amy began to laugh at him. She put her hands behind her head and rocked herself gently from side to side.

'I can't understand it,' she said. 'I haven't felt so happy for years.'

Cheerfully he crossed the landing to the small lavatory.

'A Marxist is a realist,' he said. 'After a beating up you should always check and make sure you're not passing blood.'

She turned her head and spoke shyly into the pillow.

'Pen... are you alright?'

He returned to the bedroom naked except for his shirt tied like a towel around his waist.

'Takes more than a few bluebottles to hold me down,' he said.

She stretched out her arms to him.

'What's the matter with me, Pen,' she said. 'Why do I feel so happy? What is it that's wrong with me?'

He knelt down carefully to kiss her lips and whisper.

'You are a free adult,' he said. 'Making your own choice. Your time has come. We'll explore it together. All the sweet things you are entitled to. From the great root of happiness that grows between a man's thighs. There you are, Miss Parry... you didn't know I was a poet, did you?'

Amy's eyes closed. He pulled at the pink canopy as he mounted the bed. It slipped sideways and the thin coronet hung down at a drunken angle. Her eyes opened for a moment to consider the extent of the collapse and closed again.

9

Through half closed eyes John Cilydd looked up at the sky between the branches of the oak tree. He had taken off his spectacles and they lay on the mossy ridge of the tree root behind his head. The sunlight penetrated the leaves, warming his whole body as it lay stretched out on the hard ground. The fringe of short grass that touched his elbow and his feet was dead from lack of moisture but turned by the sunlight into a threadbare carpet of pale gold. In the shade where Enid was kneeling everything was greener. She lowered her bare arm into the stream to rinse a cup. The channel was deep. Between ragged banks of damp earth and the protruding edges of flat stones draped with green lichen the water slid and slipped down stairs of wet rock. It clearly marked the end of the sanctuary created by the ancient tree: the stream was as volatile as the oak was constant. If it formed pools it only seemed to do so long enough to capture scintillating points of light before escaping with them into its own darkness. It thrust downwards towards the gorge spanned by the stone road bridge, spelling out its route in its own gurgling dialect. Bending over the moss Enid saw the water flash like a precious stone as it swirled inside the cup before sweeping on.

The sound of the stream intensified the peace that dwelt in the place. A thick coppice of hazel concealed them from the country road where the car was parked and from the stone bridge. The slope beyond the stream was covered with shrubs and young trees as far as the stubble of a high cornfield. Enid moved quietly so as not to disturb her husband's contemplative mood. On her knees she began to pack the picnic basket, setting things down with care so as not to make a noise. She picked up her tam o'shanter and pushed both her hands into it, undecided whether or not to pull it on her head. She let it fall to the ground. She sat on the travelling rug, nursing her knees and trying to school herself into absorbing the sights and smells and sounds that surrounded her. She concentrated for a time on a solitary bee working in the last blooms of the ivy on a rotting elm stump. In the bushes there were small birds fluttering about. She kept still to identify them when they appeared: tom-tits, wrens, finches. She glanced at her watch and then seemed to struggle with herself to maintain a stillness and a passivity that would match the prone figure of the man under the tree. She placed her hand over her mouth and looked upwards to observe a single leaf float down between the criss-cross of branches. It descended with such tantalising slowness it could have been selecting the precise spot on the ground where it would rest for the final stage of its unique existence.

'"A room is better if it grows."'

Her face lit up with instant pleasure and relief to hear him speak. His eyes were wide open as he considered the horizontal beams and branches above his head.

'This is perfection,' he said.

'Isn't it? Isn't it exactly?'

In spite of herself, she peeped at her wristwatch as she spoke.

'I never want to move.'

His voice was low enough not to disturb the balance and order of the natural life around the tree that now included them both, equal with the shadow of the leaves, the berries on the bushes, the small birds, the ants and insects clinging to the earth.

'If you lie still long enough you will hear the tree speak.'

She looked at him, rubbing her chin on her shoulder. She spoke even more softly.

'What will it say?'

He raised himself on one elbow. He looked at Enid and then at the broad trunk of the tree.

'The meditating cipher. The one particular key. It's here. I'm sure of that. If you could find it it would be the key to the underworld. No, not "underworld". Otherworld. Where there is no sickness. No pain. No loss. No betrayal.'

She was moved by the note of sadness in his voice. He lay down and closed his eyes. She crawled along the ground close enough to touch his forehead and run her forefinger along

366

the sharp bridge of his nose. He was as immobile as a fallen statue.

'You think I'm at the mercy of fanciful ideas?'

His eyes remained closed as if he were too embarrassed to watch her as he spoke.

'You could have made a mistake,' he said.

'What do you mean?'

His pronouncement was so solemn, she became anxious.

'I think I have a basic incapacity inside me. To connect with what I should connect with. To find what I should express.'

'O Sionyn...'

A muscle in his cheek winced at the diminutive.

'All I've got is my bit of paganism. And you don't think that's any good.'

'I didn't say that. I never said that, Sionyn. Be fair.'

'Not enough then. It amounts to the same thing. I'm not able to rise to these great occasions that are apparently opening up all around us. Hence my sense of inadequacy. That's easy enough to understand. You've been teaching me to believe in a fount of genius that isn't really there.'

'Now Sionyn...'

'Don't call me that,' he said. 'It makes me sound like a spoilt child.'

He sounded restlessly petulant. He lay back with his hands behind his head.

'I know what's happening to me,' he said. 'And I can't do a thing about it. I'm getting choked up with bitterness. It's not just Val. It's me. My own inadequacy. There seems to be nothing I can do.'

Enid sat back on her heels and nodded her head understandingly.

'You taught me to believe in my own... "genius",' he said. 'But what if it's just not there? You could be sacrificing yourself to a power that doesn't exist. Submitting to my egoism, all for nothing.'

She brought herself closer to bring him comfort. She stroked his head.

'You are tired,' she said. 'And it's not only Val. And his so called friends letting him down. We are living in a time of peculiar strain because we are so much aware of personal and public misfortune and crisis. And for a sensitive person like yourself with such sensitive antennae...'

'Lie on me.'

His instruction was immediate and abrupt, breaking in on her concentrated effort to express herself. She smiled at him patiently.

'I'm heavy,' she said.

He waited for her to obey. She tried to lie on him as easily as she could, laying her head over his heart, so that the filtered sunlight could still reach his face.

'It would be marvellous,' she said. 'To lie here for ever. With you.'

Their breathing and the beating of their hearts seemed louder than all the sounds that surrounded them. Enid lay docile and still, ready to listen to his whisper.

'I don't think I satisfy you,' he was saying. 'Any more than my work does.'

She lifted her head, but before she could slide off his body his arms held her prisoner. She struggled angrily.

'Let me go,' she said. 'You are saying things to hurt me.'

'If you loved me as much as you say you do, you could prove it here under this tree.'

'Let me go,' she said. 'I can't breathe.'

'This oak is sacred. The branches and the roots are holding the earth and the sky together. This is where we could be truly united. The exact spot. Under this tree.'

'These are pagan ideas...'

'Naked under this tree.'

He stared wide eyed at the distant sky cut up into blue archipelagos by the solid presence of the leaves. Enid tried to view the matter more lightheartedly.

'John Cilydd,' she said. 'Don't you realise we are only fifty yards from the road?'

'To be correct we should bathe first in the stream. The crystal fountain.'

'John Cilydd...'

She bent her arm to show him her wristwatch.

'We are on our way to visit Val,' she said. 'We mustn't be late. These visits mean so much to him.'

He released her. In sullen silence he put on his spectacles and watched her scramble to her feet.

'Still,' she said ' . . . It is a beautiful tree.'

She stretched out her arms to appreciate its great width. For a moment it appeared she would attempt to embrace it. Instead she moved closer so that her finger could explore a furrow in the thick rough bark. She disturbed an unfamiliar race of tiny red insects. They scurried out looking for refuge in a fresh network of crevices and hidden fissures. As she was studying them, Cilydd walked further into the wood. She saw him scramble up a slope in order to stand on an outcrop of rock overlooking the deep channel created by the stream. When she called out his name he moved away deeper into the trees. She followed him, rushing up the slope like one who fears to be left behind in a strange country. The falling water and its music were no response to her calling, only a circle of sound that could be drawn tighter around her, keeping them apart. She rushed through the undergrowth catching her skirt on the brambles, scratching her legs and the back of her hand. When she found him, he was seated on a fallen tree trunk, his feet in the yellowing ferns. She sank down on her knees before him in the breathless position of a suppliant.

'John,' she said. 'Darling. What's the matter? What is it?'

He was reluctant to answer. She shook his arm and he spoke at last.

'I don't want to go,' he said. 'I don't want to see him.'

She was eager to understand.

'I know,' she said. 'It is hard. To travel all this way to see him suffer.'

'Why should it be us all the time? What about Amy? How often does she go?'

'It's difficult for her,' Enid said.

His pent-up resentment came tumbling out.

'If you want my candid opinion, she should never have taken that job at Iscoed. Never. Quite apart from any question of principle, surely it was her place to take a teaching job as close as she could get to the sanatorium. But of course Madame Amy doesn't like teaching infants. So she mustn't on any account do anything she doesn't like.'

'John . . . don't. You sound so bitter.'

'I am bitter. Is it your place to write to him every other minute? What about her? How often does she write?'

'I don't know.'

His arm stretched out in the direction of the road where the car was parked.

'All those books and papers in the back of the car,' he said. 'It's like a travelling library. All that ridiculous research. Statistics. Facts. Figures. Government reports. Economic surveys. Why doesn't she do it?'

'But it's not just for Val, is it? It's what we all want. What we all believe in.'

Enid was struggling to be reasonable, but nothing would stem the tide of his discontent.

'Let me tell you something else. He's becoming a crank.'

'How can you say that?'

'It could be his illness of course, but what is he doing in fact? Why all this feverish activity? Making blueprints for some kind of Swiss Denmark west of Offa's Dyke. Some kind of Cymric Utopia where justice and equality and material well-being will be run on strictly co-operative lines. It's too absurd. Too divorced from reality. Flying in the face of history.'

'But you believe it,' she said. 'You've actually written it down. "All true poetry is an Utopian protest against injustice".'

'I don't believe that any more.'

'Well. What do you believe?'

'He's ill,' Cilydd said. 'He can afford the luxury of lying in bed dreaming up Utopias.'

Enid looked shocked.

'That's cruel,' she said.

'Oh, of course it is. But that's how it is in the real world. Cruel. People are cruel. Miserable. Contemptible. Just like me. Inferior clay. But in politics that's all there is to work with. Val doesn't understand that. He never did. That's why it's so easy for him to be a hero. And he is a hero. He still is. I'm not trying to deny that. I still believe in him, I suppose. But now...'

'What about now?'

She spoke so sharply she brought all his attention back to her.

'Now? Now you spend a whole day writing a letter to him. While I'm at the office. You sit up there in the empty room at the top of the house staring across the bay and writing to him. And to that American...'

'But John Cilydd... You told me to.'

Enid sounded hurt and baffled.

'Yes, but twice a week. Long letters. At least twice a week. As far as I know.'

Enid broke off a dry frond of bracken. She stood up, rubbing it between her hands, determinedly self-possessed.

'Do you know what we write about?'

She smiled at Cilydd, confident and gentle.

'About religion mostly. About theology. He talks about being forced into a spiritual posture. But in fact, I think it was always there.'

For a moment Cilydd was silenced. But when he spoke he was as despondent as ever.

'Something else that leaves me out,' he said.

Enid summoned up a burst of enthusiasm.

'I believe it's our strongest hope. In our situation, it has to be. And Val believes this too. At the moment we have lost the way. As individuals. As a society. As a civilisation. We've simply got to find the way back. If we want to rebuild we can only do that on sound religious foundations. Val agrees with that. That's what we write about.'

Cilydd behaved as if he were no longer interested in what she was trying to say. He walked through the trees and down the slope to the oak tree. Enid watched him, standing under the branches. The angle of the light had changed. He was looking down at their things as if they had been left there by another couple. The pale green trunk was alive with light. She ran down to join him.

'What is the matter?'

She looked for his hand to hold it, ready to comfort him.

'I should have thought it was obvious.'

'No, it isn't. It isn't at all.'

He studied her innocent face and looked away to speak.

'I'm jealous,' he said.

She was baffled.

'Jealous of what?'

He was calmer for having made his confession. He could

even have been pleased at the sight of trembling waves of perplexity disturbing her whole body. She let go his hand and moved away from him.

'I don't think it was ever me you really wanted,' he said. 'It was Val.'

She sat down by the bank of the stream and stared at the water.

'I'm not blaming you,' he said. 'He was so obviously the man to be preferred. But I closed my eyes to it. I wanted you so much myself. In any case I never saw it clearly until he fell ill. So much concern for him. Our lives revolve around it. All those letters. All that research.'

Enid's tears coursed down her cheek. She kept her face towards the stream so that he should not see them.

'How can you be jealous of a man lying helpless on a sick bed in a sanatorium miles away? How can you?'

Her tears prevented her saying anything more. The clear water ran on in its deep channel as though part of its natural function were to wash away the marks of time and enfold the changing seasons in its own dark light. Cilydd was immediately behind her when he spoke again.

'It costs me a lot to be frank,' he said. 'It's not my nature. I could have stored all this inside me for years. For a lifetime. But you've taught me to be frank. So you must bear the brunt of it.'

He knelt behind her and drew her shoulders towards him.

'I don't please you in the way I should. I know that only too well.'

He was whispering in her ear.

'You've got to help me please you.'

Together they listened to the sound of the water. It intensified the pain of the silence that brooded between them.

'It would exorcise my self-obsession. I believe it would.'

Her tears were dry on her face when she turned to look at him.

'Is it genius?' he said. 'Or is it a torment? You've got to prove to me that it is there. You've got to sacrifice yourself for that.'

She smiled wanly to show sympathy and understanding.

'Now you can see how horrible I am,' he said. 'I couldn't

bear to think you were serving his altar instead of my miserable ego. Will you love me now? Now you know all this. Will you sacrifice yourself? Under this tree?'

He helped her to her feet. Her movements were trance like. She dragged the rug to the further side of the oak tree. Almost hiding behind the trunk, she began to take off her clothes while he watched her. The sunlight softened the whiteness of her thigh and brought out the green edges on the furrowed bark. He touched her skin reverently with the tips of his fingers.

'This will cure my sickness. This is my salvation...'

She shook her head as she slid down to meet him but she did not dare to speak.

10

The sister's head was crowned with a small starched cap pinned securely to her copper-coloured hair.

'You've come a long way, Miss Parry,' she said. 'And of course you want to see him. But we should have been notified.'

'I'm sorry,' Amy said.

Beyond the sister's head, through the square window, there was a view of the sanatorium chapel made more ecclesiastic by the cypress trees planted around it. On the horizon there was a range of dark mountains. There was no heating in the bare room. The sister's knuckles whitened as she clutched her red hands together more tightly on the table between them: she was concentrating on the proper exercise of the authority that had been delegated her. Her solemn face shone with its own fullness and her pale blue eyes were enlarged by the lenses of her spectacles.

'We are none of us without feelings, Miss Parry,' she said. 'But the rules have been drawn up for the benefit of the patients. I can speak from experience, you see. I was a patient myself once.'

Amy looked at her with a new interest. Her plump form in

the blue uniform seemed immune from any imaginable disease.

'I hope it gives me more understanding and sympathy,' the sister said. 'I hope so. I can still remember how irksome all those hospital rules were. But every single one was necessary.'

'If you think it's better that I shouldn't see him...'

Amy showed how ready she was to obey any instruction the sister would now see fit to give her.

'No.'

The sister was firm and confident.

'I think you should see him. It would help you to understand what he has to go through. And we wouldn't want him to hear you had been turned away. But you can't stay long, Miss Parry. I think that would be too unsettling. Quarter of an hour? Half an hour? Certainly no more. Then again, you mustn't mind me saying this, but try not to say anything that would upset him. Do you know what I mean?'

Amy had begun to blush.

'I know Mr. Morris has a special regard for Mr. Gwyn. I've heard him say that Mr. Gwyn has a capacity to endure and an ability to suffer that is quite outstanding. And praise from Mr. Morris is praise indeed. And of course we all think the world of him. But even the strongest men have their weak spot, Miss Parry. And in the case of Mr. Gwyn I think we have to say that you are his.'

The sister smiled a little so that twin highlights shone in her apple cheeks. Then her solemnity returned.

'He is now undergoing a course of treatment that we call the A.P. Artificial Pneumothorax. Normally we would not allow visitors, but since you have come such a distance, a brief visit should do him no harm. And in fact may do him some good. As Mr. Morris says, the point of all treatment is to help the body cure itself. And since the mind is in control of the body, he says, a strong and cheerful frame of mind is of the first importance. So whatever you have to say to him, Miss Parry, do make sure that it is something that will cheer him up.'

With a deliberation that was almost ceremonial, the sister rose to her feet, prepared to lead the way to the hospital wing where Val was accommodated. The sanatorium had once been a country house and the extensions were built in wings that enclosed the old gardens and faced south-east. The sister's room was in the rear of the building. As they came outside, Amy glanced nervously at a column of black smoke belching out of a tall chimney stack. The kitchen garden was being tidied by patients in the later stages of recovery. Another team of men were brushing the leaves from the paths and carrying them away in wheelbarrows that squealed gently. They were enjoying the simple exercise in the pale afternoon sun. As Amy and the sister turned a corner they were met by two patients carrying garden forks on their shoulders with thermometers sticking out of their mouths.

'For goodness' sake . . .'

The sister spoke impatiently. As they saw her the patients quickly snatched their private thermometers out, to conceal them about their persons. Walking towards the east wing, the sister became thoughtful and confidential.

'Let me tell you a little more about Mr. Gwyn's condition,' she said. 'Strict bed rest has been imposed for a month. Now that means of course he can do nothing for himself. He has to lie absolutely still in a particular position and we use pillows and sandbags to lessen the motion of the affected lung. He has to allow us to feed him, wash him and help him with every bodily function. As if he were a baby in fact. Now for a proud man like Mr. Gwyn this has been something very difficult. And of course you will find that he talks in a very low voice. We encourage this. Because the more strict the stillness, the better chance the cavity in the lung has of healing up. It's as simple as that, Miss Parry.'

They stood between flower beds where red dahlias and gold chrysanthemums were blooming with a last desperate splendour. The sister held her head to one side aware that Amy was trying to formulate a question.

'How long . . . how long do you think he will be . . . in this place?'

The sister drew a deep sympathetic breath. The white cap on her head bobbed about.

'Who can tell?' she said. 'In a way it's best not to think about it. To live from day to day. That's what I do.'

'It could take years? . . .'

Amy could not resist asking the question.

'It could, of course. Every single case is different. As Mr. Morris says, it is more than a disease. It's a way of life.'

She smiled confidently but Amy did not seem to appreciate the specialist's humour. The black limousine was parked on the drive that led to the main gates. Griffiths the chauffeur in his peaked cap and uniform great coat stood by the polished bonnet as if he were waiting to have his photograph taken.

'Is that your motor car, Miss Parry?'

The sister was mildly curious.

'Not mine. Miss Eirwen Owens'.'

'Of course.'

'Miss Owens said I should try to have a word with Mr. Morris.'

The nurse was nodding understandingly.

'She wanted me to say that in the case of Mr. Gwyn she would cover any additional expense if any new treatment became available.'

'I shall pass the message on,' the sister said. 'We know that Miss Owens is a good friend of the sanatorium and of the Association. But there is no miracle cure, Miss Parry, and it's very doubtful that there ever will be. The recipe remains the same. Complete rest, good food, fresh air, clean air and peace of mind. I think it is correct to say in the case of tuberculosis the disease can be arrested but never cured.'

Amy looked at the plump sister, apparently glowing with good health.

'But you are cured,' she said.

The nurse's laugh was a comforting gurgle.

'I have my regime,' she said. 'And I have my regular check-ups. I always need to remember my illness is arrested, not cured. It hasn't gone away. It's not destroyed. It is contained. It's there, sleeping inside me. And I have to make sure I never do anything to wake it up.'

She wagged a finger, laughed merrily and led the way into the new east wing.

Val's room was at the end of a corridor on the top floor. Nervously Amy kept close to the sister. Her gloved hands lay passive and secure in the pockets of her overcoat. The large collar was turned up. She wore a small tight-fitting hat, that pushed the waves of her yellow hair close to her cheeks. Her high heels clacked noisily on the polished floor. She tried to step more lightly and make less noise. A chronic patient escaped through an open door when he heard them approach down the corridor. Amy had time to notice his face. It was as lined and as leathery as a deflated rugby ball. His dentures bulged under the skin around his mouth. There was the blue scar of the collier between his sparse eyebrows.

'No. Mr. Thomas,' the sister said. 'You know you shouldn't be wandering about. Back into bed at once, Mr. Thomas.'

'Yes indeed, sister.'

The patient's voice was a melodious wheeze. A whistle in another room was obviously a warning of the sister's approach. Amy heard scurrying noises and even the jingle of coins.

Val's room was small but it had three doors and they were all open: one from the corridor and two leading on to his section of the second floor verandah. A small desk and a stuffed bookcase looked forlorn and unused. Val's bed had been moved so that he could see something of the world outside: a bird table on the stone balustrade, a restricted view of the tops of the trees in the park and beyond the solid outlines of the mountain ridges. The patient had been placed on his side and his position firmly bolstered with sandbags and pillows under the white bedclothes. His feet were higher than his head.

'An unexpected visitor, Mr. Gwyn!'

With practised cheerfulness the sister walked on to the verandah so that Val could see her without moving his head.

'On a flying visit, shall we say. Someone you will be very glad to see, I know.'

The sister placed a chair in a position that Val could survey in comfort. Behind the chair a frosted glass partition marked the end of Val's stretch of red brick balcony. When Amy sat down something of the further side of her appearance was reflected in the opaque glass. She placed her gloved hands in her lap, aware that his eyes were fixed on her with an immobile intensity. His hollow cheeks had been freshly shaven. A fragment of dried shaving soap remained stuck like a withered pendant to the lobe of his left ear. His hair had been cut closer to the skull than Amy had ever seen before, leaving his brow large and white and unprotected. His dark eyes shone with abnormal brightness.

'Amy.'

He was whispering her name. The sister had withdrawn with tactful quiet, giving Amy a final warning wave.

'Amy. Take your hat off.'

With a smile and a flourish that was intended to please, she snatched off her hat and shook her fair curls. Val was staring at her with unblinking intensity.

'Do you know what I'm doing?'

She leaned forward to hear his low voice.

'I'm printing your image on the balcony. So that I can see you clearly when you're no longer there.'

She smiled at him, uncertain what to say: uneasy under such close scrutiny.

'Did you see Mr. Morris?'

Amy shook her head.

'He's away, I think.'

In an effort to speak naturally, her voice became unsteady, any statement she made could only be a poor approximation to the kind of truth that would be good enough for a man trapped in such extremity.

'He's a dictator,' Val said. 'A benevolent dictator. Here it works because nobody is free. It's an interesting thought to give a Marxist. Messianic dictatorship is designed for prisons and sanatoria. I've tried both. In the outside world, it's always different.'

'I don't understand,' Amy said.

Val closed his eyes.

'Just speculation,' he said. 'I do a lot of it here.'

Quietly Amy moved her chair closer to his head. She stretched out her arm so that her fingers touched his forehead. She removed the dried soap from his left ear. He opened his eyes and smiled at her gratefully.

'Tell me,' Amy said. 'I know I'm slow, but I like to hear. I want to understand.'

'I lie here and compose books about it,' he said. 'It helps to keep my mysticism in check. Stops me disappearing in a cloud of anonymous smoke.'

'I don't understand that either. You don't realise how *twp* I am.'

378

'This morning I was thinking about a Communist King Arthur.'

'Tell me. Tell me.'

She stroked his head and showed how eager she was to listen.

'Suppose there was a World Praesidium sitting at the Round Table. And these were the Elect. And they were arranging, like Mr. Morris, for all the bacilli that oppress mankind to wither away.'

Amy frowned with the effort of following his flight of fancy.

'Under those conditions, the single personal failure is more catastrophic.'

He was calmly certain about his conclusions and ready with an answer before Amy could formulate the question.

'Because of the power they possess, the selfishness, or the wickedness, or the sinfulness, or even just the weakness of only one of the Elect could bring the best system ever devised by men crashing into ruins. And that's why some form of theology must always take precedence over economics. Sin is the ultimate bacillus. We have to go on fighting it even when we know we can never be cured.'

Amy was disturbed. She stood against the glass partition and looked down into the gardens.

'I think that sounds awful,' she said. 'Is that the kind of thing Enid writes about?'

'She's very good,' Val said. 'She's a marvellous letter writer.'

Amy plucked at her kid gloves and spoke impulsively.

'I can't think why you didn't choose her, not me.'

Val seemed amused by her honesty. His face closed up tight as he restrained himself from coughing. She gazed at him, rigid with alarm.

'Sorry,' he said. 'It's your innocence. It always makes me laugh. Like the sunrise. After the long hours of darkness. The marvellous red light that hits the wall. And makes it sing.'

Amy moved about on the verandah, more at ease than at any time since her arrival. She inspected the bird table. There were crumbs there still to be eaten. She tapped the miniature trapeze on which the birds were tempted to perch.

379

Two professional gardeners were burning leaves in the central garden. As though from sacrificial altars, two columns of smoke ascended into the pale afternoon sunlight. Towards the main gates, Griffiths the chauffeur was pacing about with measured strides, his hands behind his back like a brooding emperor in exile. Val was speaking. She moved closer to him to spare him the effort of talking out loud.

'When you come to a place like this,' he said, 'when you submit to a regime, you emigrate to another continent. Another planet. It's another form of exercise ... ah ...'

The noise was between a sigh and a groan. He was too tired to speak any more. Lightly Amy touched his lips with her fingers and sat close enough to stroke his hair. While they were silent a chaffinch landed on the bird table and pecked inquisitively at the crumbs. In a while Val found the strength to speak again.

'Listen, Amy,' he said. 'I would never want to turn myself into a human prison.'

'What do you mean?' she said.

'You mustn't feel obliged ... out of pity or loyalty or duty or anything like that ...'

'What are you trying to say?'

'There are enough prisons in the world as it is. I've no right to make any demands on you. I should have said this weeks ago. All the old pledges we made to each other under totally different circumstances, they no longer apply. Whenever you want to be free, you are free. Do you understand?'

'Be quiet,' she said. 'Be quiet, will you.'

She knelt on the hard tiles so that her mouth could reach his. As if it were an act of great daring she kissed him on the lips. Then she stood up, suddenly positive and practical.

'It's your business, Val Gwyn, to get better. Do you hear me?'

His eyes looked up at her adoringly.

'Just because I can't write long theological letters like Mrs. Enid More, it doesn't mean that I'm not willing you to get better every hour of the day. Every minute of the day.'

She fought back the tears and her voice sounded harsh from the effort.

'And if you want my opinion now I've had time to think

about it, surely it's the system we should attack. The sin is in the system. That's what I think.'

His head shook with the minimum of effort and he smiled at her fondly.

'It's in us,' he said. 'Like the bacillus.'

'I'm going now.'

She had difficulty in standing still under his gaze.

'The sister said I could only have a quarter of an hour. But I'll be back in a few weeks, Mr. Gwyn. And then I shall want to see you sitting up, putting on weight and writing that book you're weaving in your head on reams and reams of paper. And then I'll read it and criticise it line by line. I promise you. I promise.'

When she left his room, she hurried down the corridor with her head down as if there was nothing more of the place she could bear to see or hear. She did not return to the sister's room. Once in the open air she walked across the gardens to the black limousine. Griffiths was already seated at the steering wheel, efficient as ever and ready to leave. There was no need for Amy to speak. With practised tact his eyes were on the way ahead and carefully averted from the untoward recognition of outward signs of another person's distress or private grief. A quick glance in the driving mirror confirmed that his passenger was comfortably settled, holding on to the leather side strap and ready to depart. The long black car proceeded smoothly down the hill between the woods where the autumn mists were already gathering to challenge the oblique rays of the setting sun. Two spans of a narrow bridge, centuries old, crossed the river that diverted the valley floor. As she watched the river the surface of the flowing water glittered in the first vapours of what would soon become its twilight shroud. Boldly the powerful car climbed the opposite side of the valley. The chauffeur's back was precise and rigid with the triumph of the machine under his control. Through the car window Amy was presented with a view of the sanatorium across the valley, all its windows set on fire by the evening sun. Holding on to her strap she moved her head to keep the awesome vision in view through the rear window until the car took another corner and her head slumped against her raised arm as her eyes closed and she shook with sobbing.

11

In the rear of the premises the alterations were still in progress. The three workmen sat on boxes, their feet planted comfortably on the rubble as they ate their sandwiches, drank their tea from the lids of their cans and chatted in muted cheerful tones. Leo Galt surveyed the front of the new establishment, his finger playing thoughtfully with his beard. In the centre of the floor a stack of shoe boxes was covered with a decorator's dust sheet. On top lay his plan of the new art gallery and he consulted it now like an orchestral conductor studying the score at an early rehearsal. When he became aware that Amy was coming down the stairs, he snatched his fingers out of his beard and waved them in what was obviously intended as an impulse of uncontrollable enthusiasm in the direction of a freshly prepared expanse of blank wall.

'What I want there is a Matthew Smith red nude,' he said. 'Nothing else will do. I don't care what she says.'

Amy stared rather solemnly at the stack of boxes.

'They still haven't collected them,' she said. 'Half of them should go down to the docks, and half to the Cwm Du Settlement.'

He was still taken up with his vision of what should be hanging on the wall.

'A soft, round, real woman. An experience in colour and significant form. Not some damned stupid dream figure. Don't you agree?'

Amy looked neutral. He was obliged to regenerate his own enthusiasm.

'Matthew Smith is the answer,' he said. 'And I think I know just exactly where I can get one. She'll need a bit of persuading, of course. Can I count on your support, my jolly eminence?'

His jocular approach met with a poor response. Amy was not even smiling.

'I don't know anything about painting,' she said.

'Well, at least you admit it.'

He persisted with his cheerfulness.

'I had an awful creature in here about half an hour ago. Did you hear him?'

Amy shook her head.

'Just couldn't get rid of him. Retired headmaster apparently. With what he kept on calling "my sister's son". His brilliant nephew in other words. A genius. He painted that thing. He insisted on leaving it here. Said he was a friend of Lord Iscoed.'

Galt was pointing contemptuously at the canvas in the corner. The painting represented five human figures in a frieze. Their elongated limbs were draped with garlands of leaves and flowers. Heraldic birds and animals were in attendance.

'"Figures from the Mabinogion" is the title. He repeated it God knows how many times. I think he was afraid I didn't know what the Mabinogion was. He was deaf too. That didn't help. Isn't it foul?'

Amy tried to show some interest.

'What's wrong with it?'

'It's bad. It's downright bad.'

'I thought we were supposed to encourage local talent.'

Leo Galt was inspired to launch a lightning attack on the picture. With a series of quick gestures he drew her attention to its faults and weaknesses.

'Cramped. No rhythm. Wooden. Imitative. Tepid with false good taste. Look at the colour! Pale, inhibited, constipated. And the brushwork. No conviction. The whole thing is a nasty mess. Provincial. Stale. Bad art. Do you see what I mean?'

Amy gave the offending picture a long stare.

'What did you say to him? To the uncle.'

'Now there was a wily bird. Proclaims nephew a genius. That makes it official. Also pulls a wire in the direction of Lord Iscoed. What you might call a belt and braces policy.'

'What did you say?'

'What could I say without being downright rude. He insisted on leaving it here so that Eirwen should see it. All I could say was he did so at his own risk.'

383

'It is a problem.'

He was suspicious of the smile beginning to show on Amy's face.

'What is?'

'Calling this place "Art for All". If that's what it is, how can you discourage the very people who show the most interest?'

He caught the top hairs of his beard under his upper lip and sucked them thoughtfully. He stalked around the stack of boxes until the answer came to him. He raised two fingers for Amy to consider, one from each hand.

'The two-pronged approach,' he said. 'The pincer. Funerals and education. Bury the smelly old fogies and Philistines and get the young back to first principles.'

'What are the first principles?'

Even as she asked the question Amy seemed to be losing interest in his discourse: she was glancing at her watch. He breathed deeply and exerted himself to retain her attention.

'The language of the morning of the world,' he said. 'No less. No less. The vitality and the truth that belong only to the dawn of creation. Make it new!'

'My goodness,' Amy said. 'You are not asking for much, are you? Anyway I must go to lunch.'

'Quite right.'

He followed her to the doorway. The words 'The Golden Slipper' were still printed in gold lettering on the tinted glass of the door.

'Man does not live by bread alone, but where, oh where, shall we eat? Down the docks?'

He offered his companionship with frank gestures of geniality.

'I'm sorry,' Amy said. 'I've got a meeting.'

His arms dropped dejectedly. He showed he was ready to set aside his own disappointment in a continuing concern for her well-being.

'Everything alright?'

'Yes. Thank you.'

'You do look a little on the peaky side. Remember I'm on the short list. For the vacant post of active guide, philosopher and friend. I ask no more, et cetera. Remember?'

Amy touched him lightly on the arm.

'You are very kind to me, Leo,' she said. 'And very patient with my ignorance.'

He looked back into the interior of the shop.

'I mean it about the Matthew Smith,' he said. 'You will help me? If the need arises. Eirwen isn't too keen on fat red nudes.'

'You know best,' Amy said. 'You are the expert.'

He was looking at Amy shrewdly as he played with his beard.

'You are the oracle,' he said. 'I don't know whether you know it. The oracle of youth or some such. If you ask me ...'

He dropped his voice to indicate a degree of confidentiality he had not ventured on before.

'... if you asked me, I'd say she was just a trifle "gone" on you, as we used to say at school.'

He stopped when he took in Amy's severe frown of disapproval.

'Anyway. Enjoy your lunch.'

She hurried down the pavement probably conscious that he could be still outside the Golden Slipper noting which way she was taking. At the chemist's on the corner the older partner stood on the threshold about to close for lunch. He studied Amy's approach with open interest. When she returned his stare, he jerked up his head and blinked at the sky, apparently calculating by some private formula whether or not a moving cloud would obscure the midday sun.

Amy was relieved to get past him and lose herself in the urgent movement of people on the pavements of one of the main thoroughfares of the city. The noise and bustle were stimulating. As she hurried along she caught a sound of human voices rising above the traffic: it was as inappropriate as if larks had suddenly burst out singing. The human melody blossomed out of the metallic roar of the traffic and the people jostling on the pavement seemed pleased enough to hear it. At the entrance to a shopping arcade Amy stopped to watch four unemployed miners singing in the gutter. They were giving themselves wholeheartedly to the music. Under their ragged caps their eyes were closed and their arms and hands were extended in stylised gestures acquired from the concert platform. They moved slowly along as they sang, passing the display windows of a furniture shop without

385

looking at their own reflections in the plate glass. They seemed pleased with the excuse the music gave them for keeping their eyes closed. A paper-seller at his pitch under the arch that marked the entrance to the arcade began to shout out his wares. Amy looked at him resentfully but he ignored her disapproval. She stood still on the edge of the pavement watching the singers' approach. Her limbs seemed paralysed by the plangent sadness of the tune. The words were traditional: it was the tune and the way they sang in doleful harmony that expressed their plight. Fumbling in her handbag she extracted a sixpence and dropped it in the mug that was held out by the oldest miner. She listened fascinated as the quartet in their mufflers and long shabby coats glided down the road like blind men guided by the kerb. She felt a strong hand squeeze her arm and looked up in fright. Pen Lewis was smiling at her.

'Pen! I'm sorry. Am I late?'

'What are you doing?. Sleep-walking or street-walking?'

She stared after the singing miners. Many well dressed people were hurrying past them now averting their eyes, as if they had come too close to a source of infection.

'Oh, just look at them,' Amy said. 'Isn't it terrible?'

Pen drew her past the paper seller into the bright arcade.

'We'll make them pay for that,' he said.

There was grim determination in his voice.

'And it won't be pennies in a hat, either.'

As they walked between the dainty displays in the arcade windows Pen unburdened himself.

'All these fancy buildings,' he said. 'Very charming, I'm sure. But do you think the snooty buggers will ever admit it was all built out of sweat and blood? Every single bloody stone. Not on your life, Miss Parry. It's run by fat little Tories of doubtful origins and they fall over themselves to get their names on the Honours List. Just think of them handing out the freedom of the city to an enemy of the working class like Stanley Baldwin. If there's anybody entitled to the freedom of this city it's the miner who created it.'

They stood outside the Elaine Restaurant. Pen's voice echoed in the arcade. Heads were turned nervously at the sound of his loud confident voice. Amy looked through the glass at the interior of the restaurant.

'There's a table,' she said. 'At the far end. Come on. I'm hungry.'

Pen went on talking as they threaded a course through the tables. Amy led the way.

'Charming city,' he said. 'No doubt about that. Good place to spend money when you've got any. Wedding cake Civic Centre and all that. But there's no power here, see. Anybody with a minimum of political sense can see that. It's what you call provincial. You know what I mean? Everything about it is essentially provincial. Cosy, no doubt. Nice and friendly in a vapid sort of way. But essentially provincial. The architecture. The newspapers. The shops. The culture. The people. Anaemic and provincial. Nice-nice and nothing-nothing. There's more real spark in one valley than the whole of this confection put together and multiplied by a hundred.'

He sat at the small table well satisfied with his own eloquence. Amy was not so impressed.

'You sound just like Leo Galt,' she said.

She glanced at the menu as something she had read often before.

'I'm going to have poached haddock,' she said. 'Will you have the same?'

As they waited for the food to arrive he smiled at her across the table.

'All theory, am I? Is that what you think? Bit of a miner escaped from the coal face and the daylight gone to his head?'

Amy gazed fondly at his startling blue eyes.

Like stars on a frost they were twinkling with an excitement she had to wait to share. He pushed a finger between the collar of his shirt and his neck. The collar was high and tight. The red tie had a small knot. He leaned over the table to speak to her more confidentially.

'I'm going to Russia,' he said.

The blood drained from Amy's face. He did not seem to notice the effect his words were having.

'When?'

She struggled to control herself.

'Soon.'

The waitress arrived with their order. Amy stared at the brown skin resting in the white pool on her plate as if it were a phenomenon she had never seen before. Pen was already eating. The fish knife and fork looked absurdly small in his strong hands. He had bitten into a piece of folded bread and butter and it was leaning against the rim of his plate with the teeth marks uppermost.

'How soon,' she said. 'How long?'

Listlessly she dissected the supine fish with the blunt silver-plated fish knife, examining the white segments with superfluous care.

'Three or four months. It's quite a privilege really.'

Pen could not conceal his pride from her.

'Another link in the chain that holds together the international struggle of miners! The spearhead of the working-class movement. It's quite an honour to be selected. It shows they have some faith in me, after all.'

He grinned at her confidently.

'Marxist economics. Marxist social history. I'll have it all at my finger-tips by the time I come back. Then I'll be a trained man. And there's the Comintern, of course. And the Red International of Labour Unions.'

Even while he was speaking he had already cleared his plate. He now had half an eye on Amy's.

'I thought you said you were hungry...'

He smiled at her most amiably.

'When?' Amy said. 'When are you going?'

'Well I'll be in London first, won't I? And then down in Abbey Wood for a bit.'

At last he seemed to be aware of the effect his announcement was having on Amy. His first impulse was to change the subject.

'So you saw old Val, then? How was he looking?'

Amy took time to answer.

'Very poorly,' she said.

'Did you tell him about us?'

She shook her head. He made an extra effort to be understanding and sympathetic.

'Poor sod. I'll tell you this much. When Communism takes over, that will be the first priority. Medical research. We'll tackle the three great evils of mankind in that order. Poverty. Disease. War. In that order.'

'I want to be honest and open...' Amy said.

She was speaking with difficulty.

'Of course you do. That's your nature.'

He was warm, friendly, and encouraging. When she pushed her plate aside he dipped his knife and fork in it to extract what was left of the haddock.

'I'm bloody hungry . . . It's not all that often I get a tasty meal.'

Amy pushed the plate closer to him so that he could substitute it for his own.

'I like to know where I am,' she said. 'I hate being confused. But I just couldn't say anything to him. He looked so ill. And anyway I didn't know what to say . . . I just don't know where I stand.'

She stared at him urgently as though she were expecting him to tell her.

'Oh I don't know . . .'

With some show of objectivity as he was eating, Pen considered her case.

'It's something new of course. Being a free woman. Being a new woman as you might say. I don't suppose it's happened in the history of civilisation before. So we're a bit weak on precedents . . . I mean it's as if you had wandered by accident into the Garden of Eden and you can't sleep at nights trying to work out where the catch is. Well, if you ask me, there isn't a catch. Freedom is freedom and that's all there is to it.'

Amy was ready to make a further appeal.

'I can't go on working for Miss Eirwen,' she said. 'How can I? Working for the boss class, as you call it. That's what it amounts to. Like the chauffeur. A lackey, you called him. A servile being. Or like Leo Galt. A hanger-on. A parasite, you called him. Do you want me to go on being a parasite? In Iscoed Hall? One of the mansions built with the blood and bones of the miners in the valleys. That's what you said.'

He was nodding understandingly.

'I know exactly how you feel,' he said. 'But just think a minute. Just think.'

He leaned over to exert his influence more confidentially.

'I think you ought to hang on to that job. Stay put. You stay there like a good girl. Until I come back.'

'I want to know where I stand.'

A plaintive note had entered Amy's voice.

'Look at it like this.'

He was eager to explain.

'It's Clausewitz again really only I can't remember the exact quotation. In a war, and that's what it is, you know, in war, the side with the best intelligence has the best chance of winning. That's the way you can anticipate the enemy's moves. Now if we organise the working class for militant action we want to know how the governing class intends to respond. Do you follow? Now what you want to do is to worm yourself right into the heart of their confidences. Right in there. There's Iscoed for instance. He and the Home Secretary are very pally. They'll be down there as sure as eggs. On a shooting party or what have you ... Hatching out their plots and plans. Deciding on their courses of action. Just think of the things you're likely to hear! This very winter that's coming. And what a winter it's going to be ... The distress ... the desolation ... the upheavals. You've only got to use a little imagination ...'

He took in Amy's reaction.

'What's the matter?' he said.

'I don't want to be a spy,' she said. 'What do you take me for?'

He ran a finger over the remnants of sauce on the plate and licked it quickly.

'You won't be doing it for pleasure, mate, I can tell you, or for profit. It's the first lesson you have to learn when you join the Party. You've got to set aside your own personal whims and wishes. Even your own scruples. The cause comes first.'

'Who said I was joining the Party?'

Amy looked indignant. Pen was laughing at her, very certain of his ascendancy.

'Well it's like this, kid. Love me, love my Party.'

'Oh. Is it?'

Amy clearly longed to be defiant, but her mind seemed to be slow in presenting her with an adequate system of argument. While she clenched her fist and lowered her head in an effort of thinking, a long-faced woman in an ill-fitting purple coat had placed herself on the edge of their table. She was staring at Pen with her mouth open, waiting for him to notice her.

'Hello, Penry,' she said.

Her voice dragged along like tired feet. He looked up at her in some alarm, apparently unable at first to identify her.

'Don't remember me then, do you?'

She seemed mildly amused at his inability to place her. She delayed revealing her identity as long as she could.

'Martha, Number 38,' she said. 'Rachel Arnold's sister.'

Pen began to look embarrassed.

'Got a job down here now then, have you? Not so easy these days, is it? To get a job.'

Pen frowned at Amy. He showed he was eager to get away. He signalled for the waitress to bring their bill and began to search in his pocket for money.

'I'll pay.'

Amy tried to whisper so that the woman standing by should not hear her.

'I'll tell Rachel Arnold I saw you.'

Martha, Number 38, showed no inclination to move.

'Funny how you bump into people in the city, isn't it? You think you can get lost in the city, don't you, but somebody's sure to bump into you, sooner or later.'

'I'm not trying to get lost,' Pen said. 'That's the last thing I'm trying to do.'

'Big Communist now, I hear. All right for some people, isn't it?'

Martha's flat voice dripped on while the waitress made out the bill and took from Pen the money Amy had pushed across the table.

'If you give me your address I'll pass it on to Rachel.'

Martha did not take her eyes off Pen.

'I dare say she'll be glad to get in touch with you.'

'Come on.'

Pen stood up and urged Amy to hurry.

'Let's get out of this place.'

He took her arm and they marched away at speed. In the arcade he looked over his shoulder to see if Martha had followed them.

'Come on. Talk about the joys of anonymity.'

'Who's Rachel Arnold?'

Amy was deeply curious.

'Some woman I used to know. Pestered the life out of me, she did. And when she got what she wanted, she wanted to own me, lock, stock and barrel. Let's go and have a drink.'

At first Amy allowed herself to be led down the arcade. At the threshold of the wine shop she showed she was unwilling to go in.

'You paid for the meal,' he said. 'Fair enough. Now I've got the money to buy you a drink.'

He jerked his thumb towards his chest. He was reasserting his command of the occasion: he wanted to behave as if he had taken possession of the city in order to provide her with a delightful day out.

'Don't say you can't go in there. It's not the same as a pub, you know. You can set all your North Walian scruples to rest. You know what I think? North Wales is so narrow it could march through the eyes of a needle without touching the sides. What's the matter? Don't you want a nice glass of Madeira? That's a nice young lady's drink.'

Through the open doorway Amy could see a row of polished casks above the barmaid's glossy black head. A man at a marble-topped table put down his newspaper to stare at her. A fluted glass with the dregs of a green liqueur stood on the table. His face was purple and his eyes floating in a colourless liquid stuck out of their sockets.

'I must get back,' Amy said. 'Miss Eirwen is coming at two.'

She looked up at him, desperate anxiety showing in her face.

'When are you going?'

'I expect I'll catch the six o'clock train to London.'

He walked her down the arcade like a casualty in an accident while she tried to grasp the reality of the situation.

'We have to be hard with ourselves,' Pen said. 'We can't go on clinging to the sloppy standards of bourgeois individualism. If we do that nothing will ever change. We've got to be disciplined. We've got to be tough. We don't have much choice if we want to win. It's just like I've been telling you, Amy. We have to sink our personal feelings...'

Amy nodded as if she understood what he was saying.

'Who was this Rachel Arnold?'

The question displeased him.

'She was a mistake,' he said. 'I can tell you that much.'

'Who was she?'

'A widow,' Pen said. 'A young widow. Her husband was

killed in the pit. Difficult compensation case. Wes Hicks made a very good job of it, fair play to him. I shouldn't have got mixed up in it really. I made a mistake.'

'What mistake?'

'She got attached to me. Look, we haven't got much time left. Let's leave it at that, shall we?'

She gazed dumbly at his face. For the first time he allowed himself to become miserable on his own account.

'I'm bloody nervous, if I was to tell you the truth.'

They walked closely together down the street. He kept his hands in his pockets, but from time to time he took a hand out to touch her arm.

'Leaving you is like cutting my heart out. You know that. And I'll tell you something else. I've never been on a ship before. Unless you count a couple of trips to Weston. Will you come to the station? See me off? Five, say? In the station café?'

Amy nodded. She was willing to listen but unable to speak.

'I haven't got two bloody words of Russian to rub together. But it's international of course. I expect there'll be plenty others in the same boat. Awful things, partings on railway stations. I can't stand them. Can you?'

They stood on the pavement near the chemist's shop.

'Don't come unless you want to. Let's leave it like that. Shall we?'

He stretched out his hands to touch her. She shrank away, pointing nervously down the street at Miss Eirwens' long black limousine parked outside The Golden Slipper.

'She's arrived,' Amy said. 'It's late. I'll have to go.'

'You can't go,' he said. 'You can't leave me. Not this afternoon. I've got a lump of stuff inside me if I knew how to say it. Can't we go somewhere? Together. In this whole damned city . . . Amy?'

Her eyes were on the limousine as he was speaking. He struggled to win her attention.

'If you knew how much I want you,' he said. 'This very moment . . . if you only knew . . .'

She looked at his pale face.

'Life is what happens to people,' she said. 'That's all it is.'

The simple proposition made him cross.

'What the hell are you talking about? Haven't you listened

to anything I've been saying? It's not just a case of sacrificing our personal lives. I've explained all this to you before. We have to go through the miseries and the distress and the persecutions of the present in order to arrive at a better and more glorious future. Damn it. That's history. It's as simple as that when you get down to it.'

'I must go,' Amy said. 'She'll be waiting for me.'

'If you want to get in touch, write to Wes. That's the best way. Through Wes in Cwm Du. Will you come to the station?'

Amy continued to stare at him. She made no answer to his question.

'You knew you were going weeks ago,' she said. 'Why didn't you tell me?'

'Oh now, come on... you can see for yourself, surely. What would be the use? I've told you from the very beginning. My life is governed by the Cause. And what that adds up to at the moment is at least three specific disciplines. On the coalfield, in the Union, and in the International Movement. Don't you remember me telling you how they all meshed together?'

She looked at his stiffened fingers as he slid them inside each other.

'You've got to come to the station.'

His appeal was insistent and desperate.

'Five o'clock. Do you hear me?'

A passer by would have imagined they were glaring at each other in the rigid grip of a wordless quarrel.

'I'll think about it,' Amy said.

He watched her walk away with his fists clenched.

12

The tiled floor of the Saddle Room was covered with clothes. Three girls in pinafores and overcoats were on their knees, sorting items according to condition, shape and size. Cards Amy had printed indicated the broad categories: infants, girls, boys, women, men. There were further sub-divisions. Amy was supervising the operation and making notes. The head gardener's daughter and a kitchen maid tied the sorted clothes in convenient bundles and carried them to the nearest stable the other side of the archway. There they were sorted in tall heaps in the vacant stalls. In spite of the fire in the grate the Saddle Room was cold. The door was open. Amy wore a scarf over her head. She was snivelling a little and often obliged to pause in her writing to wipe the end of her nose.

'My goodness! What a hive of industry!'

Leo Galt stood in the doorway. He was wearing a cloak and a deer stalker with the ear-flaps tied down under his beard. He was happily conscious of a certain eccentricity in his appearance. The village girls on their knees looked at him with undisguised curiosity. He raised his hands to wriggle them with characteristic geniality at Amy. There were spots of dried paint on his mittens.

'There are things afoot, M'mselle Parry. We are summoned. To the Presence, so to speak. *Tout de suite.*'

Amy pursed her lips while she concentrated on completing an addition.

'Molly...'

She handed her note-book to the head gardener's daughter and showed her how the record should be kept.

'Go slower if you need to,' Amy said. 'It's important that the figures should be right.'

Leo Galt sighed his admiration as they crossed the stable yard.

'Good works, good works,' he said. 'They shine out like good deeds in a naughty world.'

Amy ignored his pleasantries. They walked past the brick outbuildings where Galt's studio was situated.

'What's happening?' Amy said.

'Ah, what indeed?'

Galt lifted a finger and his eyebrows to give his rhetorical question dramatic emphasis.

'I thought at first it must be Royalty. The poor dear was so disturbed. And then of course I took further thought and realised that was completely out of the question.'

Amy was mystified. Zestfully he set out to enlighten her.

'Royalty would never come and stay with a family so

recently elevated or ennobled or what ever the correct term would be. And Welsh Calvinistic Methodists to boot. Quite out of the question.'

'Such rubbish.'

He was stimulated by Amy's muttered indignation.

'Did I ever tell you about Queen Mary spending the night at Otsford? Oh, I must have done. I was there going through the pictures. Just one night. She brought nine people with her – two dressers, one footman, one page aged forty-five, two chauffeurs, one lady-in-waiting, one maid to the same, and one detective. That makes nine, doesn't it? And the whole staff of the house at her disposal of course. How many? Thirty indoor servants? But she brought her own sheets and pillowcases.'

He almost danced, he was so pleased with his recital: the picture of royal magnificence and eccentricity he had conjured up was in some way a legitimate part of his own being.

'Scandalous,' Amy said. 'The meaningless frivolity of it all.'

'Oh, I don't know ... We've got to enjoy ourselves. Laugh a little. We can't be glum all the time.'

'The so-called governing classes.'

Amy wiped her nose.

'All play-acting their false values. Junketing about while people are starving. It's wicked and immoral. Royalty and aristocracy, the whole thing should have been done away with years ago. It's all makebelieve. It's all blind ridiculous folly.'

'I say ...'

He was taken aback by her vehemence. He stood in the entrance hall and looked at Amy as though he were seeing her for the first time.

'I knew you had views ... about Welshness and all that. But I had no idea you were such a hot Red as well. Or should I say red hot?'

Amy walked ahead of him. He was obliged to scamper down the corridor to catch up with her.

'I'm not denying that there is a lot in what you're saying.' He sounded anxious to be affable.

'Of course there is. Every intelligent person would have to

agree with a lot of what you are saying. But could I just say something personal?'

He touched her tentatively on the arm. She paused at the foot of the staircase to look at him.

'I know you have strong political convictions. And I admire you for them. Of course I do. Even if I don't agree with them myself. You've become so intense and sad these last few weeks. Has something happened?'

Amy stood with one hand on the banister and the other holding her handkerchief to her nose. She seemed on the point of accepting his sympathy.

'If there was anything I could do, I would like to help.'

Amy showed her gratitude with a quiet smile.

'That old chemist on the corner of Charlotte Street was trying to pump me about some man in a brown suit he had seen going in and out of "The Golden Slipper", as he called it. Nasty little man trying to work up a head of gossip. "Oh yes," I said, "that would be one of our associates." I don't know what he expected. Standing in that gloomy little shop of his all day. Dispensing nostrums and tittle-tattle. Nasty little man.'

Amy walked slowly up the stairs. Leo Galt followed. He seemed to be trying to make up for what he had just revealed or even to cancel it completely so that they could proceed as if it had never been said.

'The fact is, Amy, what I'm trying to say is, you shouldn't try and carry all the world's troubles on your own shoulders. What I'm trying to say is you really must try and think of yourself. Of your own well-being. Your own interests, for goodness' sake. Do you know what I mean? In this harsh world, whoever else will? We are all entitled to protect our own interests. Every single one of us.'

They stood on the landing. Amy waited for him to indicate which way they should take.

'Where is she?'

'In the small sitting-room. Amy, I hope you don't think I'm being presumptuous. I really want to be your friend.'

'Thank you.'

She was pale but polite. It was quite obvious there was nothing further she was willing to say. She knocked on the sitting-room door. They both went in. Miss Eirwen was sitting by the fire wearing a clean smock. When they came in she rose excitedly to her feet. The furniture was covered with rosebud chintz and the window curtains were made of the same material. Over the fireplace there was a bright mirror in which Amy saw the reflection of a blue painting of a Breton harbour hung on the opposite wall. Miss Eirwen had just consumed a glass of milk. There were apples and biscuits on the table by her chair. Miss Eirwen gave a short sigh of relief as though Amy in particular was bringing her immediate succour.

'It's my brother,' she said. 'He really has given me quite a shock.'

Galt waved his arms cheerfully to proclaim his innate resilience and capacity to adjust himself with complete lack of fuss to any sudden change.

'I'm sorry ... do sit down ... wherever you like.'

They settled in a triangular relationship, Miss Eirwen looking at Amy as though she wished she had chosen to sit nearer.

'Will you be warm enough there? It's such a chilly day.' Miss Eirwen sat down nearest the fire.

'I shall tell you as much as I can. As much as I'm allowed to. You know my brother is in Geneva. Things are not easy there at the moment. You've probably gathered that from the newspapers. Naval limitation is certainly not enough ... But in any case, he has arranged what he calls a private meeting with certain high-placed delegates, who, I am not allowed to name, and he wants to hold the secret meeting here at Iscoed. Isn't that exciting?'

'My goodness! Yes. Yes indeed.'

Leo Galt responded willingly.

'This will be in just over a fortnight's time.' Miss Eirwen said. 'I do apologise for this. Such terribly short notice. And of course it will affect all our plans. I don't quite see now how we can possibly open "Art for All" this side of Christmas. Sir P.O.P. wants a hand in it. I did tell you that, didn't I? He wants somebody very high up for the opening ceremony and he keeps using frightening terms like "maximum publicity"! But I suppose I do have to listen to him.'

Galt smiled and nodded wisely, plucking at his beard.

'But to return to the immediate and over-riding problem.

398

To make things easier really, my brother wants to take over the house. He wants us all out of the way for the duration.'

Miss Eirwen waved her hands to suggest their immediate banishment. She was clearly excited by the prospect of sudden change.

'And I am sure he is quite right. This is a matter of such great international importance, we have to set our own little plans and projects to one side. But, why not, I've been telling myself as I've been sitting here, why not treat the whole thing as a heaven-sent opportunity to take a little holiday?'

She pressed her hands together.

'A pilgrimage to Avignon, Arles, Aix... That's what I thought. I think we've all worked so very hard and so very well... Does it appeal to you?'

Leo Galt had slapped his thigh enthusiastically, but now they were both looking at Amy, ready to test her reaction.

'Three weeks,' Miss Eirwen said. 'We would be back well before Christmas. You would be my guests of course. I don't know about your skiing, Mr. Galt. That's usually in the New Year, isn't it? But in any case this would be something quite additional and extra. An uncovenanted blessing. We could pick up some things for "Art for All", of course.'

'Of course. Of course. Why not?'

Leo Galt was tingling with fervour. Amy had still not spoken. Miss Eirwen looked at her sympathetically.

'I'm sure Mr. Gwyn wouldn't mind,' she said gently. 'If you visited him just before we left... three weeks wouldn't be such a long time... In any case, why don't we all think about it? It's all come as rather too much of a shock, I'm sure. Let's think about it.'

Miss Eirwen stood up. Immediately the other two followed suit.

'I wanted you both to know at once,' she said. 'So that you can have time to make arrangements. Suppose you both come here at tea time. Then we'll have a council of war and decide what to do.'

Outside Leo Galt executed a brief dance step on the corridor carpet.

'You must come, Amy! You simply must. It's the chance of a lifetime. And you absolutely deserve it. You really do. The climate. Even this time of the year. And the purity of the sky. You'll see the world as you've never seen it before. Amy, I promise you.'

Amy spoke on the stairs.

'I'm not going,' she said.

He spread out his arms to show the measure of his disappointment.

'But Amy,' he said. 'Why ever not?'

'I'm leaving.'

'Leaving? Leaving where?'

They stood facing each other on the broad staircase.

'This place.'

Leo Galt was puzzled and distressed.

'I don't understand you.'

He lowered his voice.

'Giving up the job you mean?'

'If you can call it a job.'

Amy looked around at the impressive walls of the great house. Leo took her arm and led her tactfully out of the main entrance. He replaced his deerstalker on his head without bothering to tie the ends of the ear-flaps. They waved on either side of his head as he led her towards the gardens where he could speak more freely without fear of being overheard.

'Where will you go, for goodness' sake?' he said. 'Now, you mustn't be impulsive. I speak as a friend – you really must think the whole thing through. I can see that this is a very quiet place for a young person like yourself. Especially in winter. I can quite see that. And of course in your particular circumstance you do have additional strains and stresses to bear. I do understand, I assure you. But in this life we have to learn to weigh up all the pros and cons. We simply have to. I mean in my own case, it's pretty lonely for me too, at times. I have to admit it. That's why I was so delighted when you came along. You've brightened the place up no end for me, I don't have to tell you. But the thing is, I'm an artist fundamentally. I have a small talent of my own apart from my specialist knowledge and skills. So it suits me to be here. I may well be one of those tender plants that wouldn't survive the harsh winds of the outside world. Anyway, Eirwen is really very good to me. And she's very easy to live with. You must admit that. I mean one couldn't wish for a more understanding or sympathetic employer. And that's certainly true in your case. I can tell you this, if you stayed here, and just went on as you are, without any nonsense about playing your cards right or any of that sort of thing, in a matter of a few years you would become the real power behind the throne. And from there it's only a short step to becoming heir apparent. They're both childless, you know. Of course, dear brother could marry at any time if he took it into his head, but Miss Eirwen is wealthy enough in her own right, for heaven's sake ... And you couldn't be better placed when Val Gwyn comes out of hospital ... Whatever it is you have in mind for the future. And we all of us have something in mind. We have to. That's a fact of life. Amy, for goodness' sake, just tell me. What is it exactly you want?'

She looked for a dry spot on her handkerchief before wiping her nose.

'I know what I want,' she said.

'Do you? Well tell me, for goodness' sake. I can't wait to hear.'

'Independence,' Amy said. 'That's all I want.'

13

Amy sat up in the middle of the double bed, the heavy bedclothes wedged between her knees and her chin. She was staring fixedly at the view through an uncurtained window which extended almost from ceiling to floor. Beyond the sharp silhouette of the mountains the dawn was breaking: a great tide of colour was transforming the sky even as she watched it. The mud and the shallow water in the harbour became a burnished surface against which the sea birds assembled in black hungry congregations on the fringe of the ebb tide.

Amy's case was open on the floorboards. Slowly, the growing light revealed her new cardigan suit lying alongside the case on brown paper. The skirt and the coat were made of black stockingette. The cuffs and the collar of the coat were beige. And the beige jumper was patterned with black and red. Over the end of the bed was the red and beige silk scarf that completed the outfit. A folded card table leaned against the iron fireplace. On the bare wall above, the rising sun printed the watery reflection of the window frames in elongated rectangles of ruby light.

The tap on the door was so light she barely heard it.

'Amy...'

It was Enid's voice quietly whispering.

'Are you awake?'

'Of course I am.'

Enid was smiling happily when she opened the door. She was wearing a thick woollen dressing gown that did little to conceal the pregnant bulge in her figure.

'He's coming,' she said.

Further down the stairs John Cilydd was tramping his feet and blowing breathless nasal tunes through his mouth. He was carrying a well-loaded breakfast tray from the basement to the bedroom on the second floor of the terrace house. Enid opened the card table and set it near the double bed.

'Really,' Amy said. 'I could have come down. You shouldn't have bothered.'

'Just look at it!'

Enid stood in the window. She raised her hand to draw attention to the view. The light fell on her face. She was speechless with pride and wonder. Climbing the last flight of stairs John Cilydd called out.

'With the compliments of Hotel Marine Terrace!'

He entered the room in triumph. Enid pointed to the card table.

'Put it down there,' she said. 'And mind Amy's dress. On the floor.'

With bedclothes over her mouth Amy made noises of muffled surprise.

'I'm making too much trouble for you,' she said. 'I really am.'

Her gratitude expanded to include both of them. Cilydd had moved to the window. His arm lay protectively over Enid's shoulders as she gazed at the sunrise.

'There it is,' he said. 'The great curtain going up.'

He turned to look at Amy in bed and at her cardigan suit on the floor.

'Are you ready for the performance?' he said.

Amy shivered under the bedclothes.

'I'm nervous,' she said. 'I really am.'

Cilydd displayed masculine reassurance with calm authority.

'There is absolutely nothing to worry about,' he said. 'You are the headmaster's choice. Appearing before the Governors is a mere formality. A quaint local custom. A genuflection in the direction of democracy. The job is yours. That is, if you want it.'

'Oh I do, I do.'

'Geography and Elementary Biology in the junior forms?'

'I don't mind,' Amy said. 'It's music to my ears. And I'm more than grateful. I really am.'

'Well, there we are then.'

Cilydd gave his wife's shoulders a consoling squeeze as he watched Amy leaning over the tray, gazing wide-eyed at the toast and marmalade, the boiled egg, the thin brown bread and butter, the teapot under its fat cosy. Cautiously she extended one arm and poured a cup of tea.

'How on earth am I going to manage all this?'

'It's just like a happy ending, isn't it, Madame More?' Cilydd said.

Enid nodded happily. She stared wistfully at the mountains, as though she were thinking of a prince lying in a prison somewhere beyond them.

'If only Val would get better,' she said. 'Everything would be perfect.'

'He will,' John Cilydd said. 'He will.'

He spoke to Amy.

'This is where she sits to write her famous letters ...'

'No wonder they are so inspired,' Amy said. 'No, I mean it. I'm not teasing.'

Cilydd studied the cardigan suit on the floor.

'We could all settle here,' he said. 'It's funny how simple things can be, if that's the way you want them to be. He's only got to get better. And there we are ... We'll all live happily ever after.'

With her knees up, Amy sipped her tea. As the sun rose the

mountains looked colder. The noise of the birds in the harbour grew as the light invested them with their separate colours and identity. A squadron of wild geese flew across the sky in 'V' formation. In the station terminus next to the harbour, a black train blew its whistle and a plume of smoke cauliflowered many feet up in the still winter air.

'Doesn't the prospect please you?'

Cilydd was waiting for her reaction: his sketch of their future had been specially devised to meet with her approval.

'I'm sorry,' Amy said. 'Of course it does. It's this view. It's like an enchantment.'

'Isn't it just?'

Enid was excited. The word enchantment seemed to have restored her capacity to express herself.

'I sit up here watching it. And the time passes. And I don't know where I've been. But I know it's trying to say something. I do know that.'

'Divine Revelations?'

Cilydd moved jauntily to the door as he spoke, ready to go to the office.

'Make a good breakfast,' he said. 'I shall be back in no time. When I've opened the mail. Then we'll go on safari. See the wonders of my family. Glanrafon. Ponciau. You've no idea what lies in store for you.'

'You are much too kind.'

Amy was at pains now to show how grateful she was.

'My Uncle Simon,' he said. 'There's a special treat. On the local Education Committee. And a Governor, of course, of the County School. He wants a preview of the new teacher.'

'Oh dear.'

Amy made an expression of mock fright.

'With such innocent excitements is our provincial existence enlivened.'

'Sionyn...'

Enid's voice was tinged with affectionate reproof.

'You mustn't say things to put her off.'

'Indeed I shouldn't.'

Cilydd clicked his heels and nodded obediently.

'Business is waiting! The mail must be opened.'

Amy raised her voice as she heard his feet clatter merrily down the stairs.

'Thank you. John Cilydd!'

'My pleasure ... Our pleasure!'

His voice ascending was unusually carefree and youthful.

'Enid,' Amy said. 'I just can't eat all this by myself. Come and help me.'

Enid waited until she heard the front door close.

'Move over, Amy Parry. I'm coming in. To keep warm. Do you mind?'

After much laughter and giggles they settled comfortably side by side.

'He does seem much happier, doesn't he?'

Amy's interest in Cilydd was kindly, objective, confidential.

'He was pleased as Punch when you got the job. I can tell you that much.'

'I haven't got it yet, have I?'

'Of course you have.'

Amy continued to praise John Cilydd in measured tones.

'And he's doing so well. To become such a successful solicitor. And yet remain a poet. It's quite fascinating. The two sides to his character. Inspiring confidence in all those solid clients. And all the while a poet hiding inside him. It's quite romantic.'

They studied the view while they ate with uninhibited enthusiasm. With two pairs of hands they catered for each other's special preferences. Amy offered Enid a piece of toast and marmalade.

'Shall I tell you what I think is so marvellous?' Amy said. 'Really wonderful?'

'Tell me everything.'

Enid grinned and spoke with her mouth full.

'This house,' Amy said.

'We keep it empty on purpose,' Enid said. 'We are only going to put things in we really like.'

'Yes, but it's your own. Your very own and nobody else's.'

'It's yours too,' Enid said firmly. 'Whenever you need it. There's plenty of room.'

Amy passed her hand under Enid's arm to give it a friendly squeeze.

'I know it's an awful thing to say and I'd die if my aunt ever heard it, but I can't bear being at home any more. Uncle

Lucas crouches over the fireplace. Monopolising what little comfort there is. And he watches me like a hawk, criticising every little thing I do.'

'Amy, you poor old thing.'

'As if I didn't know that whatever I do, I bring it on myself. He doesn't have to tell me. I'm only too well aware of it. I mean the last night was simply awful. I sat by the table, right in the draught, pretending to read a book. Just anything for peace and quiet. I mean, anybody would think it was my fault that Val was in a sanatorium. He was behaving as if I should have been there nursing him. Such an atmosphere of reproach. I felt as if I needed a suit of armour to walk through it. Gosh, Enid. I can't tell you how glad I am to be here. These last few months I've been so miserable I can't begin to tell you.'

'You've had a terrible time,' Enid said. 'You really have.'

Amy leaned forward to put the tray back on the card table. She sank back on the pillows ready to luxuriate in the warmth and comfort.

'I suppose I should never have taken the job with Miss Eirwen. I don't know why I did. I honestly don't.'

'To avoid teaching?'

Enid made the suggestion with sympathy.

'I don't know. I think it was worse than that. With Val so ill and everything so hopeless, maybe it made me feel important to be wanted by such important people. I'm really not a very nice person, am I?'

'Don't be silly.'

'I don't know how I'm going to tell her that I've taken a new job.'

'Write.'

Amy shook her head.

'She is a good person, Miss Eirwen. I'm sure of that. Even if she is dominated by that pompous brother. She's always very kind to me. Too kind, really.'

'What do you mean?'

Amy looked at her friend with solemn frankness.

'She would have liked me to bath her, you know.'

Enid's eyes rounded with startled astonishment.

'*Bath* her?'

'Not that she said it in so many words. Just hints all the

406

time. Unspoken invitations. She probably didn't admit half of it to herself. She actually asked me to pray with her once.'

'Did she really?'

'You know I don't go in for that sort of thing. But I do recognise that she tries hard to be good. And that's more than you can say about me.'

'Oh Amy...'

'What she wants is a sort of bosom companion. Oh dear, that sounds a bit funny, doesn't it?'

They laughed together and then Enid became quietly indignant.

'Plas Iscoed,' she said. 'They treated Val abominably. Just think, if he had gone there and not gone starving himself in the Settlement, he would never have had T.B.'

'I don't think that was her,' Amy said. 'She really wanted him. I used to think at first that I was her consolation prize, if you know what I mean.'

'That awful brother,' Enid said. 'And that ghastly slimy old wire-puller P.O.P.'

They stared together at the view as if in some way it could throw light on aspects of human character and of the human condition they found difficult to understand. Amy pressed down her chin philosophically.

'I think living in that house has made me more aware of my own origins,' she said.

She frowned with the effort of expressing herself precisely.

'It's helped me to define my position. I find myself now very much in accord with the struggle of the working class.'

Enid was quick with her own interpretation.

'Ah, but that would be Val, wouldn't it?' she said. 'And all that devoted work of his at the Settlement.'

She gazed with some surprise at Amy's hand shaking slightly.

'It's a matter of feeling,' Amy said. 'A sort of emotional maturity that makes you see things more clearly.'

She became abruptly silent. Enid seemed eager for reassurance.

'But there was an influence there,' she said. 'Surely?'

Amy made herself sit up. She became brisk and forward looking.

'Shouldn't we get up?' she said.

'Amy.'

Enid spoke as if she were taking up her turn to make a confession.

'You didn't mind me writing to Val, did you?'

'Good Lord, of course not!'

She smiled at Enid with frank fondness.

'I'm grateful, I can tell you,' she said. 'I've heard about some of the notions welling up all day and night inside that funny noodle of yours. I only wish I understood half of it.'

'Amy.'

Enid was seized with a sudden bright idea.

'You know what we ought to do. Write a letter to him together. Something to cheer him up. Something funny. Every other sentence.'

Amy jumped suddenly out of bed. She stamped her feet on the floorboards to keep warm.

'You write the words,' she said. 'I'll stamp in the punctuation.'

With a shivery yell she ran down to the bathroom on the first floor. Enid lay in bed and smiled as she listened to the noises Amy was making. When she came back, Amy ran to the window.

'Isn't this view incredible?' she said. 'It changes all the time.'

'Mutations of colour,' Enid said. 'John Cilydd has been trying to write a poem about it. Not the rosy-fingered dawn. The parallel with blood. The red source of life and the red source of light. He says he has to find out more about it.'

Still in her pyjamas Amy crossed her arms over her breasts and stamped her feet again in a static dance.

'It's so cold,' she said. 'I'm freezing. Do you understand that, Madame More?'

She made her teeth chatter as she shouted. Enid responded loyally to the rush of high spirits.

'It's colder still beyond those mountains!' she said.

She bent forward in bed and stretched out her arms to suggest great distances.

'I've told you before,' she said. 'Beyond those sacred hills there's nothing but a freezing plain until you reach the Urals. Just thank your lucky stars!'

Amy stopped dancing. She was suddenly quiet. She turned her back on the window.

'I can't wait to see you in that suit,' Enid said. 'Come on, Parry. Let's see it on.'

She watched Amy dressing, with open admiration.

'You've got such a wonderful figure. You could be a model any day of the week. Or a film star, if it comes to that.'

Amy studied the lining of the coat.

'Leo Galt says a pregnant woman is the most beautiful human form. So there you are Madame More.'

Enid felt her belly under the bedclothes.

'It looks marvellous on you,' she said. 'Don't forget the scarf ... Amy ... I think I can feel something turning over.'

She gazed at her friend, her cornflower blue eyes bright with innocent rapture.

'Amy! I'm sure it's kicking.'

Excitedly she threw back the bedclothes and pulled up her nightdress.

'Put your hand here, quick. Can you feel it?'

She held her breath while she waited for Amy to confirm the movement.

'Can you?'

Gently Amy passed her hand over the stretched skin.

'You'll be like an apple,' Amy said. 'A ripe apple.'

'There!'

Enid announced the movement and Amy nodded excitedly.

'There's somebody alive inside me! Unfolding, quickening, now. Do you know what I mean?'

'Of course I do.'

'If it's a girl, we've already decided on the name. Both of us. Can you guess? "Amy." Do you like the name?'

Amy's hand slid into Enid's.

'What if it's a boy?'

Far away downstairs they heard the front door opening.

'A boy? Oh my goodness ...'

Enid took up an attitude of mock alarm as they heard Cilydd's footsteps on the stairs.

'The master's back!'

Dear Parents:

Congratulations! Your child is taki[ng]
the first steps on an exciting journ[ey.]
The destination? Independent read[ing.]

STEP INTO READING® will help your child get there. The program offers
five steps to reading success. Each step includes fun stories and colorful
art or photographs. In addition to original fiction and books with favorite
characters, there are Step into Reading Non-Fiction Readers, Phonics Readers
and Boxed Sets, Sticker Readers, and Comic Readers—a complete literacy
program with something to interest every child.

Learning to Read, Step by Step!

Ready to Read   Preschool–Kindergarten
• big type and easy words • rhyme and rhythm • picture clues
For children who know the alphabet and are eager to
begin reading.

Reading with Help   Preschool–Grade 1
• basic vocabulary • short sentences • simple stories
For children who recognize familiar words and sound out
new words with help.

Reading on Your Own   Grades 1–3
• engaging characters • easy-to-follow plots • popular topics
For children who are ready to read on their own.

Reading Paragraphs   Grades 2–3
• challenging vocabulary • short paragraphs • exciting stories
For newly independent readers who read simple sentences
with confidence.

Ready for Chapters   Grades 2–4
• chapters • longer paragraphs • full-color art
For children who want to take the plunge into chapter books
but still like colorful pictures.

STEP INTO READING® is designed to give every child a successful
reading experience. The grade levels are only guides; children will progress
through the steps at their own speed, developing confidence in their reading.

Remember, a lifetime love of reading starts with a single step!

Visit us on the Web!
StepIntoReading.com
randomhousekids.com

Educators and librarians, for a variety of teaching tools, visit us at RHTeachersLibrarians.com

ISBN 978-1-5247-1690-5 (trade) — ISBN 978-1-5247-1691-2 (lib. bdg.)

Printed in the United States of America   10 9 8 7 6 5 4 3

SHIMMER and Shine™

Magic Carpet Race!

by Delphine Finnegan

based on the teleplay "Zoom Zahramay"
by Dustin Ferrer

illustrated by Jason Fruchter

Random House 🏠 New York

The magic carpet
race is today!

Shimmer and Shine give
Leah her own carpet.
Now they can all race!

The genies and Leah
ride to the starting line.

Zeta wants
to enter the race.
She dresses up
as a genie.

At the starting line,
Princess Samira
reviews the rules.

The genies must fly
over the beach.
Then they must
swoosh through the
market and zoom to
the top of the island.

The first genie to cross
the finish line will win
the Racing Gem!

Shimmer, Shine, and
Leah are ready.

Zeta is
ready,
too.

11

Princess Samira

waves the flag.

The race begins!

Oh, no!

Leah's carpet does
not fly very fast.

Shine grants Leah's first wish.

Now her carpet flies much faster!

Zeta leads the race.
She pours a magic
potion over the beach.

Poof!

Twisty trees grow
and make a maze.
The girls are lost!

Shimmer grants
Leah's second
wish.

A sparkly path shows
them the way out.

In the market, someone throws fruit at them!

It is Nazboo!

And there is Zeta!

Her genie disguise

does not fool them!

Leah makes her third wish.
Magic paddles appear
to whack away the fruit!

Zeta uses another potion.

The girls' carpets go wild!

Shimmer and Shine fall.

They land on Leah's carpet.

The friends need
to control the carpet.
First they swing
from a star.
Then they zoom to
the top of the island.

Next they
bounce off
a bottle.

Finally, they cross the
finish line ahead of Zeta!

Leah, Shimmer, and Shine
win the Racing Gem!
It glitters and glows,
just like their friendship!